UP

FROM

FREEDOM

A NOVEL

WAYNE GRADY

DOUBLEDAY CANADA

Doubleday Canada and colophon are registered trademarks of
Penguin Random House Canada Limited.

Library and Archives Canada Cataloguing in Publication

Grady, Wayne, author
     Up from freedom / Wayne Grady.

Issued in print and electronic formats.
ISBN 978-0-385-68511-5 (softcover). ISBN 978-0-385-68512-2 (EPUB)

     I. Title.

PS8613.R337U64 2018   C813'.6   C2017-906803-2
                                           C2017-906804-0

This book is a work of historical fiction. Apart from well-known actual
people, events, and locales that figure in the narrative, all names,
characters, places, and incidents are products of the author's
imagination or are used fictitiously. Any resemblance to current
events or locales, or to living persons, is entirely coincidental.

Cover and text design: Lisa Jager
Cover images: (man) Vicky Martin/Arcangel Images Limited;
(waves) Marzufello/Shutterstock
Interior image: (bird) *Sing-Song: A Nursery Rhyme Book*, the British Library

Printed and bound in the USA

Published in Canada by Doubleday Canada,
a division of Penguin Random House Canada Limited

www.penguinrandomhouse.ca

10 9 8 7 6 5 4 3 2 1

 Penguin
Random House
DOUBLEDAY CANADA

For Tamsey's great-great-great-great-granddaughters:
Faye, Myra and Noelle.

No refuge could save the hireling and slave
From the terror of flight, or the gloom of the grave.

—Francis Scott Key, "The Star-Spangled Banner," 1814

PART ONE

⁓

When the sun come back,
When the first quail call,
Then the time is come:
Follow the Drinking Gourd

I.

Virgil Moody waded a little ahead of the others as they scouted the Rio Grande east of Fort Paredes. The south and north banks were Mexico, but nobody owned the river. They'd heard General de Ampudia was moving the Mexican army north from Monterrey, intending to cross at Las Anacuitas, and General Taylor wanted to know how many they were and what condition they were in. So far they'd heard Ampudia had from six hundred to a thousand *permanentes*, with another two hundred infantry coming up to join them, no artillery that anyone knew of, maybe a couple of twelve-pounders. There weren't more than a few hundred Americans at Fort Texas, militiamen like Moody and mostly untrained and badly provisioned volunteers. On patrol that night, splashing behind him, were Stockton Smith, Charlie Warburn, Walt Murdale, Willard Pickart and Jed Baker, with Lieutenant Endicot Millican, their excuse for a captain, bringing up the rear. None of them had any faith in Millican. They went along with him when it didn't mean anything, but when he walked them down open roads or across fields, even in the dark, Moody knew that when the fighting started, they'd follow their own inclinations and to hell with Millican. Moody thought it was safer at the head of the line. He didn't want any part of whatever went on behind him.

They happened upon the Mexican patrol at first light, a hundred yards north of the river in what the Texans claimed was the Republic of Texas. The Mexicans were so sure of their right to be there they were cooking their breakfast on open fires, smoke all over the place. The men could smell their damn fish frying. They got down on their bellies and crawled through the underbrush to a ridge above the camp. They saw the Mexicans' horses tied beside a small arroyo, the silver buckles on their saddles and bridles twinkling through the trees: regiments from San Luis de Posto or maybe San

Miguel de Allende, where the silver mines were. Cavalry, anyway, but these boys were careless. The patrol split into two groups without Millican saying a word, and Moody's group edged along the ridge to the right. They'd each need to get off two shots, and they counted on the suddenness of their attack to give them time to reload. The Mexicans' firearms, light, dependable East India Pattern muskets, were pyramided between the fires, more careless-ness. These couldn't be trained troops, they were acting like a hunting party out for a Sunday shoot. Their *capitán* was sitting on a fallen log, writing in a book. Will Pickart shot him. Moody shot one by the fire before he had time to jump up. Stockton missed his first shot and cursed. Moody could hear the others firing at the second group, and three bluecoats went down. The rest ran for their muskets. Moody reloaded and fired into them, but none fell. Then the Texans whooped and charged down the ridge with bayo-nets fixed. They had to watch their footing because of loose stones, but for a few seconds they weren't afraid of death. Two Mexicans ran across the creek, and Pickart and Moody went after them. Will chased his down, and Moody ran his into a shallow arroyo, where the *soldado* turned, put his back against a tree and raised his hands. A boy no more than fifteen or sixteen, hatless, his uniform too big for him, sandals on his feet. There was a lot of *indio* in him, dark skin, arched eyebrows and the kind of straight, black hair above dark, fathomless eyes that made Moody think of lush forest and running water. Moody stood in front of him while the boy's hands shook. He raised his bayonet, and Millican ran up behind him.

"Kill him!" he shouted at Moody. "Kill him, you fool!"

That was what he was doing, damn it. But he couldn't go through with it. Maybe it was Millican telling him to, a man he didn't respect. Or maybe it was because the boy was the same age as Lucas. But sticking a body was different from shooting at it from the top of a ridge. You had to look him in the eye, you had to hit the inverted V under the crossed *bandoleras*, you had to remember the twist that cut through the cartilage. Then you had to watch him die.

"Kill the bastard, Moody!"

"Brown said take a few prisoners," Moody said, but they both knew he was stalling.

"We got two taken back at the camp," Millican said. "This little bastard won't know anything. Finish him off, and do it now. That's a direct order."

Moody looked at Millican, the whole war, his whole life, condensed into this moment. What if he killed Millican instead? He didn't move, but he thought about it. Then Millican turned and ran back to the creek, and Moody looked at the Mexican. He was whimpering. He made a sudden movement with his right hand and Moody, startled, thrust the bayonet into his sternum so hard he pinned the boy to the tree. His feet lifted slightly off the ground and his eyes widened. He coughed once, as though he'd only had the wind knocked out of him, and finished raising his hand to his forehead, making the sign of the cross. Moody felt the rib cage settle onto the bayonet. He twisted and pulled, and the musket came away, leaving the bayonet still stuck in the tree. The boy looked at him, the fingers of his left hand curled around the bayonet's locking mechanism. Moody turned and left him.

"Nothing is forgiven," his father used to say. "Some things are forgotten, but damn few. And nothing is ever forgiven."

2.

When Virgil Moody returned to his farm on the Rio Brazos after the fighting, all he wanted was to sit on his porch with Annie and Lucas for a while, then plant some corn and cotton and not have to think about what he'd done and seen done during the war. The worst of the fighting had ended in April, when the army let the militiamen and volunteers go home to tend to their farms. He was back in time to get the crops in, and by the end of May the plants were setting squares, giving him reason to hope. But now, in July, it was too hot to do anything other than sit in the shade and watch the leaves wilt on the branches, and hope he'd watered them enough in June. The bolls opened dry and sharp, like sheep's wool caught on hawthorns. The corn stood straight up and rattled in the wind. He had plenty of time to think but not the comfort to think clearly, and the Mexican boy and his father's voice kept coming back, ambushing him where he sat.

Moody's father said a lot of things and was wrong about most of them. For example, that owning slaves was a patriotic duty. He said the Constitution guaranteed it.

"Just put the biscuits out there in the sun," he said to Annie. "I bet they'll bake." They were on the porch, their faces in shadow but the sun scorching their knees.

As a younger man he'd vowed he would never own slaves, never be like his father, but when he moved from Savannah to New Orleans, he'd taken Annie from his father's plantation. He'd first seen her at his brother's funeral, out at Plantagenet, in the kitchen house arguing with Sikey about something she didn't want to do. She was small and tough as a boot, her voice not loud but with a driving force that made you look up, like the cry of a hawk. As he watched her, he knew that if she stayed at Plantagenet, she'd be dead in a month, either by Casgrain, his father's overseer, a mean man with a fondness for the bull whip, to the ends of which he'd tied lead fishing weights, or from the yellow fever that was running through the plantations in Georgia and had already killed a thousand slaves and three hundred whites in Savannah, including his brother and two cousins. The kitchen house was hot and busy. Sikey didn't have time to stand still and talk. She was a big woman, tall and filled out in places Annie didn't even have. The top of Annie's head barely came to the cook's shoulder, and her hair was so wild that, beside Sikey, she looked like an angry cat standing under a tree. He stopped in the doorway, enjoying watching her follow Sikey about the kitchen, arguing and waving her arms, then he cleared his throat and asked if he might have a glass of cucumber water.

"Sumpin' wrong wid y'arm?" Annie said, turning on him.

"What?"

"Y'all cane fetch y'own water?"

He looked at Sikey. "Annie one of the new Gullah girls," Sikey said. "She be fine, by an' by."

Annie looked like she'd accidentally stepped on a snake. He nodded, and then fetched his own glass of water.

"Nothing wrong with Casgrain's arm, either," he said to her on his way to the door, but gently, more caution than threat. "As I'm sure you'll find out soon enough, you keep that up."

Her eyes narrowed. He stopped and turned to assess their depth, the way a jeweler might, and allowed himself to be caught in them. She started to say something else, but Sikey put a piggin of table scraps in her hands and told her to go out and feed the chickens. When Annie was gone, Sikey turned to him and shook her head. "She don't want to work in the house, Lord bless and keep," she said. "She want to work in the rice fields with her mam and the other Gullahs."

"Well," he said, watching Annie leave, the swing of her skirt, "she was right about my arm."

Two days later, when he left to go back to New Orleans, he took Annie with him. He didn't tell his father, just took her as he would a desk or a horse. No, he would have asked about the horse. He thought about taking her mam, too, and if Annie had insisted he might have, but she didn't. He'd thought they both understood what they were getting into.

3.

"You crazy or what?" Annie said, looking at him sideways from her rocker on the porch. He started, thinking, not for the first time, that she'd been reading his mind. "Cook biscuits on a rock? You been out in the sun too long yoself."

"No, I ain't crazy. Go on, do like I said."

It wasn't an order: he knew by now how she took orders. Their first day in New Orleans, she'd walked around his house like a cat looking for a place to hide her kittens, which, as it turned out, was exactly what she was doing. There weren't many such places. It was a Creole house on Burgundy Street, built in the old style, low, red brick with a corrugated tile roof and a veranda, or banquette, jutting out into the front garden, about as far from a Georgia plantation house as he could get. He'd bought it with money he made playing cards. In the parlor were his few law books, a writing table and two good chairs, and a small portrait of his mother, who had died when he was five, a miniature of the larger painting that hung in his father's house. In his dining room was a glass cabinet that held his mother's second-best china. The kitchen was in the back and, behind that, Moody's bedroom, with a dresser and a bed-spread and a stack of books beside the bed. There was a lean-to off the kitchen, with a door giving out into the back garden. After sniffing the entire house she'd retreated to that, coming out only when he called her, which was seldom, or when he was out, which was often. She did the shopping in Market Square on Sundays, when the plantation negroes came into town to sell the cabbages and fruit they grew on their own small plots, but he fixed his own meals; she washed the dishes and took what food remained back to the lean-to for herself. Moody would come home and find his bed linen changed, or the lamp wicks trimmed, or his boots brushed, but it was as though fairies had done the work. They lived in the house like refugees from hostile countries. He didn't understand until it became obvious that, sometime before they'd left Plantagenet, she had conceived a child. It bothered him that he hadn't guessed.

Gradually she grew less cautious of him, and less caustic. He wouldn't say relaxed, but after Plantagenet, with its Big House and, out of sight of the ground-floor windows, the double row of zebra houses that formed a separate village for the slaves, the New Orleans house seemed as much hers as his. There wasn't enough room in it for segregation. He never forced her to do anything. He talked to her about things, asked her if it was time to wash the curtains, or would she make pork chops for dinner, but he didn't insist and she could easily talk around him. The curtains could wait until the rainy season was over, the butcher had better chicken than pork. He would nod as if to say, *All right then. Whatever you think.* He watched her belly grow from flat bean to summer squash, and he never once asked her whose it was. He was sure he knew, and he didn't want to be told he was right. One night, after he'd been out playing cards, he came into her lean-to and climbed into her bed. There was no window, but the walls were thin and he could hear footsteps on the cobbled street outside, a dog bark, the clatter of a cab, and smell oleander and devil's trumpet in the garden. He slept. When he opened his eyes in the morning, she was still there, as though he'd always slept there. He watched her sleep. He still had most of his clothes on. When she woke, he turned to her and put his hand on her summer squash, and asked her, "What name will you give it?"

"Lucas," she said. That was a good name. He didn't know anyone named Lucas.

"And if it's a girl?"

"It ain't a girl. My mam saw three spiders when she having me, and she had a girl. I ain't seen one spider yet."

After that, he moved her into his bedroom. He remade the lean-to for the child, cut a window in it so the child would see the fig trees and the palmettos and the orange blossoms hidden from the street by the tall board fence. When it was dark, they sat on the banquette and listened to the sounds of the city. She grew. Lucas grew. Moody grew.

4.

"Put them out there on the bird rock," Moody said, pointing to the large, flat stone in front of the cabin where they scattered corn in the winter for wild turkeys and grouse, to keep them away from the chickens.

"What for?" Annie said.

He knew that wasn't how slaves talked to their owners. A slave would have said, "Yes, Massa," and kept her thoughts to herself, and got down off the porch and put the goddamn biscuits out in the sun. But this was Texas, and Texas used to be part of Mexico, and Mexico had abolished slavery in 1829. And anyway, never in all the years they'd been together had she called him "Massa." She'd never called him anything. He'd taken that as a good sign; Massa was his father, or maybe Casgrain. She got up and put the biscuit dough on the bird rock, then set a cast-iron skillet upside down over top of them, as if she were the curious one and that was the reason she was doing it. Moody didn't mind. It would have worked, too. The biscuits didn't rise, but they half baked. They would have baked all the way if they'd left them long enough, but it started getting late, and Annie took the biscuits inside and finished them in the oven. Moody stayed on the porch, content to have made his point, whatever it was.

5.

Moody had spent his childhood summers on Geechee Island, one of Georgia's Sea Islands, where Plantagenet was, and his father's two hundred slaves. Winters were passed in the family's grander house in Savannah, where they had servants and gardeners and cooks instead of slaves. Slaves worked in the plantation's cotton and rice fields. They were badly dressed, badly fed and badly treated. They belonged to the world of commerce. The Savannah servants, on the other hand, were associated with the family's comfort and refinement; they were well trained, well mannered, some even surreptitiously educated. It was thought good to have a house manager who could read and do sums. House servants were considered almost part of the family. That Annie had preferred to be a slave on the rice plantation rather than a servant in Savannah, to continue working in the kitchen with Sikey, had baffled him. It was wrongheaded; she must not have known what she was turning down. He'd thought that by rescuing her from Plantagenet he was saving her not only from Casgrain's bull but also from her own pigheaded ignorance. As soon as he'd laid eyes on her he knew that should she remain at Plantagenet, she would suffer for it; that if she would stand up to him, she would stand up to Casgrain, and she would be whipped for it until her mind was as blunt and numb as her body. He had seen it before. His father referred to his slaves as "head"; they were cattle to him. "I own two hundred head," he would say, to avoid using the word *nigger*, which had offended his wife's refinement. After she died he continued the practice, probably because he liked the sound of it.

A few years before Moody and Annie came to Louisiana, a slave revolt on a sugar plantation in St. John Parish, a few leagues up from New Orleans, had been brutally suppressed by federal troops: a hundred negroes slaughtered, their heads stuck on poles along the highway from the Andry estate to New Orleans. The rebels had refused to cut cane, which was the Devil's own crop. Moody had considered raising it when they'd first moved to the Rio Brazos, but because of that rebellion had decided cane was too hard on a body. Annie told him cane was not as hard as rice: his father had converted part of his land from Sea Island cotton to rice when Eli Whitney's cotton gin flooded the market with upland cotton. With the fields in rice, slave conditions on his father's plantation declined considerably; the slaves referred to Plantagenet as *Plant-à-genou*, and there was grumbling and talk of insurrection, which his father and Casgrain put down with a ruthlessness that had appalled him. It was as if he were being raised in a slaughterhouse, a nightmare in which everyone fought everyone else to the death. So why had Annie wanted to stay there? By the time she'd come along, the fiercest of the negroes had been made drivers, armed with cudgels and lashes and given carte blanche to wield them against troublemakers as they saw fit, and Annie was surely a troublemaker.

After Lucas was born he'd thought maybe it had had something to do with that. Who was Lucas's father? Lucas was lighter skinned than Annie, but surely if it was Casgrain, she wouldn't have wanted to keep Lucas close to him. Would she?

6.

They ate their biscuits in silence, as though they were Communion wafers and therefore signified a kind of failure, and then they got down off the porch to haul river water up to the cotton. But though it was late in the day, it was still too hot to water. Every bucketful they poured on the ground rolled into the hollows between the plants like quicksilver on parchment. They'd have to get up early and water when the earth was still soft with dew. They stacked the buckets on the wagon and went back to the porch and sat watching ants carrying biscuit crumbs off the table. Neither of them felt talkative. They fanned themselves, drank some water, listened to the crickets and admired the way the leaves on the cotton plants shimmered in the sunlight and the light breeze. Upland cotton came from Mexico, and could stand the heat. Annie went inside and brought out some beans to shuck. Beans were also from Mexico, one of the Three Sisters. The other two were Corn and Squash. But there was a fourth family member: Brother Death.

"What do you think, Annie?" he said, nodding toward the cotton. "Ton an acre? Millican got a ton last year."

Annie shook her head and went on with her shucking. He looked back at the cotton, calculating. Mentioning Millican had been a mistake. He would have withdrawn the remark if he thought she was listening. Millican's farm was upriver from theirs. It was bigger, more like a plantation, although not as much like one as Millican pretended it was. Millican had come out with the first wave of settlers brought to Texas by Stephen Austin, one of the Old Three Hundred, and he thought that earned him a place among the colony's uncrowned aristocracy. Now Jared Groce's place farther south, where Sam Houston had crossed the Rio Brazos in '36, was a plantation. Groce had two hundred slaves; Millican had twenty-seven—twenty-eight now, he corrected himself, wincing. Groce had separate dwellings for field servants and another for the overseer; he also had an ice house, a dairy and a carpentry shop. Millican had his own house, with a cook and an upstairs maid who lived in. He'd no more get down off his porch to help a slave haul water than he would help one of his cows eat grass. He told Moody he shouldn't, either. It was wrong to treat Annie and Lucas like they were human beings, it made everyone else's slaves harder to keep down. The easier Moody was on his slaves, he'd said, the harder he had to be on his.

"Millican got a lot of things," Annie said, not looking up from the beans.

He nodded, admitting his mistake. When he'd come back from the fighting, after being gone the better part of a year, the farm had been broke. Annie and Lucas had kept it going in his absence, at least they'd planted the corn, but Moody had decided it was too much to ask of them to manage cotton, too, so there'd been no cash crop last fall. He needed this year's cotton, at least a ton an acre, and prices were down because of the war and President Polk. It wasn't just the money. If he'd wanted money, he would have stayed in New Orleans and kept playing cards. But he needed some to keep the farm going. This was his home, his and Annie's and Lucas's. He stopped thinking about that, because he'd needed Lucas to keep the farm going, too, and Lucas was gone.

From the porch he could see the river, so silted up it looked like a field moving past the house. Not even a wet field. Before the war he had Lucas row out and set bottles on stumps floating by, and he'd shot at them for target practice. His old musket hadn't been good for more than a hundred yards, but it had packed a good punch. His aim improved when the militia gave him a rifle. Three winters after their arrival on the Brazos, when Lucas was eleven, Moody had spent the better part of a month cutting through the riverbank so he could get a horse and wagon down to the water. That spring, the river had flooded so wide he couldn't shoot crows across it anymore. The flood took his dock and he hadn't rebuilt it, expecting the river to flood again, although it hadn't.

Later that same summer the flood had brought him a barrel of brandy. He couldn't imagine where it had come from, maybe some Mexican army camp upriver. Texas had still been part of Mexico then. He drank some of the brandy, quite a bit of it, actually, and considered keeping the rest. In New Orleans, brandy and cards and tobacco had been his three sisters, the part of his life that hadn't been taken up with Annie and Lucas. He didn't like a whiskey drunk. Whiskey made him hate the world and everything in it, including himself. A brandy drunk was mellower, even Annie noticed it, but she still stayed away from him when he'd had too much, and when the barrel showed up she told him he should take it into Boonville and sell it to the hotel owner. Before doing so, since it was a good idea, he'd decanted a couple of bottles and hidden them in the harness room for emergencies.

After the brandy had come the body of a Mexican officer, still in his *compañia fusilero* uniform: two white *bandoleras* crossed over a blue tunic. The body had snagged in a back current behind a tree root, and Moody had waded in and pulled it out. Eagles and eels had been at the eyes. His saber was gone, but his bayonet was still in its scabbard and Moody had kept it, and buried the officer in the side of the cut. He wasn't a superstitious man, but the body drew flies and spooked the horses, and anyway, a man in uniform deserved a decent burial. In those days, before the big war, he still liked Mexicans. For him, fighting them hadn't been an act of hatred but a contest of skills between equals, more like a card game. Killing that Mexican boy had been later, when the contest had shifted in favor of Polk's army and Moody had been an involuntary volunteer. Annie had kept the Mexican's boots, they were black and of good, thick leather. She broke them up when they were still wet and made a new seat for the rocker that still sat in the corner beside their bed, unused. She never had any more children after Lucas.

Thinking of the Mexican officer he'd buried in '36 reminded him of the Mexican boy he'd killed in '45. It was one of the ways he deduced the nonexistence of God—a decent God would have known he didn't need reminding. Or else that God existed and was a mean-minded son of a bitch.

Annie stood up and carried the bowl of shucked beans into the house, leaving Moody on the porch to keep an eye on the cotton. Sea Island cotton hadn't been too bad, but this Mexican upland cotton liked to grow in pure, dry sand, and people who grew it had to live where it lived, on barren sand in open sun. At least in New Orleans they'd had crawfish and okra, and the smell of the sea when the wind shifted to the south, and Annie had had island folk to talk to. She had taught Lucas some Gullah, and told him stories about Adanko the Rabbit and Aunt Nancy the Spider. Moody hadn't asked her whether she wanted to leave New Orleans to come live in a desert where stinkbugs ate the okra and Sister Cotton made them haul water from the river to keep her alive. It hadn't occurred to him, but now he didn't think it mattered; she would have said yes. She would have wanted to get Lucas out of New Orleans. She would have wanted to stay with him.

They'd have to pick the cotton soon, Moody thought, heat or no heat. There were just the two of them now with Lucas gone, so he would have to pick alongside Annie and work some to keep up with her. She was one of those determined women who would work until she dropped. The tireder she got, the faster she worked. But there wouldn't be much to pick, three acres. Ten years and they still weren't hardened to cotton. When they finished picking and ginning and baling they'd have to soak their hands in Dr. Ball's Liniment and wrap them in muslin and still he'd barely be able to hold the reins when they drove the bales to Boonville. He often told himself he might rather ranch cattle than grow cotton, but there was something about the Brazos Bottom he liked. Before the fighting, once he got the cut dug and could get a wagon down to haul water, he and Lucas would stand in the river, passing buckets up to Annie to dump into the barrels, and the current would curl around his legs and he'd feel it trying to tug him deeper into the channel. There'd been women in New Orleans used to tug at him like that, before Annie. It wasn't a feeling you gave in to easily, but it wasn't entirely unpleasant, either.

"Come on out here and sit with me," he called to her.

She brought out some sewing. She didn't want to be with him. She sat breathing shallowly but he could see her dress move. She wasn't dead inside. He watched for a while, hoping she would look up and meet his eyes, but she would not, and when he let his gaze drift over to the Mexican's grave, like a tongue worrying a loose tooth, she sniffed. He should have pushed that dead body back into the river. He shouldn't have taken the bayonet, either. He should get up off this porch now and throw the bayonet out as far into the river as he could. Instead, a listless kind of panic came over him, a feeling that there were things he would change but couldn't do anything about. It was as though there were packages in his brain marked "Things to Worry About," and when he opened one of them—say, Lucas gone—his brain automatically opened the next package, Annie not talking to him, and then the next, the Mexican boy, until his whole brain was a mess of worries. The heat, the crop, the low price for cotton, Millican. And then back to Lucas again.

Lucas had been a quiet boy, happiest sitting by himself with something in his hands. There'd been things in the New Orleans house that Lucas would stare at for hours: a tortoiseshell hairbrush that had belonged to Moody's older brother, a pair of dice made from the knuckle bones of a pig, a wind-up brass pheasant that would strut across the dining table flapping its wings and squawking until it reached the edge of the table and fell into Lucas's lap. Moody found the boy thoughtful, but Annie said he was just unhappy, and it was true that when the pheasant waddled off the table he didn't laugh, he just gave it to Moody to rewind and put back on the table. Again, he would say. Again.

"I'll be out at the barn if you need me," Moody said, and when, as he expected, there was no pause in her sewing he got up and went to the harness room to look at the bone.

He kept it on a trestle table in the center of the room. It was a large femur, three and a half feet long, eighteen inches around at the middle, twenty-six and a half inches at each end. Annie hadn't wanted him to keep it. It wasn't part of any animal anyone had ever seen, and it frightened her. It frightened him. It had been in the harness room, coated in shellac and glowing like an ember in the pale light that came through the dust-coated window, since he found it when he was digging the cut. The dirt was red and friable when dry, easy shoveling. When his blade hit the bone he'd thought it was a rock, but there weren't any rocks that big in Texas clay, and as it emerged from the hole he could see the shape of it, considered it for a long time, looked around as though worried that the animal that lost it might be coming back to claim it. Then the rain had started. He'd had to get the bone up to the barn before the clay by the river turned to gumbo. Moody had called Lucas to come down and help. Annie came, too, but when she saw the bone she backed away as though afraid it would jump up and bite her. Lucas was quietly inquisitive, as ever. He ran his hands over the bone like a blind man, asking a mess of questions. What was it? Where did it come from? How'd it get here? Annie didn't ask anything.

"Mastodon," Moody said, thinking that knowing what it was would make Annie feel better. "Animal like an elephant," he said. "A leg bone, a femur." He ran his finger down her thigh, from her hip to her knee, to show her where hers was.

"Leave it be," she said, backing away.

"Why?" said Moody.

"Leave it be. My mam told me the Earth a man, and woman made from him, and elephant comed from woman. Elephant bones be left buried in the ground or trouble come."

She was probably right, he'd thought, just about everything brought some kind of trouble, but it wasn't like her to speak obeah and he hadn't listened to her. He didn't think she knew what an elephant was, let alone where they came from. Besides, this wasn't an elephant.

"Mastodons aren't elephants," he'd said.

She'd gone up to the house, and he and Lucas had mud-wrestled the bone to the wagon bed and up to the barn.

"How'd you know what this is?" Lucas asked him.

"I read about bones like this when I was about your age," Moody said. "And I saw some, in New Orleans." The bones had had something to do with the explorers Lewis and Clarke, were being shipped to Washington for President Jefferson and had been displayed briefly in New Orleans. He remembered the smell of the tent, the wood chips on the ground, the red sand in the boxes that held the bones. He'd had to sneak in, because his father wouldn't give him the penny.

"You learn about them in school?"

"Some," Moody said. "And later, in college."

"I want to go to school," Lucas said.

"Where?" Moody asked, evasively. There weren't any schools for blacks in Texas, or anywhere else that he knew of.

"Up North, they got schools I can go to."

"We ain't up North," Moody had said, and Lucas had looked at the bone and kept quiet. "I can teach you what I know," Moody said. "We can look for more bones up this river."

But Lucas stayed quiet. It was the first time he'd asked Moody for something that Moody couldn't give.

7.

When Moody came back from James Polk's war, after the Mexican boy and the annexation of Texas, all he'd wanted was a long period of undisturbed calm, no bloated bodies rotting in the sun, no snipers in trees, no mortars shaking the ground. A rock could go back to just being a rock. Something flying through the air could be a bird. But almost the first thing Annie told him was that Lucas, who was eighteen and restless, had taken up with a woman belonging to Millican, of all people, a house servant named Benah. He'd been sneaking over to Millican's at night and not coming back until near daybreak. Annie was worried frantic. She'd done everything to keep him back, but he wouldn't listen, and she was glad to turn the job over to Moody. "He ain't used to be afraid," she said, as though treating Lucas as a human being had been a mistake, which is what Millican had been telling him all along. In New Orleans, he and Annie had lived together openly in the Quarter, let anyone think what they would. They'd had to be more careful in Texas,

where every white farmer was a slaveholder and no one felt compelled by Mexican law to give up their slaves. Polk's war might have
been about territory, but Texans were fighting for slavery. Slavery
was their religion; the Mexican War had been a religious war. But
within their own house, Moody had gone on thinking of Annie as
his wife and Lucas as their son.

Annie hadn't been as comfortable with that as he was, he'd
known that. The consequences for her were far greater than they
were for him, even in New Orleans, but she'd gone along with
it, wore her *tignons* and scarves and walked beside him as if her arm
were in his, as if she were his fancy lady. At the very least, he'd
thought, she and Lucas could be taken for his house servants, and a
grand house it must be to have such well-dressed, fine-looking servants, must be a mansion, maybe she was more than a servant, look
how yellow that boy is. And see how many *tignons* she was wearing.
She was a fancy lady for sure. As long as they didn't let it go to their
heads, people turned a blind eye. *Louisianais* could detect differences of color in two glasses of milk; it didn't bother them much
but they noted it for possible future use. They didn't think Annie
was trying to fool anybody. They treated upper servants in a grand
house like they were family, because in many cases they were. Until
trouble come, as Annie would say. Then they turned on you like
Sarah turned on Hagar, as if all the time they had had no idea.

And trouble always comes. If Millican caught Lucas with Benah
he'd send him back home in a pork barrel. Moody asked Annie how
she could have let it happen, Lucas out alone at night, a target for
all kinds of things, even apart from Millican. He could be nabbed by
a slaver and taken down to Galveston and sold. Even being seen
by a white man could mean trouble; if anything went missing
anywhere within ten miles, a farmer mislaid a pair of gloves, a horse
run off, a child woke up crying, people would say they saw Lucas
out that night, he must have been up to no good, and before you
knew it a rope got thrown over a branch. Moody didn't have to tell

Annie any of that, she knew it better than he did. But he told her anyway.

"What you want me to do?" she said. "Chain him to the barn?"

"Didn't you talk to him?"

"'Course I talk to him, da. He think shit flies don't land on honey. You talk to him."

"Me?" he said. "He's your son."

Annie threw her hands in the air. "But he your slave!"

That rocked him back, hit him in the chest like a mortar shell. It was a betrayal, her saying that. It wasn't the first time the word had passed between them, but it had always been thrown in anger— Annie's anger—and the word had always seemed to him to be leveled at him unfairly. He hadn't bought her, he hadn't fathered a child on her, he had never treated her or Lucas like slaves, or even thought of them as such. Had she? When Austin was handing out land in the Brazos Bottom, Moody hadn't taken the four-thousand-acre *sitio* allotted to a family with slaves, as Millican had, he took what a single farmer was entitled to, six hundred and forty acres, enough for a good-sized farm but not so big it would require slaves to run. He'd wanted a small holding, a life of hard work but with time for sitting on the porch with Annie and Lucas, for reading at night, for Sundays in town. He'd studied law in New Orleans, and had had some idea of being a frontier lawyer, maybe helping Austin in his negotiations with the government in Mexico City. He and Annie and Lucas had been a family in New Orleans, they'd been a family here. And now here she was calling him a slaveholder.

The next morning, when Lucas was at breakfast and Annie was in the garden cutting onion tops, Moody sat across the table from him and said, "What's this business with Benah, Luke?" It wasn't the most judicious of inquiries, he knew, but it was man to man, not owner to slave. In lawyering it was known as the approach direct. It was supposed to elicit trust, not resentment.

Lucas shrugged. "She receiving me," he said.

"She is receptive to your intentions?" Moody said for clarity.

"Yes."

"What are your intentions?"

"We want to marry."

"Marry," Moody said. "You mean in a church, with a preacher?"

"There's a man works for Millican will jump us over the broomstick."

"What do you mean, works for?"

"All right, he's a slave, but he's also a preacher."

"Do you think Millican will let you marry one of his servant girls?"

"I'll talk to him."

"You'll have to buy her from him."

"I'll talk to him."

"You can't talk to Millican."

"Why not?"

"Because Millican only talks to whites."

"He thinks I'm your son."

"Maybe so, but he doesn't think you're white."

Lucas tore a corner off a loaf of corn bread, spread some middling on it and ate it. "So what happens?" he said.

"If you promise me you'll stay home at night," Moody said, "I'll speak to Millican and see what I can do."

"What can you do?" Lucas said.

"I'll offer to buy Benah, and bring her here."

"But then you'll own Benah."

"No, I'll free her as soon as she gets here. One step at a time."

"What about me? You free me, too?"

You already are free, he was about to say, but stopped himself. "You've always been free here, but now we'll have to get you your free papers."

"We? You'll free Ma, too?"

Moody hesitated. Fatally. "We aren't talking about your mother now," he said. "We're talking about you and Benah."

"But will you free her?"

Moody drank a mouthful of coffee. "If she wants."

"What do you mean, if she wants. Of course she wants."

"Jesus," Moody said. "I thought you two were happy here. What's going on?"

Lucas stared at the table. "Why were you fighting the Mexicans?" he asked.

"What? Because they were fighting us."

"That ain't it."

"When I signed up with Austin," Moody said, retreating to the easy answer, "part of the deal was that if there was trouble with Mexico or the Comanche, I would fight in the militia."

"I know that," Lucas said, "but why were you fighting the Mexicans?"

"Because Texas was a state of Mexico, and we didn't like the way they were treating us," Moody said, feeling his way. "We wanted to be an independent republic."

"So Mexico owned you," Lucas said, looking up.

"Yes."

"And you said to Mexico, 'We don't want to be owned by you no more. We want to be free.' "

Moody was quiet for a while. "Yes," he said, "that's what we told them."

"And Mexico said to go to hell."

"Yes."

"So you fought Mexico to set yourselves free."

"It was a bit more complicated than that," he said, feeling out-lawyered. "But you're right, essentially, that's what happened."

"Well," Lucas said, "that's what I'm saying to you."

"I take your point. But I still need to fix it with Millican."

"Now that Texas is part of the United States, we're slaves again. You better fix it. This whole damn thing is your fault."

"Not *my* fault, Lucas. I've been against slavery all my life!"

"That so?"

"Yes, that's so."

"Then what are you to me?"

So, another betrayal. What was happening here? "I'm your . . ." But he couldn't finish the sentence. Whatever was catching in his throat, it wasn't a word.

"When we lived in New Orleans," Lucas said, speaking more gently, "I kept asking Mam if you were my father. I thought that's what you were. She always said, 'No, he ain't your father. Your father in Georgia.' 'Then what is he?' I asked her. She never said. It's like there's no word for what you are to me."

There were tears in Lucas's eyes, but he wasn't crying.

"I always raised you like a son," Moody said.

"Did you? Wouldn't you have sent your son to school? Would you have even moved out here if you had a son? I mean a white son."

"Yes, of course I would have. I'd have done the same for him as I did for you."

"Then do this thing for me now. Fix it with Millican."

8.

After chores the next morning, he'd saddled Justice and ridden to Millican's. It was warm for June. The cottonwoods had yellowed out and early-summer heat was releasing cicadas and crickets from the soil. He felt separated from it. He sensed the burgeoning in the air but didn't feel it in himself. Millican's corn was six inches high, the rows neat, the fields watered and weeded. His own corn was hand-spread, unevenly spaced. It grew just as well, for the most part, but it didn't look as good and it was harder to weed and water. He started to blame the war. Polk. Even Austin. How far back did he need to go before he could blame himself? Not that far.

Lucas and this Benah must have been considering running off, but to where? Most runaways from Texas went south, into Mexico, or east, to the Atlantic seaboard and farther, to Haiti. Tales of runaways living in the lap of luxury in Canada, where slavery had been abolished years ago, were also circulating in the South and had, of course, been loudly dismissed as pure fantasy by preachers and plantation owners. Free land, separate schools for negroes, paid labor, protection of the law, who could believe such things? Moody could. Slavery was slipping everywhere but here in the South. There'd been talk among the soldiers who'd come to fight for Texas from places like Tennessee and Virginia that the old ways were unraveling and new ways hadn't been invented yet. Millican believed them, and the news had made him more adamant about keeping his slaves under the whip. By buying Benah, Moody would be rescuing her as he had Annie, but he couldn't let Millican think that. He would have to say he needed a second kitchen hand. He'd put in an extra acre of cotton and needed Lucas in the field. He didn't like the idea, he didn't want to end up owning another slave, even for the short time it would take to set her free. He would manumit them both, as long as they agreed to stay close and work for him, but he wouldn't tell Millican that, either.

He rehearsed the story as he rode. He would say he wanted his fields to be as well tended and free of burdock and goat weed as Millican's. He wanted a big, white house and slave quarters. To be more like his father and Millican. He thought he might get six cents a pound for his cotton this year, which would give him two hundred and forty dollars, and he would offer that to Millican. He thought it was a good plan. He thought all his plans were good plans.

Millican invited him into his office in what he called the Big House and settled him in a chair across from where he had some papers spread out on a library table. Moody hadn't seen him since Fort Brown, more than a year before, and the sight of the man still irked him. He had the eyes of a ferret. His fingernails were yellowed and pointed. He was wearing a white planter's suit and had started growing side-whiskers. Maybe he thought they made him look dignified, but they only made him look more ferret-like. Beside the papers were a glass of whiskey and a pistol, as though he'd been expecting a long session of gloating followed by a break-in. He didn't offer Moody any whiskey.

Moody told about him his idea of buying Benah.

Millican shook his head. "Now that we're a state," he said, "I have to petition Congress for permission to sell a slave. Even one. You ever petition Congress for anything? The bitch would be a grandmother before I heard back from them. We can work out some other kind of arrangement."

"What kind of arrangement?"

"You don't want Benah, anyway," Millican said. "You want some field slaves."

"I want to increase my holdings," Moody said.

"Then here's what you do," Millican said, leaning forward in his chair. "I'll give you four hundred dollars for Lucas. You take the money to Galveston, and you buy yourself two, maybe three field niggers. Two males and a mare. Or better yet, one male and two mares."

"What? No!"

"Ain't that what you said you wanted?"

"Yes, but I'm not selling Lucas! I'm offering to buy Benah!"

Moody thought Millican had mentioned four hundred dollars because that was what he wanted for Benah. Millican knew he would never sell Lucas, because Millican believed that Lucas was Moody's son. This was a poker game, and Moody realized too late that he had tipped his hand.

Millican poured himself another whiskey. "I couldn't think of letting Benah go," he said, setting down the bottle. The whiskey sloshed in the glass like angry waves in a small harbor. "Congress or no Congress, Mrs. Millican needs her in the kitchen." He looked at Moody. "All right," he said, "five hundred for Lucas."

"No," Moody said. "I will give you two hundred and forty for Benah when I sell the cotton."

"This is low," Millican said, making a sour face.

Moody knew he'd lost. He was bidding now to save face. "Four hundred for Benah."

Millican shook his head. "My offer stands."

"Five hundred."

Millican sat back and folded his arms over his chest.

Moody rose from the table, took up his hat and started for the door.

"I know what you want Benah for," Millican called after him, and laughed. "Annie getting on, is she?"

9.

"Of course I said no," he told Lucas and Annie that night at supper, but Annie set down her knife and fork and started shaking, like she could see into the future. "Millican's a mean man," he said. "I served under him, I know how weak he is, and there's nothing meaner than a weak man."

Lucas looked downcast. "Benah says he whips her."

"Of course he whip her," Annie said sharply. "You think he stop whipping her when you there? He'll whip her and you, too."

"Maybe," Lucas said. "Maybe once."

Annie sat back and shook her head. "He'll whip you a hundred ways from Friday," she said. "He'll whip you any time he want to. And when he done whipping you, he'll whip Benah in front of you. Maybe worse."

"My father had an overseer like him, name of Casgrain," Moody said. He looked at Annie and then away. "Casgrain would have whipped your mamma soon as look at her. That's why I took her away from there."

"I know," said Lucas. It wasn't the first time he'd heard that story. "And that's why I got to take Benah away from Millican."

"What that?" said Annie. "You and Benah planning to run off?"

"If we have to."

"Lucas," said Moody, "you're smarter than that. You know what your chances are of getting away from here? You'll have every blackbirder and pattyroller in Texas after you. You won't get five miles down the road."

"Let me go to Millican, then. I'll take it from there."

"I will not let you go to Millican!"

"Sell me to him and give me the money," Lucas said. "You won't be selling me, you'll be buying my freedom. Actually, Millican will be buying my freedom, and Benah's, too."

Lucas's innocence recalled to him Annie's back in Sikey's kitchen—*Sumpin' wrong wid y'arm?*—and it momentarily broke his resolve. The words to a Creole song they had often heard in New Orleans came into his head: *Pou la belle Layotte ma mourri 'nocent.* For the beautiful Layotte I must die like a fool. For the beautiful Benah, it seemed, Lucas would put his fool head in a noose. Annie was holding her sides, rocking forward and back on her chair. He didn't know what she was thinking. She was humming a song she had taught Lucas as a child, a song in a language Moody didn't know. More distance.

"If you think I'm a slaver," he said, "just wait until Millican has you."

Lucas got up and left the house.

Moody knew he should go after him, bring him back and talk to him. But he sat at the table and stared at his hands. What was it? Stubbornness? Cowardice? But he told himself it was time for Lucas to go. He told himself he did nothing out of respect for Lucas.

"You lettin' him go?" Annie said.

"He isn't going anywhere," Moody said. "He probably just went out to the barn."

"No, he gone. You let him go."

"He'll be back."

"No, he won't!" she yelled at him, clutching at his shirt. "You fetch him back! You have to go get him, Virgil!"

But he didn't. He'd convinced himself that Lucas was out at the barn with the bone, or down by the river, or taking a piss off the porch. That he would come back on his own. Annie got up and ran outside, and twenty minutes later when she came back inside she wouldn't speak to him.

10.

That night he went to bed early, telling himself that Lucas had gone to see Benah and would be back home when he woke up. He'd checked the barn, he'd stood in the harness room with the bone for a time, noting its stillness and finality, feeling the enormity of his inaction. The sky had remained light until almost ten, and he lay in bed waiting for Annie. If he'd left her in Georgia, Lucas would have been gone long before this, sold the moment he was weaned. He'd saved Annie from that, he'd done right by Lucas. He fell asleep in the dark and woke up an hour or two later in a panic, his heart pounding wildly, still alone. He got up and lit a candle, thinking Annie had fallen asleep in a chair, or couldn't sleep because of Lucas. He thought maybe Lucas had come back and they were up drinking tea together, that she had talked sense into the boy and they could go back to living the way they had been. But she wasn't anywhere he looked. He went outside and checked the porch, where it was cooler and he could hear the river, restless in its shallow bed of clay. He finally found her in Lucas's room, curled up on his bed, sound asleep. She still had her clothes on. Her face was beautiful in the soft candlelight, and she looked more peaceful than he'd seen her in a long time, maybe not since New Orleans, when he would lean on his elbow in bed and watch her sleep, her eyes moving under their lids, afraid to touch her and pull her from her dream.

He put a blanket over her, careful not to wake her, to let her know he'd been there, then went back to his own bed.

II.

Early the next day a man rode into Moody's yard and dismounted. Moody was in the cornfield, pulling weeds, but when he saw the dust on the road he started toward the house, thinking it was Lucas come back on his own, without Benah. By the time he got to the yard, whoever it was had ridden off again, and he saw Annie standing on the porch, holding a leather pouch. Moody knew what was in it, and Annie knew what it meant.

"Your thirty pieces of silver," she said, tossing the pouch onto the table.

"That's Lucas's money," he said. "I'll give it to him, and he and Benah can get away."

"First you make him a slave," she said, "and now you make him a fugitive."

So he hadn't gone.

I2.

He still hadn't decided what to do about Lucas when, on the fifth of August, three days before the auction, he hitched up Max and Carlota and he and Annie started out to Boonville with six bales of cotton on the wagon. It was a forty-mile ride, mostly uphill. The thermometer read a hundred and six degrees. With three tons of cotton the horses couldn't get up to much more than a walk, and in the heat even that exhausted them. They had to stop to water and rest the horses every couple of hours. Annie had barely spoken to him since June, and Lucas was as pigheaded as she was.

Millican's corn was so high it blocked their view of the Big House. Annie stood up in the wagon to try to see Lucas, tottered, then slumped back down. When they passed the mouth of the lane, she turned in her seat and stared at the tree above the slave house, as if she expected to see Lucas hanging from it. Moody was curious, too, and slowed the horses so they could see he wasn't there. He wasn't.

"He's likely gone to Boonville with Millican's cotton," Moody said. "We'll see him there. I'll convince him to come home and I'll return Millican's money."

She sat in the wagon staring down the road as though she could see the whole forty miles to Boonville, hear the drivers slapping their horses and owners shouting out numbers, the creak of block and tackle as bales were hoisted onto weigh scales. She shook her head.

"I worry he won't," she said.

"I know."

"You don't know," she said, closing her eyes. "You don't know what worry is. He Millican's slave now. I hoped I never see my boy a slave with a hard massa, and now I see it. You don't know."

She'd gone to Millican's a few times to see Lucas, and told Moody about her visits. At first Lucas was well treated, she said. He and Benah were married by a tall, hungry-looking man named Bongo. But Benah was still sleeping in the Big House, on a pallet of corn husks on the floor of the pantry, while Lucas lived in the slave quarters. Millican wanted to make him a driver, give him a bullwhip and put him in charge of the field hands, but Lucas wouldn't take that job. Millican told him that as a driver he'd get a house of his own, and he and Benah could live in it together, but Lucas still didn't take the whip. Moody and Annie both saw trouble ahead. Why did Lucas think he could tell Millican what he would and wouldn't do? Annie said Moody should never have touched that bone. Moody had offered to give her the pouch to secretly pass on to Lucas, but she hadn't taken it. If Lucas had the money he would run off with Benah, and they'd both be caught and killed, or as good as. At least at Millican's she knew where they were. Moody was tired of having his best offers turned down.

They arrived in Boonville on the morning of the seventh. They'd slept under the wagon at night, Annie seeming to relent, to need the comfort of his nearness, though she'd cried throughout. He'd needed her comfort, too, although he was not sure she'd given it. She asked him what he would do if they found Lucas, could they take him back with them? Moody said he thought so, if Lucas would come, and if Benah could come with him.

"Millican lied about having to apply to Congress to sell a slave," he told her. "Nobody does that."

But what if Lucas wasn't there? she asked. What would they do? It would be like Millican to keep Lucas out of Boonville, to show him who was running his life now, not him and not Moody. Millican would sink his teeth into anything soft. At Fort Brown, during lulls in the fighting, the men would sit around in Sarah Boggins's tavern drinking Mexican beer and talking about why they were killing Mexicans. They each had their ideas about it. Some just liked fighting. Some were glad to be anywhere but home. A few, the older men who had fought in the War of Independence, said this was different, the cause in this war was unclear. They weren't defending their own land, they were pushing the Mexicans out of theirs. Moody realized now that Millican hated him, and would do everything he could to break him. That was why he wouldn't sell Benah. In his *sitio* days, Moody had been a friend of Stephen Austin's, they'd studied law together in New Orleans, played poker and drunk rum, and Millican couldn't stand the fact that, despite being one of the Old Three Hundred, Millican had never so much as spoken to Austin, never been slapped on the back and asked how his daddy was, never invited into Austin's tent for a game of cards. Whatever Moody had, Millican would want to destroy. And Millican thought Moody had Lucas, even though Lucas now belonged to Millican.

Eventually Annie slept, her head pressed against his chest, while Moody lay awake listening to the night, the horses cropping grass beside the wagon, the water slipping quietly through the *charco*, to Annie's troubled breathing.

Millican's six wagons were in line when they got to the cotton exchange, but Lucas wasn't on any of them.

"You said he'd be here," Annie said.

"I said he might," Moody said. "Maybe he's gone for a walk."

Annie looked at him as if he were a moron. As soon as he pulled into line behind the last wagon, Annie jumped down and went over to talk to a group of Millican's teamsters who were standing inside the entrance to the warehouse, no overseer in evidence, probably at the saloon or the whorehouse. They kept their eyes away from her, looking down at their feet, or up and down the street as though for a wagon to come along and save them. Annie came back to the wagon and told Moody that Lucas had disappeared and they didn't know where he was, or else they weren't saying to his mam.

"What we do now?" she asked him.

"Wait here," Moody said. "Move the wagon up if our turn comes." He handed her the reins and got down from the wagon. At the warehouse, he asked Millican's men straight out where Lucas was. The men looked at each other and then at him.

"Lucas bain't here," one of them said.

"I can see that. Is he somewhere with Benah?"

"Benah bain't here, neither."

"Benah be sold," the first man said.

"Sold?" Moody said, stunned. "Sold where?"

"Massa sell she, up away."

Up away meant the auction block north of Boonville, on the Camino Real, a stockyard meant for cattle and horses but owners sometimes took slaves there who were trouble and couldn't be sold locally. Too wild, too old, too crippled up. Most of the buyers were speculators passing through, looking for a bargain. Benah would have been a prize. If that was where Millican had sold her, she could be anywhere between Santa Fe and Galveston.

"What about Lucas?" he asked the man, but he already knew the answer.

"Him gone after she, da."

He went back to the wagon and told Annie what he'd learned. "As soon as we sell our cotton," he said, "we'll go up to the auction yard to see if Lucas is there. If he isn't, I'll go see Millican, get him to say who he sold Benah to, and then we'll go find her, and when we find her we'll find Lucas."

"Go now," she said. "Buy Benah yourself."

"I need the cotton money."

Annie looked at him as she had when he'd told her to put the biscuit dough on the bird rock. There'd been some warmth in her then; this time she just stared, her hands clasped on her lap. She hardly breathed, sipped air into the tops of her lungs like she was floating on her back on the ocean, afraid to empty them for fear she'd drown. She'd warned him. She'd told him trouble would come.

They waited two hours. Finally, their bales were lifted off the wagon and weighed, their weight debated, their value calculated, and more time consumed in counting and signing. Annie was almost comatose. There was little point in going after Lucas this late, the auction would be over. Moody's gloom increased with every dollar that was passed to him. Annie hadn't moved.

Lucas wasn't at the auction yard. Whatever commerce had taken place there that day was long over. Moody spoke to a white-haired man who was sweeping the office, but the man didn't know if a woman had been sold that day or not. Annie sat quietly beside

Moody the whole way back to the farm. Only once did she speak.

"I knew trouble come the day Lucas born. When I saw his light-light skin I started waiting for this day. It no good, white on black, it pain at the start and worse pain at the end."

He supposed she was talking about Casgrain. "I'm sorry," he said.

"Maybe it ain't your fault. Maybe he'd have run off anyway." But she didn't look convinced. "You been good to Lucas," she said, "you raise him like your own."

"I tried."

"But he not your own, he mine. You didn't have that right."

13.

Millican was sitting on his front porch, a drink in one hand and a fly swatter in the other. Moody didn't dismount. He sat on his horse in the sun and left his hat on to let Millican know he was in a hurry. There was a table beside Millican with a scattering of dead flies on it and a Colt Paterson revolver lying on its side, like a dog sleeping with one eye open, staring at Moody. Millican must have kept it as a war trophy. Moody had heard him say that if they'd had revolvers at the Alamo a lot of good men would still be alive. Moody thought it unlikely, given the odds had been a hundred and seventy to one. Millican always thought he could beat the odds.

"I don't know where that boy of yours went," Millican said. "But I will tell you this" —he pointed the swatter at Moody— "he gets brought back here I'll whip him so hard his own mammy won't recognize him. I've a good mind to ask you for my money back, plus something for the filly."

"You shouldn't have sold her," Moody said. "You knew he'd go after her."

"I sold Benah to pay for Lucas."

That was another lie, and both men knew it. Millican took a drink to cover it.

"I offered to buy her myself," Moody said, "but you told me you couldn't part with her."

"I knew why you wanted her."

"No, you didn't."

"You're too soft on your help," Millican said lazily. "I told you that before."

"I treat them like sensible human beings."

"That's just what I mean. They ain't sensible and they ain't human beings. Somebody treated Nat Turner like a sensible human being and look what he did. Slaughtered a dozen innocent people in their beds, is that what you want to happen out here?"

"I doubt there's a dozen innocent people in the whole territory," Moody said.

Millican laughed and touched the revolver. "Get down off a that horse and have a drink," he said. When Moody didn't, he said, "You want those niggers to start thinking they don't have to go out and pick cotton if they don't want to, if it's too hot or they got better things to do, like rut all day in the barn. All right," he said after a pause, "I sold her because Lucas was making her forget her station. I caught her saying things like 'It's hot, Lucas. I wish I didn't have to wash these bedclothes,' and him saying, 'You shouldn't have to, Benah dear. What's wrong with leaving them till tonight when it cools down?' "

"Sounds sensible to me. What's wrong with waiting until it's cooler?"

"Because that's how it starts is what's wrong with it. What's wrong with it is my wife told her to wash them bedclothes now, not whenever she damn well felt like it. My wife and I tell people what to do around here, not Lucas. And not you, neither." He pointed the swatter at Moody again. "Like I said, the kinder you treat your niggers, the harder I gotta be on mine."

Moody turned in the saddle and looked over Millican's cotton fields, dark now after the harvest. A few balls blew along between the rows. Cicadas whined in the heat.

"Who'd you sell her to, Endicot?" He kept his voice casual, as though he were only conversationally interested.

"Why, you going after her?"

"I'm going after Lucas."

Millican gave him a long look. "Some slaver, I didn't catch his name."

"He say where he was heading?"

"No. South, I reckon."

Moody's and Millican's cotton was being barged down the Rio Brazos from Boonville to Galveston probably that very day. If Lucas knew Benah was headed south, he might have stowed away on one of the barges. Maybe their best chance was to go down to Galveston and wait for Lucas to show up there, with or without Benah.

He turned his horse to leave, but Millican stopped him.

"Virgil Moody," he said, "you find that nigger you bring him back here. I don't care in how many parts."

He'd gone to Millican because he thought he had to do something. But he didn't have to do something, he had to *undo* something. And maybe that wasn't possible. It would have been like unfinding the bone. Once a thing is done, it can't be undone—was that what his father had meant? That nothing lost can ever be found again? But the bone had been lost for ten thousand years, and he had found it. Lucas had only been lost for a few months.

14.

When he got home, Annie wasn't there.

He called. He walked through the house, the barn, the corn-fields and the pasture, the bare, red hills above the lane. He climbed down the hollow behind the house to where the bodark grew thick above the river. He sat on the porch, dread growing in him. There weren't a lot of other places she could be. He got up and went down to the river, past the Mexican's grave and where he'd found the bone. The water made a steady, rushing noise, a kind of gravelly hiss. He looked into it, but it was too silted up and he couldn't see more than a few inches down. He thought about wading in but knew that wouldn't tell him anything he didn't already know.

Something he'd seen when he was looking for her snagged in his mind, and he tried to remember what it was. Something in the barn. He ran back up the cut and on his way glanced at the house, half expecting to see her sitting on the porch shelling beans or mending one of Lucas's shirts. In the barn, he went to the harness room and flung the door open so hard one of the leather hinges snapped.

He looked at the empty trestle table for a good two minutes, waiting for the bone to reappear, then ran back to the river. He might have yelled "No!" He might have called her name. He knew what she must have done. She must have carried or more likely dragged the bone down to the river, tied herself to it, walked out into the water and let it go. Let the elephant drag her in. He could see her doing it. He was running to stop her, untie the rope from her waist before the river grabbed her, tell her they would find Lucas, get him back, start again. Undo everything. He remembered her almost-last words to him, that it wasn't his fault, that Lucas would have run off anyway. He'd known it wasn't true when she said it, but he hadn't understood she was saying goodbye.

Sometimes, where his shadow lay on the water, he thought he could see deeper into it. He waded in, felt around with his foot, moved out deeper to where the bottom dropped off sharply and he was nearly pulled in. That was where Annie would be, down there with the catfish and the alligator gar. He knew better than to dive in, but maybe if he had a pole. He ran back up to the barn and looked around. Didn't he have a pole? It was like he was in a stranger's barnyard. The top rail of the corral gate was about four inches around. He grabbed it, worked the spike at the other end of it out of the post, and ran back to the river. He edged his way out to the drop and stuck the pole in. The current was so strong he could barely hold the pole against it. He braced the pole against his left leg and moved it around like a tiller. He thought he felt something solid come up against it. He thrashed around in the water, trying to pull and at the same time keep upright and away from the drop.

It was a post from his old dock, broken off two feet below the surface. And there was something attached to it, like a crosspiece, smooth and hard. A rope. He turned the pole until the nail hooked on the rope and began pulling it in. It didn't come at first, and then it began coming faster than he could keep it taut. He pulled until he could grab the rope, then threw the pole away and hauled on the rope. He felt the cloth of her dress, and he pulled harder. Her face came into view, floating like a caught fish, just beneath the surface. The rope wasn't around her waist, it was around her neck. Jesus, Annie. The more he'd pulled, the tighter he'd choked her. She'd done that on purpose, in case he came back before she drowned; when he pulled her in he'd have lynched her.

"Jesus, Annie," he said again, aloud this time.

He carried her to the cut and set her down. When he loosened the rope around her neck, water streamed out of her mouth.

After a long while, he fetched a shovel and blanket from the house, and dug a hole beside the Mexican soldier big enough for Annie and the bone, too late but he did it anyway. He said a few words as he filled in the hole, whatever came to mind. He was sorry. He'd tried his best. No, no, he hadn't tried his best. But he would, he would from then on. He would try his best.

15.

He went up to the house and drank some water, standing at the bucket looking through the window down toward the cut. The house was clean, everything in the kitchen washed and put away, the beds made. Annie's farewell. Whoever found the place would have no complaints that way. He opened a satchel and ran around the house like he was grabbing things to save from a fire. Did he need a hairbrush? No. Soap? No. A change of clothes? Put it in. The pistol. Put it in. The envelope with Millican's money in it was lying on the table. Put it in. He still had the cotton money. Put it in. The Cuvier paper? He hesitated over that, then put it in. When he was done, he took the satchel out to the porch and set it down, then went out to the barn. He saddled Justice and fed and watered Max and Carlota. He'd stop up the road and tell Harry Goodfellow he could have the horses. The corn, too, if he wanted to bring it in. The whole damn farm. He went into the harness room one more time. The bone was still gone. He dug the two bottles of brandy out of a chest and put them in the satchel. Then he went down to the river and stood at the bank, looking across the water at the line of trees on the other side. He thought he could see crows in the tops of them, working their way south. It was nearly sunset, he'd best get on the road.

"Lucas isn't lost," he said to Annie. "I'll find him."

PART TWO

The River's bank am a very good road,
The dead trees show the way.
Lef' foot, peg foot goin' on,
Follow the Drinking Gourd.

I.

The bullet caught him somewhere on his left side below his waist, and knocked him off his horse. He'd been half asleep, dreaming he was sifting through a wooded valley, peering into the trees for Lucas, and the next thing he knew he was lying on his back in the dirt, the air squeezed out of his lungs and Justice dancing above him, trying not to step on his head. There was no pain yet, but he was a soldier; he knew it was coming. Two faces appeared above him: one small and gray, with sharp, shrewd features like those of a merlin; the other blotched and bloated, the texture of a boiled *nopal* cactus. The big one held him down with one foot while the smaller one flailed at him with his boots, then the smaller one said, "Your turn, Brother," and they switched. Then the pain started. The small one's eyes, the last things Moody saw before passing out, were as pale and blue as thin ice on a skim of clear water.

When he opened his own eyes again, pain like an electric current was running up and down his spine and his hip felt like a bag of eggshells. He raised his head and looked around. His tormenters were gone, as was his horse and saddle. The satchel lay open beside him; reaching into it, he felt the Cuvier paper and some linen, but no pistol, no bayonet—and no pouch containing Lucas's money. He couldn't move anything from the waist down. Blood flowed from his groin. It wasn't a good sign.

After a long while, he began pulling his way toward the road. Before he got there he heard a horse and wagon approaching. With a tremendous effort, and ignoring the squelching and crackling noises in his hip, he pulled himself halfway onto the road and tried to raise an arm. A lone woman on a buckboard looked down at him disapprovingly and was about to continue when she reined in.

"Are you drunk?" she said. Her horse snorted. "I passed thee on my way into town three hours ago. I could smell the liquor from here, and there you are still."

"Not drunk," he managed, although his tongue was swollen. "Shot and robbed."

"Indeed."

"Look," he said, pointing to the blood-soaked region of his trousers. Her eyes flickered to it. "They poured brandy on me so you would think what you did and keep going."

Her eyes relented, slightly. "You can't stand," she said, but she might have meant it sympathetically.

"I think the ball is still in there," he said. "I need a doctor. Is there a field hospital nearby?" He paused. She was staring at him. Maybe she'd been speaking Spanish. "*Señora*," he said. "*La misericordia, por favor.*"

At which the ground slipped from under his hand and rose swiftly to meet his face.

2.

When he woke again he was lying on his back on what appeared to be an artillery cart or mortician's stoneboat. He'd been collected with the dead. The sky was gray and smelled of cordite. It looked as if it would rain, which meant the men would be fighting in mud. Someone had removed his trousers and placed a wad of cloth over his pelvis, but blood was still running down his hip and pooling under the small of his back. He lifted his eyes and saw a woman's back, a black bonnet outlined against the sun, which haloed her hair. Not the war, then. Unless he was already dead.

"Annie?" he said, and passed out.

3.

The woman was not Annie. Apparently, he was among the living.

"Where is this?" he asked, looking up at the sky.

"Alabama," she said without turning.

He absorbed the information.

"I was going to Huntsville," he said.

"Why?"

"I'm looking for someone."

"For whom?"

"He would have just been passing through."

She was quiet a moment, maybe waiting for him to give a name. "Not many pass through Huntsville," she said. "How is thy side?"

Plain speak. He'd heard it in Georgia, where Quakers weren't welcome because of their opposition to violence and their uncompromising views on slavery. They wore their formal speech, their *thees* and their *thys*, like a badge, and paid for their pride with beatings and burnings. But he'd found them interesting. They were educated and didn't go around bleating about God.

"What part of me is broken?"

"Thy *os ilium* is intact," she said, "the acetabulum damaged but not irreparably. Most of the damage is to the upper femur, especially the greater trochanter. It's shattered, I'm afraid."

He tried hoisting himself up onto his elbows, a mistake. When he moved, his hip throbbed and bled. During the war, more men had died from bleeding to death than from the shot itself. Or their wounds turned putrid and poisoned their blood. Or the pain drove them mad and their hearts burst like overripe tomatoes.

"You should lie still until the bleeding stops," she said.

"Why are you helping me?" he asked.

"The Lord flung thee in my path twice," she said. "I ignored him the first time, and I almost ignored him the second time, too, but since you seemed determined to crawl before Satan, I stopped."

"Before Satan?"

"My horse," she said, nodding to the big black that was pulling the wagon. "She would most assuredly have trod on thee."

"How do you know I'm not dangerous?"

"You can't move enough to be dangerous," she said. "I would know thy name."

"Virgil Moody," he gasped.

"Good day to thee, Mr. Moody."

"What's yours?"

But he was gone again before she could answer.

4.

For four days and nights he drifted in and out of consciousness, long periods of feverish sensation broken by brief moments awash in agony. Cannon fire roared in his ears, men shouted in anger and pain and terror; large, black wings flapped over his head. He reached for Annie, caught his fingers in her hair as she pulled away, saying, "Don't." When awake, he lay clammy and cold, his chest shivering, legs twitching, candlelight breaking up into tiny hexagons behind his half-closed eyelids before fading into darkness. At night, he heard his father asking where his mother had put his hat, the flat one with the wide brim that made him look like a Quaker; Sikey asked him if he wanted a glass of cucumber water; wagon wheels rattled over ruts and Casgrain's shod horse splintered the stable floor. Stephen Austin dealt him a hand of strange-looking cards: a snake, a coffin, a woman who looked like his mother sitting on a swing. He smelled urine. He tasted gunmetal. Gradually the hours he was awake and writhing in pain and horror outlasted those spent in vivid oblivion. He grew conscious enough to believe he was dying, then that he hadn't died, and then that he probably wouldn't die.

5.

Her name was Rachel Tanner. She was from Philadelphia, which surprised him at first because he'd detected a Southern gentleness in her voice and manner. But Philadelphia was where most Quakers came from, and so his sense of reality was shifting back into focus. Her eyes were bright and brown, even in the dark, her auburn hair pinned at her nape with a stick and, under a starched bonnet black as a raven's eye her forehead was smooth and childlike. Her breast pressed against his shoulder when she reached across him to rinse a cloth, and when she tied his bandages her face almost brushed his. She swaddled his ribs and bound his left thigh to his right, to prevent him from moving it, and he lay inert in a tangle of damp sheets on a cot beside the cookstove in the house's main room, which served as both kitchen and parlor, and there was another room toward the back, her bedroom, he guessed, to which she retreated at night. There was an unheated pantry behind that, from which she brought him cold water and compresses. The house was well made, the joints square and the windows and doors properly framed and sealed. Where was the maker?

His intention was to rest another day or two, until she released his leg and he could ride, then find the men who'd stolen his horse and gun and money and resume his search for Lucas. He'd come to Alabama on the assumption that Lucas, either with Benah or following her, had gone east, because traveling north from Texas wasn't sensible unless he wanted to find seven extremely unpleasant ways to die: Comanches (Lucas killed, Benah taken), desert (dehydration, snakebite), mountains (bears, wildcats, cliffs), starvation, freezing, wandering around the Colorado wilderness forever, looking for the right canyon. It was the same south of Texas, in Chihuahua country. No, Lucas would have gone to Galveston and taken a steamer to New Orleans to look for Benah, or else to Mobile if he'd already found her, and then come up through Alabama, from where he could turn either downriver to Kentucky or upriver to

Tennessee. Moody had therefore been making his way to Huntsville, thinking that was where Lucas would have met the Tennessee River. He figured he'd arrived a week or two ahead of him, but he couldn't be sure. In either case, he couldn't afford to remain idle for much longer.

His leg had other plans.

"Your assailant did not stint on powder," Rachel told him. "You were lucky."

"Lucky," he said.

"That I came along when I did, otherwise you would have bled to death. My father was a doctor."

There was boot damage to the rest of him. His body was so islanded with bluish-green bruises connected by red streaks she said that naked he looked like a calico crab. Six weeks before he could stand, she told him, if an organ didn't fail, if the bleeding stopped, if the lead ball hadn't splintered when it struck his thigh bone, if she'd got all the bone fragments out, and if the wound were kept properly drained so that putrefaction didn't set in.

Now when he drifted it was into more decipherable dreams: Lucas calling to him from the barn, Annie from the river, the Mexican boy nailed to a tree and spitting up blood. He awoke drenched in sweat, hair plastered to his forehead, Rachel dabbing his hip with a damp cloth and talking, always talking, as if to herself while he'd been listening to voices he could not tell her about.

"Who made this house?" he asked one day.

"Robert," she said, pausing in her ministrations. The cloth was warm; he must still have a fever. "My husband."

"Where is he?"

"My late husband," she said.

Robert had died that spring. He'd come in from planting corn unable to speak, his jaw opening and closing but no sound issuing from his mouth. He'd pointed to his throat and fallen dead at her feet.

"There wasn't a mark on him," she said. "It was as though he'd been struck down by Divine Providence, as if God had reached into his throat and plucked the life out of him." She didn't think it could have been for anything Robert had done, he'd been a pious man, a virtuous husband, steadfast in his faith and his love for her. Perhaps it had been something he'd thought. "Can we die from our thoughts, do you think, Mr. Moody?"

"If we could," he said, "I'd be dead long ago."

"But people don't just up and die for no reason," she countered, "with no warning, and no sense to be made of it afterward."

"Yes, they do," he said. "That's exactly what they do." Annie had had no reason to die; he would have found Lucas. He would find Lucas.

"Just because we don't see a reason, Mr. Moody, doesn't mean there isn't one."

"If we don't see the reason," Moody said, "then what's the good of there being one?"

"To make us look harder."

"I've got more important things to look for."

"Ah, yes, the man who was passing through Huntsville."

He tried to talk to her about Lucas, but in his semi-delirious state he could barely explain Lucas to himself. "He's my son," he said, inadequately. Rachel wrung her cloth above the basin of cold water and didn't say anything. "His name is Lucas, and he's my son."

"Robert and I were not blessed," she said.

6.

Two weeks, then a third. Rachel unbound his thigh but left it tightly bandaged up to his waist, and his ribs still hurt like hell when he moved. He was able to sit up in his cot, slide on a pair of Robert's trousers, take a few cautious turns about the room, but he sank back exhausted after a few minutes. The wound puckered and oozed a pinkish liquid he recognized from the war, and he knew that if it turned green he would die in a matter of days. For another week, however, the effluent remained the color of rosewater, and he was almost able to sleep through the night on his back, though still prey to feverish dreams in which Annie's face floated up to him through various surfaces, and Lucas's body dropped silently out of sundry ceilings. He carved himself a pair of crutches from two ash poles, and during the day, Rachel escorted him on undemanding promenades, first up and down the porch, then across the yard to the barnyard gate, then into the barn itself, where he inspected the stables and the granary. He admired the harness room and the hay-loft. A week later she took him down to the river, Moody leaning heavily on his crutches, and he saw Robert's grave and his gold workings, his sluice and screens, his mounds of tailings, looking as fresh as if they had just been worked that morning. He didn't look into the river itself, afraid of what he might see there. When he dis-covered that he could manage on a single crutch and carry a pail of oats in his right hand, he began feeding and watering the horses. He was elated; the action produced a thrill of pain in his ribs, but did not start the wound bleeding. At night, Lucas no longer cried out from the barn. Instead, he beckoned from the road.

"You can't ride, Mr. Moody," Rachel said, anticipating his thoughts. "You can barely walk."

The thieves had taken his army greatcoat. Rachel gave him Robert's winter broadcloth, which had pockets and a collar and a single button, but was thick and warm if the wind came from behind. As the nights grew colder, her woodpile became depleted; it was on her mind, because she talked of Robert and the many things he had done that she now had to do, such as cut and split firewood. Moody found that by leaning on a single crutch he could work the bucksaw and a six-pound splitting maul. He toiled in the mornings, the broadcloth secured by the button and his leather belt. He balanced the wood on the chopping block, then brought the maul down, trying not to split his foot in half. Waiting for the throbbing in his hip to stop, he watched Lucas disappear over the horizon, looking back only once to see if Moody was following him. Benah danced on the clothesline. To ease his conscience, or perhaps to cover his lack of one, he told Rachel about Lucas. "Not my son," he told her, "Annie's, but he was like mine, as good as mine." He knew Rachel believed she was harboring a warmonger, and now a slaveholder, and he tried, with only middling success, to explain to her that he was neither. "We raised him together."

"She belonged to you?"

"We belonged to each other," he said. "I took her from my father's plantation because I wanted to save her."

"But you owned her, did you not, Mr. Moody?"

Rachel was adept at asking innocent yet damning questions. He had saved Annie, damn it. He had saved Lucas, too. He was proud of that. Rachel's questions came at him like the ticking of bullets through undergrowth.

"I didn't own her," he said. "I rescued her from slavery. Isn't that what you do?"

"Were you and Annie man and wife?"

"No, how could we have been?" The law forbade marriage between blacks and whites, as Rachel well knew. That hadn't been his fault. "She stayed with me because she wanted to."

"How do you know that?"

"Because she didn't leave," he said. It was a circular argument, useless in law, he recalled from his studies in New Orleans, but useful in life.

"Women don't leave," Rachel said. "What choice did Annie have, do you think?"

"I don't think she had any regrets," he said, "at least not before Lucas ran off."

"Lucas ran off?"

"Yes. That's why I'm here. I'm trying to find him."

"It must be hard for thee to dawdle like this."

"I'm not dawdling," he said. "I can't use my leg."

"Do you not have regrets, Mr. Moody?"

"Regrets?" he said, startled. "Of course I do. Too many to count."

But he did count them. When kept awake by his hip, he lay on his cot listing regrets like a miser. That his father was a slave owner; that he had left Annie and Lucas to fight in a war he didn't believe in; that he had killed that Mexican boy while he was praying; and, most of all, that he had allowed Lucas to leave, and had not gone after him in time. And then came the thousand smaller cuts: that he had left law school without taking a degree; that he had become mixed up with Stephen Austin, sold his own house in New Orleans, moved to Texas; that he had ever met Millican. He was awash in regrets. He tried to think of one that he could safely mention to Rachel that would stand for the rest and yet seem trifling.

"I wish, for example," he said, "that I had buried the elephant bone."

"The elephant bone?" she asked, as though feeling his forehead for fever.

He told her about finding the bone, and about Annie foretelling that trouble would come from it, and that she had been right. Lucas had run off, Annie was dead, and now he'd been shot. He didn't say how Annie had died.

"It wasn't an elephant bone," he said. "It was a mastodon femur."

"A mastodon?"

"A kind of elephant."

She smiled. "All your answers seem to go around in circles," she said. "Like wagons."

7.

He still had the Georges Cuvier paper—the thieves hadn't thought it worth taking—and the sketch of the *incognitum* that was mounted in Peale's museum in Philadelphia, which Cuvier had identified as a mastodon.

"I've seen it," Rachel said happily. "My father took me to the museum when I was a girl. I was more fascinated by the stuffed birds than by any pile of old bones. I remember a pelican, and a bird with a name I shan't forget: a blue-footed booby."

He placed the sketch on the table and showed her the femur, explaining what Cuvier had said about extinction, that there were animals that had lived on Earth for eons and then vanished overnight.

"Thine was broken right here," she said, pointing to where the mastodon's femur fit into its hip socket. "This is the greater trochanter. I still don't know if I got it turned properly, but it seems you'll be able to walk."

"Without hobbling?"

"I don't know. Probably not." She looked at the drawing. "Why would God create a creature this magnificent and then allow it to disappear?" she asked.

"I don't know," he said. "Jefferson thought there were still some woolly mammoths out west, and told Lewis and Clark to look for them. They traveled all the way to the Pacific without seeing one, nor even any sign of one."

"That's because they were all in Texas," she said. She was making fun of him.

"No, they weren't," he said, "at least not then. They weren't anywhere. They'd already died out."

"But how?" she asked. He admired the curve of her neck, the fine hairs that had escaped from the bun and were dancing in the sunlight. In the drawing, a man, possibly Charles Willson Peale himself, stood beside the reconstructed mastodon skeleton, his head barely reaching the monster's knees.

"Mr. Cuvier," Moody said, "thinks some kind of catastrophe killed them off."

"What sort of catastrophe?"

"Something big. A volcano, maybe."

"Would a single volcano be big enough to kill every mastodon on the face of the Earth, do you think?"

"Maybe there was a whole string of volcanoes."

"Could it have been the Great Flood we are told about in the Bible?"

"Mr. Cuvier doesn't think so."

"Why not?"

"Well, the bones are too old, for one thing."

"How old are they?"

"About ten thousand years."

She shook her head. He knew that according to the church fathers, the Earth was a little under six thousand years old—some bishop had added up the ages of the patriarchs listed in the beatitudes—but she didn't say that. Maybe Quakers didn't believe in beatitude, maybe all their stories were secular. He remembered how easily Annie could slide from quoting the Bible to relaying a story her mother had told her from a dimly remembered past where the Bible had never been. Women as seeds from which elephants had sprouted. All the wisdom of the world hidden in a calabash squash. Rachel, too, had the capacity to step, however fearfully, outside the known, but she kept her other foot on firmer ground. She reached out and, with her forefinger, moved the sketch a fraction of an inch on the table.

"God gave us the ability to ask questions," she said, as if arriving at the end of a long series of thoughts, "and therefore to doubt. He put the tree of knowledge in Eden to test us."

"Six thousand years is a long test."

"Because we keep failing."

"But if God is all-knowing, he would have known we would fail."

"Maybe we didn't fail," she said. "Maybe Adam was meant to eat that apple."

8.

His thigh was taking God's own time to heal. Summer passed and haying season was upon them. He felt he could ride, but not all day, day after day, and also that if he was well enough to ride he was well enough to stay and help with the haying. He owed her that much. If he stayed until the end of September, Lucas would have a two-month start on him. He chafed at the delay, cursed the two thieves who had shot him, but didn't feel he could leave Rachel to scythe and fork hay by herself. And even if he could, he didn't have a horse, or a gun, or money to buy either. Swinging the scythe hurt his hip, but also strengthened his thigh, and he liked the way Rachel's eyes widened when she thought about something that frightened her, such as his leaving.

"If I were God and I wanted to make up new creatures," he said to her one day in the hayfield, "how would I go about it?"

He had spent the week sharpening blades, sweeping out haylofts, repairing and greasing the hay wagon. Now, in the evening, the heat of the day subsided, he was leading the horses from rick to rick while Rachel forked hay onto the bed, the sun's low light slanting through the wheels. Grasshoppers fled the onslaught of her fork. She was quiet, but he knew she had heard his question. She no doubt suspected another attack on her beliefs, and was wondering how to go about defending God.

"So, now you are going to assail the Creation?" she said, not stopping her work. The hay on the wagon was high, he would have to climb up to level it.

"If it were me," he said, "I'd start with something close to my own image. What creatures did God make first?"

"Ocean dwellers," she said. "Fish. You're saying God looks like a fish."

"He might, at that."

"Very clever, Mr. Moody. You're saying that God is not a man who made a fish, but a fish who made a man. Mightn't God have started with something simpler than himself, like a fish, with no arms or legs or even a neck. And then with each successive creature he added more complex features, until he arrived at something as close to perfection as himself?"

"So God wasn't always perfect? He had to learn how to make humans by practicing on simpler life forms?"

She stopped to consider, leaning on her pitchfork. "You are what Paul the Apostle called a 'natural man,' " she said. "An unbeliever. 'The natural man receiveth not the things of the Spirit of God.' "

"As you say, God gave us the ability to question authority."

"Is that what Annie did?"

"All the time." He smiled.

"I think," she said, "that by *natural* Paul meant a thing as yet unformed, or misbegotten. A thing like Caliban."

That startled him. He hadn't thought of himself as a Caliban. He'd attended a performance of *The Tempest* in Savannah, in which both Caliban and Ariel had been white actors with burnt cork on their faces, playing the characters as slaves, Caliban a field slave and Ariel a more privileged house servant. "What is't thou canst demand?" Prospero had asked, and Ariel said, "My liberty." Ariel had gone over well with the audience, and they had laughed at Caliban's misery—until he talked about how he would like to ravish Miranda, and then they had stood up and shouted him off the stage, threatening to tar and feather him if he so much as glanced her way. Moody had thought the whole thing clever at the time; it was before he'd met Annie. Now he didn't know what to think.

But he liked the image of himself as a natural man, a thing as yet unformed. He would cry with Caliban: "Freedom, hey-day! Hey-day, *Freedom!*" He would hang on to that.

9.

"My father was killed by the British," she said. It was a clear, mild evening, and they were sitting outside, wrapped in blankets and looking up at the stars. "I was a baby at the time. It was after the Battle of New Orleans," she said, "when the British came up to take Fort Bowyer to cut off New Orleans's supply route so they could attack it again. They didn't know the war had been over for months."

"No war is ever over," he said.

"This one was supposed to be."

"Annie and I went to New Orleans fifteen years after that, and the war was still talked about in the taverns, how brave Andrew Jackson had led his men into battle and kicked the British out of America. Jackson was the president then. That was a time when men died for no reason, yet somehow that didn't diminish Jackson's stature as a hero."

"The British bombarded Fort Bowyer for two days," she said. "My father was in it and was killed."

"What was your father doing in Fort Bowyer?"

"We may not approve of soldiers, but we don't just let them die. As you have seen. My father was treating the wounded."

"We're not supposed to fire on civilians." But they did, all the time. Blowing up a supply train made a hungry army, and a hungry army made mistakes. They weren't supposed to fire at a retreating army, either. Or bayonet prisoners.

"My mother and I came north to Huntsville after that and she opened a boardinghouse. I stayed with her until I met Robert."

"You were married in Huntsville?"

"Quakers don't marry, at least not in the sense you mean. We have no parsons or ministers, no church, as such. We express our commitment to each other before Friends, and henceforth we are considered man and wife."

"And then you came here?"

"Robert heard there was gold in the rivers out here in the hill country," she said. "Nuggets the size of walnuts, they said, and we thought that with gold we could do much good." He imagined her smiling in the dark. "So we moved here and homesteaded, and Robert panned for gold in Blue Creek."

"Did he find any?"

"Certainly nothing as big as walnuts, but enough to keep the farm running and to buy some cows and a half-dozen pigs. We liked the country," she said. The sound of late-season frogs filled the darkness. "The land here is fertile and gentle, and Blue Creek will take you all the way down to Mobile if you have the patience for it. Alabama was a new state then, and it was growing like twitch grass. All those cotton mills in Huntsville were built since we arrived."

"I didn't know there were cotton mills in Huntsville."

"Oh, yes. It's a modern manufacturing town."

"And slaves work in them?"

"Yes, Mr. Moody. It's why we chose Huntsville after my father was killed."

Lucas might still be in Huntsville, then, working in a cotton mill. Had he guessed Lucas's route after all? Could he find him, with Rachel's help? He tried to divine in her the rabid abolisher that most Southerners imagined Quakers to be, and saw a gentler version of it: headstrong, determined, as Annie had been, and undaunted by life, compelled by the rightness of the Quaker cause. She would be good at whatever she put her mind to.

They fell into a companionable silence. He imagined himself finding Lucas in Huntsville. When Rachel took him into town, he would look about. He would also keep an eye out for his two thieves.

"We were out here the night the stars fell from the sky," Rachel said. "Have you ever seen stars falling out of the sky, Mr. Moody?"

"A few," he said.

"This wasn't a few, this was almost all of them, or so it seemed. We thought it was the end of the world. It was as though whatever held things together up there had just let go. We were told that people in Huntsville fell on their knees and prayed."

"Is that what you did?"

"No, we don't pray like that. We took our blankets and sat out on the porch, as you and I are, and watched the fireworks. Robert fell asleep, but I couldn't stop watching. It wasn't a meteor shower, more like a torrential downpour of heavenly bodies. They fell for two whole nights. Fire and brimstone, Mr. Moody. Perhaps it was something like that that killed thy mastodons? But what amazed me was that when the stars finally stopped falling, there were just as many of them in the sky as there had been before. Was that God, do you think, Mr. Moody, replacing fallen stars with new ones as fast as the old ones fell? Like creating new animals when the old ones become extinct?"

"Maybe he was replenishing his supply of ammunition."

"That was what Robert said."

"What was Robert like?" he asked.

"No, Mr. Moody," she said gently, "I don't think I can tell thee about Robert. Maybe one day, but not now. It's like he's here on this porch with us, sitting in that chair over there, and it would be rude to talk about him as if he weren't." Her voice sounded strained. "I know you can understand that," she added, "because you haven't really told me about Annie, have you?"

"Some," he said, "but not all, no."

"The dead are hard to speak of," she said. "We know so little about them."

10.

He had to consider not only when but also how he would leave. Would he stand up after breakfast one morning, wash the dishes, wipe off the table and announce that he was taking a horse and leaving when the chores were done? Would he tell her one day that he would be gone the next? Or would he just not be here one morning when she got up, leave a note on the kitchen table? There had been some talk of taking him into Huntsville to show his leg to a proper doctor; maybe he would just keep going from there. It was the end of October. He would have to decide. If he didn't leave soon, Lucas would be God knows where, too far ahead for Moody to catch up. The thought of not finding Lucas because he was unable to decide how to leave Rachel threatened to make him resent Rachel, and he didn't want that—another reason to leave soon. He wanted to leave her, but he also wanted to remember her fondly.

It had become his custom at night to wait until the thin strip of light under her bedroom door went out before he retired to his cot. Rachel's father had brought a crate of books from Philadelphia, and she had kept them. She read each night before going to sleep. She must have read each one many times, because there weren't that many of them. They were mostly medical texts, some philosophical and religious books, and there was some poetry, which he borrowed and read, and which seemed to feed his growing sense of urgency. He read John Greenleaf Whittier's poem, "The Fair Quakeress":

> There are springs
> Of deep and pure affection, hidden now,
> Within that quiet bosom, which but wait
> The thrilling of some kindly touch, to flow
> Like waters from the desert-rocks of old.

"That quiet bosom." He lay on his cot imagining Rachel reading, wondered if it were her deep and pure affection that was preventing her from sleeping, or something darker. Loneliness, the temptation to dwell on the deaths of her husband and her father. He felt the kind of protectiveness toward her he had toward Annie. When he could be still no longer he would slip quietly outside, look up at the stars and listen to the sounds of the night, at first for danger but then for the simple pleasure of listening. Owls and bats in the trees, coyotes on the ridge above the house, aware of him yet unconcerned by his presence. Reassured, he would go back in, stoke the fire and blow out all but the stub of the candle he kept beside his cot, resting on a chair atop the Cuvier paper, worn and tattered from many readings. He didn't like to undress in the dark, he wanted to see where his clothes were, especially his boots, in case he had to jump up in the night and feel for them in the dark. If he'd had his pistol it would have been the last thing he looked at before blowing out the candle. He hadn't lost the habit of that from the war.

One night, not long after their starry vigil on the porch, when the light had faded from beneath Rachel's door, he was awakened by a movement on the cot: she had joined him. He couldn't deny it had occurred to him that she might, that they might. He had often thought about it, but hadn't let it build up into anything like an expectation. They hadn't so much as brushed against each other in the months he'd been there, except now and then, by accident, as two people must who live together in a confined space. Sometimes they said "Excuse me," at others they pretended it hadn't happened. Occasionally, as they sat up evenings after dinner, he'd caught her looking at him over her needlework with a peculiar, speculative intensity, and he had no doubt he'd looked at her the same way. But they had settled into a cautiousness that had come to feel comfortable. They'd been close, but it was not a closeness based on touching. He supposed they both knew that the kind of accord they were developing couldn't last on its own, that sooner or later it would reveal itself as a prelude to a more tangible intimacy, as a stone vault might be built to support a more elaborate structure on top of it, and after living in that stone vault for a while a person might want to move upstairs. But if they had seen their situation that way, neither of them had let on.

He didn't turn right away. He gave her time to change her mind, or to just go to sleep herself, if all she wanted was his company. As he had that first night with Annie. But when she put her arm around him and pressed herself against his back, he turned, put his left hand behind her head, and held her to him as delicately yet as fervently as he dared. Moonlight sifted through the window, enough that he could see that her eyes were open. Her hair was unfastened and smelled of lavender. There followed a bit of awkwardness with his hip, and when finally everything was lined up nicely they paused, as swimmers do before jumping in.

"I hope you don't think I'm being too aggressive," she said.

"Not at all," he said. "I hope you don't think I'm offering too much resistance."

"No, none that I can see. We'll make a Quaker of thee yet."

There was no frenzy, as there had often been with Annie, but rather a kind of concentration. They had waited long enough to know exactly what the other wanted and to give it. He hadn't missed the "we" in her sentence, meaning, he supposed, she and Robert, but it didn't bother him. There were things she didn't want to forget, and things he didn't want to remember.

Eventually frenzy set in, and neither of them slept much after that. His hip throbbed. At midnight, he lay looking up into the darkness, she with her head on his left shoulder, the cot barely wide enough for both of them.

"You may come to my bed from now on, Mr. Moody. That is, if you want to."

"I do," he said. "Although I fear for your soul."

"We don't believe in souls."

"No souls? No sin, then, either? Nothing to lose?"

"The only sin is causing pain and suffering in others. This

would be a sin if Robert were yet alive, but he is not. Nor is Annie. We are harming no one, and only giving pleasure to each other."

"Then why did we wait so long?"

"Because I wasn't ready to meet thee halfway."

"And you are now?"

"I think so. But no further."

Whittier had foreseen it: her passion had been unleashed *like waters from the desert-rocks of old*. But as he lay in the darkness while she slept, his arm under her head and her knee over his, but cautiously, he thought about what would happen next. How could he leave now, as he'd planned? He felt the weight of panic in his chest, her leg pinning him to the bed.

II.

He was sharpening an ax in the kitchen. Rachel had asked him to take it to the barn, but he said it was too cold and he was almost finished and he would clean it up when he was finished. She was dipping candles on the stove when they heard footsteps on the porch. Moody stood and went to the door: two runaways, a boy and a girl, threadbare clothes and no shoes. He had been wondering when something like this would happen. Rachel ushered them into the kitchen. The boy said they'd waited down by the creek until it was dark, and had come up when they saw light in the kitchen window. The boy was all right, a little muddied and cold, but the girl's dark skin was pebbled and scabby around her nose and mouth, her hair like matted river weeds, and her eyes rimmed with green pus. The cold seemed to have kept her intact, but now that she was inside she was shivering herself apart.

Rachel inspected the girl and took her out to the barn with a pan of warm water and some soap and towels. Moody stayed in the kitchen with the boy, who was scared to death of Moody, possibly because he was still holding the ax. He kept looking to the window, maybe after the girl, maybe just out into the night. There was a bad smell in the room.

"How'd you get here?" Moody asked him, to pass the time.

"Follered de ribber," he said.

"Where from?"

"Massa's." He pointed south.

"That your sister?"

He didn't answer. He looked as though he didn't understand the question.

"You hungry?" Moody asked.

No answer this time, either. Moody guessed he hadn't taken it as an offer of food. He got up and put some fried catfish left from their supper on a plate and set it in front of the boy, who stared at it like he thought it might flip up and bite him if he touched it.

"Go ahead," Moody said. "Watch out for bones."

Carefully, the boy broke the white meat in half, shoved one piece into his mouth and set the other back on the plate. Then he sat back and looked at Moody while he chewed. Moody got up again and put another portion of fish on the plate along with a slice of crackling bread. The boy did the same with those, broke both in two, ate half and left the other for the girl.

"What's your name?" Moody asked him.

Before he could not answer again, Rachel came in with the empty pan. "Julius," she said, "take that food out to your friend. We'll be along in a minute."

When the boy was gone, Rachel looked at Moody and he looked at her. She set the pan on the stove and poured more hot water into it. Moody remained seated at the table, letting her see how calm he was.

"How long have you been hiding runaways?" he asked her.

"Since we came here. Before that, really. My mother hid them in her boardinghouse in Huntsville."

"Do you have some place you hide them?" he asked, thinking someone would be along shortly looking for them.

"Robert built a false wall in the back of the barn," she said. "I haven't put them in there yet, but I will."

"We better tend to it now," Moody said. "They don't seem to have come from too far away."

They went out to the barn, Rachel carrying the pan with more hot water and some fresh towels, Moody scanning the ridge above the road and wishing he had a rifle. His leg hurt. Dante and Beatrice, both stolid horses, looked up from their stalls and fluttered at them when they came in, expecting grain. Satan was in the fourth stall. There was no horse in the third stall, and that was where Rachel had put the two runaways. The girl looked less terrible than she had. She was sitting up eating. Rachel had washed her and given her a clean dress. Julius still looked terrified and Moody wondered if something wasn't wrong with him after all, something less visible than whatever was wrong with the girl.

Rachel led Moody to the end stall. Satan looked mean, but she was in fact the gentlest of the three. Moody backed her out, and Rachel moved aside a piece of burlap that was nailed to the side wall, revealing a jagged hole about the size of a hand and looked like it had been kicked in by a demented horse. She reached through the hole, turned a wooden catch, and the wall slid open. Expert carpentry; no visible hinges or saw lines in the wood, weighted so it would slide quietly. Moody wouldn't have seen it was a door even if he'd been looking for one. Behind it was a narrow space, no more than four feet wide, that ran along the width of the barn. He put the lantern through and saw a table at the far end with a jug of water and a few candles on it. Room for maybe ten people, if they didn't fight. Rachel brought Julius and the girl.

"You'll be safe in here," she told them. "There's good air and no light gets out. Stay until one of us fetches you, do you understand that?" The girl nodded. "You hear anything going on outside, horses or voices or anything, you just stay put. Not a peep, you got that?" She nodded again.

Rachel closed the door and replaced the burlap, and Moody put Satan back in the stall. The big animal seemed to take her role as guard horse seriously.

When they were in the house, Moody refilled the kettle to make tea. He'd have preferred whiskey, it might have helped the pain in his leg, but he'd told Rachel he didn't drink, which was true because he didn't have any. He felt virtuous. She sat at the table and rolled up her sleeves as though readying for a fight, but he wasn't going to fight her.

"What's wrong with the girl?" he asked.

"She's fifteen and she's had two babies already. Whoever owned her kept her in a cage and bred her like an animal. She doesn't seem to have been given a name, Mr. Moody, not so much as a name. I don't know what all's wrong with her. Starvation. Parasites. Infection. She needs a doctor."

"Where we going to find a doctor who will treat a slave?" he asked.

"They're not slaves," Rachel said. "We don't recognize slavery as a human condition. They are children who are suffering."

"Still," he said, "where're we going to find a doctor who will look at them?"

"I know of one in Huntsville. The same one I would have taken thee to if thy wound hadn't healed."

"That's a day's ride from here."

"What do you suggest, Mr. Moody? That I send them on their way with her in that condition? You've seen her. She needs proper care."

Moody reached across the table and took her hand. "How soon can we move them?" he said.

"She needs a day or two."

"If anyone's coming after them, they'll be here before that.

I don't suppose you have anything here we can defend ourselves with?"

"We don't defend ourselves. We have done nothing that requires defense."

"I doubt they'll see it that way," he said.

12.

They came the next afternoon, a father, son and another man who had the surly look of an overseer. Moody caught the sun glinting off their buckles and heard their horses coming down off the ridge, and readied himself on the porch, keenly feeling the lack of a weapon. He suggested Rachel go inside, but all she did was take off her bonnet.

"At least let me do the talking," he said.

They stood on the porch trying to look like two people receiving unexpected company.

"Huddy," the older man, the father, said.

"'Day," Moody answered. "What brings you boys up here?"

"We're just out huntin'," the man said. "Followed some tracks up the crick."

"Oh?"

"Two of them. They stop just here."

"What kind of tracks were they," Moody asked, "this time of year?"

The man looked at Moody as though wondering if he were new to the Earth. "You're Robert Tanner, ain't you?" he said.

"No," Moody said. "Name's Moody."

"I heard your name was Tanner and you hide runaways."

"You heard wrong, then. There's no one named Robert Tanner living on this farm."

Rachel gave a kind of grunt beside him, but he hadn't told a lie and he kept his eyes on the men. The son was short with a large head, hair cropped close to his scalp. His ears stuck out and he didn't seem to have any eyebrows. He grinned all the time, as if looking forward to doing something he loved doing. He reminded Moody of men he'd known in the militia, the kind they were sorry they had to unleash on the enemy, but they did. The one Moody thought was the overseer had an old muzzle loader sitting crossways on his lap and he kept his right finger on the trigger. To shoot, he'd have to raise the barrel over his horse's head, which would give Moody a few seconds. To do what?

"My name's Judd," the father said, raising his eyebrows. "Silas Judd. This here's my boy, J.J., and that there's Sam Lerner, my overseer."

"'Afternoon to you all. There's no slaves here, Judd, neither yours nor ours. I come from Texas," he said. "I know how much trouble runaways can be."

"They surely can," Judd said. "Fun to hunt, though, ain't they?" He turned to his son, laughing. "Well, I guess that nigger we whipped was wrong, we'll have to whip him again. He said you was Quakers and you helped a lot of my runaways." He looked speculatively at Rachel. "Mind if we look in your barn, ma'am?"

"I surely do mind," said Moody. "That would be the same as calling me a liar."

"They might have snuck in there in the night."

The son made a noise that sounded like air escaping from a bloated cow. He got off his horse and walked to the barn. Moody contrived to look unconcerned. Judd looked unsure, as though he could stop the lad if he wanted to but didn't want to embarrass him in front of the others. He must have been losing a lot of slaves to be placing such a large bet on these two.

"J.J. has something wrong in his head," Judd said, touching his hat. "But sometimes he's right."

The overseer thought it was his turn to speak up.

"We just want the buck," he said. "J.J.'s done with the female."

Moody looked calmly over to him. There were just two of them now, the father and the overseer, both waiting for something to happen. He could see Lerner gauging the distance between himself and Moody and how long it would take him to get his musket over his horse. Maybe too long. Maybe the ball had dropped out of it. He wouldn't know about Moody's bad leg; Moody himself didn't know how fast he could move with it. The overseer yawned and Moody tensed. Yawning usually signaled a stupid move on the way.

Just then the boy came out of the barn alone, and the moment passed. He looked at his father and shrugged, which Moody took to mean he hadn't found anything but wasn't convinced there was nothing to find.

"Sorry to bother you, then," said Judd. "We'll be on our way."

"If I see any slaves I'll let you know. Where's your place at?"

"Just up along," he said, nodding back the way they'd come.

"We're neighbors, then," Moody said.

"Yep," said Judd, turning his horse. "We'll be seeing a lot of each other. Come on, boys."

Moody and Rachel watched them ride off. Only J.J. looked back, like a child being pulled away from a carnival.

13.

They waited until it was dark, then another half hour, before going out to the barn. Moody was certain the Judds would be watching from the ridge. The moon was almost full and the night cloudless. They took an unlit lantern and kept to the shadows as much as possible, then darted across the barnyard like a pair of foxes. Satan was in her stall, eyes as big as teacups when they lit the lantern. Moody led her out and Rachel opened the door to the hide. Julius came out first, and Rachel went in for the girl. Then she called, "Mr. Moody, please." Moody told Julius to stay where he was and not stick his head outside or even stand near the door, and went into the narrow room. The girl was lying on a bundle of sheets; she seemed to have shrunk. He put a blanket around her, picked her up and carried her out. Even soaked in sweat she was as light as a dead sparrow. Moody stood inside the barn door with her in his arms and Julius behind him while Rachel went out to look around. When she called they made their way to the house the way they had come. In the kitchen, Rachel blew out the lamp and told Moody to put the girl on the cot, which was still beside the stove. Then she made up a bed for Julius on the floor beside the girl.

"Her fever's gone up," Rachel said. "We'll have to get her to town soon."

"How soon?"

"First thing tomorrow, I'd say. She might not even make it that long."

Moody considered their chances of getting past the Judds in daylight.

"I'll take a look around before it gets light," he said. Maybe he could get behind one of them, take him down with a club or the ax and get the man's gun. He was thinking like a soldier, weighing the consequences of having a weapon, that it would escalate a simple confrontation into a two-against-one shoot-out. He was confident he could win such an encounter, and wanted to go ahead with it.

"You try to get some sleep now," Rachel said. She was kneeling beside the cot, looking down at the girl's glistening face. "I'll stay up with her for a while."

Moody took a candle and went into the bedroom. Of course he wouldn't sleep. On the small table beside the bed was the book Rachel had been reading the night before, *A Letter Concerning Toleration*, by John Locke, her place marked by a Quaker tract condemning slavery "in all its forms: viz. the slavery of Negroes, the slavery of women, the slavery of children." When he met Annie she had been all three. "Whosoever will list himself under the banner of Christ," he read in the Locke, "must, in the first place and above all things, make war upon his own lusts and vices." Moody's lusts and vices remained unassailed. If they made it to Huntsville with the runaways, he would try to buy a rifle or at least a pistol, and he would defend Rachel from people like the Judds.

"Mr. Moody, come quickly! The barn!"

He jumped up and put his britches and shirt on and grabbed his boots. He was in the main room in time to see Rachel flying out the door. When he looked through the window all was luminous black and yellow. Julius and the girl were in the kitchen, looking scared but not getting up. He ran after Rachel and sat on the porch step to pull on his boots. The back half of the barn was blazing, smoke rolling out into the blackness through the spaces between the boards and under the eaves. He ran to Rachel, who was struggling to get the double doors open. They each opened one side, then ran in to release the horses. He threw an armful of harness into the wagon and pulled it through the door, letting it roll out into the barnyard. Rachel let Dante and Beatrice out of their stalls, and he ran to Satan. She was rearing and whinnying in a dead panic, her head going up into the smoke and then coming down hard. He opened her stall with her front hooves whistling past his ears, and she was gone. Three horses and the wagon. The smoke was so low by the time he and Rachel left the barn that they had to double over to run under it.

They ran to the house without straightening, then stopped to look back. J.J. must have paced off the distance from the front of the barn to the back wall when he was inside, then come back later and paced off the outside, and known what the difference meant. He didn't need to find the door to know there was another room back there. Rachel stood beside Moody, coughing and shivering. She and Robert must have known something like this was at least possible, if not likely. Quaker barns had been going up in flames all over the South. Robert had built his far enough away from the house that fire from one wouldn't leap to the other.

"Do you think the Judds are still up there?" she asked, looking up to the ridge.

The fire was burning furiously, roaring and crackling as the hay they had recently put in the loft caught. The heat branded their foreheads even on the porch.

"Yes."

"What will we do?"

"I'll go catch the horses," he said. "We'll take the children into Huntsville tonight."

"The children!" She turned and ran into the house. The kitchen was still dark but the firelight coming in through the window let him see the girl sitting up on the cot, squeezed into the corner like she was afraid of what was coming through the door. There was no sign of the boy.

"Where's Julius?" Rachel asked the girl, who shook her head but didn't speak. "Where is he?" Rachel said again.

"Massa take he."

"What?" Rachel cried. "What did you say?"

"Massa J.J., him take Julius, da."

14.

Back in Texas, if a man burned your barn down, you did what it took to teach him that, in general, burning down barns was a bad idea, and that burning down your barn in particular was monumentally stupid. It wasn't for revenge, exactly, and you didn't get your barn back, but it discouraged that person from burning down barns. It benefited everyone, including, if you wanted to be philosophical about it, that person. But this wasn't Texas, a fact about which he was otherwise glad, so he let Rachel talk him out of going after the Judds.

"I can't counsel violence, Mr. Moody," she said.

"What if Julius got away from them somehow, what if he's out there wandering around in the dark? I might find him."

"We need to get this girl to a doctor," she said. "They won't stop us taking her, now that they've got Julius. We should leave as soon as we find the horses."

"They'll kill the boy," he said.

She looked at him wildly. "Why would they do that?" she asked. "It's to their advantage to get him healthy again and put him back to work. Killing him would be a waste."

"They think running away is a disease that slaves get," he said. "A kind of rabies."

"That's nonsense."

"I know it is, but it's what they think. They'll kill him so he doesn't infect the others."

"I want you to go find the horses," she said. "We'll save the girl. And our souls."

Dante and Beatrice were standing head to rump in a clump of alders near the creek, and Satan was at the water's edge, about twenty feet downstream, keeping her nose close to the water, where the smell of smoke wasn't so strong. Moody scouted around briefly for the Judds. It was dark but there were signs they'd been there, a shoe scrape in the mud, a cigar end. Not properly dealing with the Judds was a mistake. The Judds were Millican with backbone.

The horses let him lead them until they realized where he was taking them, then they balked and would be led no farther. He didn't flail at them, they were already scared enough and would probably try to kill him. He tied them to the fence and dragged the wagon to them, thankful he'd had the sense to throw the harness into it. He hitched up Dante and Beatrice and tied Satan to the tail-board because he didn't have a saddle for her. By the time he headed back to the house, the sun was beginning to outline the eastern end of the ridge, and he thought about the stars Rachel and Robert had watched falling from the sky, portending the end of the world. There was violence all around, he would tell her, murderousness in everyone. The meek shall not inherit the earth: the meek are swept away while the mighty head for higher ground.

Rachel had readied the girl and a few other things. She'd been busy. Clothes in a bundle, the books in a crate beside the door.

"You're leaving for good?" he said, astonished. "I thought we were just taking the girl to a doctor."

"I'm taking some things with us," she said, "because I don't know when I'll be back and I don't want to leave them here in case the Judds come and burn the house down. Besides, we now have no hay for the winter."

She had Moody carry the mattress from her bed out to the wagon. When he got back, he saw she had also removed a floorboard from the middle of the kitchen, and placed a tin canister on the table.

"What's that?" he asked.

"Robert's gold," she said. She took the lid off and stepped back to let him see inside. "He kept going down to the sluice every once in a while, and this is what he got." It looked like ordinary river sand to Moody, but it glinted dully in the morning light, and he took her word for it that it was gold. He'd never seen raw gold before. Some of the pieces were as big as grains of rice, and when he hefted the tin it felt heavier than he expected.

He gathered his own gear, what there was of it: his satchel, the Cuvier paper, some clothes of Robert's that Rachel had given him. Everywhere he looked he saw the shattered past. Annie drowned, Lucas lost, Robert dead, the barn smoldering as after a battle, the dying girl. What could he do that would not just add to it?

15.

Rachel tried not to look back, and succeeded until they reached the curve in the road, then she asked Moody to stop. They both turned. Smoke rose lazily from the barn, broken, charred timbers pointing like black fingers at the sky, but the house looked peaceful, as though they were still in it, still lying in bed thinking of breakfast and the day's chores. Any minute now he would get up and light the stove, then crawl back into bed to hold her while the room warmed up. The girl lying on the mattress moaned. He slapped the reins and they began the ride to Huntsville.

"Maybe it was a mistake for Robert and me to come here," Rachel said after a while. "We thought we could help end some of the violence, at least the violence of slavery. We did help a few."

"How many?"

"Maybe twelve or fifteen."

"That's something," he said.

"I can't have violence around me, Mr. Moody," she said suddenly. "I won't. It frightens me. That was why my mother left Mobile, why I left Huntsville, with its hellish mills squeezing the lives out of those poor people. Violence, anger, hatred, intolerance, cursing, drinking, fighting. What's wrong with people, Mr. Moody, that they choose those things over happiness and friendship and community? We are told that poverty leads to despair, but I believe it is the other way around. Poor people don't have to hate or curse or beat up people who are poorer than they. It's poverty of the spirit that leads to poverty of the body. Out here on the farm we rarely had two pennies together, but it was peaceful and quiet and we could believe that that was how things were meant to be. As in Eden. We worked the fields, we tended the animals, we went months without seeing another soul. Robert built the house and the barn and once in a while we'd put fugitives up and take them to Dr. Carson, in Huntsville, and he would pass them on to another Friend along the way."

"Dr. Carson is a Quaker?"

"Yes. He may know something of the son you are seeking."

Moody unconsciously slapped the reins.

"Sometimes they'd help us on the farm for a few days," Rachel said, "if it was planting or harvest. Two young men helped Robert shingle the barn roof. We had a girl once who taught me how to make proper pastry. We thought we'd found a new way to live. We put high sides on the wagon and filled it with corn or potatoes, things we'd grown from the earth with our own hands and our own love, and we hid the runaways in it and delivered them to the doctor. It was like we were setting them free, like they were birds and we were letting them out of their cages, and then we'd go home and resume our peaceful lives. There was no violence in our lives, or so we thought. But it was like playing a game, wasn't it, Mr. Moody? That's what you're thinking, I know, that's what you have been trying to show me. We were like children playing a game with the Devil and thinking we were winning."

"That isn't what I was thinking. I was thinking that you are actually helping the people you want to help, whereas every time I try to do the right thing it turns out to be exactly the wrong thing."

"You are feeling sorry for thyself?"

That stunned him. He was sorry for Annie, he was sorry for Lucas, and for Rachel, but was he also sorry for himself? What if he was? He was still going to find Lucas.

"Even if we went back to the farm," she went on, "and you 'took care' of the Judds, as you put it, it wouldn't be the same. It would be peace paid for with violence."

"As after a war," he said, agreeing with her.

"And more Judds would come, and more. I would always be aware of living in the eye of a storm, which is perhaps how I have been living all these years without knowing it. You taught me that, Mr. Moody. I could have withstood Robert's death if it hadn't been for thee. I was withstanding it. At night, when the work was done and I was sitting alone in the house with a candle lit and a book in my lap, the grief would hit me with such sudden force it would knock me to the floor, and I would lie there throbbing with the sheer physicality of it. But after a time I would get up again and resume my reading, and gradually my hands would stop shaking and my breathing would return to normal, and I would be able to sleep in the same bed in which Robert and I had slept together."

"But not now?" Moody said.

She was quiet for a moment, her breath coming in gusts as she stopped to compose herself. The road took a dip, and holding the horses back made him think of the trip from Boonville with Annie. That had been a kind of farewell, too.

"It has been pleasant these last few nights," she said.

"But?"

"But I would not keep thee from thy search for Lucas."

16.

Huntsville was a sizable town, surprising given its remoteness. Thirty years ago there had been nothing there but rocks and trees, not even a trading post. It was Creek land, and the Creeks had sided with the Cherokee against whites expanding into their territory. Unsuccessfully, it turned out. The Creeks and the Cherokees had been evacuated, replaced by cotton mills. Moody drove slowly down the main street, the girl covered with a blanket, past hotels, a couple of saloons, and a number of smaller establishments, gun shops, haberdashers, all closed and dark at that time of night except for the saloons. Rachel directed him to Dr. Carson's, in a section of town maintaining a semblance of gentility by keeping its curtains drawn and its gates closed. The large clapboard houses had been built by mill owners who had since moved to the more salubrious air up on Green Mountain, and had turned their former residences into repositories for their white workers. The colored workers lived in the lower part of town, closer to the mills and the dockyards and the truculent Tennessee River.

Dr. Carson was a small, bespectacled, energetic man, brisk and businesslike in his movements and careful in his speech. He wore a gray tailcoat and small, tight-fitting boots. Moody could easily imagine him risking his practice for the Quaker cause, and was reminded of Stephen Austin, who had set aside his law degree to settle Texas. The doctor took in runaways and passed them on to other Quakers farther north, either through the Appalachians into Tennessee or else down the Tennessee River into Kentucky. Moody guessed that the mill owners did not send their daughters to him.

Once they settled the girl in a room behind the clinic, the doctor examined Moody's hip. "You won't be able to ride for a while," he said, "but the wound should heal without permanent damage. You may have a slight limp. Rachel did a fine job keeping it clean."

Moody asked him if he'd ever sheltered a fugitive named Lucas.

"What is your interest in him?" Carson asked.

"I have news of his mother," he said. "I want to find him and deliver that news."

Carson frowned. "Nothing more than that? Has he run away from you?"

"No, from a neighbor of mine. You may be assured I have no intention of bringing him back. If anything, I want to help him get farther away."

"Can we believe him?" the doctor said to Rachel.

Rachel looked at Moody. "Yes," she said. "I think so. He's not a bad man."

Carson removed a ledger from a lower drawer in his desk.

"I don't know what last name he would have given," said Moody. "Maybe Casgrain."

"We don't ask for last names," said Carson, taking a sheet of prescription paper from his desk. He dipped his pen and wrote on it, and handed the paper to Moody.

"It's an address in Knoxville," he said. "Lucas stayed here for three nights while I arranged transportation for him. Normally I would have sent him east, up the Tennessee River to Paducah, but boats aren't getting past Muscle Shoals these days, the water being so low, so instead I sent him upriver, to Knoxville."

"How long ago?"

"A month."

"Did he have a woman with him, named Benah?"

"No. He asked if I'd seen a young woman of that name, and I told him I hadn't."

"A month," Moody said. "Would he be in Knoxville now?"

"I have no idea," Carson said. "We don't communicate such things. The hill country between here and there isn't entirely friendly, with bands of Cherokee and Creek still trying to evade removal. But they are hostile mainly to whites. We've put what we call way stations in the caves above the river, caches of food and water, some warm clothing, where a runaway can hide for a day or two. If you take a steamboat up the Tennessee to Knoxville, Mr. Moody, and keep your eyes open along the way, you might catch up with him."

"Thank you, Doctor."

"I advised Lucas to avoid Chattanooga, which is about halfway between here and Knoxville."

"Why's that?"

"It's the old staging area for the Cherokee Removal of 1838. Most of the Cherokee are long gone, sadly, but some evaded capture and others are sneaking back, and the army maintains a camp there to protect the town. The place is swarming with soldiers with nothing much to do. I found Lucas work on a flatboat, but warned him to get off before Chattanooga and take to the hills, then pick up the flatboat again farther upriver."

"Why?"

"The army is dragooning what they like to call 'personnel' to work at the camp. They take negroes off any boat that passes through. He'll be safe enough if he takes to the trails, but you never know. Some people don't like to take advice."

Moody smiled grimly. "That sounds like Lucas," he said. "But he's no fool."

17.

Rachel offered him Satan, but though he liked the mare for her wild looks and gentle ways, he didn't accept the gift. He wouldn't be able to take her on the steamboat, and if there were card games on board, which he had no doubt there would be, he would be able to buy a horse and saddle in Knoxville. And a gun, he thought, a revolver, a Collier, like the one he'd lost, or maybe one of the new Colt Patersons. He would find Lucas and together they would ride north to Ohio, or even up to Canada. Maybe they would find Benah first. They would set out as master and servants, in case anyone asked, and arrive as father and son and daughter-in-law. In her mother's boardinghouse, he lay in bed beside Rachel, who was sleeping, and thought about the cabin Lucas and Benah would make, the crops they would sow. The children they would have. He thought about bringing them back to Rachel's farm, but then he'd have to "deal with" the Judds, or else pretend that Lucas and Benah were their slaves. He couldn't do that, nor would Rachel let him. He rose early without having slept, left the house without waking Rachel, and walked through the dark to the dockyard. A layer of heavy, white dew furred the trees and settled onto the grass and the boardwalks and the roofs of the houses, lightening the morning but chilling the air. When he reached into the pocket of Robert's coat for his gloves, he found a small leather pouch, a heavy packet of Robert's gold. Rachel must have put it there the night before. She had foreseen everything.

18.

He woke slowly and opened his eyes, lying still for several long moments trying to place the room. Low, paneled ceiling. Wide, four-poster bed, uncurtained but the rods were there. No one beside him. Against the opposite wall, a low washstand with a white-and-blue basin, and a matching pitcher strapped to the wall beneath a framed mirror. A door on his right, another on his left, with light coming in through the louvers. How long had it been since he had left the Rio Brazos? And he had yet to wake up in a room he recognized.

A steady pounding coming up through the floor reminded him that he was on a steamer. Ah. He'd boarded the SS *Mary White* in Huntsville after saying goodbye, or not saying goodbye, to Rachel. To his right, a door opened onto the great interior lounge, where he remembered there had been tables and a bar and a card game. He looked frantically around for his coat and satchel, found them on the floor and dumped their contents on the bed. The pouch with Robert's gold was still there, along with a handful of coins—dollars and eagles—and in the satchel a rat's nest of paper money drawn on Huntsville and Knoxville banks he'd never heard of. He must have drunk a considerable amount of whiskey. He didn't remember playing cards, and had no recollection of coming into this stateroom and falling fully clothed onto the bed.

He was on his way to Knoxville, to find Lucas. So much of his life had been spent on or near water: the inland passages between the Sea Islands and Georgia's mainland, where in the heat of August he had lowered fishing lines from summer docks and caught fathead sculpins, a fish so ugly and full of bones that Sikey refused to cook them; Lake Pontchartrain, where, when he had money, he had taken Annie and Lucas sailing, letting Lucas hold the tiller while he opened the wine and Annie unpacked the fried chicken and okra salad; Blue Creek, the trickle of water that ran past Rachel's farm and had yielded up Robert's gold; the Rio Brazos.

He put the banknotes in his pocket, returned the rest of his few belongings to the satchel, stowed the satchel under the bed, and stepped outside to the gallery, to see what fresh air would do to his head.

The *Mary White* was a stern-wheeler, a hundred and fifty feet from paddle to bowsprit, and the deck he was on was ten feet above the waterline. Below his deck was the open engine deck, where all the thumping was coming from, and below that the ship's hull, which, like everything else on board, was painted gleaming white. He'd been on bigger boats on the Mississippi, but this one had a light draft that was right for the river. He studied the trees along the shoreline, calculating the ship's progress against the strong current: about two knots. Sixty hours from Huntsville to Chattanooga, sixty more to Knoxville. How many of them already passed? Say twelve. Five days to go.

He filled his lungs and set off around the gallery. Scenes from the previous evening came back to him. His card-playing skills had returned; he patted his pocket, wondering whom he had to avoid, and squinted at a gull flying level with the deck rail, twenty feet to starboard, its gray head dipping back and forth, its yellow eye studying the water below. He imagined himself in Knoxville, handing the pouch of gold to Lucas. Here, he would say, find Benah, buy some land, build a house, start a new life. Lucas would look at him with astonishment and forgiveness and, yes, love. Not since Lucas had been eight or nine, not since they left New Orleans, had Moody held him in his arms, but he would hold him then, pat him awkwardly on the shoulder. They wouldn't speak for a moment, a bond stronger than words having formed between them. On the

riverbank, smoke curled up from the chimneys of log cabins cen-
tered in clearings hewn out of the dense forest. A house like that, he
would say to Lucas, but not here, not in the South. Get as far from
here as you can.

He made his way forward along the deserted gallery, looking
through open stateroom doors to where colored servants were
making beds and picking up clothes and emptying washbasins and
chamber pots into slop buckets. In one room he saw a young woman
dressing a white child. She could have been Benah. The previous
evening, he remembered now, he had asked several white women
in the ladies' lounge if they knew a servant girl named Benah. They
told him what they knew of servant girls. They had no morals.
They would rob you, but only of trivial things: a comb, a cheap
brooch, a silk handkerchief. The women allowed their servants to
bring their tea, but not to pour it. Why should Annie not be on
the *Mary White*, fetching a white woman's tea, dressing a white
woman's child? But of course she wasn't. He tipped his hat to the
servant in the stateroom and strode on.

The foredeck was strewn with bollards and vents. He admired
the thickly coiled hawsers, the way their ends were braided back
along their shanks to prevent fraying, and the swaying gangway
suspended on ropes over the prow. Barefoot crewmen scurried
back and forth, tightening this, unwinding that, obedient to the
bellowing boatswain, a red-faced Irishman who nodded brusquely
to Moody as he hurried past. Moody looked up at the oncoming
river, shielding his eyes from the sun glinting off the waves. More
of the previous night came back to him, the first mate remarking
that the river was so low they would be taking on a pilot at Ross's
Landing, just before Chattanooga. "There's more exposed rocks,
more sandbanks, more snags than in wetter seasons," he'd said,
"but the snag boats have been out and the main channel is cleared
and mapped and marked with buoys. The pilot has been guiding
boats up and down the Tennessee River his whole life."

Moody had been a competent *bouillotte* player in New Orleans. He didn't cheat, although he knew how. He could palm a card or spot an ace, but he'd decided that a ball in the temple wasn't worth the risk, and he was a good enough player to win more often than not without resorting to trickery. He'd tried teaching the game to Annie, but she had shown so little interest in cards he'd given up. He hadn't played at all in Texas, not even during lulls in the fighting when, between brushes with death, there'd been long stretches of idleness in Sarah Boggins's tavern, during which the men gambled away their small sums, their saddles, their horses, their farms. By the time some of them died in battle they wouldn't have had much to go home to had they lived. He'd avoided gambling because he didn't want to be responsible for another man's despair going into battle. He'd won last night, though, at least until he'd had so much to drink that he was playing recklessly, and even then had had enough sense to gather his winnings and excuse himself from the table. What happened after that was still a mystery.

At the stern paddle he watched the buckets, each one a plank eighteen inches wide and ten feet long, churning into the river behind the boat and glistening in the boat's shadow as it rose, the mechanism giving off a blast of steam at the top of each revolution. It reminded him of the steamer that had brought them from New Orleans to Galveston. Annie and Lucas had remained below, in steerage, allowed above only for brief spells during the day. How Annie had fumed. Such rules had largely been ignored in New Orleans. He and Annie would walk along Rue d'Orleans openly together, Lucas rolling hoops on the brick sidewalk, or chasing pigeons ahead of them into Congo Square. On the ship, he'd told her it was only for a few days, counting himself virtuous for having noticed her anger, thinking she would appreciate the difference between his concern and the other passengers' lack of it. Annie and Lucas were more to him than slaves: wasn't he a fine chap? He had slept comfortably in his cabin, on clean sheets and in fresh air, while they, his adoptive family, suffocated below on straw mats and were fed gruel. But what could he have done? More.

He looked downriver at the mottled gulls swerving above the boat's wake, landing and bobbing on the furrowed surface, their piercing cries like squeals from a paddle wheeler's ungreased axle.

He completed his circumnavigation and came again to the door of his stateroom, where Henry, the ship's steward, was leaning on the rail, casually observing the passing shoreline. Henry was well dressed for a steward, fingernails clean, hair neatly pomaded and brushed back. He wore a thin mustache, a mere black line on his upper lip. Moody had known his type in New Orleans. He stopped at the rail, and they listened to the sound of the engines coming up from below and mixing with the cries of gulls, the boatswain's shouts and the wind whistling through the rigging far above their heads.

"Fine day, boss," Henry said.

"Yes."

"How you feeling this morning, sir?"

"Fine, Henry, fine," he said. "Never been better, thank you."

"I'm glad to hear it, sir. You were kind to me last night."

"I was?"

"You gave me ten dollars."

"I did?"

"Yes, sir," Henry said, taking the bill from his pocket and showing it to him.

"Well, you earned it, Henry." He now recalled the steward getting him to his stateroom, helping him off with his boots, placing a glass of water on the nightstand. Had he been that drunk? "Unlike me," he said. "I just won it."

"And you offered to do me a kindness," Henry said quietly. "A favor."

"A favor?"

"Yes, boss. Do you not remember it?"

"Remind me."

"Tomorrow," Henry said, "we be coming up to Chattanooga. Before we get there, the pilot boat will come alongside with the new pilot on board, and to take off the old pilot."

"I see," Moody said, although he was able to make nothing of this apparent diversion.

"There be soldiers on the pilot boat," Henry continued. "They come on and take all the freeborn and freed men and women to be in the army. They call it 'recruiting.' "

"Yes, I've heard something to that effect."

"To dig latrines. To do laundry. Slave work, not army work."

"Yes."

"They don't take anyone who already owned. Only freedmen, like me."

"Ah," Moody turned to Henry and squinted into the sun. "You want me to be your owner, is that it?"

"Yes, boss. You did offer to do so. You being the only passenger on board without a body servant."

"I'll help you. And maybe you can help me."

"Anything I can."

"I'm looking for a runaway," he said. "A man about twenty years old."

Henry's expression started to go blank. Moody knew what he was thinking, that he was being asked to secure his own freedom by helping someone else be caught.

"I don't want to bring him back," Moody said quickly. "I want to help him get away. His name is Lucas."

"I'll ask around," Henry said. "Lots of people come and go on the river."

"Thank you," he said. "So what do you want me to do?"

Henry grinned. "Take off your clothes."

"My clothes?" He looked down at his shirt. "What's wrong with my clothes?"

"I'll wash them and try to get you some new ones. Maybe I can find you a hat and polish up them boots, too. No self-respecting servant let his massa out in public looking like you do. You'll see, everything be all right."

19.

At ten o'clock the next morning, Moody, barbered, brushed and clothed, was sitting in the lounge with the other passengers, the mill owners and planters and their wives and body servants. Henry had scrounged him a suit of clothes, complete with a fresh shirt and cravat and even a gold watch chain, sans watch, to drape across his midriff. In the tall, gilt-framed mirror affixed to the lounge's central pillar, he was startled to see his father staring back at him, a fixed scowl on his face; his son, or maybe his horse or his walking stick, had let him down again. Henry stood behind him, dressed in a spotless white jacket and trousers, with white gloves and a blue bandana around his neck that matched the silk kerchief in Moody's breast pocket. He would have looked overdressed at a masquerade ball in New Orleans. Henry had been unable to find him a good pair of boots. He pulled his feet under the table, where they were hidden by the low-hanging tablecloth. He knew how to deal with the army: the less explaining he did the better. His father scowled at the array of liquor bottles behind the bar. A few of the male passengers were already drinking, ignorant of or ignoring what was taking place elsewhere on the ship.

"We'll pick up replacements a few miles above Chattanooga," Henry said quietly to Moody, "them as had the presence of mind to abandon ship and go around. There's always a few that don't, though."

The patrol leader, when he entered the lounge, was an elderly sergeant in the uniform of the Third Tennessee Foot, the yellow stripe on his trouser legs faded almost to white and his tunic buttons tarnished except for the two directly beneath his chin. He wore a ribbon from the First Seminole War on his chest, and stood at the entrance, flanked by two privates, trying to establish an attitude of authority. He gazed about the room, his eyes halting at every black face in it, of which there were a dozen, men and women, all suddenly attentive to their masters and mistresses. No one seated on the chaises or around the dining tables stopped talking or drinking to acknowledge the soldiers' presence. Moody kept his eyes on the sergeant, who, perhaps for that reason, or because of Henry's flamboyant finery, crossed the room and stood at the table, looking down at Moody.

"Major Brant's compliments, sir," said the sergeant, giving a perfunctory salute, "and I would know the name of your servant."

Moody turned to Henry. "Lucas," he said in his best Georgia accent, "bring us two whiskeys, and none of that unwholesome rotgut they served us last night, mind you now."

"Yes, Massa," Henry said, bowing and moving off toward the bar.

"It's 'Lucas' now, is it?" said the sergeant. "I believe when I saw him two weeks ago his name was Raleigh and he was the servant of a Louisiana gentleman by the name of Major Allenhurst."

"Impossible," Moody said.

"Why so?"

"No man can be both a gentleman and a major," Moody said.

"Might I know *your* name, sir?"

"I doubt it."

"I mean, what is your name, sir?"

"Moody," Moody said, standing in the most insolent fashion he could manage, as his father would have stood to see around whatever obstruction had had the temerity to position itself in his field of vision. "And you are . . . ?"

Moody watched permutations and associations parading behind the sergeant's eyes. Moody, Moody, wasn't there a . . . ? Didn't Colonel Fain's daughter marry a . . . ?

"What is your business on this ship?" he said.

Moody sat as Henry returned with two glasses of whiskey on a silver tray. Henry removed the glasses, set them on the table beside Moody's left hand and resumed his place behind Moody's chair. Henry's former master, Moody thought, must have been a card player.

"My business," he said, raising one of the glasses, "is my business." He drank the whiskey and set down the empty glass. "But I can assure you," he added, raising the second glass, "it has nothing to do with army recruitment." He tossed back the second whiskey and set the glass on the table beside the first. Henry put both glasses on the salver and returned with them to the bar.

"I believe your servant is a freedman, and as such is subject to conscription into the United States Army. We are at war with the Seminoles, as you know."

"Not here, surely. The Seminoles are in Florida."

"We are preventing their insurrection from spreading north."

"Let us not dissemble," said Moody. "I have been a cotton planter in Georgia, I have been a cotton planter in Texas, and am now, since you ask, a cotton planter in Alabama, and I know perfectly well why the army is eager to rid the country of Seminoles. For the same reason they rid Georgia of the Cherokee: because the Seminoles hold the only productive land left in the state, and we want it. It isn't war, Sergeant, it's commerce."

"I'll relay your sympathies to the major, Mr. Moody."

"He already has my sympathies, Sergeant," Moody said as Henry returned with two more whiskeys. "As do you. But you shall not have my servant."

He raised a glass to the sergeant, surprised and more than a little dismayed by how easily Georgia planter manners had come back to him. The other gentlemen in the lounge, who knew for a certainty that Moody was not an Alabama cotton grower, some of whom may even have recognized his frock coat, were silent, ostensibly paying no attention to his charade, but Moody knew they were listening. Many of them would remember him from the previous night's card game, and all of them knew Henry. The sergeant glared but pushed his claim no further. He seemed as aware as Moody was that he was playing a role in a preconceived farce. He leaned dramatically over the table and picked up the fourth glass of whiskey.

"To your good health, Mr. Moody," said the sergeant, and drank.

20.

Moody found the atmosphere in the lounge awkward after the soldiers had taken their leave, as if the other passengers expected him to change back into his own clothes and start talking like a Texan again. He stood up from his table and walked out onto the foredeck. The vibration under his feet diminished as the *Mary White* slowed to tie up at the dock in Chattanooga to take on new passengers. The gangway settled on the dock, and Moody descended to look about for Lucas, although he had not much hope of finding him here. The army encampment was east of the settlement, down a dry, rutted road that followed the shoreline. No one came out of the guardhouse to challenge him at the gate. The camp itself was small, with a few permanent buildings for administration and officers' quarters, a parade square with a faded Union flag on a pole at the center and, farther back, rows of white canvas tents for the lower ranks. A few soldiers loitered before the post office. Moody asked them about Lucas, and they looked suspiciously at him and shook their heads as if Lucas's whereabouts were a state secret. He poked his nose into the mess tent, where half a dozen colored men were peeling potatoes and washing cast-iron pots. None of the men looked up, none of them was Lucas. He nodded to them and left. When the *Mary White*'s five-minute departure whistle blew, he gave up and returned to the dock. He was certain that Lucas wasn't there;

he had most likely gone up into the hills and was now in Knoxville, or somewhere beyond, in Virginia or Kentucky, where he would be hiding behind a false wall or under a load of hay or lumber. Moody boarded the ship with the new passengers, a few commercial travelers, a handful of soldiers on furlough, and stood again on the foredeck, gazing across the river at the hills above the old stockade, where the Cherokee had been held until their removal to Oklahoma. All that remained of them within the stockade walls were a few naked tepee poles and stone fire circles. As he looked, darkness settled over the scene like a curtain drawn slowly across an empty stage.

"That sure a sight, ain't it?"

Henry had come quietly onto the deck and was standing beside and slightly behind Moody. He was still wearing his white frock coat and the blue scarf.

Moody nodded. "I've been thinking about what I said to that sergeant," he said. "About how I couldn't go along with the Seminole War because it was simply a way of freeing up land for cotton planters. It sounded good, but I was forgetting that the same thing happened years ago in Georgia. My father benefited from removal then, and I did, too."

Although Annie hadn't, he thought. Or Lucas.

Henry considered the stockade. "At least," he said, "they didn't make them pick cotton." He turned to Moody. "Why do you think that was, Mr. Moody? The white man come here and find the place full of Indians they could beat down and turn into slaves if they wanted to, and instead of that they brung us over all the way from Africa to do that work. Why did they do that? I heard the government paid the Cherokee four million dollars for their land, and give them the same amount of land out in Indian Territory. What they pay us? What they give us?"

Moody made no reply; they both knew what had been given, and only Henry knew what had been taken away.

"I did ask about your runaway," Henry said. "I asked the cook. The cook knows everything that happen on a ship."

"No luck?"

Henry shook his head. "I'll keep looking. Where he from?"

"Texas," Moody said. "Like me."

"I thought you was from Georgia," Henry said.

"I'm from Georgia the same way you're from Africa," Moody said.

"Africa," Henry said, looking past Moody at the stockade. "I ain't never been."

The ship's horn gave an all-clear blast and the *Mary White* eased back into the dark river current to resume her torturous ascent.

"Well," Moody said, "you're still free. But I guess I didn't make many friends today."

"You made one," Henry said, "and that's one more than you had last night."

"How long before we get to Knoxville?"

"Another thirty, forty hours."

"What's it like?"

"It a rough, dirty town, Mr. Moody," said Henry, shaking his head. "Bigger than Chatt. Plenty of tippling houses. It got three tanneries, two churches and twenty-seven bars. But it has its good points."

"What are those?"

"It a place where a black man might find some sympathy for his situation."

21.

Three days later, the *Mary White* gently nudged the steamboat wharf below a long sign with KNOXVILLE, TENNESSEE painted on it in white block letters. Moody looked up at the sun: a little after noon. The city above the wharf was quiet, as though everyone in it were

hiding. Moody said goodbye to Henry, who had insisted on carrying his satchel down to the end of the gangway, and, leaving the
dock, climbed into a coach with a half-dozen commercial travelers
to be transported to the Knoxville Hotel. There was a scramble for
the five rooms still available. Moody got one because he wanted it
for three nights and paid his four dollars in advance.

"You have the room that was occupied by Jim Polk when he was
governor of Tennessee," the manager told him. "We ain't changed
a thing, except for the sheets."

"Glad to hear it," said Moody, signing the register. He asked the
manager for directions to the address on Dr. Carson's prescription
slip. He had assumed it was that of a private home, but the manager
looked at the address and then back at Moody.

"You a newspaper man?" he asked suspiciously. Evidently, giving James Polk's room to a mere newspaper man was against hotel
policy.

"No, why?"

"Because this is the address of the *Register*."

"The *Register*?"

"The *Knoxville Register*, our weekly newspaper."

He left his bag in his room, went back downstairs and stepped
briskly out onto Gay Street. The sky, which had been clear all morning, was still cloudless, and a sharp wind whistled down Main Street
from the north. The town swarmed with early-morning pedestrians,
women wearing long blue or black dresses with gray shawls pulled
tightly around their shoulders, and men, most of them in slouch
hats and buckskin, still managing to give the decidedly Southern
impression of being engaged in gentlemanly activity. Most of the
doors along the boardwalks were entrances to shops or law offices or
eateries. Some concealed stairwells leading to apartments above the
shops. Away from the river, everything appeared new, as though
the town had been built in the past few weeks. And dusty, for wind
and the lack of rain had filled the air with a coarse grit. Even horses

tied to the rails had dust on their backs. He found the *Register* office at the corner of Main and Locust; it was in a smallish clapboard building bearing a sign above the door that read THE KNOXVILLE REGISTER, FREDERICK HEISKELL, PUB., HUGH BROWN, ED.

The first thing he noticed about Frederick Heiskell was his beard: it grew to the edge of his lower lip, so that when he closed his mouth his whiskers merged with his mustache. Watching him talk was like seeing a forest reclaiming a pasture. Above the beard, his narrow, lined face and piercing gaze suggested a bright fanaticism. Moody had avoided such men in the war; they were the kind who rushed headlong into battle without first checking their escape routes or their ammunition pouches. You wanted such men on your side, but not in your unit. But there was kindness in Heiskell's eyes, too. His bushy eyebrows, turned up at the ends like horns, were satanic and comical at the same time. He read Dr. Carson's letter twice, turned it over to see if anything had been added on the other side, set the paper on the counter that divided the public third of the room from the cluttered two-thirds behind him, and leaned on his elbows with his hands folded together in an attitude not suggestive of prayer.

"It's Friday," he said, "the busiest day of the week for us. We have a paper to get out. What can I do for you?"

The space behind Heiskell was dominated by what Moody supposed was the printing press, a large, cast-iron, flywheeled contraption that looked like a spinning wheel built by someone who had never heard of wood. Around it were narrow tables laden with boxes of metal type, cans of black and red ink, torn and crumpled sheets of paper, filthy rags, paintbrushes, wooden paddles, wrenches and rubber hammers.

To the right of the machine, under a small window through which light crept cautiously in, was a large desk at which sat a second man, presumably the editor, Hugh Brown, who didn't look up from his work when Moody entered and appeared not to have done so for a good many years. He wore gold-framed eyeglasses and a visor, above which his head was as bald as Heiskell's was shaggy, and gleamed through the dusty light like a round hole in a granary wall. His work seemed to consist of reading pages of writing, muttering, and then, with a thick Salem pencil and a look of utter disdain, drawing heavy lines through what he had read and writing something else above it.

"I'm looking for a friend," Moody said to Heiskell.

"So are we all, Mr. Moody," said Heiskell. "What makes you think you'll find one here?"

"Dr. Carson said I might," said Moody.

Heiskell's eyebrows rose slightly. "What's your friend's name?" he asked.

"Lucas," Moody said.

Heiskell frowned. "I don't know anyone by that name," he said. "What else can you tell me about him?"

Moody described Lucas, putting as little emphasis as he could manage on the color of Lucas's skin, lest Heiskell draw the usual wrong conclusion. He said Lucas might have asked about a woman named Benah. He realized he'd been expecting to walk into the office and find Lucas helping with the printing press, or sweeping the floor, that a look of pure joy would spread across Lucas's face when Moody walked in, and they would leave together to continue the search for Benah. At the very least he'd hoped to find that Lucas had been here and moved on. So certain of this had he been that he had given no thought to what he would do if Lucas weren't there. It would mean he must have passed Lucas somewhere along the Tennessee River.

"What's your friend done," Heiskell asked, "that you're looking for him?"

"He hasn't done anything. I told his mother I'd find him and help him."

"Help him do what?"

"Get to wherever it is he's going."

"His mother being?"

Moody felt Heiskell reading his face as intently as Brown was reading his papers.

"Someone I knew," Moody said.

"I see. Well, you're welcome to wait, Mr. Moody. He may show up. But I've got work to do. Have a seat, if you like. I can talk and work at the same time."

Heiskell raised a flap in the counter and Moody stepped through into the print shop. Heiskell climbed onto a high stool set before a tilted table and began picking up tiny pieces of metal with a pair of tongs and arranging them in rows within a large, metal-and-wood frame, like a child playing with a set of blocks. Moody sat on an ordinary wooden chair that looked clean.

"Of course," Heiskell said, "if this friend of yours had been to see us, we would freely admit of it. Dr. Carson's note is quite sufficient proof that you are trustworthy in that regard."

"If he had been through here," said Brown, not looking up, "he'd be long out of harm's way by now. But he wasn't."

"How long should it have taken him to get here from Huntsville?" Moody asked. "He was supposed to come by flatboat."

"Flatboats wait until they're loaded to the guards before setting off upriver," Heiskell said. "He might still be in Huntsville, or he might be in Chattanooga. He might have changed his mind and gone downriver to Paducah."

"What about Muscle Shoals?"

"Oh, he could have gotten around Muscle Shoals, if he was determined enough. The flatboats downriver of the shoals are still going up to Paducah."

"Well," said Moody, "I think he found out that Benah was coming this way, and that's why he asked Dr. Carson to send him to Knoxville."

"All we can advise, then," said Heiskell, "is that you wait until he shows up."

"Is there anyone else he might have gone to for help?"

"Well, just about anyone," Heiskell said. He had finished filling the wooden frame and, using a rubber mallet, had tamped the type evenly flat and was tightening bolts on the side of the frame with a wrench. "We're a forward-looking town," he said, "with a forward-looking newspaper. We were anti-Removal, we're still antislavery, antiwar and antitaxes. We print what we want without fear of reprisal, for the most part, unless we run an article about the appalling working conditions in the tanneries, then we hear about it, eh, Mr. Brown? Blount County, just south of here, is mostly Quakers. The rest of the town is Presbyterian. Your fugitive would find sanctuary at just about any house in the area. And we have Maryville College. Have you heard of Maryville College, Mr. Moody? Founded some thirty years ago to train Presbyterian ministers, opened with five students, one of whom was George Erskine, a former slave whose fee was paid by the Manumission Society of Tennessee. He became an ordained minister, and took his family to Africa to preach the Gospel to his own black brethren."

"In other words," Moody said, "Lucas could have come through Knoxville a week ago, found help somewhere other than here at the *Register*, and have long since moved on. He could be anywhere by now. Would you have heard if he came through?"

"Mr. Heiskell is a former mayor of our city," said Brown. "Added to which, he's the publisher of Knoxville's only newspaper. Not much gets by him, and what does, I catch."

"Then I guess I'll wait for a few days," Moody said. "There ain't much else I can do."

"If we hear from Lucas," said Heiskell, "we'll let you know. Where are you staying?"

"At the Knoxville Hotel."

"Can your friend read?" asked Brown.

"Yes, I taught him myself. Why?"

"You might place an advertisement in our newspaper," Heiskell said. "A message, cryptic yet clear. 'LUCAS: for news of your mother,

ask for Mr. Virgil Moody at the Knoxville Hotel, No. 8, Gay Street.'
Something along those lines. In case he doesn't come here, you
understand. It will come out today. He might see it, if he's here, or
someone who knows him."

"Yes," said Moody. It was something. "All right."

"Good," said Heiskell. "That will be one dollar."

22.

Moody left the *Register*'s office not knowing which way to turn. He
wanted to press on, to hurry to the next station in the Quaker chain
to see if Lucas had been there. But he realized that if Lucas had
gone ahead without going to the newspaper, then going to where
Heiskell would have sent him wouldn't be much help. Three days.
He would give it until Monday. If Lucas hadn't shown up by then,
he would go back down the Tennessee to look for him.

There was no shortage of places to wait in Knoxville: saloons,
ordinaries, tippling houses, hotels, whorehouses. The hotel boasted
a billiards room, and in a smaller, adjoining, room he was informed
by the desk clerk a weekly poker game took place on Saturday nights.
"Modest stakes," the clerk confided. "Friendly games." No opportu-
nity for idleness, it seemed, went uncatered to, which Moody
thought was odd in a town that was half Quaker and half Presbyterian. He spent the rest of the day walking along Gay and Main
Streets, looking at faces. He got to know which boards in the sidewalk squeaked, which nail heads needed to be driven in, which
stores sold honest goods, which signs needed repainting, the
clerks who smiled and nodded to him as he passed and the sales-
ladies who looked through him as though he were a speck of
plasma floating across their field of vision. When he reached the
south end of Gay Street he continued down to the docks and talked
to the men who came in on the flatboats and passenger steamers.

Three or four boats had arrived since the *Mary White*; men emerged from the holds and the engine rooms blinking in the sudden sunlight and taking in deep drafts of air. No one had seen or heard of Lucas. He stood at the end of the longer of the three docks and gazed across the river, which was wide and deep this close to its source; watched gulls drifting in the air above the hills on the far side with their rising folds of green. Lucas could be over there. Three different rivers converged at Knoxville, and Lucas might at this very moment be following any one of them north. Moody's task seemed hopeless. When he turned back toward town he saw Lucas at every moment, on every corner and in every shop, climbing into carriages, dressed as a white gentleman with a female servant following, or wearing buckskin and walking with a woman toward the train station. He began to feel as though he were living two lives: his own, looking for Lucas, and that of Lucas, looking for Benah. Every movement of Lucas's life caused a corresponding movement in his. It was as though he and Lucas were twins, entangled in each other like the roots of two trees. He sensed that if he were itching to be on the move, as he was, it was because Lucas was already on the move somewhere else. He was Lucas's shadow, and could no more move independently of the figure who had cast him than a locomotive could move independently of its tracks.

His room in the hotel contained an ordinary table and one chair, a washstand with a looking glass, and a feather bed. Moody wondered if Polk had conceived the idea of annexing Texas while lying on the bed, as he was, staring up at the cracked ceiling, seeing in a line of broken plaster the erratic course of the Rio Grande. Had he considered then the lives to be lost, the widows and fatherless children, the destroyed villages, the hollow-eyed men? Or had he thought only about history and his place in it? Most likely he had blindly assumed, as Moody had, that doing what was good for him was good for everyone else concerned.

23.

On Saturday, he bought a gun. The clerk in the gun shop on Main Street tried to sell him an old pepperbox, a multibarreled monstrosity that Moody knew was wildly inaccurate and prone to explode in the user's hand. He asked for a Colt Paterson, but the clerk said the army had bought up all Colt's stock, and showed him instead a Collier, similar to the one he'd had before he was robbed. It was lighter than the Colt and, the clerk assured him, more accurate. He imagined Rachel watching him from farther down the counter: Why do you need a pistol, Mr. Moody? she would ask disapprovingly. He was going north, he would say; there would be bears, wolves, mountain lions. People, she said; handguns are used only against people. She followed him through the back door of the shop to the shop's proof house, where he tested the gun's accuracy. The kickback awakened a small pinpoint of pain in his hip, which brought a look of concern to Rachel's face, but he placed two bullets within an inch of the target's center. A bull's-eye, he told her, not a man's heart. And he didn't buy a holster, for the Collier was a belt gun. He admitted to her, though, when he had carried it and the ammunition back to his hotel room, put them in his satchel and slid the satchel under the bed, that he felt the world right itself a little.

Why do you need a gun to look for a boy, Mr. Moody? What are you afraid of?

He wasted more time. He read the *Register*. A disagreement over taxes in the general assembly in Nashville. General Zachary Taylor defeated Santa Anna in Buena Vista. A new law school opened in Boston. Colson's Dry Goods had received a shipment of the latest in ladies' hats from Charleston. Miss Annabel Johnson from Baltimore was spending the weekend with her sister, Mrs. Charles Sterngood. "LUCAS: for news of your mother, ask for Mr. Virgil Moody at the Knoxville Hotel, No. 8, Gay Street."

But there came no knock on his door.

24.

On Sunday, he lunched with Frederick Heiskell at Martha's Hearth, an ordinary located on Main Street that took its name not, as he had guessed, from its owner, whose name was Catherine Slough, but from a large portrait of Martha Washington that hung on a wall above the serving table. The first president's wife had apparently been a well-fed woman of gentle demeanor who, except for the scalloped lace bonnet tied at the top of her head with a silk ribbon, looked very much like her husband, George. Moody wondered if the artist had begun her portrait too soon after completing that of the first president. The room she overviewed contained a dozen tables and was reached by means of a long, narrow hallway leading from the street. On the wall of this passageway hung a series of portraits of other women from the Revolutionary era: Moody didn't know any of the names engraved on brass plates at the bottom of the portraits: Jane Mecom, Esther de Berdt Reed, Sarah Franklin Bache.

"They all helped raise money for the cause of freedom," Heiskell said, passing the portraits without a glance. "And they all owned slaves."

Seated at one of the tables, Moody told Heiskell of his conversations with men from the steamboats. Heiskell told him to be patient.

"Time passes quickly," he said. "We are in an age of great change. Those steamboats used to arrive carrying food and household goods, tanning supplies, paper for our press. Now," he said, "half their cargo consists of machine parts."

"Lucas was on a flatboat," said Moody, trying to keep the conversation about Lucas.

"Same thing," said Heiskell. "It's the Industrial Revolution. Everyone's getting in on it. 'The age of steam,' they're calling it. A vaporish age. Steamships on the rivers, steam locomotives on the railroads, steam engines running the cotton and sawmills. Even the presses, although not ours. I don't know what to make of it, do you, Moody? I mean, from an abolitionist's point of view? On the one hand, steam should be the black man's salvation. Imagine a steam-driven harvester, operated by a single man sitting atop his automaton like a pasha on his elephant, the machine doing all the picking, sorting and cleaning in a matter of hours that now takes a team of slaves weeks. That's what they're promising. An end to hard labor. An end to forced labor. We'll have to let our slaves go, wouldn't you think?"

Heiskell stopped talking to munch on a square of corn bread.

"So the *Register* supports mechanization?" Moody asked, intrigued by the logic. "Because it will free slaves?"

"Not necessarily. We support immediate emancipation, of course, but we recognize that it will take time to bring about the changes that need to occur before emancipation can take place. Mechanization would make emancipation happen virtually over-night, but imagine four million slaves being set free in an instant, with nothing to do and nowhere to go. Nobody feeding them, hous-ing them, clothing them. How are they going to live? Pros and cons, Moody, pros and cons. That's what makes a good newspaper story. On the one hand emancipation means freedom—schools where black children can learn to read and write and work at a trade or a profession. And on the other hand, it could lead to hordes of starv-ing desperadoes roaming the land, killing their former masters and taking over plantations, then villages, then whole towns, four mil-lion emancipated slaves, think of it, the army couldn't begin to stop them, whole states going down to savagery and butchery. All it would take would be one Nat Turner. Slavery was born in violence, and it could very well end in violence. What if the negroes joined forces with the Seminoles, as some of them already have? 'Maroons,' they call themselves. What if France or England helped them? Supplied the maroons with arms? What then? Why, it would be the end of the Union."

Heiskell was a philosophical abolitionist, a man of principle who believed that, all things considered, slavery was a bad idea. Moody admired that. He himself was more practical. He just wanted Annie and Lucas back so he could free them. Maroons, though. Had Lucas joined the maroons? He'd certainly been angry enough. And he'd always wanted to be a soldier, like Moody, although he wouldn't have fought in the Mexican War, which had brought slavery to Texas. Lucas had his own war to fight.

25.

As a young man, Moody had gone to Franklin College, in Athens, Georgia, where he'd taken courses in biology, engineering and law. After, he'd gone to New Orleans. He'd read books from the college library, novels and poetry and some philosophy, but it had been the law courses that had most stimulated his imagination. Biology had interested him for what it taught about how the world worked, but after a while a frog splayed out on a dissecting table looked too much like a human body, an unborn baby's, for example, for him to feel entirely comfortable cutting it open to see what was inside. But when he'd found the mastodon bone, he wished he'd paid more attention to biology. At least he had learned enough to know how to learn more.

The law, he found when he first moved to New Orleans in 1830, had fired his imagination because it was open to so many idiosyncratic and perverse interpretations. The law was not an ass, it was a Hydra. Cut off one spurious argument and two more sprouted to take its place. Spend hours following a line of inquiry only to find that it led to two other lines. The law, he realized, had prepared him for this search for Lucas.

26.

Later that afternoon, as he stood by the fireplace in the hotel lobby trying to decide whether to have a drink or ask someone other than Heiskell about Lucas, the desk clerk appeared and said there was someone outside who wanted to speak with him.

"Is it Brown?"

Heiskell, born Presbyterian, had become a Quaker when he married Eliza, Brown's sister, who was a stout member of the Society of Friends. Brown was a lifelong Quaker, and preferred lunching here at the hotel, where the food was plainer and there were no portraits of hypocritical heroines of the War of Independence on display.

"He didn't give a name, sir," replied the clerk. "He's waiting outside."

"Outside?" Then it wasn't Brown. "Well, show him in, man, show him in."

The clerk looked embarrassed. "He's a negro, sir."

Moody stared at him. "You don't say," he said. "I'll see him outside."

He hurried out onto the street, expecting to see Lucas standing by the entrance. He had been right to put the advertisement in the *Register*, and to wait for Lucas to see it. He looked up and down the street. There were the usual shoppers and saunterers, but no Lucas. He was about to set off toward the river, thinking Lucas had changed his mind and run off again, when a dark figure emerged from the narrow confine between the hotel and the adjacent building. A tall, well-dressed man with a cane, a dove-colored jacket and a plain, rounded hat. Moody hoped his disappointment was not overly evident on his face.

"Henry!" Moody said, and the *Mary White*'s steward held out a gloved hand, which Moody warmly shook. "It's good to see you."

"A great pleasure, Mr. Moody," Henry said, removing his hat.

"What favorable wind has blown you to me?"

"I saw in the paper you was here at the hotel," Henry said, gesturing toward the door.

"Well, I'm glad you saw it. It doesn't seem to have come to Lucas's attention, though. You're back in Knoxville already? You left only on Friday."

"The *Mary White* broke a rudder shaft just past Chattanooga," said Henry. "Hit a rock. The water sure is low. There wasn't no rock there the last time we went by. We comed back for another one."

"Wouldn't it have been easier to continue downstream to Huntsville?"

"Captain wife live in Knoxville," Henry said, laughing. "There sure are some irated passengers on that boat. Now we have to wait for a new rudder shaft."

"How long will that take?"

"A week or two, maybe more. They have to send a long way for it, maybe to Charleston or Pittsburgh. And me all that time with no pay."

"That's a shame, Henry. Is there anything I can do to help?"

"I don't think so this time, boss. Unless you need a body servant for a couple of weeks?"

Henry flicked an invisible flake of ash off Moody's shoulder and eyed the hotel's facade as though considering its suitability as a temporary abode. Moody thought about being his father again, this time for two weeks.

"I'm not stopping," he said. "I'm going on to Philadelphia."

"Philadelphia? What's in Philadelphia?"

"I'm convinced that Lucas must have gone that way without coming into Knoxville."

Henry pursed his lips. "You don't think he might have gone more north, into Kentucky? Lexington almost due north of here, closer than Philly."

"You think he went to Lexington?"

"Well, I brung you some news," Henry said. "I heard something at Chattanooga, when the *Mary White* stop to take on new crew. I talk to a man said he talk to a man the week before asking about a woman name Benah. He say he remember particularly because Benah such a nice name he like to meet her himself."

"Did he say what the man looked like?"

"He said this man didn't have no nicks in his ears or his nostrils, and he had all his fingers and toes. That a rare condition for a runaway, you remember something like that. He said this man was at the dock waiting on a white man was going to hire him to take a wagon up to Louisville."

"Louisville?" Moody said. "From Chattanooga? Would he have to come through Knoxville?"

"No, he couldn't," said Henry. "There ain't no good road from here to Louisville. But from Chattanooga he could cut up through the hills to Lexington and be in Louisville in a few weeks."

"Did he say who this man was who was sending him to Louisville?"

"No. He only say he driving a team of horses for this man, and that he was going up to Louisville because he heard this Benah going there."

"Thank you, Henry. I don't suppose you'd like to come with me?"

Henry looked down at his immaculate coat and trousers, the spats on his shoes, and smiled. "No, sir. I be all right on the *Mary White*, though I do wish she had a different name."

"Stay away from soldiers."

"You, too."

"And speculators."

"Thing is," Henry said, leaning toward him, "there's lots of men out there that promise to help runaways. They get what work they want from them, then sell them to a speculator. Louisville ain't exactly a safe place for a black man."

He would go to Louisville. He would leave that very day, after saying goodbye to Heiskell and Brown. The livery stable behind the hotel would sell him a horse and saddle, and if he rode hard he might even intercept Lucas before he reached the Ohio River.

27.

The trail through the hills above the Tennessee River was far from inviting. Bands of Cherokee were rumored to have secretly returned from the Indian Territory to hide out in the Smokies, waiting for the collapse of the Union to reclaim their traditional lands. Maybe the Union *was* falling apart. The more he thought about it, the more his horse skidded on the hard-rock hills, as though his own concentration and the horse's were the same, the more he was tempted to turn back. The wind threatened to blow him out of the saddle, and his hip ached from the bouncing and the cold. He couldn't manage much more than a trot. He began to doubt Henry and his tale of a stranger helping Lucas get to Louisville by giving him a wagon and a team of horses. Henry's own final words proved that he wasn't sanguine about the arrangement, either. Why would Lucas trust anyone? This benefactor sounded like a character in a story the *Register* might have published, a warning about the kind of smooth-talking speculator a runaway might run into on the long road to freedom. Moody thought Lucas was too smart to fall for such tricks, but he also thought Lucas might think he could outsmart a crooked teamster. And so he wavered. He should turn back. He would press on.

Eventually the hills gave way to flatland, reminding him of parts of Texas, except here there were trees he didn't know, grasses he'd never seen before. He recognized most of the birds in the trees and on the rivers; he stopped to water his horse and watched a great blue heron staring so intently into the water he thought it must have been frozen, until the bird took a slow, cautious step toward something and stopped again. In a small blue lake, a family of green-winged teals dabbled for whatever bottom dwellers they had up here. Would Lucas take the wagon all the way up to Louisville, or would he take it as far as he dared, or until he caught up with Benah, and then ditch it, or else turn off the main road to head for somewhere else, Cincinnati, maybe, which was closer than Louisville? No, Lucas would do what he said he would do. Moody had raised him to keep his word. If Lucas said he would take the wagon to Louisville, he would take it to Louisville. If he heard Benah was in Cincinnati, he would take the wagon to Louisville and then head for Cincinnati. Moody thought he could take a lesson from the heron: patience, focus, faith.

He stopped one night beside a river where two trappers had a cabin. The pain in his leg had become all but unbearable, and he half expected to see blood when he climbed down from the saddle. The trappers were twin brothers named Tim'n'Tom, which was to say one was named Tim and the other Tom, but since they were so identical that no one, not even the two of them, knew which was Tim and which was Tom, they both answered to Tim'n'Tom. They'd built the cabin at the fork of two rivers and called the place Twin Forks. They'd added a skinning shed some distance from the cabin, because of the smell, in which pelts stretched on loops of willow branches hung from the rafters: beaver, muskrat, a few minks and otters. Moody asked them if they'd seen a wagon train go by lately.

"Yep," said one.

"Nope," said the other.

"We seen plenty wagon trains go by," said the first.

"But not lately," said the second.

"Why d' you ask?" said the first.

Moody told them about Lucas. They seemed to absorb the information without really understanding it. He suspected they were simple, that maybe, being identical twins, they were each born with half a brain. The *Register* had run an article about Chang and Eng Bunker, P. T. Barnum's Siamese Twins, two brothers who'd been born joined at the waist, each of them sharing a single liver. Tim'n'Tom weren't joined, but they seemed to share thoughts, as though each knew exactly what the other was thinking, or as though there was just the one thought and they were each having half of it at the same time.

"It's a big country," said one.

"Needle in a haystack," said the other.

He slept on the cabin floor, which didn't do his leg any good but at least he was warm, and when he woke in the morning Tim'n'Tom fried him a breakfast of some unidentifiable meat— beaver, said one, muskrat, according to the other. They told him that if it had been summer they'd have had mallard eggs. "Mallard's good to eat," they said. "Coot not so much." He was eager to get back on the road, but allowed himself the pleasant confusion of conversing with his hosts as they ate. They told him he had crossed a divide—all the rivers now flowed north, into the Ohio. He was in Kentucky, but he was out of the South. Kentucky called itself neutral, although it was a slave state. Moody told them about the bone he'd found beside the Rio Brazos—not what had ultimately happened to it, but what it had meant to him before that. It seemed to have brought him to a new way of looking at the world. They told him they saw bones like that all the time, just sticking out of the riverbanks. Whale bones, they supposed they were, belonging to behemoths beached by ancient storms, buried by floods, bathed by more recent rains and bleached by the sun. Bible bones.

"During the Flood this whole area must have been underwater," they said.

"Water was so deep it had whales in it."

Moody packed his bedroll and satchel, bid goodbye to Tim'n'Tom and, once back on the road, cantered as fast as his horse and his leg would let him. The half-tamed land around him, still gently hilled, became flatter and dotted with farms and crossroad villages—two or three rough houses beside a tavern or a smithy—and then opened to

plantations, with large, white, verandaed houses, smoke rising from
stone chimneys, and slave quarters and barns tucked into the closest
woods. He rode in his horse's breath, stopping to rest and change
mounts in Richmond, Lexington, Frankfort. Always asking the livery-
men about Lucas, who might also have changed horses at those same
stables.

"Tall man, lightish skin, no nicks or parts missing," Moody
would say, "likely driving a team and wagon with a load on it."

A man in Lexington asked him, "Light skinned? Quadroon?
Octoroon?" and Moody didn't know what to say. Annie was light,
but Moody had never seen her mother.

In any case, no one had seen a wagon go by, or a young man
hightailing it to the border with or without a woman. Moody climbed
back on his horse and resigned himself to the road. When he came to
the Ohio River he followed it west, downstream, to Louisville.

28.

The city was bigger than he'd expected, it wouldn't be easy to find
Lucas in it. It was built beside the Falls of the Ohio, a ten-mile set of
impassable rapids that had forced riverboats to stop, unload and go
back to where they came from. The goods they unloaded had then
been carted to the other end of the rapids and reloaded onto other
boats and taken down the Ohio to the Mississippi, and on to St. Louis
or New Orleans. But enough goods had stayed in Louisville to make
it a well-supplied city with direct links upriver to Pittsburgh and
Philadelphia, even to Boston. The Ohio River joined the country
east and west, and separated it north and south, with Louisville at
the hub. Louisville men had their hair cut square across the backs
of their necks, washed and shaved every morning, and wore boots
that seldom stepped on anything but wooden or carpeted floors.
They decried slavery, calling the men and women who worked for

them for nothing servants. The women's dresses were hemmed above the ground and unmuddied, their sleeves and necklines trimmed with lace, sewn on by their black housemaids. None wore bonnets, but pinned starched muslin caps with trailing ribbons to their hair. There was an opera house and a concert hall, and notices in the newspapers for chamber concerts and visiting poets. Along with the luxury goods that came downriver from Philadelphia came an attitude, a sense that it was the rest of the world, not Louisville, that had to justify its existence. That the goods arriving daily by steamship and keelboat were not trade goods, but tribute from a grateful nation. Louisville didn't need the Falls of the Ohio; the Falls of the Ohio needed Louisville. Even now that the city had dug a canal around the Falls, boats still stopped, people continued to get off, the city would go on forever.

He kept his eyes open, convinced that he would find Lucas trying to cross the Ohio. Every day, his steps brought him to the dockyards, which were extensive and, seen from the road above them, chaotic. Barges, snaggers, dredgers, flatboats and keelboats jostled the shore for space between fancy riverboats and steam-driven freighters. Crews and stevedores, carters and draymen swarmed the docks. Huge Belgian workhorses maneuvered heavy wagons up and down the piers. Riverboat traffic was becoming increasingly heavy by the day, and most of the steamboats he saw were burning coal. As was the city in general. Wagon trains and coal barges arrived from Pennsylvania and Tennessee, and Moody watched their cargo of coal being dumped onto mountainous, flat-black, bituminous stockpiles beside the river. Bales of cotton and hemp were off-loaded at a different pier, away from the pervading coal dust.

Moody figured that Lucas would likely have been hauling cotton from the South, not coal or hemp, which were Northern products. He sat in an ordinary across Ohio Street from Pier 9, the cotton pier, making his breakfast last as long as he could, into the lunch hour if possible, and studying each face as it passed, and every wagon that turned down to the loading docks, all the time thinking Lucas could be over at Pier 2 shoveling coal, or delivering lumber to Pier 4, or bags of salt, or sugar, or grain, anywhere but at Pier 9. After a few days he began to be noticed in the eatery, a white man surreptitiously watching the docks. People started to avoid him. The waitresses became less friendly, the coffee older and colder, they'd run out of dessert, would that be all, sir? He said he was looking for a job, which in a way was true. He couldn't keep counting on winning at poker, because he was getting to be known in the saloons, too, and the desk clerk at the Hart House Hotel was snooty whenever he returned to his room at night smelling of cigar smoke and whiskey. He sensed he'd also begun to exude an air of disappointment, with maybe a dash of desperation, like a gambler down on his luck. He wasn't drinking much, but he wasn't abstaining, either, and he was aware of it when his tread on the stairs above the clerk's desk sounded halt and unsteady. He paid his bill weekly, but his tips became less generous, his smoker's squint more habitual and less discerning, his cuffs and collars more frayed. And still there was no sign of Lucas. He could have found Benah and been in Sierra Leone or Liberia or Nova Scotia by now. But Moody remained certain that they hadn't crossed the Ohio River. He had to be certain about something, and he chose that.

One day, a week after his arrival in Lo'ville, as he was learning to call the city, he wandered into a section of it he'd been avoiding because of his skin. Shacks and doss houses made from discarded packing crates and heated with coal picked up on the roadways and in the railyards huddled along streets ripe with caked mud and horse droppings. Everything seemed temporary, everyone who lived there was waiting for the end of something. The fugitives looked hunted, defiant, achingly close to their goal but without the wherewithal to cross the last river. The free blacks ignored him, looked away as though his presence were an annoyance but not a concern. He felt the overhanging gloom, the sense that soon the camptown would be struck and they would be moved on. Fugitive or freed, they had only to survive until they could cross the Ohio. He calculated the odds of happening upon Lucas at around a million to one, about as likely as a mastodon dying and, a hundred thousand years later, its bones turning up at his doorstep.

A team and wagon stopped in front of what appeared to be a church or a meeting hall, a young man about Lucas's age holding the reins. Was that Benah sitting up beside him, carrying a doll or a child? No, she was lighter, and the young man wasn't Lucas. He was seeing Lucas everywhere. The day before, he had followed a man for five minutes down Huckabee Street, something about the man's shoulders, his gait, but when he turned he didn't look anything like Lucas. This couple in the wagon looked at him nervously as he approached, aware of his scrutiny.

"'Morning," he said to the man, taking off his hat. "Fine day."

The man and woman stared down at him as if from a scaffold. Neither seemed inclined to return his greeting.

"I'm looking for a friend of mine, name of Lucas, and his wife, Benah. Have either of you come across him in your journeys?"

He received the usual blank stares. They didn't even look at each other. He knew that if he offered money he'd be taken for a catcher, if he wasn't already.

"I ain't out to harm them," he said. "I want to help them across. Tell them that. I want to help. I knew his mamma."

The man looked down at the reins he was holding, as if he would haw the horses into motion if he could get his hands to work, and the woman continued to stare at Moody as though waiting for him to take something from her. The wagon, her husband, her child. There was something so elemental in her stare, it contained none of the sentiments of normal discourse, no curiosity, no fear, no pleasure, no alarm. He hated to think what had reduced this woman to this state.

He put his hat on and backed away. "Tell them if you see them," he said. He'd remember the church and come again when it was quieter. A church that helped runaways might have helped Lucas.

29.

In the dining room of the Hart House Hotel, he read the notices in the Louisville *Bulletin* as he ate his breakfast:

$75 REWARD

Ran away from the Subscriber in South Carolina on the night of Oct 11, a negro man named SILAS, about 30 years of age, 5 feet 6 or 7 inches high; of dark color; heavy in the chest; several of his big jaw teeth out; upon his body several marks of the whip, one of them straight up the back and curving over the left shoulder. No other identifying marks. Took with him a quantity of clothing, mostly white cotton, and several hats. A Reward of $75 will be paid for his apprehension and security, if taken out of the State of Kentucky; $50 if taken in any county bordering on the Ohio River; $25 if taken in any of the interior counties. John Hitchcraft.

Catchers were paid better, he noticed, if they let runaways cross the Ohio River into Ohio or Indiana before catching them. This improved Lucas's chances of reaching the river. There were a dozen such dispatches every day, men run from plantations or roadwork or even from households, women gone with their children, children just gone. Moody read them as he drank his coffee, notices from hard-done-by plantation owners in the Carolinas, angry shopkeepers in Georgia or Mississippi: "absconded wearing linen pantaloons," "accompanied by his wife BETTE," "of a pleasant disposition when spoken to." He wondered if he should post a notice for Lucas in the

Bulletin as he had in the *Register*. Inquire at the Hart House Hotel, 23 Wooler. Would Lucas suspect a trick? He was a fugitive, after all. But what else could Moody do, other than roam the city like a wraith? He didn't know any Quakers in Louisville, but they wouldn't be hard to find. He should have asked Heiskell for a letter of introduction. He continued to surveil the dockyards, walk out onto the ferry dock, stare across the Ohio at the Indiana shoreline as if expecting Lucas and Benah to step out of the trees, wave at him to come join them. He would row across the Falls of the Ohio. But no one emerged from the Indiana forest. He walked back through the shantytown and sat in workingmen's saloons drinking poor beer and returning their vacant stares. Once he knocked on the door of the church where he had seen the couple in the wagon, but no one answered. No one in this part of town was going to open their door to a white man, no matter how often he said he wanted to help.

He considered going back to Twin Forks and holing up for the winter, but discovered he didn't need to, because Twin Forks came to him. On one of his daily meandering waterfront checks he saw Tim'n'Tom driving a trace-galled horse and a loaded wagon along Ohio Street, past the exits to the docks, past Webber's Livery Stable and Matsen's Coal Yard, heading east toward a section of the riverfront reserved for private wharves and warehouses. He called to them, but there was too much clattering and whinnying, and so he walked briskly in the wake of their wagon, unable to run because of his hip. They moved at a decent pace, as though eager to put the city's dust behind them, and eventually turned down a disused, rutted track leading through some scraggly trees to the water's edge. Moody caught up with them as they were untying the tarpaulin that covered their load. They looked up and waved as though they'd known he was behind them all along.

"Pelts," said one.

And the other nodded and said, "Furs."

"Auction house in Wheeling."

"Beaver and muskrat."

"Mink, otter, ermine."

"Couple of lynx."

"Whooping crane."

"Whooping crane?" asked Moody. "A bird?"

"Yep, big whooper."

"Museum buys 'em."

"Sold 'em a brown pelican last year."

"Named our boat after it."

"The *Pelican*."

One side of the dock was a long, shed-roofed structure perched, like the dock itself, on stilts. Two side doors opened into it. Tim'n'Tom slid one aside and they stepped through it onto the deck of a keelboat. There wasn't much light, but Moody could see the boat was about fifty or fifty-five feet long, with a large cabin aft. He could also see that the vessel was well made, the joins tight and the deck pumiced smooth as a Savannah dance floor.

"Did you make this?" he asked, running his hands along the cedar-sided hull. The boat stirred gently in the water, nodding against the dock.

"Built the boat," Tim'n'Tom said.

"Built the shed."

"Built the dock."

"Built the wagon."

There was a brief pause.

"Bought the horse."

Moody helped them unload the bales of furs through a hatch into the keelboat's hold.

"We'll advertise for help," said Tim'n'Tom. "Hard poling in places, going upriver, especially with the water low like this."

"Wind helps."

"Sometimes."

All during dinner, which they ate aboard the *Pelican*, at a table and chairs set up on the boat's ample foredeck, Moody considered signing on with Tim'n'Tom. He was still thinking about it as they sat outside on the dock, hands wrapped around warm tea mugs, and watched the sun go down over the city. His high estimation of Louisville as the place where he would find Lucas was also setting. Lucas wasn't anywhere near Louisville. Why would he be? The Ohio was a long river and there were safer places to cross it, where Lucas would be less scrutinized than he would have been in Louisville. He'd been wasting his time, first in Knoxville and now here. Weeks had been lost.

"What's Wheeling?" he asked, and they told him it was a town in northern Virginia, on the edge of the East. From there you could get upriver to Pittsburgh and even Philadelphia by train. Although it was Virginia, they said, slavery wasn't as deeply entrenched as it was in the eastern half of the state. If Lucas was hiding out somewhere along the Ohio between Louisville and Wheeling, looking for a way to get across, then sailing up the river on a slow-moving, fifty-five-foot keelboat wouldn't be a bad way of finding him.

"Do you ever see runaways on your trips to Wheeling?" he asked them.

"Lots of them," said one.

"Working in Wheeling, mostly," said the other. "And Malden."

"What's in Malden?" Moody asked.

"Salt mines."

"Salt furnaces."

"Supply all the meat packers from Louisville to Pittsburgh."

"Huge operations."

"Hot work."

"Slave work."

"Most runaways get themselves caught crossing the Ohio end up in Malden."

"If they ain't sent back South."

"Or killed."

"We stop there on our way to Wheeling, to pick up salt."

"I'll come with you," Moody said.

"Thought you would."

"Needle won't come out of the haystack by itself."

He returned to the hotel, paid his bill, sold his horse to the livery yard, and took a cab back to Tim'n'Tom's dock, his optimism renewed. He felt as though he were running away to sea.

30.

On the upriver trip he scanned the trees and beaches for signs of runaways. He would set his pole on the bottom, feel it nestle into sand or jam between rocks, fix his end of it against his shoulder, then look up to see if anyone was watching from shore as he pushed. There must have been hundreds of fugitives lurking in those bushes, eyeing the *Pelican* as it passed, calculating the risks of hailing it, but he saw no trace; no marks in the sand, no broken branches, no small fires or stacks of blackened driftwood, no smoke sifting through the leaves. He supposed that by the time fugitives reached the Ohio they had learned how to be invisible. A runaway who had made it this far was a smart runaway. Moody poled on the starboard, or shore, side of the boat, so that Lucas, if he was out there, would see him and come out. But *would* he come out? Would he trust Moody, or would he think Moody had come to take him back into slavery like any other catcher? The thought pained him, but as he inched the *Pelican* against the current he had to admit Lucas had little reason to trust him. Moody had let him go to Millican's, which had caused Millican to sell Benah, and perhaps by now Lucas even knew what had happened to Annie, and held Moody responsible for his mother's death. Moody had to find Lucas and prove to him that he'd changed. To acknowledge to him that he, Moody, had made terrible mistakes in his life, but that essentially he was a good man, that he hadn't known they were mistakes until after he'd made them. Not that that made it all right, but it might make it easier for Lucas to forgive him.

Some things are forgotten, but nothing is ever forgiven.

He felt an overwhelming need to be forgiven. Annie and Rachel were behind him, only Lucas could forgive him now. He would keep on.

31.

The Kanawha River drained into the Ohio a day's poling west of Wheeling, and they turned into it. At Kanawha Salines, a settlement a few miles upriver, Tim'n'Tom stopped to take on sixty fifty-pound bags of salt.

"Why not pick them up on the way back from Wheeling?" Moody asked.

"Auction's Wednesday."

"This is Monday."

"Save a day on the way back."

While the brothers loaded, Moody walked about, looking for Lucas among the furnace workers. There were fifty-two salt operations, fifty-two mine heads housing steam-driven contraptions that pumped river water down to the salt beds four hundred feet below the surface, and pumped the liquid brine up into heated evaporation pans that had to be constantly stirred and raked by slaves, male and female, children and uncles. Smoke from fifty-two coal-burning furnaces choked the entire valley. Moody started coughing the minute they tied up. Louisville had been dingy from coal burning, but nothing he'd seen there matched this. Coal smoke blackened the trees and the roofs of the houses, the tops of the fenceposts, the washing on the clotheslines, the surfaces of the water in the horse troughs and drinking barrels, the flanks of the horses, the faces of the men who drove them, even the bread they put in their mouths. The very ground seemed to be made of coal dust and cinders. It was hard to see how anything as white as salt could come from it.

More than five hundred slaves worked in the Kanawha Salines. Moody spent the day searching among them, and in the evening walked through Malden's shantytown, without learning anything. No one had heard of Lucas. It had been months, but he felt he'd been looking for Lucas forever, since the day Lucas was born, even before that, when Annie was still carrying him. She never said how Lucas had been started, neither at the time nor that day coming back from Boonville. When Lucas was born with such light skin and it was clear that his father had been white, Moody settled on Casgrain. The overseer was unmarried, lived year around on Plantagenet and devoted himself to siring slaves as if it were part of his job. Fat, leering, stupid Casgrain. Moody had hoped he'd got Annie away in time, but Casgrain never missed a trick. It explained his swagger, the way Moody's father deferred to him in all matters concerning slaves, and why Moody's mother treated Casgrain as though he were a plague imposed on her by her husband. The thought of Casgrain had infused an awkwardness between himself and Lucas that Moody had never been able to breach. He thought about that as he walked through Malden, looking into the workingmen's blackened faces. Would he recognize Lucas beneath the grit? Would Lucas reveal himself if he didn't? He was almost relieved when it was time to go back to the *Pelican* and set off up to Wheeling.

32.

Never had he seen such excitable people as there were in Wheeling, Virginia. Everyone was always worked up about something: dogs running after carts, children running after dogs, women running after children. Men starting up this, launching that, getting something else going, all moving in a direction they vaguely described as "ahead" but to Moody simply looked like "around." Work had begun on a new suspension bridge connecting the city to Zane's Island, in the Ohio, even though there was nothing on Zane's Island except a few farms. Papers in Philadelphia were calling it "the bridge to nowhere," but nowhere was being connected to somewhere, and that was deemed progress. Coal mines on the mainland supplied the salt furnaces, the salt furnaces supplied the meat packers, the meat packers supplied the bridge workers. Someone had discovered iron in the area, and that had set off a run of eager speculation: Wheeling could supply Pittsburgh with iron ore as well as coal for the smelters, and get back steel for the bridge. Maybe Wheeling could get the Baltimore and Ohio Railroad to lay some tracks to haul the ore, coal, salt, and of course passengers possibly from Boston on their way to points west. New stores would be needed, hotels, eating houses, the land registry office would have to be expanded, they'd need a chamber of commerce, and someone would have to build a hotel on Zane's Island. They should take a vote on paving the streets. So much delving and scheming. In the agrarian South, even in Louisville, resources tended to lie on the surface—cotton, tobacco, hemp, cane, rice—whereas here in the North everything seemed to be under the ground, and require a great effort of digging to get it up and greater efforts of planning to ship it off and sell it somewhere.

As Tim'n'Tom had said, the real work in Wheeling was done by slaves, even though the city was officially antislavery. They didn't call it slavery, they called it free labor, but all the laboring was done by blacks. Colored men worked on the bridge and in the salt mines and the manufactories: "Far from lessening the intolerable burden of the black man," he wrote to Fred Heiskell, "industry appears to have increased his suffering, for it is far uglier labor in a factory than on a cotton plantation, where at least he has the benefit of sun and air, if we could but banish the whip. The factories are dark, noisy, and dangerous—men are dwarfed by the size of the machinery, bludgeoned by the clamor of metal hammering metal and boiled alive like lobsters by steam. In the coal mines, men work underground from see to can't, as they used to say in Texas, never seeing the light of day except on Sundays, when they are too tired, discouraged, and demoralized to worship the deity that has landed them in these deplorable circumstances."

The blacks in Wheeling were runaways who'd been caught and put to work locally instead of being chain-ganged South. They had glimpsed freedom across the Ohio River before that Holy Grail was snatched away from them. Looking across the river, Moody saw a drift of ascending hills covered by tall, leafless oaks and maples, latticed by rivers. Too far to swim, but close enough to be a torture as they loaded boats or dragged metal girders off the docks.

He helped Tim'n'Tom stack their pelts on a cart to be taken up to the auction barn, then stayed down at the water to ask after Lucas. He talked to men working in the coal yards first. Most were from Georgia or Mississippi; they were quiet when they heard his accent, but relaxed when he explained that he was trying to help a friend get to Canada. They had seen the *Pelican* come in. "You could take us across the Ohio in that," they said. "Take us all the way to Canada in it." They were right, he could have.

"If it was my boat, I would," he said, recklessly. The men nodded and went silent for a moment, then turned back to work before the overseer came along and caught them talking to a white man about a boat.

33.

Tim'n'Tom returned from the auction barn to get the whooper skin and take it to the museum, and this time Moody went with them. The museum was housed in a small building attached to the side of the town hall: THE WHEELER MUSEUM OF NATURAL CURIOSITIES

AND HISTORY, the sign above the door read. Inside, the emphasis seemed to be more on curiosities: among the shelves of the usual stuffed birds and bottled reptiles, Moody saw the skeleton of a two-headed calf; a large jar of yellow liquid in which floated the lightly haired fetus of a one-eyed horse; another jar, labeled "The Malden Mermaid," contained an unborn human child whose legs were fused to form a single, fish-like appendage; a large ostrich egg on which a sailor had etched a whaling scene; and beside it, a bone, slightly smaller than the one Moody had found by the Rio Brazos, with a drawing of a giant wearing a panther skin and holding a wooden club the size of a tree trunk over his shoulder. An arrow pointed from the bone to the giant's upper thigh. Nature, it turned out, was filled with such a variety of oddities that no accounting of it, no matter how far-fetched and outlandish, could be disbelieved. Giants once roamed the Earth, mermaids inhabited the oceans: here was the proof. Everything was possible.

The museum director was a short, fair-haired, balding man whose enthusiasm did not appear to have been dampened by the evidence of life's treacherousness by which he was surrounded. His name, Lester P. Underhill, was engraved on a lump of coal set on the edge of his desk. He gave Tim'n'Tom ten dollars for the whooping crane skin, and told them he was happy to have it, but next time could they get him a great auk or a penguin? He was, he said, pretty well fixed for ducks and geese. "What I don't have," he said, "are critters we don't see in these parts. This whooper's a migrant; we see 'em from time to time, a few days each year, but there ain't always time to shoot one."

Moody asked him where he had gotten the mastodon femur that he was passing off as a giant's leg bone.

"Big Bone Lick," said Underhill, making a face and eyeing Moody speculatively. "I seen a whole set of them in old Bill Peale's museum in Philadelphia, but I ain't never had but the one bone here. How'd you know what it was?"

"I used to have one myself," Moody said.

"Where is it?"

"I lost it."

"How in hell do you lose a four-foot, hundred-pound thigh bone?"

"I just did. I heard Peale's came from somewhere along the Ohio River."

"That's Big Bone Lick, but his came from the Hudson Valley, up to New York. The Ohio bones were dug up by a bunch of damn Frenchmen a hundred years ago, and the bastards sent them to France. I've written to the president to tell him he should demand their return. Those bones belong right here in this museum. Or in the museum in Louisville at the very least, seeing as they came from Kentucky. You been to Big Bone Lick?"

"No."

"It's in a loop of the Ohio, just south of Cincinnati. Captain William Clark was there in 18-ought-7, that's where he got the mastodon skeleton he gave to Thomas Jefferson. Big Bone Lick got more bones in it than a catfish. Mastodons and giant sloths and cave bears must've went there to get a lick of salt and fell in. We got our own salt lick down to Malden, but nobody's found any bones in it yet that I know of. You got any training in geology?"

"Took a course in it one time, at Franklin College, in Athens, Georgia." This was more recklessness. His roommate at Franklin, a young hellion named Keith Barrett, had taken courses in natural science, and Moody had glanced from time to time at his textbooks and been fascinated by drawings of coiled shells, stone shrimps, petrified snakes. He hadn't needed giant leg bones to convince him of nature's strangeness. "That was a long time ago."

"No, it wasn't," Underhill said. "Them bones was a long time ago. Big Bone Lick is old hat, got too many amateurs digging it up and bringing me their junk, knucklebones and such, never a skull. Tell you what, you find me some fossils that ain't from Big Bone

Lick, and draw me a map of where you found 'em, I'd be happy to put them in the museum. Especially a skull. Bring me a whole skeleton that don't come from Big Bone Lick, gentlemen, and it'll make your fortunes."

34.

"You can't find bones without a boat," Tim'n'Tom said to Moody as they strolled in contemplative silence down the dusty, board-walkless street from the museum to the river. The fur auction was two days off and they would sleep aboard the *Pelican*, with the stove going to forestall the chill winter weather. At night the temperature dropped below freezing. "We can show you where some more bones are, and where Big Bone Lick is, but you'll need a boat to get to 'em, and you don't have a boat. You need a boat."

"What about you?" Moody asked them. "Aren't you interested in finding him a mastodon skeleton?"

"Nope."

"We like the way we live now."

"We like the outsides of animals better 'n the insides."

"You need a boat."

"Where can I get a boat?" Moody asked.

"And a shed to put it in," they said.

"And a dock to tie it to."

"Are you selling the *Pelican*?" he asked.

"We been thinking of it."

"We ain't as young as you."

"You need a boat to find Lucas."

"All right," he said. It would cost him the rest of Robert's gold, but he could earn money with the boat, hauling cargo. And when he found Lucas and Benah, he could take them the rest of the way to Canada.

35.

At some point before dawn on the morning they were to leave Wheeling, Moody was awakened by a commotion on the foredeck. Not a commotion, he realized when he was fully awake, more like a suppressed disturbance, something furtive. He looked through one of the cabin's forward windows and saw dark figures moving in the moonlight; they appeared to be huddled against the wind, smoking cigarettes, he thought at first, but then saw their breath condensing in the cold air. There came the dull thunder of the hatch cover being rolled aside. He dressed quickly, jammed his pistol under his belt, pulled on his coat and went out to investigate.

He saw Tim'n'Tom talking to three figures, two men and a woman, obviously fugitives; black, even in the darkness he could see they were dressed in rags, coughing. The woman was older than the men.

"They heard we's goin' to Lo'ville," Tim'n'Tom said to him.

"Want us to take 'em."

"So we're takin' 'em."

"There's catchers behind 'em."

"Guns."

"We'll hide 'em under the salt."

Their names were Jonah and Sully, the woman was Mary. Sully said they'd been working in a coal depot, shoveling coal off steamboats, and heard they were being sent to work in one of the salt furnaces in Malden; they knew that would kill them, so Mary had brought them here. Mary was their landlady, a free woman.

"All right," Moody said, peering at the two fugitives. Neither of them was Lucas. "Let's get them below, and we can close the hatch and light a lantern."

"That's what we was thinkin'."

"We gotta shove off at first light."

Moody climbed down into the hold with the two fugitives and one of the Tim'n'Toms. The other closed the hatch and began untying the *Pelican*. Moody lit a lamp in the hold, then the four of them arranged the sacks of salt into rows forming a trench down the center. Tim'n'Tom laid boards across the trench and they piled more sacks on top of the boards to form a kind of cavern, and the two fugitives crawled into it. Tim'n'Tom placed more sacks across the opening. No one spoke much. Tim'n'Tom seemed to know exactly what to do.

"You done this before," he said.

"Yep."

"You knew they were coming."

"Happens."

"That's why we stopped for salt," Moody said, "so the bags would be here."

He felt the *Pelican* rock as it slipped away from the dock. Fifty sacks of salt gave enough weight that the rocking and drifting were slow. Moody heard shouts coming from above and blew out the lantern. He and Tim'n'Tom scrambled up the ladder and opened the hatch a crack. It was still dark. The opening was filled with stars. Tim'n'Tom paced along on the deck, poling the *Pelican* away from the dock, and two men on the dock were yelling at him.

"Stop, goddamn it! Stop or we'll fill yer boat so full of holes she'll sink and, and you and yer goddamn niggers with her!"

Tim'n'Tom continued poling. Moody pushed the hatch cover the rest of the way open and he and Tim'n'Tom climbed out on deck. The boat wasn't more than twenty yards from the dock, but once out into the current it would be easier going. Moody grabbed a second pole and pushed. One of the Tim'n'Toms ran into the cabin and came out with a rifle, and Moody felt that now the whole thing was coming undone. Guns in the dark: no one could see anything, no one thought they could hit anything, and so everyone felt justified in firing at anything that moved.

"I'll shoot the first one of you sons of bitches fires at this boat," the Tim'n'Tom with the rifle shouted. It was the longest sentence

Moody had heard from him. Then, from the dock, he heard the crack of a rifle. Moody jumped and Tim'n'Tom dropped backward through the open hatch into the cargo hold. There were more rifle shots. Moody brought out his pistol and fired blindly in the direction of the dock while the Tim'n'Tom who was poling ran to the far side of the boat, putting the cabin between himself and the catchers. Moody fired two more shots. The boat was far enough out now that the dock blended into the darkness. A final rifle shot came their way but hit nothing. Moody climbed down into the hold.

When he lit the lantern, he saw Tim'n'Tom lying on his back on the sacks of salt. His eyes were open and there was a hole the size of a ten-cent piece in the middle of his forehead.

36.

There'd been nothing dramatic about it, just men shouting at one another, some shots fired and a man killed. It was like the war.

They lifted Tim'n'Tom out of the hold wrapped in a blanket and laid him on his cot in the *Pelican*'s cabin. His brother was taking him back to Twin Forks to be buried. He and Moody worked the poles, easier now they were going downriver but still necessary to keep off the rocks. At night, when they tied up to the shore, Jonah and Sully came up on deck to cook and to scrub Tim'n'Tom's blood off the wooden planks. The result looked good at night, but in the morning the stain was still there beside the hatch cover. During the day they kept to the Ohio side, in case the catchers followed after them, or new catchers became interested. Tim'n'Tom kept his rifle handy, and sat beside the cot in the evenings, reading or staring off into the darkness above the candle. It rained most of the way, a cold, slanting drizzle that knocked the leaves off the trees and made the deck slippery under their boots. Moody rigged a tarpaulin over the foredeck, where the cookstove and some chairs were set up, and to give Tim'n'Tom some privacy he carried his cot down to the hold and slept there with the fugitives, leaving the hatch cover open for air. There was blood on some of the sacks, and they shifted those to the back and replaced them with clean burlap, on which Jonah and Sully slept.

Neither of them knew anything of Lucas or Benah. They'd been caught by a posse coming up from Tennessee, but had never been near Chattanooga, didn't know anyone who ran delivery wagons up to Louisville, had never been west of Nashville before. They were sorry, they would have liked to help, especially because they felt responsible for the death of his friend.

"You didn't kill him," Moody said.

Moody brought Tim'n'Tom food, but it was barely touched. He would sit with them for a while, then put a hand on Tim'n'Tom's shoulder and leave to go sit out on the deck with his pistol on the table beside his chair.

"The trouble," said Tim'n'Tom one night as Moody was at the door, "is that I don't know which one of us is dead."

37.

By the time the *Pelican* nudged sluggishly against its home dock, the rain had become colder, bordering on sleet, and the river was a midnight blue stirred, at its shallower places, into whitecaps. They transferred Tim'n'Tom's body to the wagon, and Tim'n'Tom drove it back to Twin Forks. Moody offered to go with them, but he had to deliver Jonah and Sully to a Quaker household in the west end. Tim'n'Tom gave him the address, and Moody watched him drive off.

They waited in the boathouse until after dark, then made their way along darkened back streets, through the workers' neighborhood, until they found the address. After delivering his charges,

Moody told the man who took them that he would ferry fugitives across the Ohio River, or to whatever station was next on the Railroad line. They invited him in and gave him dinner. They talked guardedly about their activities, but assured him he and his boat would be welcome. "It gets harder from here on up," they said. "More catchers, bigger fines. Jail sentences." Moody said he'd be careful. Cincinnati, they told him, or, if he went the other way, downriver, then Paducah. Moody had the impression he was at the center of a large but nebulous network, each junction of the web knowing only the next junction, nothing beyond that. He inquired after Lucas, more out of habit than hope, and was told that the name didn't ring any bells, and the family didn't keep records. They seemed as frightened of being discovered as Jonah and Sully were. Remembering his experience with Rachel and the Judds, he didn't press.

From that night on, however, his boathouse was a gathering place for runaways. Charcoal or chalk markings appeared on the trees by the road, and often when he emerged from his cabin in the morning fugitives would slip out of the woods and come down to the dock; families, single men, single women, small groups of children who had been through more than they would ever recover from. Moody took them in, fed them, hid them in the *Pelican*, and took them across the river into Ohio or Indiana. For a while he imagined Lucas and Benah showing up at his dock, the surprise on their faces when they realized who their ferryman would be, their joyful reunion, his hallelujah day. But the fantasy faded as the winter went on and the hardship and the disappointment mounted. The river froze over in places, some mornings he had to chop his way out into the current. Still, he felt he was inching toward Lucas by helping his charges reach whatever degree of freedom might await them on the other side of the river.

In February, a merchant offered him twenty dollars to deliver a hundred kegs of blasting powder to a coal mining company in

Paducah. He was certain by then that he was not going to find Lucas in Louisville, or anywhere east of it. He couldn't have said why, except that he hadn't, he'd lost confidence in the eastern stretch of the river. West, however, was all new territory: the promoters were right. What if, after leaving Chattanooga, Lucas had decided to take Dr. Carson's advice and go west, down the Tennessee instead of up? What if he'd gone to Paducah? He'd be long through by now if he had, but he might have left some hint of where he was going from there. Moody's new Quaker contacts would tell him where the next station north was. Paducah seemed a better bet than Louisville. He made the five-day journey with a single passenger, an old man named William, a fugitive from Mississippi, who after a long separation was joining his daughter in Canada. He had a letter from her. Moody read it to him every night, after he'd tied up and William had climbed out of the hold for supper.

"'Well, Father,'" Moody read aloud:

"I have found my Canaan at last, for here I am surely in the land of milk and honey. We arrived in the village of Amherstburg, across the Detroit River which here is called the Straits, without any thing, and went straight into the bush cutting wood, and in a short while earned enough to buy our land from the Children of Peace Society. The Society has seventeen hundred acres of good land that only refugees from the house of bondage can buy. They expect to have fifty thousand acres in a few years, and a town with a free-labor store and a school where we propose to send our children if we are blessed with any, and a Zionist church where we will hear the Gospel on Sundays."

Moody noticed William's lips moving as he read. The old man had memorized the words. Moody marveled at the faith it must have taken for a daughter in Canada to send a letter to a Virginia slave who couldn't read. And yet he had received it.

"'Slavery been abolished here a long time,'" he went on:

"Whites up here be used to it by now. They don't like us much, but they don't like each other much either and they don't abuse us any more than they abuse themselves. Last week a catcher come across the Strait in a boat and a group of whites gathered on the shore with firearms and would not let him arrive. Us they do not regard as Southerners, simply victims of the cursed Southern institution, and so they harbor us as refugees."

"That's a nice letter," Moody said, refolding the paper.

William nodded. "That the Gospel truth," he said.

"Your daughter," Moody said, "how did she get to Canada?"

"She follered the Drinking Gourd."

"The Drinking Gourd? What's that?"

"In the sky." William pointed up, and Moody looked.

"The Dipper? You mean she followed the Big Dipper?"

"It always point north."

"Toward Canada."

"Yes. The North Star shine over Canada like the Star of David shine over Bedlehem. It guide us the same, too."

"How did it get her there?"

"I don't know how, exactly. She wrote it took her up the river to Paducah, Kentucky, and then up another river to Indianapolis, and from there it took her straight up to Canada. I expect there was some difficulties, but that the way I been going. She foller the Drinking Gourd and I foller her."

If Lucas came this way, that's the route he'd have taken, too. Indianapolis.

"I'll take you to Indianapolis," he said. "Soon as we deliver this blasting powder."

38.

"Construction fever has hit the North," Moody wrote to Heiskell. "Louisville has a canal, Paducah has a rail yard, Cincinnati has a canal tunnel, and Indianapolis has dug a canal that carries boats from the west fork of the White River right into the heart of the city. The National Road is due to reach Indianapolis from Baltimore by 1850, and tracks are already being laid to bring the Madison and Indianapolis Railroad into town by the middle of next year.

"But who builds these canals and railroads and highways? Not slaves, for our Northern states are proud of the fact that their constitutions do not allow slavery. No, the workers on these industrious projects are free blacks—a designation that usually signifies a man is free from slavery, but that here has come to mean also a man who works for free. Or for wages so low that he can't afford to do anything about his situation.

"It was a dark day for America when our antislavery Northern states discovered that it is cheaper to pay for labor than it is to feed and house the laborers."

Only nine miles of the canal from the White River to the city's center had been completed when the state ran out of money, but it meant that Moody was able to tie the *Pelican* within walking distance of the legislature building, which sat on a patch of snow-covered grass planted sparingly with bare trees at the center of a ring road called the Circle. Other roads radiated out from the Circle like the spokes of a gigantic buggy wheel. Indianapolis was like a child's drawing of a city; it looked good, but nothing worked. The defunct canal had been part of something called the Mammoth Internal Improvement Project; no one knew why it was called "mammoth," unless it was because it was big. But Moody saw the irony in the name, because the project, like the animal it was named for, was extinct.

In Paducah he'd been given the name of the Indianapolis Quaker who helped runaways: Solomon Kästchen, who lived on one of the ring roads behind the Masonic Temple. Moody and William walked to the address from where the *Pelican* was docked in ten minutes. The sign in the shop window said KÄSTCHEN'S GENERAL STORE, SOLOMON KÄSTCHEN, PROP. WE SELL FREE-LABOR GOODS ONLY.

They went in and stood by the door until the little bell stopped ringing and their eyes adjusted to the gloom. Moody assumed that the man behind the counter was Solomon Kästchen, because the store didn't look profitable enough to support hired help. Solomon Kästchen didn't look all that profitable himself. He was tall and thin and mostly bald, with fine, whitish-blond hair feathering the sides of his head, and side-whiskers reaching almost to the point of his chin, stopping about an inch from each other, so close that Moody wondered why he didn't just let them grow together, call it a beard and be done with it. He wore a threadbare woolen frock coat over a cream silk vest, a woolen shirt and gold-rimmed spectacles that gleamed in the weak light coming through the windows. Behind Kästchen were shelves crammed with all manner of dry goods, none of which had been made using slave labor: bolts of cloth, presumably not cotton; balls of frayed yarn; spools of silk thread and ribbons; gray-and-blue woolen blankets that reminded Moody of his army bedroll. The rest of the shop consisted of barrels of nails and staples, bags of flaxseed, flour, corn, crocks of honey. Farm and garden equipment hung from ceiling beams or leaned against the walls, and in the back a tack shop, with harnesses and bridles and metal bits and a couple of uncomfortable-looking saddles. Moody tried to find something he could buy. No guns, no tobacco, no liquor. It was amazing the things the store didn't have. He figured Kästchen would count himself lucky if two people a week came in and bought something. There were jars of penny candies on the counter, none of them made with sugar. Kästchen watched Moody and William eagerly as they approached the counter, Moody with a spool of fishing line and two hooks.

"Twenty cents," Kästchen said, "or I could sell you the fish for ten."

"I'll take the gear," Moody said, "and tomorrow I'll sell you eight fish for a nickel each."

"You think like a Northerner," Kästchen said, taking his money, "but you talk like a Southerner. Where are you from?"

"Georgia," Moody said.

"Never been there," Kästchen said, looking at William. "My father came here from Germany when I was a child."

"Do you miss Germany?"

"I hardly knew it," said Kästchen, "but yes, I am fond of what I do remember. In Germany," he said, looking at William, "we didn't treat people like animals."

Moody put his hand on William's arm. "This here is William. I'm delivering him to you. Daniel Hornby in Paducah told us you would help him."

"Daniel Hornby?" Kästchen said. "Never heard of him."

"He said to ask you for a length of chain with five links to it."

"Did he now? And what would you do with a length of chain with five links?"

"I would break it."

Kästchen nodded and looked at William with kindness. "Go up those stairs, my friend," he said, indicating a set of steep stairs set into the corner of the shop. "Mrs. Kästchen will look after you." To Moody he said, "You took a chance coming here in daylight. But it's winter, not too many people about."

"We've come a long way," he said, "all the way from Louisville."

"You have helped a great cause."

"Now I wonder if you can help me."

Kästchen favored him with a helpful expression.

"I'm looking for someone."

The helpful expression vanished. "We sell goods here, sir," he said, "not people."

"I don't want to buy someone, I want to find someone."

Kästchen regarded him blankly.

"The man's name is Lucas."

Kästchen's eyes did not flicker. He didn't look as though he were trying to remember anything. He spared himself and Moody the charade of rubbing his chin and scratching his forehead.

"You disappoint me, sir," he said.

"Mr. Kästchen, my name is Virgil Moody. I'm on your side. I brought William today and I have helped many other fugitives cross the Ohio River to freedom. But I am looking for one fugitive in particular who is a personal friend of mine. He ran away because of something I did, well, because of something we all did, and now I would find him and help him get to where he wants to go."

Moody saw the man relenting. He came out from behind the counter, locked the front door and pulled down the window blind. Moody thought that locking the door wasn't obviously necessary. Kästchen led Moody through a door behind the counter that gave into a small, cluttered, windowless office with a desk and two chairs, a medium-sized safe and shelves above it lined with thick ledgers and marble-edged account books. For a store that didn't do much business, it seemed to require a lot of bookkeeping. Kästchen shut the door, sat at the desk and gestured toward a second chair. Moody sat across from him.

"What is it you want?" he said, taking his spectacles off and polishing them with a handkerchief. Moody waited until he had put them back on.

"I want to know if you remember a man named Lucas coming through here within the last few months. Young, smart, well built, light skinned, no marks on him. He would have come from Texas, but by what way I don't know. Perhaps through Cincinnati, perhaps by way of Paducah. He might have been with a woman named Benah. I don't want him back. I just want to know if he made it this far."

"Mr. Moody," said Kästchen. "My wife and I have helped more than two thousand fugitives come through this city in the past ten years. We don't ask them their names. We don't ask where they come from. Most of them wouldn't tell us anyway. It's best that we don't know. And we don't talk to anybody about our activities, not even to other Friends. My wife's sister lives in the city, and we do not discuss our activities with her, at least not in detail, and she is a Quaker. Indiana is, generally speaking, antislavery, but it is also antislave. Even those who support our cause, and help us with private donations from time to time, wouldn't think of opening their doors to our unfortunate friends, let alone their hearts. If the mood in these parts changed tomorrow, as it very well could in these trying times, we and our activities would be denounced on every street corner and from every pulpit in the city. We're immigrants, Mr. Moody. If they didn't denounce us for being antislavery, they would denounce us for being anti-American. Even the Religious Society of Friends has disowned us, did you know that? They feel that the best way to achieve emancipation is through political channels, amendments to the Constitution, lobbying congressmen in Washington—most of whom, as you know, are Southerners. Everything above board, nothing that would hurt their chances of gaining sympathy with the population at large, and therefore with the people the population at large votes for. That is what, in this country, is called democracy. So you see, we have to be very cautious. Very cautious indeed."

Moody hadn't known about the Society's change of position, and he wondered if Rachel had. He imagined her alone in her farmhouse, or in the boardinghouse in Huntsville, at the mercy of people like the Judds without even the Society to turn to for support.

"I appreciate your position, Mr. Kästchen," he said. "I have to be cautious myself, though less so here than I was in the South."

"Do not assume you can be less cautious here."

"Two thousand saved," Moody said, wondering how many of them he had ferried across the river.

"The Society believes that helping a few thousand individuals into Canada is nothing compared to freeing four million with the stroke of a pen, but the way I see it, our few thousand will still be alive when the change comes, if it does, whereas if we didn't help them, they almost certainly would not be."

"I'll keep bringing you as many customers as I can," Moody said, rising.

"What is your interest in this man Lucas, if I may ask?"

"His mother was a particular friend of mine. I promised her I would help him."

"I see." But he sounded as though he had no idea what "a particular friend" meant. Neither did Moody.

"If he did come through here, where would his next stop be?"

Kästchen looked up in astonishment. "I cannot tell you that, of course," he said. But at the door, he hesitated before raising the blind. "Mr. Moody," he said, "if you ever happen to be in Newport, a village about sixty miles north of here, you might stop in to visit Mr. Levi Coffin. He's a dear friend, and he owns a shop very similar to mine. All free-labor goods."

"Thank you."

Moody stayed on the *Pelican* that night. He lay awake for a long time thinking about Lucas and Annie. Lucas had been an inquisitive child, wanting to know what everything was for, what things did, how things worked. Maybe he'd wanted to believe that Moody was his father, but had Moody let him? They hadn't talked about it, but he must have wondered how they had all come to be together, how the family worked. Moody assumed that Annie had explained things to Lucas when he was old enough to understand them. But he and Annie hadn't talked about it, either. He thought of Lucas driving the team and wagon into the barn for the first time by himself, the nonchalant look on his face, and Moody watching him, trying not to grin. He thought of Annie kneading bread dough by candlelight, her sleeves rolled up and her golden-brown forearms sprinkled with flour. But after that the images grew progressively more sinister: Lucas standing in Millican's yard, believing that servitude was the only way he could be with Benah, and not knowing what servitude meant. Annie saying she forgave him, but then dragging the bone from the barn down to the river. He had to stop himself from seeing the drag-marks in the sand. He sat up, lit a candle, thought about getting out of bed to make coffee and piss over the side of the boat. He heard drums in the distance, then realized it was his own heart pounding in his ears.

He had James Hutton's *Theory of the Earth* on the shelf beside his bed, and to calm himself he took the book up and opened it at random.

"It is the little causes, long continued," he read, "which are considered as bringing about the greatest changes of the Earth."

His was a little cause, finding Lucas, and it had long continued.

39.

The failure of Indiana's mammoth canal and road-paving schemes meant there was still plenty of work for keelboat owners, and Moody found himself taking cargo regularly between Indianapolis and Terre Haute, a town in the western, less settled, part of the state, and bringing fugitives back with him as crew, whom he then passed on to Stationmaster Kästchen. He spent many happy evenings in the Kästchens' apartments above the shop, where Catharina, Solomon's wife, poured schnapps and set out small cakes and cookies, and joined in the conversations. The three talked at length about the changes taking place in the North: as more and more slaves were emigrating, as Kästchen quaintly put it, from the South, states like Indiana and Ohio were passing stiffer laws to keep them out, which the Kästchens saw as further evidence that the Society's plan to convince politicians in Washington to abolish slavery was never going to work. Although he remained a Quaker in his heart, in his mind Kästchen was having serious misgivings about the Society's right to dictate individual morality. He talked about the need to separate morality from religion.

"Morality," he said, holding the schnapps glass delicately between his thumb and forefinger, "is acting according to the dictates of your conscience. Religion is acting according to the dictates of your church. But when your church is in conflict with your conscience, as it must at times be, since conscience is individual and church is collective, then you must, you *must*, obey your conscience."

"What about your government?" Moody asked. "What if your conscience is at odds with your government?" Was it his conscience that had made him fight to free Texas from the Mexican government?

"Still your conscience is your true guide."

"This is why Solomon's father leaves Germany," said Catharina. "After the defeat of Napoleon, everyone wanted to go back to the way things were, with thirty-seven little duchies, each with its own little monarch and its own little constitution. They want to stick their heads in the sand as if Napoleon had never happened."

"Thirty-seven little Strausses, *ja?*" laughed Kästchen. He stood up and retrieved a book from a set of shelves in the kitchen.

"Disobeying your Society," said Moody, "sounds like mutiny to me."

"*Ach,*" said Kästchen. "Catharina and I are both seditious by temperament, with our opposition to slavery. And look at you, aiding and abetting us."

He handed Moody the book he had taken down.

" 'Theodore Parker,' " Moody read. " '*History of the Jews.*' "

"He writes that the so-called miracles recorded in the Old Testament were really naturally occurring phenomena, easily explained by modern science. The parting of the Red Sea, Aaron's walking stick turning into a serpent. Moses getting water from a rock. Manna falling from heaven. All, he says, can be explained without recourse to magic and superstition. Beliefs that have endured for thousands of years crumble into dust when examined in the light of reason."

"You are Jewish?" Moody asked.

Kästchen laughed. "*Ja*, we're agnostic Jewish Quakers."

" 'All fails,' " Moody read, " 'and all fails equally.' "

He recalled his conversations with Rachel and wished she were with him now, sharing his doubts, the way Kästchen and Catharina shared their convictions. He had felt, at the farm, like a schoolboy making fun of Schoolmaster God behind his back, hoping to impress a pretty girl in the classroom. Here was a more mature way of thinking. He even began to question Cuvier. "Fossil organic remains are the relics of a primeval world long since past," Cuvier's paper began, "proclaiming with a loud voice the instability of earthly affairs, and impressing upon the minds of those who seriously consider them, sentiments of piety and feelings of devotion." But surely Cuvier's conclusions were a direct challenge to piety and devotion. What was Cuvier up to? His own reading of Lyell and Hutton, and now of this Parker fellow, convinced him that Cuvier hadn't taken his own argument far enough. Turning the accepted tenets of science on their heads, as Cuvier had, sowed the seeds of doubt, not piety. Scripture was quoted by slaveholders and anti-abolishers to defend the institution of slavery. If slavery was to be defeated, religion would have to be defeated first. And that would have to be done by men and women of conscience.

"To sedition," he said, raising his schnapps.

40.

He ferried dozens of fugitives from the Mississippi to Indianapolis, where he delivered them to the Kästchens, who passed them on to Levi Coffin. He talked to them as they helped him pole, listening to their stories, asking about Lucas. They didn't talk about the conditions from which they had escaped, all too well known, but rather about how they had come, the hardships of the road, the occasional bright spots: the crates they had squeezed into, meant for glass or machine parts; "Best to find one marked 'Fragile,' " one said, "if you can read." The wagonloads of lumber or coal; the train cars carrying pigs or chickens: "Burn your clothes after." One woman spent seven days in the chain locker of a riverboat, in the point of the bow, buried under a stack of cordage and oakum. "A kind stoker brought me food," she said, "until he killed when a boiler exploded." Some just walked out of the woods and appeared to him like wraiths, half starved, half clothed, half eaten by deer flies, half crazed by fear. He took them all on. If they could work he handed them poles or set them to the bilge pump, if not he lay them on a cot in the hold during the day, carried food down to them after he'd tied up at night, or brought them up on deck if there was no traffic, talking quietly and keeping an eye out for lights. They were cautious at first, especially when they heard his Southern accent, but they were also desperate, and being from the South, he knew how to talk to them. He knew where they had come from, what they were running from: they were running from people like him. Or rather, he began to allow himself to think, from people who were like he used to be.

None of them had seen or heard of Lucas. He was either too far north or too far south, too west, too east, too early or too late, too eager or too resigned. But he kept asking, and never stopped listening for the rustle of leaves beyond the light from the fire, or scanning the shore as he poled, only half expecting Lucas to emerge from the woods, brush the twigs from his shoulders and wave down Moody's boat, like a New Orleans dandy hailing a cab. He bought a cabin near a town called Spencer, Indiana, where he planned to spend his winters, and wondered if it was big enough for himself and Lucas and Benah. Maybe he should add another bedroom? He stocked the larder for the coming winter with enough flour and beans and molasses for three.

Early in the winter of '49, he took on Otway Tull, a former cotton slave from the Green Mountain plantation in Virginia who had stowed away on a Mississippi steamboat and jumped ship in Cairo, a mosquito-infested town at the confluence of the Ohio and Mississippi Rivers. Moody was delivering a load of salt when Tull approached him and offered to help unload, saying he wanted to go to Indianapolis. He was so scarred over Moody couldn't say how old he was, or whether he was handsome or plain. His left arm was crooked and he walked with a limp. He said yes to Tull, he said yes to everyone, but when they set off upriver first thing the next morning, he found Tull so defeated and bitter he was sorry to have him on board. When he asked Tull about Lucas, Tull spit over the side of the boat and shook his head.

"Fugitives crazy to come this way," he said. "They gwan down to Mexico, or San Domingo. Some are took by abolitionists, who juss want us gone, and sent back to Africa. Others go to secret colonies deep in de Carolina swamps or de Florida Everglades, where dey mix with Seminoles and others who hiding there, and live by piracy and cunning, waiting for Armageddon dat dey think will come to end our bondage and set us free."

"You came this way," Moody argued. "Lots of people come this way."

"Dat don't figure. Some of us is like sticks floatin' in de water. Us wash up here and come to groun dere. Dis Lucas, he from Texas, nuh? Why come all de way up here, den da? Dis de longest way to freedom dere be. He wun't be here."

"I heard he was in Paducah."

"Paducah, nuh."

"They said he crossed the Nuther River. What river's that?"

"De Nuther Ribber," Tull said, spitting over the rail again. "Who tol' you about dat? Dat just a song our mammies sung us at night when our heads achin' and de stripes on our backs keepin' us awake." He cleared his throat and sang a wavering, tuneless song:

"When de sun come back
An' de first quail call
Den de time be come
Foller de Drinking Gourd.

De ribber's bank am a very good road
De dead trees show the way
Lef' foot, peg foot, goin' on,
Foller de Drinking Gourd.

De ribber ends atween two hills
Foller de Drinking Gourd.
Nuther ribber on de other side
Foller de Drinking Gourd."

"Dat how yuh get to Paducah," Tull said when he was finished. "But dey ain't no 'nuther ribber.' Or dey always a 'nuther ribber,' take yuh pick."

"The Ohio's another river."

"An' where does crossin' dat get you?" Tull said. "Cross de Ohio from Paducah an' you in Illinois. From dere yuh gets to Indiana. Den dere's de Wabash. Den de White. Cross dat an' you still in Indiana." He spat. "Ain't no Paradise fo' black folk."

"Then why are you going to Indianapolis?"

"'Cause it a longer way from Virginia."

Moody put him ashore in Indianapolis and felt like scouring the *Pelican* when he was off it. He wished Tull hadn't been his last passenger before winter lockup. Rachel's gold was gone, he'd lost Millican's money; he had nothing to give Lucas, except the *Pelican*. As full winter set in, he retreated to his cabin in the village of Freedom, near Spencer, where he played cribbage with his neighbor, a freedman named Randolph Stokes. Ice locked the *Pelican* to its dock and frosted the cabin's windows and door latches. He wouldn't hear if Lucas came through Indianapolis now. Maybe Tull had been right. Wrapped in blankets, playing cards, reading his geology books and staring into the fire at night, Moody thought a fugitive would be crazy to come this way in winter. And anyone trying to find him here would be crazier still.

PART THREE

MARCH–MAY 1850

～

The River ends atween two hills,
Follow the Drinking Gourd;
Nuther river on the other side,
Follow the Drinking Gourd.

I.

Randolph Stokes showed Moody the first returning robin on March 15, but there was still snow on the ground, and it was another three weeks before the wind shifted from north to east, and another week after that before the ice receded from the *Pelican*'s dock, although not far enough to allow him to get the boat out into the river. He checked the hull for damage and found none, and brought his mattress and chairs down from the cabin. During his long period of hibernation, he'd thought about Otway Tull and the song of the Drinking Gourd. Would Lucas have known it? He'd often heard Annie singing quietly to him, but had she been singing that song? Had she been teaching him to run away even then? It was possible that Benah knew the song, or that Lucas heard it from someone after running off, but it seemed a fragile thread to plan an escape with. Judging from the number of fugitives turning up in Paducah and crossing the Ohio, however, the song seemed to be working. He and Stokes talked about it over cards while he waited for the ice to leave. Stokes said he'd followed the song and it had led him here to Freedom.

"The Drinking Gourd," Stokes said, "that's what we call the Big Dipper, and it always point you north. You follow that long enough, you end up in Canada."

"I know that much," Moody said. "But what's the rest of the song mean?"

Stokes thought for a moment, to bring the song back to mind.

" 'When the sun come back,' that the spring, the best time to go because you want to get to Canada before wintertime. The 'river' is the Tennessee, and you follow it downstream to Paducah. 'Dead trees show the way, left foot, peg foot goin' on' mean when you see a foot carved in a dead tree, you turn left, and when you see a round mark on a tree, like it made by a peg, you turn right. 'The river ends atween two hills'—that's where the Tombigbee empties into Mobile Bay, near Woodall Mountain, where you can see it has two peaks. It ain't hard to figure out. Lucas have no trouble with any of that."

"If he knew the song."

"I expect he did. I expect his mam sang it to him when he was a baby." Stokes paused his dealing and looked at him. "It wasn't meant for white folk to hear," he said. "What you think? We gonna say, 'If I ever run away from you, here's the route I'm gonna take'?"

Is that what he'd been to Annie and Lucas? White folk? Someone to run away from?

2.

When the ice released its choke hold on the river and he was almost out of firewood, he closed the cabin, said a temporary farewell to Stokes, and moved the *Pelican* a few days downstream, to a jetty he'd built the previous summer not far from where the White River joined the Wabash. From there he could sail north on the Wabash, east on the White, south on the Mississippi, and even, after a day on the Mississippi, sail east on the Ohio to Louisville or even Philadelphia. He felt like a spider at the center of his web, ready to pounce as soon as Lucas touched however distant a thread. As a bonus, he'd found a fossil near the jetty, a curious kind of skull, which he had started to take out last summer, and now wanted to finish, so he'd have another crate full of rocks to add to the pile in the *Pelican*'s hold he already didn't know what to do with. He thought of taking it all to the museum in Wheeling, but he was unlikely ever to be back there.

The day after tying up, a cold, steady drizzle set in, pewtering the river and keeping him from working on the skull. His leg stiffened from lack of use. The wound had healed well, but the damp made his hip bones ache and he had trouble lifting his foot when he walked. He drank endless cups of tea, to save coffee, and played solitaire in the *Pelican*'s cabin, keeping the coal-oil lamp going all day. By evening the score was Moody, sixteen; the Devil, ninety-two; and he could hardly walk without bending over like a crab. He was thankful he hadn't brought a case of whiskey, because he would have drunk it. Bored with cards, he read. He had his geology texts with him, but decided to give Walter Scott another try. He had *Old Mortality*, but couldn't stick with it, it reminded him too much of the South. When he was growing up, the Waverley novels had been much admired and emulated in Georgia. There were plantations with names like Claverhouse and Midlothian, and families who named their sons Dugald and Evan and Guy, and their daughters Lucy or Meg, after Scott's characters, not all of them worthy of emulation. The South venerated old families, engaged in decades-long clan wars, worshipped pride and honor above reason or even common sense.

He tried Hawthorne's *Twice-Told Tales*, and made it through two of the tales, "The Gray Champion" and "Sunday at Home," before putting the book down without marking his page. These Yankees, he thought, but it wasn't Hawthorne or even Scott, it was him. He couldn't concentrate. After a winter of enforced idleness, he felt, like Hawthorne's Mr. Ellenwood, "a shy but not quite secluded man, selfish, like all men who brood over their own hearts, yet manifesting, on rare occasions, a vein of generous sentiment." The rain and the pain in his hip were making him too introspective; he was no longer a spider at the center of his web, but a mole trapped beneath a flooded field. He brooded over his own heart. He was only generous when it suited him. He transported fugitives only because he thought they might help him find Lucas. And he didn't even want to find Lucas for Lucas's sake, but for his own. For forgiveness.

What if he gave up the search for Lucas, where would he go? He was forty-four (Mr. Ellenwood was sixty-two, and brooded still). How much longer could he push this boat around, heavy as it often was with rocks and salt and fugitives? How many more families could he transport upriver? He thought, more often than was his custom, about New Orleans, where he and Annie had been happy, where Lucas had been a joy that, like the sun in Texas, he wished now he'd appreciated more at the time. He could go anywhere. He could, simply by untying the *Pelican*, drift downriver, to wash up like a stick, like the odious Otway Tull, wherever spite and the current took him.

He dealt out another tableau of solitaire, to let the cards decide. The Devil won handily. As usual when his luck was down, the cards refused to cooperate.

3.

The rain stopped on the fifth day—he would later remember it was April 10, his mother's birthday. He'd been to the quarry, and now stood on the *Pelican*'s foredeck drinking coffee, to save tea, and timing a flotilla of early-migrating Bonaparte's gulls as they bobbed past him on the river. About five knots, he reckoned, a good pace: the river was high with spring runoff, the rocks not so threatening to his hull. He could be in New Orleans in May. He'd finish taking out the goddamn fossil, then throw his tools in the hold and cut the *Pelican* loose. He didn't know what kind of animal the skull belonged to, but he knew it was odd, something he'd never seen before, either in the ground or in a museum. It was big, about the size and shape of a dinner plate, flattened and rounded, like a giant frog. Why not? Mr. Darwin had found a giant sloth in Argentina and not thought it unlikely that the Earth had once been inhabited by giants. He considered the mastodon. He noted the flooding of the White River, which reminded him of the flooding of the Rio Brazos that had taken his dock. Then he tried to think of something else. This morning the skull had been delicate and the claystone around it soft and wet from the rain and snowmelt, which had meant slow work. He'd tried using an awl, but his hands shook and the point kept puncturing the bone, especially around the eye sockets. Each time it happened he'd jumped back as though stung. He didn't know how much damage he was doing to the braincase, so he'd come back to the boat to see what else he had that he could use, and ended up making lunch and a pot of coffee and thinking about giving up on Lucas. And just, well, giving up.

As he turned away from the river, he felt himself being watched. It was a sense he'd developed during the Mexican War: not a prickling, exactly, the hair on the back of his neck didn't stand on end, it was subtler than that, more like an instinct to duck and look hard at the line of trees on the other side of the jetty. A red squirrel scolded, and a jay gave its alarm call.

He knew who it was. An hour earlier he'd heard a commotion on the towpath downstream and had gone to investigate. There were five of them, three women and two men, with two horses. They were trying to get the horses onto a flatbed barge so they could pole them across the river, he'd guessed, but they weren't having much luck. The older woman and the older of the two men were standing in the water, pulling on the first horse's halter, urging it to step onto the barge, but the horse had locked his forelegs and wasn't budging. The two youngsters, a boy and a girl, were watching, and a third woman stood with her back to them and her arms crossed, like she didn't want to be taken for someone belonging to the party. She was the first to see him. She jumped. She was so light skinned he thought at first she was white.

"You need a blindfold," he said, to no one in particular.

They stopped and turned to look at him. No weapons.

"If it were me," he said, "I'd swim them across."

They continued to stare at him, the way deer stare before bolting. He was still holding his coffee cup. He took a sip.

"This here your barge?" asked the older woman, who was wading ashore.

Her dress was sodden and torn at the hem but of good quality. Was she wearing shoes? She was. A house servant, then, or else a free black. All three were well dressed. The older one's hair was gray at the temples, like his, full but not wild like Annie's, and she had tied it behind her neck to keep it out of her face. She was bigger than Annie, fuller in the bosom, but she looked at him with Annie's intensity, as though she would know what he was thinking. He liked that. He missed it. He'd like to know what he was thinking, too.

"No," he said. "Somebody left it here. You're free to use it, I guess."

"What's on the other side?" the man asked, pointing across the river. He was maybe twenty, the same age as Lucas.

"Just more Indiana," he said, thinking, reluctantly, of Otway Tull. "You're a ways from Canada yet."

"But Canada come after Indiana, ain't that so?" said the woman.

"That's so," said Moody, "if you don't count Michigan."

They stood in silence then, contemplating the far shore as though the existence of Michigan were debatable. He'd left them and come back to the *Pelican*, but he could hear them still trying to load the horses onto the barge, still without success. There was a lot of splashing and neighing and yelling for a while, then silence, and he imagined them admitting defeat and moving through the trees in his direction. A horse won't step onto an open barge in fast-moving water, Moody could hardly get one onto the *Pelican* in flat water with a plank and a sack over its head. He removed his gaze from the line of trees and refilled the kettle to make more coffee. He wondered if he would offer to take the horses, too. He hoped not.

4.

It was the woman who showed herself first. She'd straightened her bodice and he could see creases where she'd squeezed some of the water out of her skirts. Her caramel-colored skin and dark hair shone in the overhead sunlight. The others made themselves visible behind her.

"We ain't runaways," she said.

"I know that," Moody said. "Runaways generally run away."

She studied him. "You a bountyman?"

"No, ma'am, I'm a boatman." He'd once asked Kästchen if there were a sign he could give to show runaways that he could be trusted, a flag hung a certain way or a word spoken, something like the five-link chain, and Kästchen had said no, because if there were, catchers would use it.

The woman looked the *Pelican* over. "It a fine boat," she said. "We come down the Ohio on a boat like that, maybe a bit bigger. Where this river go?"

"Downriver," Moody said, pointing, "it joins up with the Wabash and then on down to the Mississippi. Upriver it doesn't go much past Indianapolis."

"How far's that?"

"A couple of weeks, maybe more with this fast spring current. There was a lot of snow this winter and the river's full. Tough poling. Got to use the cordelles in places." He was talking too much. He stopped.

"Horses could tow it," she said. He nodded.

The man joined the woman, and he took in the two of them standing together. They reminded him so powerfully of Annie and Lucas he put his hands on the boat rail to stop them from trembling.

"Where you live?" the man asked him.

He was taller than his mother, and strongly built. He wore a black hat that Moody hadn't seen on him earlier.

"Right here, at the moment," Moody said, flustered. "I built this dock last summer. Good wood, it should last a few winters. And I got a place up in Freedom."

"Freedom?" Annie said. "Freedom a place?"

"A settlement upriver," he said. "Mostly me and old Randolph Stokes, who bought himself a few years ago and came north. We get along fine. My cabin's beside his, but summers I live on the *Pelican*."

"Why do you call it the *Pelican*?" piped up the younger one.

They had stepped out of the trees. The lighter-skinned woman still had her arms folded across her chest and was looking curiously at him, as if wondering when he was going to notice that she wasn't dark. The others seemed both bold and afraid, except Annie, who looked at him and knew exactly who he was.

"That's the name she came with," Moody said.

"What you got in her?"

The woman turned to the younger one. "Granville," she said.

"A pile of crates full of useless rocks," Moody said. "There's lots of room."

"We're going to Indianapolis," Annie said.

"No, we ain't, Mam," Lucas said to her.

"Will you take us?" Annie said. "We can pay you."

"I'll take you, but not for a few days."

Annie and Lucas went back to the others for a conference. There was a lively discussion. Lucas wanted to go north, to Canada. The younger woman, the one who looked white, who maybe was Benah, said something sharp and Lucas stopped. Annie said a few low words, then came back to the jetty and said they'd go with him if he'd take them. They didn't mind waiting until he was ready. But when might that be?

"Maybe a week," he said. "Depends on how hard the rock is."

Although that must have sounded like a riddle to her, she took it in stride.

"What your name?" she asked him.

"Moody," he said. "Virgil."

"I'm Tamsey," she said. "Tamsey Lewis. This here my son Leason, and his wife, Sarah, and these are Granville and Sabetha, my other two. My husband, James, be along shortly."

"Pleased to meet you all," Moody said, turning to watch a line of crows skipping along the treetops across the river. Annie had a husband. "I got me a frog to dig up, anyway."

Granville couldn't let that go. "You going to dig up a frog?" he said.

"Well, it looks like a frog," Moody said. "It's all bone now. I'll show it to you."

"I'll get our things," Leason said.

He went back into the trees and Moody watched the forest edge where he vanished, until he returned with two saddles and a saddlebag.

Moody limped toward a chair on the *Pelican*'s foredeck. "Come aboard, if you like," he said. "I made coffee."

"Somethin' wrong with your leg?" Tamsey asked.

5.

Whenever he knew he was going to be in one place for more than a day or two, Moody set up the *Pelican*'s foredeck as a place to sit: he set out an easy chair for reading, and a table and a second chair for working and eating, two coal-oil lamps on the table, he even threw a small rug on the deck, beside the hatch cover, mostly to hide the bloodstain. The woodstove was already on the deck, tied down and sitting on a pallet of sand. When it rained, he'd thrown a tarpaulin over the stove and moved everything else into the cabin, but now he had it all in place again. He called it his parlor.

He set out extra chairs and helped Leason and Granville pitch the tarpaulin as a tent on the ground beside the jetty. He lent them some blankets to wrap themselves in while their clothes dried by the stove. When they were ready they came up into the parlor. He poured coffee and they talked as though the *Pelican* were the *Mary White* and they were about to embark on a pleasure cruise. Tamsey offered to make soda biscuits, and he went into the cabin to fetch flour, baking powder, butter and salt.

"Back in Texas," he told her when he came out again, "it got so hot you could bake biscuits on a flat rock in the sun."

"Hmm," she said. "What you grow down there?"

"Cotton."

"It ain't too hot for cotton?"

"Mexican cotton."

She frowned. Her features were similar to Annie's, and he wondered if her people were from Angola. She was talkative, as Annie had been at first. Toward the end, though, Annie would go days without saying two words together, at least to him. With Tamsey, everything was a story. The sun on her face reminded her of South Carolina. They'd had a stove like his in Kentucky. Making soda biscuits brought to mind the time she baked soda biscuits for Massa Somebody-or-other and the missus complained because she hadn't put enough sugar in them, and she'd replied that where she came from soda biscuits with sugar was shortbread, and Massa asked for soda biscuits, not shortbread, so she made soda biscuits. She never got on with the missus after that, she said, stirring, and did Moody have any milk? She could make soda biscuits with water but milk made a better biscuit, and was there any salt in the butter? If there was she'd put less in the dough, because too much salt made the biscuits hard as rocks and taste like seaweed. So she was a cook, he asked her? She was cook and housekeeper and upstairs maid and anything else the missus wanted her to be, except dead. She'd learned to make better biscuits in New Harmony, where they lived after leaving Kentucky. She was freed, all of them were free, the whole family, she could show him their free papers. In New Harmony, she'd used buckwheat flour and sweet butter. What kind of wood was Moody burning? It smelled like slippery elm, which was too bad because elm burned cold. Where was he from? Georgia? Didn't he say he was from Texas? Georgia then Texas? She was from

South Carolina then Kentucky. "I surely do miss honeysuckle and smoke pipes when the weather turn warm like this," she said, "and pecans on the roadsides and laurel along the creek beds. I'll miss them even more when we get to Canada."

"I know a man in Indianapolis," Moody said, "who can get you to Canada."

"You mean put us on the Underground Railroad?"

"You're on it now."

She looked at him. "How I know you ain't a catcher?"

"You know," he said.

"Indianapolis then Canada?"

Moody nodded. "A few stops along the way. You were in New Harmony?"

He'd heard of New Harmony, a Utopian community in the southwest corner of the state, one of many that had sprung up and then gone back to forest. Fred Heiskell had written about them in the *Register*, because most were against enslavement. New Harmony, he recalled, had been started by an Englishman named Owen maybe twenty years back, who thought if society had a new beginning we might get it right this time. But that was all Moody knew about it, except that it had been abandoned after a year or two, as had most of the rest. *All fails, and all fails equally.*

"We live there for a time," Tamsey said, putting the biscuits in the oven. "My husband still there, but he'll join us presently. We don't mind the wait. James won't think to look for us in Indianapolis, he'll cross the river and go on up to Canada."

"Which," said Leason, "if we had any sense we would do, too."

"Canada be there in the morning," she said.

"And catchers be here tonight."

"You don't need to worry about catchers on my boat," Moody said. "I've carried a good few fugitives to Indianapolis and I ain't lost one yet."

"We ain't fugitives," said Leason.

"How long ago did you leave New Harmony?"

Tamsey looked at Leason and shrugged.

"Not long," she said. "We traveled about a week, then waited for three days at the top of the track for James. Leason scouted on ahead and came back saying they a lake close by and the track end at it, and a meadow with a fire pit where Rappites used to smoke fish."

"I know that lake," said Moody. "Didn't know Rappites used it, though."

"Rappites built New Harmony before the Owenites took it over," she said. "I told Leason I didn't know what the hurry was. Once we lost the track James couldn't follow us. We didn't know where we was. I said to him, take the others and push on. I'll stay here and wait for James. Leason said he'd go to the lake and wait three days, then I had to come. I couldn't think of James being taken back into slavery. If I went on without him, it like I sending him downriver myself. I can't do that. Every step I take into these woods without him be like death to me. All my life I be thinking of him back there somewhere looking for me."

"Why did you leave New Harmony?" Moody asked.

"That what I telling you," she said, "but I have to go on before I go back."

"All right."

"This my story," she said. "Let it come, let it go."

"All right."

"I told Leason go on up to the lake and figure out how to get around it, I be along. Granville wanted to stay with me, bless the child, but I sent him, too, saying Brer Moses need him, that was Leason, and Sarah and Sabetha went and I was alone. I had some squirrel meat and a saddle blanket and Jezzy, my horse that didn't like getting on the barge. There were blackberries down by the riverbank, and fresh water. I wished I had a pot to boil water in, I was tired of roasted punk roots, but I didn't even have a knife, we left so fast. Maybe James would have one, and some corn meal. And a roast of beef. And a kettle and some tea."

She paused. Moody didn't want to interrupt her, but he thought maybe she was saying she didn't like coffee. "Would you rather have tea?" he asked.

"No, thank you, this coffee fine. And our feather tick, James might bring that. I would make him a proper supper, and we would lie down on the feather tick and he would tell me how good life was, and then we would join Leason and the others at the lake, and go on to Canada. I walked up and down that track. I sat by the river and watched it go by, but it was too loud and I couldn't hear anything behind me, so I run back, but there wasn't never anything behind me. It like I sitting in the Garden of Eden and God hain't made Adam yet."

She paused again, this time to check the oven.

"Biscuits ready," she said. "You all want one?"

Moody handed around the plate of biscuits and some butter. Honey would have been good, but he didn't have any.

"Where were you and James married?" he asked.

"In Louisville. Same time as Leason and Sarah."

He sat up suddenly, as though looking for rocks on the river. Lucas had been in Louisville.

"We're going to bed," Leason said, and he and Sarah stepped off the boat and ducked under the tarpaulin. Granville and Sabetha took a last biscuit and followed them. Moody poured more coffee for himself and Tamsey.

"How many fugitives you carried up this river so far?" she asked him.

"I don't know. Dozens."

"What happen to them there?"

"I hand them over to Solomon Kästchen, and he sees they get to Canada."

"How?"

"I don't know. I'm not supposed to know."

She nodded. "Where was I?" she said.

"Getting married in Louisville."

"No, before that."

"Alone in the Garden of Eden."

She smiled at him. "You a good listener," she said.

"I'm learning to be," he said, startled.

But she was back in her story. "I waited until almost dark on the third day," she said. "I knew he wasn't coming. There was life in the garden, but he wan't part of it. A deer come. A fox trot up the track. A dead leaf fall from the tree I sitting against and land beside my hand. I shivered under that tree, looking down that empty road. My blanket around my shoulders and I still couldn't get warm. I always cold. James a forge beside me at night. Sometimes if I sit in a chair he left I feel the warmth of him in the wood. When it too dark to see, I climbed on Jezebel and let her take me to the lake."

"You still think James is coming?"

"I hope he is."

"Do you want to go back to look for him?"

She was quiet a moment. "No," she said, "we can't go back there."

"Why not?"

"Let it come," she said, "let it go."

6.

After breakfast the next morning, Moody took them all to see the frog. The quarry was a half mile upriver and a short way in, at the rim of a clearing that had once been a swamp surrounded by a clay bluff and was now all roots and stone. He carried a bucket with an awl and a hammer, several paintbrushes, a pot of glue, a jar of shellac, a roll of burlap and a bag of plaster of Paris. At the edge of the clearing they pushed their way through dense mats of panic grass, marsh marigold and joe-pye weed to a spot where Moody set down the bucket and removed a tarpaulin from what looked like a broken tooth sticking out of the face of the cliff. They stood in a semicircle, looking down at his giant frog's head.

"It's pretty big," Granville said.

"Pretty flat," said Leason.

"Crushed by the weight of all that clay on top of it," Moody said.

"How long you reckon it been there?"

"I don't know," Moody said. "Thousands of years, anyway. However long it takes for bone to turn into stone. Maybe there were giant frogs back then."

"Were there people?" Granville asked.

"Not yet," Moody said. "I'd wager ours are the first human eyes to see this thing."

"Why you digging it up?" Tamsey wanted to know. Moody waited for her to warn him about disturbing the bones and bringing trouble into the world, but she didn't.

"It's history," he said. "It tells us what happened."

"How much longer you need to dig it?" she asked.

"The rock is pretty soft," he said, "and I have to be careful. A week. Less, if Leason and Granville help."

"I will," said Leason.

"Me, too," Granville said.

"Good," said Moody. "Then we'll be out of here in a few days."

He showed them how to loosen rock from around the skull using hammers and cold chisels, without touching the bone. The rock broke away easily, which was dangerous because it drew them into working too fast. Moody examined the debris for bone, hoping the rest of the animal had been buried with the skull. After an hour, Moody took up an ice pick and began to flick away bits of stone from close around the bone.

Tamsey, Sarah and Sabetha stayed with them at the quarry, not wanting to return alone to the *Pelican* in case catchers showed up; they walked back to the towpath from time to time, though, in case it was James who came out of the woods.

A day or two later, Tamsey came to the quarry and up to Moody.

"I been thinking of a thing my mam told me," she said, and he thought this was when she was going to warn him about trouble. Once again, he was wrong. "She say Earth a big head, and when a person die and buried, that person become part of the Earth memory. All the buried men and women are the Earth thoughts, and if a person ain't buried, he be forgotten. Maybe this frog you digging up is the memory the Earth have of it."

"In that case," Moody said, "the Earth has a long memory."

"It does," Tamsey said, and he was glad he had buried Annie.

7.

That night, on the parlor deck after the children had gone to bed, he asked her again why they had left New Harmony. She showed him her free paper and asked him to read it to her. Sarah had read it once or twice, she said, but she wanted him to read it. The pages were soft from being folded and unfolded so many times they had almost separated into small squares. Light from the lantern shone through the creases, which made him think of William's letter from his daughter in Canada, the terminus of the voyage Tamsey's free paper had been the start of.

"It says your name is Thomasina Lewis," he said.

"Tamsey," she said. "No one but my mam ever call me 'Thomasina,' and then only when she mad at me. 'Thomasina,' she say, 'what I tell you about wash your hands befo' touchin' white folks' clothes? Thomasina! Don't you ever speak to Massa like that.' "

He laughed. "Your mam is buried in your head," he said.

"She surely not forgotten."

"What else did she tell you?"

Tamsey was quiet, sitting at the table with her hands folded on her lap, as though remembering her training. The lantern drew sulfur moths; she watched them fly their figure eights for a while.

"How many slaves you own, Mr. Moody?" she asked him.

" 'Virgil,' " he said. "Please call me 'Virgil.' " If she could dissemble, so could he. "And I don't own any slaves. Your paper says you and Leason were manumitted in the Commonwealth of Kentucky on the eleventh day of January, 1833."

"Two years after he born, about. He a slave for that long."

"Well," said Moody, "he's free now."

"I show our papers to catchers, you think they leave us alone?" she asked.

"They have to," Moody said. "But no, I don't expect they would."

"And Granville and Sabetha and Sarah are free born. They don't have papers. How we prove to catchers they ain't runaways?"

"A catcher has to take you to a magistrate," he said, "and then you show your papers to him. He'll see that Granville and Sabetha were born after 1833." Then he ventured, "Sarah might not even be asked."

"She be if she with us." Tamsey's hands twisted on her lap. "How you get mix up with Quaker business?"

"I always had trouble with slavery," he said, "ever since I was a child."

"Me, too," she said, and they both laughed.

"My father owned a plantation in Georgia," Moody said. "Still does. Rice and Sea Island cotton and two hundred slaves. I hated it from the start. My mother hated it, too, but she died. I had two older brothers who I thought were going to inherit, so there wasn't anything I could do but leave, so I left."

"Rice comed from Africa," she said. "It the hardest to work."

"In Louisiana they say cane is the hardest."

"Everything hard," she said. "In Kentucky it tobacco. James worked in the kills. He say tobacco finish you before it grown. Make you crawl on your belly in the dirt."

"What did you work on?"

"I worked on a stud farm in Kentucky. Before that I work for Massa Lewis in the Big House, and before that, in South Carolina, for Massa Lockhart.."

"Oh, yes, I remember. As cook, scullery, upstairs maid, parlor maid. You preferred that to working outside?"

"Preferred?" she said. "No one ask me what I preferred. Inside was cleaner, and I had help. But outside was safer."

"Safer?" Annie hadn't wanted to work in the house, either. Did she feel safe from Casgrain out in the rice fields? More men around to protect her? "Safer from what?"

Tamsey looked down at her hands. "I never talked to a white man before about slavery, except to agree that it a good thing, a necessary institution, how much more civilized we be here than in Africa, where we went naked all the time, with no true religion or morals. How better off we be as slaves, where we given houses and clothes and food and taught the Bible."

"I'm sorry," he said. "I didn't mean to pry."

"Go ahead and pry. Safe from the massa, what I meant. It safer at night in the slave quarters than sleeping alone on the pantry floor or in the kitchen woodshed."

Then why would Lucas not take the driver's job, and get Benah out of Millican's house? Unless he knew Millican would go back on his word, and Lucas would end up being a driver and still not have Benah. That sounded like Millican.

"We talked about slavery in New Harmony," she said, "almost nothing but. New Harmony started by white people, but they abandon it and left they slaves behind, and the slaves stayed on and worked the land, and when I got there more 'n a hundred coloreds been living there nearly twenty years. Brother Joshua said we finished the social experiment."

"I didn't know that," Moody said. He was glad she'd got around to talking about New Harmony, because Lucas might have been there. He didn't seem to be anywhere else.

"We didn't tell too many whites. The people all live in five communes. We in the Morning Star commune, that the horse and tobacco commune, because I worked with horses in Kentucky and James worked tobacco. Everyone did what we did. We all had stories about what we suffered and what we lost, a child, a husband, a mother, a finger or toe, brands on our cheeks, nicks in our ears, wales on our backs. And how we escape from the South, whether set free, bought free or run free, hiding in cane brakes or the woods, listening for dogs, filing off ankle and wrist and neck brackets, starving but afraid to steal because of the hounds or just because we honest. Brother Joshua say we already come through the Valley of the Shadow of Death and we should fear no evil. But you always got to fear evil. You never catch the Devil. My mam say, 'Yu cyan ketch Kwaku, yu ungle ketch him shirt.' "

Moody laughed. "I've lost a lot of card games to Kwaku," he said.

"Brother Joshua preach the wrongness of slavery, how in the Bible there be slaves, but they weren't stolen from they own countries and sold like cattle, like us, they live in the same house as they massas and set free after six years."

"We had that kind of slavery in Texas," Moody said, "except for the six-years part. We called it 'indentured servitude for life,' but it was slavery, if you were the indentured servant. It was how we got around Mexico's antislavery laws. Now that Texas is part of America, they've gone back to good old-fashioned slavery."

"That why you left?"

"Partly."

"Brother Joshua say New Harmony the last lick of the New Moral Order, where no slavery be, and everyone share they work together and prosper."

"Who's Brother Joshua?" Moody asked. "And you still haven't said why you left."

Tamsey sighed. "All right," she said, as though reluctant. "Let it come."

8.

"We left New Harmony when the catchers come," she said. "A whole army of them. They come at night, when we sleeping. I woke in darkness hearing a horse whicker, and when a horse make that sound it talking to another horse close by. I lay still as dead, listening, not breathing, until I hear the other sounds I knew would follow. A hoof stepping onto dirt. The creak of saddle leather when a rider put his weight on a stirrup. I clamped my hand over James's mouth and kept it there until he hear it, too, then I got up and looked out the window onto the common. Twenty men on horseback, taking they positions in front of our houses, two men to a house. James come up beside me, pulling on his overalls.

"I wasn't afraid yet. It was like I seeing a prophecy come true. They was bound to come sooner or later, I always knew that, but I never did anything about it. That what we do. If we don't know what to do, we do nothing. In Kentucky when there was talk of a tornado coming and no one knew what to do about it, everyone did nothing except go around saying a tornado coming, a tornado coming. Then the sky got dark and the wind bent the locust trees, and the slates blowin' off the houses, and suddenly we all knew what to do, we had to get down into the cellar and pray to Jesus not to kill us for our own stupidity. So I knew catchers would come. Every time it was quiet, that was what I was listening for. Every time

I saw dust on the road, that what it was, catchers coming. And now they come."

"Where'd they come from, so many together like that?" She was describing an army of catchers. He'd never known them to be so organized before. A whole army of slave catchers, sweeping north of the Ohio River. Sweet Jesus. The Ohio Grande.

"I wonder that now," she said, "but then I just had to move, like they a tornado and I left the chickens out."

"Looks like you saved the chickens."

"Hmm, so far. I look out back and don't see anyone between the house and the barn, or on the road beyond the barn that come north, so I get dressed and go into Granville and Sabetha's room and wake them up. I told Granville, 'Go out the back door and snake along the fence to the stable, then run through the pines into town and tell Brer Joshua'—he like the headman of the town, preacher and head-man together—'to bring help. Catchers may be in town, too,' I said, 'so be careful. Stay off the road. Stay in the pine trees.' They a double row of pines that run from the houses to the main road. 'Stick in that,' I tell him, 'then get back here and wait in the woods back of the stable. You know that big rock down by the creek? Get down behind that rock and wait.' Then I said to Sabetha, 'Go wake up Leason and Sarah. Tell them to get some horses ready, but do it dead quiet. Then go down to the creek and wait for Granville.' "

"What was happening out front all this time?" Moody asked.

"I don't know, I didn't look. I took our papers and some money that we never give to the commune, our freed money, and put it in my dress. I heard the back door open, that Leason running out. I heard Sarah pulling on her clothes and I prayed: Dear Jesus, don't let them come before she decent. From the house to the stable is thirty running strides, thirty chances to be caught or shot, but no shots come and no catchers riding around to the back. Granville gone, and no shots. Leason gone, and no shots. I push the back door open and look out. Chicken house, buggy shed, the backs of the other houses, barn, stables, road. James come up behind me. He say we got to wake the others.

" 'Let's get to the stable first,' I said, 'then you fire Old Kentucky and we make for the woods through the tobacco.'

"So we set off across the yard to the stable and nobody shot us. I guessed Leason was getting the horses ready, and Sabetha and Sarah were down by the big rock. I couldn't think why the catchers weren't coming around the back. I looked through the trees above the creek, but I couldn't see if more catchers waiting there for us to run into they arms. Then a sound come from the stable corner and Sabetha run around it, then Sarah and Leason with two horses.

"Then I heard Old Kentucky crack, that old musket sound as loud as a cannon, and then James calling 'Halloo! Catchers in the yard!' And two catchers come around the side of the house, headed straight for the stables. James had Old Kentucky reloaded and he fired again, I couldn't tell if he missed or if he fired above they heads, but both men rein up. 'Catchers!' James calls again. 'Everbody up! Catchers in the yard!' He starts reloading. Windows and doors fly open, men come out pulling they braces on, carrying whatever they could find to fight with. There was shouts and gunfire and the sound of breaking glass. James hopping up and down like he at a country fair.

" 'Take the children and run,' he shouts to me. 'Never mind the horses, I'll bring 'em later. Stay on the road. I gotta go back.'

"This knock the wind out of me. He always had to do what was right. Not right for him, not right for us, even, but right for the people. He ran back into the house, like he forgot something, and I felt a sadness settle over me, like he been pulled out of me, like some powerful hand come down and grab he away. I couldn't move. It like my soul left me. Maybe you know what that like."

Moody looked down to the river. The pale bodies of catfish circled in the oblong patch of lamplight falling on the water's surface.

She *was* like Annie. She could see into him and didn't always like what she saw. "What happened to James?"

"He stayed back."

"And you ran."

"I ran. He held the catchers off for us to get away, and then, in some life we was all being pulled into, he would join us and he would give me back my soul. At the river, maybe, or by the lake. Maybe in Canada. I had to believe that or I couldn't run. I still believe it. What you think?"

"I hope you're right," he said. "I don't believe much in souls. I once killed a Mexican soldier while he was praying. I saw life leave him, but I wouldn't say it was his soul."

"Oh, glory, his soul fly to heaven."

"I wish I could believe that."

"Don't matter what you believe. It only matter what you do."

"What did you do?"

"I ran to save the children. Leason had two horses saddled, Jezzy and the roan. He said nothing, just turned and ran back to the house to be with James. I let him go."

"You did the right thing."

"I told Sarah, 'Take the horses and find Granville by the big rock, then head up the road. I be along.' "

"You went back, too?"

"The noise from in front of the houses was louder now, the catchers must have charged. Muskets and pistols, then silence, then more firing and shouting. I imagined catchers storming the houses and James and Leason fighting them off. The silences frighten me more than the noise. At least gunfire meant the fighting still going on. I listen for Old Kentucky and hear it once more, then the sound of battle grew louder. I didn't know if men from town got there or more catchers showed up, then I saw that the fighting was in the backyard. I turn and run alongside the field toward the creek. I had to think of the children now. Then I turn and see the back door of our house open and James and Leason run out, bent double like they running under trees. But the catchers are there and James pushes Leason into the pines and turns and fires Old Kentucky, and one of the catchers raise his rifle and fires back, and James goes down. I see him go down. He on one knee, trying to reload that cursed musket, and then he is down hard, like a hand reach up from the earth and pull him into it. Leason run out of the pines for him. I start to run, too, but Leason sees me and stands up to wave me away, so I stop. No, don't stand up, Leason! I can't see James, he should be up with Leason, but Leason still waving for me to go. Run! A catcher took aim and fired again, and I see Leason fall. I run toward him, then stop and turn around and run for the creek. And we didn't stop runnin' till we got here."

"What about James?" Moody said quietly.

"That my story," she said. "A story a story. Let it come, let it go."

Moody wanted to reach over and touch her arm, but he didn't dare, not even a reassuring pat to tell her she was safe. She wasn't safe. He wanted to ask her if she'd seen Lucas in New Harmony. The possibility of him being there had reawakened his hope as well as his pain. Lucas and Benah could have gone to New Harmony after Paducah, it looked like hundreds of others had, but he didn't want to disturb the calm that had come to her after she had told her story. There was time, he thought, and he would ask her. In the morning, or the next day. Asking her would mean he'd have to tell her his story, and he wasn't sure he could do that yet. Not that he didn't trust her. He didn't quite know what his story was.

9.

It took them longer to get the skull out than he'd thought it would, and everyone was getting nervous. Moody couldn't rid his mind of the notion of an army of catchers out there in the woods, moving north, and was anxious to untie and move upriver. But the skull resisted their efforts, refusing to budge even though it was three-quarters exposed, and then the weather joined in. After five dry days came a morning of pelting rain, turning the quarry into a pool of wet clay and gravel, when even stepping off the *Pelican* was a risk none of them felt like taking. Moody threw the tarpaulin over the quarry while the others brought the parlor inside. It was warmer and cozier, but the noise on the cabin's flat roof kept them from talking. Moody and Sabetha read, Granville looked out one of the windows at the fidgetous river, and Leason and Sarah sat on the bed, holding hands and looking sideways at each other. Moody studied the family over his book, Mr. Darwin's account of his voyage aboard the *Beagle*, when he found the giant sloth and then turned his attention to birds. Sabetha was quiet and watchful, not as absorbed in Jane Austen as she let on. Granville was all surface, like a puppy; he missed his father and wanted to keep busy so as not to think about him. Tamsey was mending one of Moody's shirts so that Leason could wear it.

But it was Sarah who mystified him. She rarely spoke, rarely had an opinion that she shared with the others, but there was obviously a lot going on behind her placid facade. She was the opposite of Tamsey, who spoke first and only realized afterward that what she had said was true. Sarah thought about what she was going to say for a long time before saying it, and what she said wasn't always the whole truth.

As he expected, it was Leason and Sarah who broke first. Sarah announced they were going for a walk, never mind the rain, it was dry under the trees. They should check on the horses. Tamsey stuck her finger with the needle and said, "Oh, *fine*."

Shortly after the midday meal, cold pork, white bread and black tea, the rain stopped and the sun turned the still-bare branches of the trees into living skeletons against the sky. Granville was out the door and headed down to the quarry before Tamsey could caution him against catchers and panthers, both of which she said came out after a rain. Moody put Darwin down and said he'd go with him.

Leason came, too, so Moody told Tamsey he wouldn't be long. He'd get the boys started and then return to the boat.

The three of them walked down the towpath, breathing the mineral-rich post-rain spring air. Even with the tarpaulin in place, the unshellacked sections of bone were so soft they had to scrape the claystone away, like dried glue off the shell of a raw egg. Arrayed around them were the tools of their trade: awls and brushes, cold chisels, two or three claw hammers, a small sledge, a marlin spike, a hatchet, a handsaw for cutting away tree roots, and an assortment of glass jars for keeping the bits of bone that they accidentally broke off and he would glue back on later. Moody envied Mr. Darwin, who found his *Megatherium* skull in the loose gravel of southern Patagonia. Indiana was all mud and mudstone. Alongside the box, Moody had a pick and a couple of shovels, with which Leason cleared away the rubble that had washed into the pit. Leason said a wheelbarrow would work better, and Moody told him if he saw a hardware store anywhere nearby to let him know and he'd get him one.

Moody was ready to return to the boat when Granville sat back and shook his head.

"I don't know what this thing is," he said, "but it ain't no frog."

"You don't think so?" Moody said, stopping. "Why not?"

"Because frogs don't have teeth," Granville said. "And this here thing got more teeth than a sawmill." He pointed to the mandible, which was lined with tiny, needle-sharp teeth.

"What do you think it is, then?"

"You ever seen a hellbender?" Granville said, and Moody shook his head. "It's the god-awful ugliest thing I ever saw. A kind of lizard fish. We had one at our school in New Harmony. Erasmus caught it and brung it in. I didn't know what it was because we didn't see them down in Kentucky. But Brer Arkwright, he was our teacher, he said it was a hellbender. About this long," Granville said, holding up the pick handle, "and a head on it looked like this frog's, flat and round in front, except it had real squinty eyes and a whole bunch of little teeth, like this thing has. We took it apart in anatomy class, and then we boiled it in a big cauldron we got from the laundry house, and we got the bones out, and damn if the head didn't look just like this except smaller."

Hellbender. The skull didn't belong to any creature still roaming around Indiana, but it might have been a distant ancestor. He wondered if any of his books mentioned hellbenders.

"Did Brother Arkwright say what else hellbenders are called?" he asked Granville.

"He said they were giant salamanders. We had a salamander skeleton, too, a normal-sized one, and it was pretty much the same, bone for bone, and so we used it to put the hellbender skeleton together."

"All right," Moody said. "Giant salamander. We'll look it up tonight."

They walked back to the *Pelican*, where they found Tamsey, Sarah and Sabetha sitting quietly in the cabin. Tamsey had laid the shotgun across her knees. When he came in she asked him if he would move the *Pelican* upriver, closer to the quarry, so that they wouldn't be so alone when he was digging up his damn frog. He told her that was a good idea, and he was sorry he hadn't thought of it earlier. They'd move the boat first thing in the morning.

After supper, he was in the cabin immersed in drawings of extinct amphibians, when Tamsey came to the door with two mugs of tea. She held one out to him without coming in, and he followed her out to the parlor deck. It was a clear night and the living frogs were making their usual racket. Moody tried to imagine how much noise a chorus of giant salamanders would make.

"Where's Leason and Sarah?" he asked her.

"Off somewhere it best not to inquire after," she said. They leaned against the boat rail, looking upriver toward the dig.

"Granville thinks our giant frog is a hellbender," he said.

Tamsey shuddered. "Granville a smart boy. A man caught one of them things in a swamp near New Harmony when he was cat-fishing," she said. "Scared him so bad he never went fishing again, couldn't even *eat* fish, said even the smell gave him night sweats. Don't you go bringing one of them Devil things home," she said. "We got enough to have nightmares about already."

Home, he thought. "No sign of James?" he asked gently.

"He'll find us," she said.

"We'll have the skull out tomorrow," Moody said. "I'll move the boat, but we can leave any time after that."

"I know."

"What are you thinking?"

"I talked to Sarah today, when you were down at the quarry. She told me when she was little James used to let her help him comb the horses, and if she was feeling bad about anything, he told her she could talk to her favorite horse, a small chestnut named Beulah that wouldn't let no one ride her but Sarah. When Sarah got sick Beulah got sick, and when Sarah got better Beulah got better. Once when Beulah had a rheumy chest, James made her some medicine, but she wouldn't take it unless Sarah did, so he mixed up some watermelon water the same color as the horse tonic and Sarah drank that and Beulah drank her medicine. She told me some other things about James that she remembered." They listened to the frogs for a moment. "Sarah don't usually talk to me so sweetly," she said.

"She don't talk to me at all," he said.

"I think she was trying to tell me that James ain't coming," Tamsey said. "I think Leason knows something about James he not telling me."

"Why don't you ask him?"

"I thought maybe you could. He might talk to you."

"Me?" he said, and almost, *almost*, added, *He's your son.* "All right," he said. "I'll talk to him tonight."

10.

Later that night, Moody found what he wanted in a paper by Georges Cuvier. Granville was right, it was a giant salamander. The first specimen had been dug up a hundred years before, in Germany, by a Swiss naturalist named Scheuchzer, who'd thought it was the skeleton of a child who had drowned in the Great Flood. The drawing showed a flat head and a spine no more than three feet long. No tail or legs, which made another Swiss scientist, Johannes Gessner, think it was a giant catfish. Finally, in 1822, Cuvier got hold of it, cleared more stone from around the specimen, discovered it had forelimbs with four toes, and identified it as a salamander. Good for Georges. And good for Granville. The fossil was still called *Andrias scheuchzeri*, though; *Andrias* meaning "in the image of Man." Moody sat back in his chair and scratched his head. How could salamanders have been made in the image of Man if Man was made last? It must have been Adam who was made in the image of a salamander. Rachel would have liked that.

He heard Granville moving about on the parlor deck and went out to join him, taking the book with Cuvier's article. He found Granville looking at a jar of tadpoles he'd collected for fish bait. Moody showed him Cuvier's drawing.

"Don't look like no child to me," Granville said.

"They thought he was flattened by the weight of all that water."

"I thought only sinners got drowned in the Flood," Granville said.

"Sinners," said Moody, "and the innocent children of sinners."

Moody picked up one of the lanterns. "Come on," he said. "Let's go to the quarry and take a look."

The skull now sticking out of the cliff matched Cuvier's draw-ing, the same holes in the snout for the nostrils, two bigger eye sockets near the top. Moody explained as best he could that what they had wasn't a hellbender but the many-times-great-granddaddy of a salamander, that with each generation there had been a tiny change that eventually turned this creature into a salamander.

"Why'd it get smaller?" Granville asked.

"Everything got smaller," Moody said.

"But why?"

"I don't know. Maybe they didn't get enough to eat."

"Why'd it lose its teeth, then?"

"Maybe when it got smaller it ate smaller things and didn't need teeth anymore. I knew a man in Texas who lost his baby teeth and never grew new ones. Never ate anything harder than bread and potatoes after that. Maybe the same thing happened to *Andrias scheuchzeri*. Maybe coming to America from Europe it found softer food and didn't need teeth, so just stopped growing them."

"You going to get a lot of money for this thing when you take it to the museum?" Granville asked.

"Not a lot, no, but some. And maybe some scientist will study it one day and write a paper about it, and name it after you. *Andrias granvillii*."

"Me? Why me? You the one found it."

"Yes, but you figured out what it was. That's the way it works."

Granville looked at Moody and grinned.

"You and Sabetha went to school in New Harmony?" Moody asked.

"We did," Granville said.

"What did you study?"

"Biology, geography, and literature."

"Did you like school?"

"Yep. After you spent three years in school, you helped out in the communes and the gardens. And then you had to learn some-thing useful, like carpentry or mechanics."

"How long were you in New Harmony?"

"I don't know how long. Maybe three, four years."

"How many people lived there?"

"All told?" Granville said. "A lot. Hundreds."

"All runaways?"

"Most of them. Some freed, I guess. Like Mam and Leason."

"Did you ever come across a fellow named Lucas?"

"Lucas?" Granville said. "Maybe. Why?"

"I knew a man in Texas named Lucas. I've been looking for him so I can help him. He'd be about Leason's age."

"A man named Lucas came last summer. I didn't know him very well. He had a woman with him."

"Benah?"

"Maybe. They were in the North Star commune."

Moody sat down beside the skull. He thought Granville hadn't heard him right. "Are you sure?" he said, keeping his voice steady. How far was it to New Harmony? Five days? A week?

Granville nodded. "He worked in the hat factory," he said. "He made Leason's hat. I think Benah worked in the nursery, but I ain't sure. We were in the Morning Star, and then it was winter, so we didn't see them much."

Moody got to his feet and walked away from the quarry. He had a sudden urge to see the river. Granville followed him. The moon-light made the water look like liquid silver. The river was still high, but there would be rocks in the shallow places, and any one of them would rip the bottom out of the *Pelican* if they hit it. It would be lunacy to take the boat downriver in the dark, but that's what he was considering. He knew the White, the Wabash not so well. With lights on the bow, lookouts, poles, luck, he could beat the Devil.

"Are they still in New Harmony, do you think?" he said to Granville.

Granville looked uncomfortable. "I don't know. I don't know if anyone there anymore."

"Why not?" Moody turned to look at him. "Did the catchers take them?"

"Maybe ask Leason. He stayed longer."

"Let's go back to the boat."

Tamsey was sitting at the table on the parlor deck. Moody took a chair beside her.

"Granville tells me there was a couple in the North Star commune named Lucas and Benah," he said. "Did you know them?"

"I knew of them."

"Did you see them anywhere after the raid?"

"The woods was full of people running," she said. "They might have been there, they might not. It was dark. I wasn't looking for them. Why?"

"Lucas is why I left Texas. I've been looking for him all this time."

"What for?"

"I lived with his mother," he said. Tamsey started to say something, then stopped. "He was like a son to me. Did you see if they escaped or not?"

"They wasn't catchers in the woods when we ran, I know that. Me and Granville went back to the horse barn, but we didn't see Leason or James, and I thought they went a different way, maybe through the North Star's cornfield. The barnyard was full of catchers with torches. I thought they was going to set the barn afire, but I guess they wanted us alive. We watched from the edge of the woods, and then we turned and run up the track to find Sabetha and Sarah."

"So you don't know what happened to Lucas," Moody said.

"I don't know if the catchers raided every commune or just ours. I didn't hear shooting at the other communes but there was a lot of noise at ours. And Brer Joshua didn't come, Leason told me that much. Granville couldn't find him in the town."

"It doesn't seem likely catchers would attack just one commune, does it?"

"I don't know. Nothing seems likely to me now."

"Do you think James is alive?" he asked.

Tamsey turned to look downriver. "I knew a woman in New Harmony was brung over on a slave ship," she said, "and the ship sank and she and her husband clung to each other in the water, keeping themselves up, and they clung like that for two days until another ship come and pick them out the water, and she saw her husband been dead the whole time. She was saved by his gassy body. I think I like that woman, keeping James alive in my head when he just a memory of James."

"I need to go there," he said. "I need to see where Lucas was with my own eyes." He put his hands in his jacket pockets and took a deep breath. "His mother lived with me in New Orleans, then in Texas. Then she died and he ran off before I could explain things to him."

"What things?"

"How it was between me and his mother. Between me and him."

"How was it?"

"Good, I thought."

"He your boy?"

"No, but we raised him together."

"You own him?"

"It wasn't like that."

"His mother die by your hand?"

"Good Lord, no," he said, glad to be able to give a clear answer. "Her own."

Tamsey looked at him with such sadness it was as if his own guilt were staring back at him. No, not guilt, because there was no judgment in her eyes. His guilt was still safely inside him.

"You ain't much good at telling stories, are you?" she said.

"I don't have your knack for it, no."

Granville came up on deck with an armload of firewood. "Where you want this?" he asked. "There's more coming."

"Just put it by the cabin," Moody said. "I'll move it to the hold before we go."

"We're leaving? When?"

"First thing in the morning."

"What about the giant salamander?"

"We'll get him on the way back. I'm still taking you to Indianapolis. But first we're going back to New Harmony."

II.

The threatened rain hadn't materialized by morning, which Moody took as a good omen. Tamsey said she didn't like omens. "What come, come," she said. She placed one of the parlor chairs at the prow of the boat and sat staring downriver, oblivious to the rocking waves. Moody would have moved her, but he thought she knew her own mind. Sarah retreated to the cabin, pleading seasickness, where she lay on Moody's cot beside Sabetha, who was reading *The Rime of the Ancient Mariner*, which Moody thought was a good choice under the circumstances. "The ship was cheered, the harbor cleared, / Merrily did we drop." Leason and Granville posted themselves on the foredeck with their poles, and Moody stood on the cabin roof, holding the tiller tightly against his good hip. The current was strong, the main channel squirming under the river like a dark snake. He swung the *Pelican* sharply back and forth to stay in deep water. He watched Tamsey's back, unmoving as a bowsprit, and wondered what she was thinking. Did she expect James at every bend, as he did Lucas? Her questions of the night before came back to him. Had Lucas been free in Texas? Moody would have said he was, for a while, when Texas had been part of Mexico, but he knew now that that was an excuse. Lucas hadn't been free, which meant he was a slave. That was how she meant it, and how Lucas must have seen it. There was no middle ground, and Moody desperately wanted to let him know that now he understood that. The woods were alive again with the possibility of Lucas. Moody kept his eyes on the towpath whenever he was able to wrest them from Tamsey's back.

The rain crept up on them from behind. "And now the stormblast came, and he / Was tyrannous and strong." First the sky turned pewter, then purple, the temperature dropped, the wind pressed Moody's wet shirt to his back. He didn't feel the rain until he noticed it pebbling the surface of the water. At about the same time, Granville turned as if to say something and there was a flash of lightning, and before the light was gone thunder cracked over their heads and the *Pelican* was caught in a deluge of cold, hard rain. Granville slid his pole onto its rack, grabbed Tamsey and her chair and pulled them both toward the cabin, staggering against the weight and the wind. Leason remained at the bow, gripping his pole. Rainwater streamed off their hats and shoulders, the roar around them was deafening. The river swelled and the *Pelican* picked up speed. This wasn't so bad, Moody thought, but when they slipped the channel and swooped down the center of the river, narrowly missing rocks he didn't see until they were behind them, he changed his mind. This was bad. He looked for a cove or a tributary to pull into, but there was no slowing down or turning into quieter waters. Leason held on to one of the stove's guy ropes as the boat bucked, its hull alternately leaping into the air and scraping the riverbed. Through the rain and the tossing waves, Moody managed to keep the boat pointed more or less downriver. Leason looked up at him for a moment and their eyes met. Leason laughed, and Moody grinned. "The ship drove fast, loud roar'd the blast, / And southward aye we fled."

12.

The noise abated and they slowed down, but the river continued rough until evening, when under a clear, studded sky they reached the mouth of the White. Moody considered it wise to tie up before making the turn into the Wabash. By lantern light, Tamsey made them a quick supper of fish and bread and tea, and rather than pitch a tent on land, everyone except Moody crowded into the cabin. He brought out the parlor furnishings and a blanket, saying that with the rain finished he would sleep under the stars. Tamsey came out and sat with him. His arm ached from holding the tiller; Tamsey rubbed his shoulder and talked about the virtues of horse liniment. He was content with their progress. The Wabash was deeper and slower than the White, and from then on they wouldn't travel as fast, but they wouldn't have to worry about rocks, either. He listened to the woods, but if there was an army of catchers in it, they weren't making any noise. An owl called.

"We might get there tomorrow," he said. "More likely the day after."

"If there be anything left to get to," she said.

13.

They tied the *Pelican* upstream from New Harmony, nudged into a marshy stretch and hidden from ascending or descending vessels. Moody put his revolver in his belt—"I *told* you," he heard Rachel say—and he and Tamsey stepped ashore. It took them half an hour to walk to New Harmony, along a footpath that followed the river but was out of sight of it. "This the track we came up on," Tamsey said, but otherwise they barely spoke, each wrapped in private forebodings. Moody tried to prepare himself for what they might soon see: smoke rising from the remains of barns, the smell of burned horseflesh or pig fat or worse, fieldstone chimneys left standing in the charred remains of houses. A group of solemn men with shovels in their hands, hats and coats on the ground, burying their dead. They wouldn't welcome a white man.

From a knoll at the edge of the woods they saw a line of intact houses across a plowed field that was beginning to show green. No smoke from the houses, barns intact, no sound anywhere except the wind in the trees behind them. The path they'd been following continued along a low pine windbreak that led up to the closest houses.

"That the Morning Star," Tamsey said.

"Where's the North Star?"

"Across that field," she said, pointing to their right. "You can't see it from here."

Moody wanted to hurry but, remembering his militia training, forced himself to stay alert. They turned toward the Morning Star, Tamsey peering between the pines.

"Which was your house?" he asked when they were closer to the commune.

She pointed to a row of six houses aligned along a smaller track that branched to the left from the lane. "That first one," she said. It was two floors, unpainted and rough, four windows per side, bigger than the Creole house he and Annie and Lucas had had in New Orleans. No porch, no gingerbread, no orange trees in the yard. This was Tamsey's home, he thought. If she found James alive she would stay here with him, since the danger appeared to be over, at least for the time being. She would fetch the children from the *Pelican* and start planting corn. He'd be left to fight his way upriver by himself, unless he found Lucas and Benah and they went with him, which seemed improbable. Improbable that he would find them, even more improbable that they would leave with him, or want him to stay. His knees began to give him trouble.

All the buildings were deserted. No horses in the paddocks, and the front door of Tamsey's house hung open.

"You going in?" he asked her. "I'll come with you, if you don't mind."

They went up to the open front door and stepped cautiously through it. There was an air of haste and confusion in the rooms, but none of the signs of fighting he had seen in Mexico. In the kitchen, Tamsey straightened a chair at the table and picked up a cloth that had been left on the counter, after which they went from room to room, looking for something to tell them what had happened in them. There was nothing. The rooms were as they had been left— beds unmade, a few personal items lying on dresser tops or hanging in tallboys: Granville's geography book, Sabetha's rag doll, Sarah's comb, James's neckerchief. Tamsey put all these in a sack and they went back outside by the rear door, then through the gate leading to the barn and stables.

"This was the horse commune?" Moody asked.

"Catchers must've took them, too."

He pictured the drive south. A hundred men, women and children on foot, bound at the wrists and neck, catchers riding, some herding the captives, others herding the horses. There'd have been boats waiting at Mount Vernon, down on the Ohio, ready to take them on to the Mississippi, where they'd be transferred into river scows. They'd be in New Orleans by now. Those who'd survived.

"Let's look for Lucas," he said.

They set off along the pines and turned to cross the plowed field to the North Star. A short way from the house, Tamsey stopped to examine the spot where she'd seen James fall, set her hand on the soil, lifted it and looked at her palm, wiped it on her skirt and moved on without looking at Moody. He saw something metallic sticking out from under a pile of dead branches and bent to pick it up. A musket.

Tamsey turned. "Old Kentucky," she said. He kept it, and they walked on.

The North Star was as still and empty as the Morning Star had been. They looked in a few houses, but there was little to be learned. In some there was still food on the table, coats and hats on hooks behind the doors, boots beside the cold kitchen stoves. Flies buzzed everywhere. In one sitting room, a chair was overturned and a Quaker Bible lay open on the floor.

"Which one was Lucas and Benah's?" Moody asked, and she led him to a small house at the end of the row, facing north, away from the plowed field. It was much like the others they'd searched, littered with signs of a hasty departure. In the bedroom, Moody picked up a pair of braces Lucas had had in Texas. The room, with its double bed and a woman's shawl hanging on a hook, belonged to a Lucas whose life he didn't know, but the braces on the floor were pure Lucas. On the dresser was a reticule that must have belonged to Benah. Inside it was a folded piece of newsprint—the drawing of the mastodon skeleton from the Peale Museum that he had given Lucas when they found the bone. Annie must have brought it to him at Millican's, which meant Lucas must have asked her for it. He put the clipping back in the reticule and the reticule in his pocket. There didn't seem to be anything else in the house Lucas might come back for, and he went outside to join Tamsey.

"I want to go back to the *Pelican* now," she said. "I want you to take us away from here," and he nodded. If he was still a gambling man, he would bet that Lucas and Benah were at that moment running north, the way their house faced, the way Tamsey and her family had fled, and that his best chance to find them was to take Tamsey to Indianapolis. Why would anyone run south from here, back into the slave states, unless it was dark and they were panicked and confused? But he was no longer a gambling man. He'd lost confidence in his ability to play the right card, and when you started second-guessing your bets, it was time to walk away from the table.

14.

"The closer we get to Indianapolis," Tamsey told Moody one night, "the less I want to get there."

The boat was tied to the branches of a huge, dead oak that had fallen almost into the river, its giant trunk stretched along the graveled beach like Goliath after his encounter with David. Woodpeckers had been at its bark, and someone had started cutting it up for firewood. Which meant there were people living nearby.

"If you want to go north," Moody said, "you have to go through Indianapolis. Kästchen will put you on the Railroad."

"I know, but I feel safer on the river," she said, looking into the woods. "The river wider now, and a catcher have to ride right out into it to get at us, and if that happen I got Old Kentucky to hand. And you," she added after a pause.

"Kästchen and his wife will keep you safe in Indianapolis," he said, "for the short time you'll be there."

Leason and Sarah had gone off into the woods to look for something, kindling or drinking water, they said, and Moody and Tamsey were sitting on the parlor deck, talking end-of-the-day talk. How far they'd come. How far they had to go. She talked about James and he talked about Lucas, both surprised at how free they had become with each other. Moody would see Annie and Lucas standing in the trees. Sometimes he saw Rachel, which solaced both him and Tamsey, since as far as he knew Rachel wasn't dead and so they weren't just being haunted by dead people. Tamsey talked about New Harmony, nothing specific; it felt to him more like seeing shadows moving behind a drawn curtain. They were patient. He agreed there were more boats on the river than he remembered from the last time he was this way.

"What you say if someone ask about us?" she asked. "Would you tell them we your slaves?"

"I don't need to tell them anything," Moody said. "No one owns the water."

"Which don't answer the question."

"I know," he said.

"So, what you say?"

"I'd say you're my crew. You work for me."

She didn't say anything to that. He still hadn't answered her question.

15.

The answer came the next day. Two men hailed them from a bare spit of land that jutted out into the river from the south shore. Moody stepped into the cabin and came out with his pistol under his belt, then he and Leason poled until they were nearly at the spit.

"What is it?" Moody asked the men.

They wore cotton shirts of an unknown color, leather braces such as bricklayers wore under brown wool vests. One had a red bandana and the other a dirty white cloth wrapped around his neck like a bandage, like they'd both escaped hanging and were hiding the burn. Tamsey was at the stove on the parlor deck with the poker in her hand, and Sabetha and Granville and Sarah were in the cabin.

"We need some help," one of the men said.

"What kind of help?" asked Moody.

"We got a wagon wheel come off back there on the road. Wagon's too heavy to lift by ourselves."

"You take everything off of it?" Moody asked.

"Yeah, we done that. Still too heavy."

"Use a long pole for a lever."

The man lifted his chin toward Leason. "He got a pole right there in his hands."

Moody looked through the trees without seeing a wagon. He didn't think there was a road there, either. "We can't help you."

"Lend us your boy for a minute," the second one said.

"I don't think so."

"We'll pay him."

"Get inside, son," Moody said to Leason. He looked at Tamsey and she followed Leason into the cabin.

"I'm sorry for your trouble," Moody said to the men, trying with one pole to keep the boat from being carried too close to the spit, "but we can't help you."

"How many you got in there?" said the second man.

"They ain't runaways," Moody said. "They work for me."

"Why you hidin' 'em, then?"

"I ain't hiding them, I'm protecting them."

"We just want to borrow the buck. We'll help you tie up."

"Nope."

He pushed the boat farther from the spit, remembering the scene at the dock in Wheeling, Tim'n'Tom falling into the hold. He couldn't take the pistol out of his belt without letting go of the pole, and he couldn't let go of the pole without being pushed onto the spit. Sending Leason inside might have been a mistake. If the men went for their guns he'd have to shoot them and let the boat go where the river would take it, which would be onto rocks. He was considering shooting them anyway, when he heard one of the windows open and saw the business end of Old Kentucky showing itself, aimed at the two men. The men saw it, too.

"You boys get back on your horses," Moody said. "We ain't doing any business here today."

The one who had spoken first put his hat on his head and nodded to Moody. "You just bought yourself a whole lot of trouble, friend," he said. "Helping fugitives is a federal offense. We could come back with a posse and impound your boat."

"These people ain't fugitives. I told you, they're my crew."

"All right, whatever you say. Tell your woman there she can put that old museum piece away."

"Leason!" Moody called. "Come on out and take a pole. We're leaving."

Leason came out of the cabin, and Old Kentucky remained pointed at the two men. Moody and Leason poled the *Pelican* across to the north shore and they continued upriver. Once they were under way, Tamsey came out of the cabin.

"Would you have shot those catchers?" he asked her, and she shrugged.

"I couldn't find the powder," she said. "Where you keep the powder at?"

He showed her.

16.

She felt better about Moody after that. Moody noted it, how she talked about things that didn't directly concern their immediate survival. For instance, why the river they were on was called the White River. "It ain't white, it brown as cane sugar. We don't drink it, we don't cook with it, we don't wash clothes in it." They had tied up on the north shore for the night, beside a sand beach where he had stopped a few times before and made a fire pit. They sat around the fire, letting it push the night back into the trees, the coffeepot resting on a flat stone surrounded by coals. He said it was called the White River because it was milky, and they argued gently about that for a while.

"I never see milk that color," she said. "Milk supposed to be white."

"Looks more like milk than water," he said.

"Look more like mud than milk."

He sighed. "Why do you have to be so cussed contrary?"

"I ain't."

"I say a thing is so and you say it ain't without even thinking about it."

"I been thinking about it all day. Why's it called the White River?"

"Maybe because it has a lot of rapids in it," he said.

"It for sure does that," she said. "A lot of rapids and shoals and places hard to pole over. See, I ain't being contrary."

"Agreeing with me when I say you never agree with me is being contrary."

They sat quietly for a few minutes, contemplating the way the setting sun turned the water into fish scales spread out on a wrinkled tablecloth.

"No, it ain't," she said.

"We'll be in Freedom in a day or two," he said. "Maybe we should stop there. I'd like to show you my cabin."

"How a Southerner come to be in a place called Freedom?" she asked him.

"Long story," he said.

"You goin' somewhere?"

She was sounding more like Annie every day. He was drawn to her in a way he hoped wouldn't frighten her off, as his talk of guns and war had frightened Rachel. After so many years with Annie, he'd forgotten how to be with a woman who wasn't Annie. But Tamsey was becoming Annie.

"Like I said, my mother died when I was five," he said, throwing a piece of driftwood on the fire and watching the sparks fly up into the night. "I don't remember much about her except that she was too good to be married to my father. My oldest brother was an army engineer, he built things like bridges and redoubts, but he was killed in New Orleans in 1812. A powder magazine blew up when he was in it. I still had one brother left, so I still didn't expect to inherit. When I was sixteen I went to the academy in Savannah and studied whatever interested me. Literature, geology, some law, a little of this, a little of that, I didn't think at all about who was doing the work that was paying for it. I didn't like my father much, but not because he owned slaves, it was because he treated them badly. In Georgia, slavery's like bad air, you keep on breathing it and after a while you don't notice the smell anymore."

"If you white," she said mildly.

"Yes, of course if you're white. That's what I meant, sorry."

"Don't stop."

"When my oldest brother died, my father took me to New Orleans to collect the remains. All that was left of my brother fit into a boot box, and most of that probably wasn't him, but it took us two weeks to get it, what with the war coming and army paperwork, and during that time I saw a lot of New Orleans. It made a powerful impression on me. Colored people playing music in the street, women dressed like Gypsies, blacks and whites mingling together—'amalgamating,' they called it. I liked the way everyone drank wine like we drank water, how they walked like they were dancing, like their feet weighed nothing at all, how the women laughed. And the sun going down over the Mississippi delta at low tide, the air smelling of swamp water and life. So when I finished at the academy in Savannah I told my father I wanted to study law in New Orleans. I bought a house in the Creole quarter and read books all day and played cards and drank all night, and I got by. I met a woman and we were together for a while, but she wasn't impressed by my qualifications for a husband and married a major who went to Washington on the coattails of a congressman."

"You learning to tell a good story," she said. "But you forgot to say it maybe not all true."

But she was teasing him. "It is all true," he said.

"Then let it come," she said.

"When I was at law school, I met Stephen Austin, a man my own age and of a similar bent. We eyed each other across various card tables, and we agreed on most things. He'd already run for Congress in Arkansas and lost, and then the government in Washington seized his property in Little Rock, and now he was losing what money he had left to me. He was broke and angry and thinking about moving to Texas, where his father had a *sitio* from the Mexican government to start a colony. He wanted me to go with him, but I said no, he wanted families and I didn't have one. And I couldn't see myself busting sod in some dreary corner of Mexico. Then I met Annie."

"Annie," Tamsey said.

"She was a slave on my father's rice plantation," he said after a pause. "She was smart and pretty and could have worked in the house in Savannah if she wanted, but she was like you."

"How like me?"

"She preferred to work outside, for one thing, with her mother. She was at Plantagenet, that was the name of the rice plantation, and I was there for my second brother's funeral—he died in the yellow fever epidemic, along with thousands of others, mostly slaves who worked in the paddies. I wanted to get Annie away from that, and also away from Casgrain, my father's overseer, who was a hard man with the bullwhip and also had a reputation for interfering with the female slaves. Annie was a beauty, but she was spirited, and she wouldn't have survived both Casgrain and the fever."

"Then she not like me."

Moody smiled. "No, maybe not. Or maybe I was wrong about her."

"I know that fever," Tamsey said. "We call it swamp fever. You fine one day, then you start to sweat and throw up your food, then suddenly you feel better. That when you got to worry, when you start to feel better, because inside a week you dead. There was a lot of it in Carolina, but I didn't get it."

"My brother did. The doctors scarified him and gave him quinine and calomel and some concoction made from tree bark, but none of it did any good. They wouldn't have bothered at all with Annie. So, I took Annie with me back to New Orleans."

"You buy her from your father?"

"No, I just took her. If he missed her at all, he probably assumed she died, too."

"You ask her did she want to go?"

"She would have said no, unless I took her mamma, too."

Moody watched the fire for a long time. He sensed her trying not to say something, but she never could stay quiet. "You knew she would say no, that why you didn't ask."

"Maybe."

"You don't ask a slave what she prefer."

After a while he looked at her. "But I saved her," he said. "And Lucas."

"Not her," Tamsey said, keeping her voice soft. She moved to put her hand on his arm and he didn't take it away. "She already lost when they took her mam from Gullah."

"But we had a good life in New Orleans," he said.

"And after that?"

"We should have stayed there. It was hot, but not hot the way it was in Georgia, even in the Sea Islands it never got so hot. In Georgia you bake, in New Orleans you boil. The heat seemed to come from under your skin, like it was part of you, and instead of fighting it or resenting it you just relaxed into it. In Georgia we had to destroy what was there in order to live, but in Louisiana we were creatures of the tide pools. Annie and I sat on our banquette at night, watching the fireflies and listening to the *bamboulas*. We should never have left."

"Why did you?"

He shook his head. "Lucas was starting to ask questions, notice things, want to know why they were the way they were. And the city was changing. After the war, Northerners began moving down, people who wouldn't just relax into things. The drinking and the gambling became more serious, almost vicious, it was a kind of desperation, and the Creoles started moving out. Suddenly all our neighbors spoke English and beat their servants. And looked at us like they wanted our house. Eight years seemed enough."

"Eight years old a difficult time for a child."

"I thought the move would be good for him. Stephen Austin kept talking to me about Texas, how there was no slavery in Mexico, and the land was free. When Lucas was old enough he could get his own farm. So I signed us up. It was 1838. We farmed for ten years, Annie and me and Lucas. After Texas became a republic, slavery was back, but it didn't seem to matter."

"How you mean? Slavery didn't matter?"

"No, I mean between us. Nothing changed between us."

"Muddy," she said, "everything changed."

She had taken to calling him "Muddy" after their talk about the White River. He didn't know if it made her feel closer to him or more distant.

"We worked together," he said. "We were a family. We worked in the sun, in the cold, in the rain and the lack of rain, insects and lack of insects, blight, rust, gall, root rot, canker, crumble, little things in the ground you never heard of before and can't see, hurricanes, lightning bolts, flash floods, hail, snow. It wasn't like farming in Georgia, where you sit on your porch and let your slaves do the work for you until your land turns to dust and blows away, like a judgment on laziness, and you pack up and move to another piece of land and do the same thing all over again, generation after generation, failure after failure. In Texas, it was our land, we needed each other to survive."

"How Annie feel about the move?"

"Annie? She was happy, I think. At first. But I thought she was happy in New Orleans, too, so maybe she wasn't. I don't know anymore. I thought she liked the way Lucas was growing into a fine, strong lad. She was a slave in New Orleans, even if we pretended she wasn't. I thought she would like life in Texas better, where she wasn't a slave because there was no slavery. It was hard work, but she was used to hard work. And in Texas she didn't have to worry about Lucas so much."

"Why not?"

"Because even when he got old enough, he couldn't have joined the militia. If we'd stayed in New Orleans, he could have joined the Louisiana Battalion of Free Men of Color, but there were no black troops in Texas."

"Would he have been a free man of color?"

"Yes," he said, staring into the flames, "I probably would have let him go."

"Why would he want to join the militia, anyway?" she asked.

"Because I did," he said. "Lucas would have gone to war with me if he could."

"To fight for slavery?"

"Crazy as it sounds."

"What happen to Annie, if she was so happy?" She said it as gently as she could, but it still came out hard. He took a long look at the river, like it was a glass of whiskey and he would drink it all down before answering.

"She drowned," he said. "When Lucas ran off, she threw herself in the Rio Brazos and drowned. Lucas doesn't know."

"And you want to bring that bad news to him?"

The coffee was cold but they drank it. He stared into the trees and the darkness beyond the fire. Her hands started shaking.

"If you want to keep moving," he said, "I'll take you to Kästchen. But maybe you want to rest up for a while first?"

"I want to rest and I want to be somewhere safe," she said.

"Then I'll take you to Freedom. You can stay in my cabin. When you're ready to move on, I'll take you to Indianapolis. I'd say that from now on you can relax."

"See?" she said. "I told you not everything you say be true."

17.

After several days of seeing little more than solitary skiffs and barges and, to either side, the untracked forest, they began to encounter cleared patches of greener grass, with yellow-topped stumps and smoldering brushfires, scattered at first but gradually becoming more frequent. They passed sprinklings of small islands, some empty, others with a single log cabin and a cow or a pig in the yard. The White River was wide and sluggish at this point, as though the weight of its own silt were slowing it down. When they saw a homestead, alerted to it by a skiff pulled up into the reeds or tied to a cottonwood limb, the white homesteaders straightened from their hoeing or wood splitting and watched them go by, as if the *Pelican* were a strange new animal, possibly hostile to humans. Sometimes Moody waved at them, and sometimes they raised an arm or a hand in return, but there was never any welcome in the gesture. Look what the river is sending us this time, it said. Last time it was an eagle on a dead cow.

Just before dark, when the air was beginning to cool, Moody steered the *Pelican* into the mouth of a creek that looked more like a tunnel through the trees, which were beginning to leaf out. Away from the river, it was too dark to see anything until he stopped at a dock with a path leading into the bush. When they'd tied up, he led them up the footpath with a lantern toward the cabin. It was a good size, he told them on the way. Three rooms, one about twenty feet square, and two that were half that. There was plenty of room, he said, but he would sleep in the *Pelican* until they got things figured out, and to give them some privacy. He added that Randolph Stokes next door had an extra room that Leason and Sarah could probably rent for nothing, he'd talk to him about it in the morning.

At the cabin, he watched Tamsey standing at the door looking around, and tried to see it through her eyes. There was no back door. There was a broom in the corner to her left, and an ax and a poker leaning against the wall behind the stove. The cooking area had some knives and a heavy iron skillet. She was taking inventory of things she could use to defend herself and her family. He'd seen Annie do the same when he first brought her to New Orleans, the way she prowled about the house looking for the exits and the safe places. Tamsey surely didn't think she would need a weapon against Moody, but maybe she did. And there was no guarantee that the next white man to come through the front door would be him.

While the others arranged themselves, he showed Tamsey into one of the smaller rooms at the back, the one he usually slept in, and told her she could have it. There was a double bed and a dresser and a window looking away from the river. He watched as she took the few poor things she'd saved from their trip to New Harmony out of her bag and set them on a table beside the bed: a cowrie shell, a button, her and Leason's free papers. It felt like an invasion to be watching her, so he left and went back into the main cabin to tend the fire. Sabetha and Granville were in the other small room, arguing over whose bed was whose, and Leason and Sarah were spreading blankets on the floor by the stove, with the intention of moving over to Stokes's in the morning. Moody sat up with them for a while, talking quietly, until their new surroundings felt more familiar to them. Before the candles burned down, Leason put two more logs in the stove's firebox and Moody took a lantern down to the *Pelican*, wondering what he'd meant by getting things figured out.

18.

Randolph Stokes was dozing on a chair on his porch when Moody brought them over in the morning, his face upturned to the sun, an unlit pipe in one hand and an empty cup in the other. Tamsey stood beside him for a while, as if reluctant to disturb his peace, but Moody's footstep on the porch startled him awake.

"Brought you some new neighbors, Randolph," he said.

"Thought I saw lights," Stokes said, opening his eyes. When Moody had completed the introductions, Stokes ushered them into his cabin and set them around a large, square table.

"How long you been here now, Randolph?" Moody asked when they were seated.

"Been here fifteen winters," Stokes said. "Never touched a drop of liquor, never married, worked every day but Sundays from before sunup to after dark, clearing all this here land right down to the river, built this here cabin, made a nice patch for my garden, grow enough truck to feed myself summer and winter. I never have any trouble with rabbits or deer, but hawks sometimes get my chickens, and mice get into the cabin in the fall. Can't seem to keep 'em out. I grow cabbages, turnips, potatoes, beans, anything you want. Collard greens and black-eyed peas I have plenty enough to share."

He crossed the room and moved the tea kettle to the middle of the stove. His cabin was about the same size as Moody's, well kept and comfortable, and also obviously lived in by a bachelor. Everything he might use in the course of a day was close to hand, and hardly anything else. There was a shovel and a hoe leaning against the wall beside the door, a loaf of corn bread and a knife on the cutting board, a jacket slung over the back of his chair, and a fairly dirty towel on a nail beside the basin. Moody could see Tamsey wanting to get up and wash something. One of the rooms off the back he knew was used to store root vegetables and empty jars and chairs, but Stokes said Leason and Sarah could have it if they helped him clear it out.

"That's a fine garden," Tamsey said. "It must take a deal of work."

"It does, Sister, it does, and I ain't as spry as I used to be."

He had lived a contested life, he said, and the prospect of another summer alone had been weighing on his mind. "I be glad of the company," he said. "Virgil here a good neighbor, he help me out some, but he away a lot." He told them he was born in Halifax County, North Carolina, on a plantation on the Roanoke River that had grown everything from indigo to pigs. When Old Massa Willie was alive, Stokes had been the plantation manager, lived in the Big House, dressed like a gentleman and learned to read and write and do sums. When the old massa died, the young massa brought in a new manager, a white man from Virginia, and hired Stokes out to do labor he was not used to doing, but he did it. He gave most of his pay to the young massa, twenty-five dollars a month, but anything over that he kept for himself, and eventually he bought himself with it.

"Working out," he said, "building walls or digging wells, it nearly killed me. But if I worked overplus, stayed until nine o'clock doing extra chores, I could keep that extra money. It took me ten years, but then I had enough to buy my freedom."

"My husband did the same," Tamsey said. "On a tobacco farm." Stokes nodded but didn't ask where her husband was.

"Why's this place called Freedom?" Leason asked.

"When I got here it didn't have no name at all—did it, Virgil— just the bush and this cabin and a couple others used by hunters in the winter. Virgil wasn't here yet. When they put the post office in in Spencer, that's the nearest town, about a half-hour ride from here, they said we all had to have a name so we could get letters. 'I don't get no letters,' I said, 'but all right, let's call her Freedom.' I was the only one at the meeting, so that's what they called it."

"Black folk welcome here?" Tamsey asked.

Stokes looked uncomfortable. "I wouldn't say welcome," he said. "I don't go out much."

They settled on a price for the room, which was free if Sarah would do a little housework and Leason would tend the garden in the summer and get the firewood in the fall. "We only here for a short while," Tamsey said, and Stokes said that the ground was already dry enough to be dug. Leason went back to Moody's cabin to get their things. Sarah looked so pleased she didn't seem to mind about the housework. When Stokes cut slices of corn bread, she stood up and poured the tea, and Moody realized she was staking her claim in Stokes's cabin. He and Tamsey exchanged glances.

They'd be all right here for a while, he thought, even when he was away for a few days. No one knew they were here, but word would soon get around.

19.

Moody had to take the *Pelican* to Spencer to pick up a load of salt for Terre Haute, and told Tamsey he would hire Leason to help him if Sarah could spare him. Tamsey went to Stokes's to talk the matter over with Leason and Sarah, who agreed, then all three walked back down to the *Pelican*, where Moody, with Granville's and Sabetha's help, was stowing the parlor furniture in the hold. Tamsey wanted to give him Leason's free papers in case they were stopped, and he said all right, remembering the two catchers who'd tried to stop them on the river. Personally, he didn't think the catchers, had they nabbed Leason, would have asked politely to see his free papers. They'd have hit him over the head, searched him, burned his papers and carried him off to New Orleans. He didn't say any of that to Tamsey. He took the papers and put them in the strongbox he kept chained to a staple in the boat's cabin. To make room for the salt, he and Leason unloaded some of the crates of fossils, including the one containing Granville's giant salamander skull, and took them up to the cabin.

Sabetha asked Moody if she and Granville could read his books when he was gone, and he said, "Help yourselves. That's what books are for." Then Leason kissed his mother and Sarah, mussed Granville's hair and smiled at Sabetha. Moody untied the *Pelican*, jumped on board, and, ducking under the branches and sparse foliage overhanging the bayou, poled them out into the current.

20.

Two weeks later they were back. In Terre Haute, he'd asked after Lucas with the usual result. He'd had Leason ask around, too, with the same answer each time. No Lucas, or Lucius or Rufous. No Benah. No one had even heard of New Harmony; Brother Joshua, too, seemed to have vanished. Moody regretted involving Leason in his search, as it had served only to make them both feel bad. At night, on the parlor deck, they talked about the raid, the army of catchers that might now be on the march again. Leason was certain James was either dead or captured, and more willing to admit it than Tamsey was, at least to Moody.

"Your mother thinks you know more than you've told her," Moody said.

"I saw him go down," Leason said. "I didn't see him get up. But even if he's still alive, the catchers took him."

Moody waited.

"I hope the catchers didn't take him," Leason said.

"He wasn't your father, was he?" Moody asked.

"He was in most ways that count," Leason said. "I guess like you and Lucas."

Moody was taken aback by that. He'd been too tangled up in the differences to see the similarity. Whoever Lucas's natural father was, it was Moody and Annie who'd raised him. "Do you miss him?" he asked.

Leason raised his eyebrows and nodded. Moody read the gesture as saying something between *Of course* and *What does that mean?*

When they were back in Freedom, Leason gave Tamsey his free papers and five dollars, his wages for the trip, and ran over to

Stokes's to see Sarah. Moody stayed with Tamsey. He told her he'd enjoyed his time with Leason. "If you stay awhile," he said, "I'd be glad to take him on again." After supper, Sabetha read to them about a free black child in Boston who was so clever and obedient his teacher wrote a book about him. Little Jimmy Jackson, his name was, and he could do sums and read books when he was four. But when he was six he came down with yellow fever and died, and Sabetha cried so hard she had to put the magazine down and wipe her eyes. Tamsey said the story made her think of Sabetha and Granville in the school in New Harmony, how she fretted every day she saw them walk down the road that something like that would happen to them. Sickness, or wolves, or a tree falling on them, or the school burning down. She told Sabetha maybe she could find a happy story next time. Sabetha said none of the happy stories were about black people.

Moody said maybe someday Sabetha might write one. Tamsey looked at him oddly, and not long after that he walked down to the *Pelican* and went to bed.

In the morning, he and Tamsey went next door to see how Sarah and Leason were getting on. "They doing fine," Stokes said, sitting out on his porch. "I wouldn't go in there just now, though," he said with a wink, and Tamsey sighed and settled herself in a chair, while Moody leaned against a post. Stokes lit his pipe. "I'll make us some tea in a little while," he said when it was going. "I be sorry to see you go to Indianapolis, though," he added. "It ain't no place for us."

"Why do you say that?" asked Moody.

"Dangerous."

"In Louisville," Tamsey said, "I knew a man name Outlaw. He the deacon of the African Methodist Episcopal church there, down by the dockyards."

"I know that church," said Moody. "I looked for Lucas there."

"Then maybe you saw Outlaw, a funny, twisted-up man, like a

tree grown in steady wind. He had irony hair, and his arms, you could see them through his shirt, looked like they was once muscled but now was soft and folded, and deep hollows in his neck look like they would hold water when it rained. Close up I saw a slit on one side of his nose, so he a plantation slave before he was a deacon, and he grinned all the time, another sure sign, and his hands always doing something, scratching at his leg or tugging at his shirt or hitching up his britches. He had nice eyes, though, kind, and he let us stay in the church when we first got to Louisville and had no other place to sleep. He told us we be wise to stay away from Indianapolis."

"He say why?" Moody asked.

"In Indianapolis, he say, you got to pay your bond, which is five hundred dollars, and then you got to get out of the state, no ifs ands or buts, or they sell you back into slavery, bond or no bond. He say they had a riot there killed twenty negroes and chased two thousand more up to Canada. Burned down they houses."

"They sure don't want us in Indiana," said Stokes. "Look at this." He took a piece of newspaper from his shirt pocket. "I saw it in the Indianapolis paper the other day when I was in Spencer. It says here that the Indiana militia should keep out 'all dregs of off-scourings of the slave states,' because we 'too incurably affected with that horrible gangrene of morals which slavery engenders to be welcomed among a virtuous and intelligent people.' "

"I always thought north of the river was free states," Tamsey said.

"They is, freer than Kentucky, anyway," Stokes said. "Nobody own us in Indiana. It safer here than in Indianapolis, because nobody know we here. But they don't want us to get too settled anywhere. They think it too late for us to be decent human beings after more 'n two hundred years being slaves. Decent to them, anyway."

"We ain't all bad," Moody said.

"No," said Stokes, consideringly, "no, you all ain't. But enough of you is. And the cities get more catchers in them every day. This paper I read," he said, holding it up, "says negroes is organizing vigilante parties to protect theyselves from catchers." He shook his head. "Something bad going to happen before too long. If you folks leaving, I'd say best to go sooner than later."

21.

Moody stayed for a few more days, making repairs to the cabin roof and putting in the garden. He was still sleeping on the *Pelican*, but going down to it later and later each night. He didn't know how Tamsey felt about that, she gave no indication that she even noticed, and he also wondered about Granville and Sabetha. Even thinking about what might lie ahead made his pulse quicken. What he felt for Tamsey was different from what had happened with Rachel, different even from his feelings for Annie. As he worked on the roof he thought about the differences. With Annie he'd been protective; Rachel had made him querulous. Tamsey didn't need protection, she'd made it this far without much help from him. And she didn't argue so much as ask questions that cut into his prevarications like a bayonet through cloth. She made him feel ashamed and cowardly, and though he couldn't say he enjoyed the feelings, they at least seemed to him to be honest ones.

When he told Tamsey he was going to Spencer to collect a cargo of bricks to take to Indianapolis, and would like Leason to come along if he was willing, she asked him to take her to Spencer, too, so she could get copies of their free papers made.

"Randolph say there a good lawyer in Spencer," she said.

"Cliffington Parker," said Moody. "He's from South Carolina, but he knows the law up here. He'll help you sort out your papers, and tell you whether you need to pay the bond. Sarah doesn't have free papers, does she?"

"She say she don't need them."

"She should have them drawn up anyway. Up here a person can never have too many papers."

In the morning, Sarah decided to go with them, to see the shops, she said, if Tamsey would comb her hair out for her on the way. "She like her hair straight when she in town," Tamsey told Moody. "In Louisville she wore it part down the middle and hung in loops at the back. She say she look like a white woman, but to me she look like a horse at a county fair. Turned a few heads, though, including her own."

Sarah and Tamsey going to Spencer meant leaving Granville and Sabetha alone in Freedom. Granville had found a limestone bluff not far from the cabin, above a dried-up creek bed, and said it looked so much like where they'd found the giant salamander he was sure it held more like it. Muddy said he should take a look, but Tamsey told him to stick close to the house, fossils or no fossils.

"What if Mr. Stokes comes with me?" Granville said.

"And leave Sabetha alone in the cabin?" Tamsey said.

Sabetha said that was fine, she just wanted to read. Tamsey sat at the table and tried to keep calm. She wanted everyone to stay where they were, to not move until she got back. "Muddy teaching you your figures," she said to Granville, "and you can work on them when we gone. Sabetha am not to be left alone in this cabin, you hear?"

"*Is*," said Sabetha, not looking up from her book. "Not *am*."

Tamsey looked at Moody, but he stayed out of it. Tamsey placed some fried catfish and a loaf of bread under a damp cloth and told them she and Sarah would be back later that night, probably after dark.

"At least we acting like a family again," she told Moody as they walked down to the dock, and he remembered Lucas at Granville's age. Lucas had never been much for books, but he'd been hard on Annie. Annie, though, had never turned to Moody for support.

In Spencer, he left Leason to load the bricks into the *Pelican* while he accompanied Tamsey and Sarah into town, saying he had some business with Cliffington Parker, too. He assured them they would have no trouble in Spencer, there were plenty of negroes, some of them owned property and worked in the stores. There was no need to be nervous. "No one will even notice you," he said.

"Townspeople notice everything," Tamsey said. "And anyway, I feel better if they notice us. That way they might notice us missing."

Spencer was built around a red-brick courthouse that sat in the middle of a grassy meadow with trees and shrubs growing in it, and paved streets making a square around it. Stores, a church and other buildings, all brick, shouldered on the streets like a bulwark against invasion. The streets radiating out from the square had large, dignified houses on them, and shade trees left standing here and there, oaks and elms. The shrubbery along the four paths leading through the square to the courthouse's big, white double doors, one on each side of the building, were tinged with pale green. All four doors were flung wide open, like it was spring-cleaning day, and they could see people milling about inside.

"I don't see many coloreds," Tamsey said. They were walking along the boarded sidewalk toward Parker's office. "I thought you said there was lots of us."

There was hardly anyone outside the courthouse, black or white. A black man in a straw hat sat on a wagon parked in front of the hardware store. When they came up to him, he jumped down and removed his hat.

"This is Cecil Fountain," Moody said to Tamsey and Sarah. "He lives up Vandalia way, out past Freedom. He makes hog feed, and Leason and I haul it for him when we have a load of salt going that way." He turned to Cecil Fountain. "Sarah is Leason's wife," he said.

"Yes'm," Cecil said, keeping his hat off. "I sell feed to Buzz Crawford, down to Terre Haute." He shook his head and laughed and looked at Tamsey. "That Ol' Buzzard Crawford, he the cussing-est buzzard I ever met. That man butchering a hog is practically fratricide."

Sarah was quiet, as though she considered Cecil's words a disparagement of her husband's work.

"Have you been up here long, Mr. Fountain?" Tamsey asked.

"A fair while, yes. I was born on a pelican farm north of Baton Rouge," Cecil said. "We raised pelicans and sold them downriver in New Orleans. Now I raise them here."

"Pelicans?" Sarah said. "Why would anyone buy a pelican, Mr. Fountain?"

"For their feathers, ma'am," Cecil said to Sarah. "To make hats."

"Oh, I see."

Tamsey asked him how he came to Indiana. One day, he said, when he was ten, a white man snatched him off the pelican dock and locked him in a cabin on a steamboat, took him all the way north to Louisville, where he sold him to a hemp planter named Elijah Haynes.

"I always wondered where the hemp bags I stuffed feathers into came from," he said, "and after that I knew."

"My family is from Kentucky," said Sarah. "The Franklins of Adair County."

"Pleasure to meet you, ma'am," said Cecil. "My new massa, Massa Haynes, he wanted his two daughters to learn French, so I spoke to them in French every night, after I finished my work in the fields. 'Voulez-vous promener avec moi?' 'Aimez-vous danser?' Not that they'd ever be seen walking or dancing with me, but I could say anything I wanted to them as long as it sounded like French. I didn't live in the Big House, but I was in it every evening, and them girls dressed me and fed me and Miss Haynes let me go to church with them on Sundays. The Methodists had a slave gallery in the back.

One Sunday I met Mrs. Packenham, she the wife of the visiting Methodist preacher they had from Cincinnati, Ohio. When I told her my story she took me to Cincinnati, got me my free papers and put me on the 'mysterious road,' as what we called the Railroad in them days. That was winter, it was cold as a nun's kiss and I didn't want to go any farther north if I could help it, so I got off in Indianapolis. I shined shoes, I cut hair, I cleaned stables. I worked there ten years, saved my money, and then came here and bought my farm."

"You lived in Indianapolis?" Tamsey asked. "What it like?"

"It like slavery without the privileges."

"But you had your free papers," Tamsey said.

"Nobody ask me for papers," he said. "I was nearly grabbed a couple of times, but I got away. Now I keep a loaded pistol right up here under me," he said, pointing, "in case I run into catchers on the road."

"You'd shoot a catcher?" Sarah asked.

"No'm. The pistol for me."

Tamsey and Sarah said nothing to that. Moody thought it a good time to intervene.

"After Cecil takes the feathers off the pelicans," he said, "he dries the rest of the bird, puts it through a shredder, mixes the shred with some grain and sells it to Buzz Sawyer for hog feed."

Cecil Fountain beamed at them proudly.

"Are there many other black families out where you live, Mr. Fountain?" Tamsey asked.

"There's plenty in Vandalia," he said. "Not many here in town."

"Why that?"

Cecil Fountain looked at Moody. "Not everybody treat us as good as Mr. Virgil here," he said. "Some of 'em wishes we stayed in the South."

"We just passing through," Tamsey said.

"Some of us am," Cecil said. "And some of us just too tired.

I usually stay in Vandalia, but I need some more hemp bags. Mr. Harris inside, he say he sell me some but I have to wait to the end of the day, in case some white man wants them first."

"How many you need, Cecil?" Moody said.

"All they got."

Moody went into the hardware store and bought a bale of hemp bags. He brought them out and lifted them into the back of Cecil's wagon.

"Thank you, Mr. Virgil," said Cecil, looking nervously into the hardware store, where Harris was standing at the window, watching them.

"Now you can do me a favor, Cecil," Moody said. "You can wait for a while until these ladies are finished in Cliff Parker's office, then you can give them a ride back to Freedom. I've got to go on to Indianapolis."

"Sure thing," said Cecil. "I'll just be waiting down the road a ways, under them trees."

Parker's office was three doors from the hardware store. Parker was at his desk reading a book when they entered his office from the street. There was not much to indicate his profession: a desk and two chairs, a bench by the door that served as his waiting room, a low shelf behind him with more books than files on it, and a safe at the back with its door swung open, as though it had just been blown open. When they came in, he closed the book, keeping his finger in it, and stood up.

"Good day, Virgil," he said. "Looks like you brought me some business."

"These ladies need some papers copied," Moody said. "Copied and notarized." Parker said his scrivener was at lunch; they could come back in an hour, or he could make the copies himself if they were in a hurry. The fee was one dollar.

"We'll wait," Tamsey said.

"I'll wait with you," Moody said.

"You don't need to, if you got business elsewhere," said Tamsey.

"I don't mind. I'll need to take a copy of Leason's free paper with me to Indianapolis. Maybe, Cliff, you could make an extra copy and I'll just keep it on the *Pelican*."

He also wondered if Tamsey was going to ask Parker about free papers for Sarah.

They sat on the long bench by the door, watching Parker as he wrote. He wore a cloth sleeve to protect his shirt cuff. With a ruler and pencil he drew a few light lines on a sheet of paper as guides, smelled his inkwell and tested the sharpness of his nib with his tongue. His pen scratched across the paper with a curious, insectile sound, like a cockroach in dry leaves. A pendulum wall clock above Parker's bookcase ticked hollowly. Solomon Kästchen had one much like it in his parlor; he said his father had brought it with him from Germany. Moody wondered if he would soon be handing Tamsey over to Kästchen. He supposed he might ask her, but he didn't want her to think about it. After a while, Sarah sighed dramatically, stood up and walked over to the notice board on the wall beside the door.

"Oh, look, Tamsey," she said, startling Moody from his reveries. Sarah had never called Tamsey by her Christian name, she'd always been *Mam*. "This is Owen County. I wonder if it's named after Mr. Robert Owen."

Parker looked up from his work. "No," he said, "it's named for Abraham Owen, an officer at the Battle of Tippecanoe, against the Shawnee. He fought alongside William Henry Harrison."

"Oh, yes," said Sarah. "I do recollect that name."

"Which one?"

Sarah turned back to the bulletin board. Moody and Tamsey exchanged glances. Moody was amused; Tamsey was furious.

"In fact, this town is named for Captain Spier Spencer, who was also killed in the battle. Harrison won the battle," Parker said, "so he got to be president. Owen and Spencer were killed, so they just got a county and a town named after them."

"Well," Sarah said, "it feels like a connection to New Harmony, don't it, Tamsey? And look at this." She pointed to another notice on the board. "There's property for sale, near Vandalia: two hundred acres of mixed hardwood and cedar for eighty dollars. We got eighty dollars, don't we? We could buy our own land."

"Aren't you going to Canada?" Moody asked, wondering what she was up to.

"Where is Vandalia?" Sarah asked Parker.

"About ten miles thataway," he said, getting up and moving to the window, where Sarah joined him. He pointed, his arm nearly touching Sarah's shoulder. "See that man on the buckboard out there? That's Cecil Fountain. The land's right next to his. You can ask him about it if you're interested."

"We ain't," Tamsey said. "We're going to Canada."

"I'll go out and talk to him," Sarah said. "I want to see the shops, anyway."

"We both go, then," she said. "We be back shortly." She looked at Moody, and he got up and followed them out onto the street.

"What was that about?" Tamsey said to Sarah.

"What was what about?" Sarah said.

"Calling me my name," said Tamsey. "Putting on airs for that lawyer. You never done that before."

"I thought it made you sound more dignified," Sarah said.

"Dignified?" she said. "It made me sound like I your servant. Don't you ever do that again."

"I don't know what you're talking about," Sarah said. "Do you, Moody?"

This time Moody didn't stay out of it. "She's right, Sarah," he said. "You sounded disrespectful."

"Well," Sarah said, and marched on ahead of them.

They let her go and returned to Parker's office, where Moody led Tamsey to a chair and asked Parker to bring her a glass of water.

"That sun can be terribly hot," Parker said.

"It ain't the sun," Tamsey said, fanning herself. "It the daughter-in-law."

Parker smiled. "Would you like me to keep the originals here," he asked, "where they'll be safe?"

Moody nodded, and she said yes.

Sarah came back and sat down on the bench as though nothing had happened.

"If you're interested in purchasing that land," Parker said to her, "I'd be honored to take care of the legal aspects. I helped Moody buy his cabin in Freedom, and I think he found my work satisfactory?"

"Very," said Moody. "But I don't think they're interested."

"I'll have to talk it over with my husband," Sarah said, as if her husband were a grand duke and not the man whose free paper Parker had just copied.

Moody walked with them to Cecil Fountain's wagon. On their way, they passed a ladies' dress shop that had a sign in the window, which Sarah pointed to and read out: "SALESLADY WANTED." The shelves behind the window were stacked with finery: shawls, gloves, bonnets, even shoes.

"When I came out here to speak to Cecil Fountain," said Sarah, "I went in there and applied for that job."

Tamsey stopped walking so abruptly that Moody almost bumped into her.

"You did what?" she said.

"I don't want Leason and me to be farmers," Sarah said. "I want us to live here in town, I want our children to go to school." Moody looked at her and thought it was the first honest words he'd had from her. "I want things, Mam. I want the same things white people have. There, I said it."

"But you ain't white."

"I'm white enough."

"White enough ain't white enough."

"Then why'd we leave the South?" Sarah said angrily. "I want our child to have things."

Tamsey stared at her. "You with child, child?" she asked.

Sarah nodded. Tamsey clapped her hands.

"How long you been?"

"Hmm," Sarah said, "I think almost four months."

"Oh, Lord," Tamsey said, smiling at Moody and hugging Sarah. "Oh, Lord. No wonder you acting strange."

22.

On their way back from Indianapolis, Moody and Leason stopped at Spencer to pick up supplies for the cabin. After securing the *Pelican* to the dock they walked up to town. They'd been two days in Indianapolis and three days on the river, and Moody was eager to get back to Freedom. So was Leason. Almost all they'd talked about on the trip was his coming fatherhood, a subject about which Moody was both knowledgeable and detached. He felt he was learning more from watching Leason than Leason could ever learn from him.

The two stopped at Parker's law office. Parker had drawn up a contract for the regular supply of salt to Buzzard Crawford, in Terre Haute, a job Moody hoped to hand over to Leason by the end of the summer, if they were still there. The contract was Crawford's idea. A handshake would have been good enough for Moody, but Crawford was expanding his meat-packing business and said his bank wanted to see some assurances on paper. That would be a Northern bank. In the South, a bank was a place where you kept your money so you didn't spend it, and it lent you more when you did; up here, banks were businesses out to make a profit, or rather to take a portion of Moody's profits. Maybe he should get Parker to draw up a contract between him and Leason, make Leason a full partner. He didn't want to make the same mistake with Leason that he'd made with Lucas, but hoped he was past the point of being in danger of that.

Parker had his feet on his desk and was reading the *Indianapolis Daily Herald*. "Congress is pressuring Taylor to sign Clay's Compromise bill," he said by way of greeting.

"Zach Taylor won't sign it," said Moody. "I served under him in the Mexican War. He's quiet, but he's a tough son of a bitch, and he hates slavery."

"If the South takes over Congress," Parker said, "it'll force the North to send every last fugitive it has back into slavery. I worry Taylor will sign the Compromise if he thinks it'll stop the South from leaving the Union."

"How's the Compromise going to keep the South happy?" Leason asked.

"The North wants the new territories Virgil here stole from the Mexicans to be slavery free," said Parker, "and the South wants them to be slave states. The Compromise will let them decide the matter for themselves, whether they're free or slave, so all the South has to do is make sure most of the settlers in them come from the South, so they'll vote for slavery when the time comes."

"Can't the North do the same thing?"

"A lot more people are moving west from the South," said Moody. "People up here already got as much free land as they can use, and it ain't drying up and blowing away like it is down there."

"The Compromise also says the North will have to send all fugitives back where they came from," said Parker. "It'll make it against the law to interfere with a catcher coming into Indiana to catch a fugitive. In fact, we'll have to help him or go to jail ourselves."

"It's legalized kidnapping," said Moody.

"How's that different from what happened in New Harmony?" Lucas asked.

"What happened in New Harmony wasn't legal," Moody said.

"With the Compromise in place, those catchers will be able to get the militia to help them. But Taylor won't sign."

"People change, Virgil," said Parker. "Anything can happen."

"I guess it's not a good time to be a runaway," said Leason.

"When is?" said Moody. "But you aren't a runaway. And we've paid your bond and you've proved you can keep the peace. You and your family have as much right to be here as I have."

Leason looked unconvinced. Moody signed the Crawford contract, and they left the office and headed for the hardware store, where Leason wanted to buy a keg of nails with a view to repairing and expanding Stokes's woodshed for him. On the way, he said next week was Sarah's birthday. He wanted to buy her something, but he didn't know what.

"What's she fancy?" Moody asked.

"She likes lacy things. I don't even know where to get 'em."

"Here's the ladies' shop," Moody said. "How about some fancy lace handkerchiefs?"

"Maybe," Leason said.

The shop was owned by Etta Pickering, the sheriff's wife, a woman Moody knew to be a tight-mouthed termagant who looked like a heron that had just spotted a frog. Her husband, Melvin "Pudge" Pickering, was a damn nuisance. In an ideal world, a sheriff wouldn't have anything to do. The world being something short of ideal, Pickering spent long hours in his office thinking of ways to justify his stipend by making everyone's life miserable. Pudge and Etta were a well-matched pair. Etta once hired Moody to bring her a china cupboard from the freight depot in Indianapolis, and when he got it to Spencer she expected him to haul it up from the ferry dock to her house. He had to hire a horse and wagon and wrap the thing in blankets so it wouldn't get scratched and none of the glass doors would crack. After he had it in place in her dining room she thanked him and gave him a dollar. "I surely didn't expect you to do the work yourself," she'd said. "Ain't you got you a boy to help?"

She greeted Moody when they entered her shop, no doubt wondering what she had in there that would interest him. He told her they wanted to see some silk handkerchiefs.

"Really?" she said. She looked like she wanted to say more, but evidently thought better of it. She went to the back and brought out a box of handkerchiefs, and spread them on the counter.

"What do you think, Leason?" Moody said. "Would Sarah like these?"

"I suppose," Leason said. "She likes pink. What do you think?"

"Sarah?" said Etta Pickering. "Sarah Lewis? She was in here just the other day. Seeking employment. I told her we hadn't any vacancies."

"Then what's that sign in the window for?" asked Moody. He hadn't told Leason about Sarah applying for the job, but Leason didn't look very surprised. If anything, he looked as though he'd just had some bad news confirmed.

"I hired a new girl last week," Etta said stiffly. "I just forgot to remove the sign."

"Well," Moody said. "You keep Sarah in mind if the new girl doesn't work out."

"I need someone who lives in town," said Etta. "Someone I can count on to be here on time. Someone reliable."

"Well, that's all right," said Leason, "because Sarah and I are planning on moving into Spencer. Didn't she tell you that?"

"Sarah and you?" said Etta Pickering. "Whatever do you mean by that?"

"Sarah and me," said Leason. "Sarah's my wife."

Etta Pickering's hand went to the top button of her blouse. "Oh," she said. "Oh, yes. She did mention she was married. That's another reason I didn't hire her."

"We hear there's a house for sale right next to yours. Would that be close enough to make Sarah reliable, do you think?"

Etta Pickering glared at Leason but said nothing. Moody smiled at her as Leason paid for the handkerchiefs. Her mouth looked more like an unhealed knife wound than ever, and Moody wondered if she were a secret drinker. She wrapped the handkerchiefs in tissue and tied them into a package, which Leason put in his jacket pocket.

"I hope your wife enjoys them, Mr. Lewis," she said.

When they were outside, Leason said, "How do you enjoy a handkerchief?"

"I expect they're softer on the nose than oak leaves," Moody said, giving a troubled laugh. "I didn't know you were thinking of moving into town," he said as they walked toward the general store.

"We're not," said Leason. "I just said that to give that old vulture something to chew on."

"That old vulture runs this town," Moody said uneasily. "Best not to wave dead meat in front of her."

23.

Moody was on his dock in Freedom, transferring a hundred bags of Cecil Fountain's hog feed from his wagon into the *Pelican*'s hold and contemplating the irony of stuffing pelican meat into a boat called the *Pelican,* when he heard footsteps on the dock behind him. It was a warm sunny day, late June, but the creek, which he called the "bayou," was in deep shade and he couldn't at first see who it was. Leason and Sarah were in Indianapolis for a couple of days—Kästchen was taking Sarah to a doctor he knew. Tamsey, Granville and Sabetha had gone back with Cecil to look at some pelican chicks. Moody had been thinking about himself and Tamsey. He hadn't slept on the *Pelican* for a week, he'd been sleeping in his old bed with Tamsey, a development that hadn't surprised either of them. He'd been getting up early and coming down to the boat before Granville and Sabetha woke up, but this morning they'd tarried a bit and Granville had come out of his room earlier than usual and found them eating toast, Tamsey still in her nightclothes. Granville hadn't seemed too surprised, either. He'd come over to the table and sat with them, taking a piece of toast and pouring himself some coffee. Tamsey sat as still as if she were waiting for an explosion, Moody could see the toast shaking in her hand, but the morning had gone on without incident. Before Tamsey left for Cecil's, she'd come down to the dock and they'd spent some undisturbed time in the *Pelican*'s cabin. Moody hadn't felt so good since he'd taken Annie to New Orleans.

When his eyes adjusted to the shadows, he saw the outline of a man standing just where the dock joined the creek bank. Large hat, rotund middle, spindly legs that splayed out from the knees down. He had to move to one side to see who it was for sure, but he already knew it was Pudge Pickering.

"Morning, Sheriff," he said. "What brings you this far from your padded chair?"

Pickering always reminded Moody of one of Buzz Crawford's hogs. His small black eyes peered out from their caves of flesh, his chins stayed in place when he turned his head, his clothes were as tight on his arms and legs as sausage skins, and he had small hands and feet. Moody straightened. There was still enough guilt in him, especially after this morning, to make him cautious.

"You taking that hog feed down to Buzz Crawford, are you?" Pickering said.

"Yep, this and forty bags of salt. You got something you want me to bring him?"

"Oh no, no, just askin'." Pickering looked around as if for something else to ask about. Moody waited him out, watching the sweat run down the side of the sheriff's face and over a bulge of chewing tobacco, which he dislodged from time to time to relieve the sting and then tucked into a different corner. "I knocked up at the cabin, weren't nobody home."

"How'd you know that? You go in?"

"No, no. Just looked through the winder. Went next door to Stokes's place, and nobody there, either."

"Randolph's getting hard of hearing. You have to knock hard."

Pickering nodded, or at least his jaw disappeared into his throat a couple of times. "Sarah Lewis," he said. "She living in there with that boy of yours, Leason?"

Moody took off his gloves and set them on the *Pelican*'s rail and pushed his hat back off his forehead. In Texas, his action would have been taken as a sign of aggression. It would have been saying, *I didn't quite catch that, you mind saying it again so I can hit you?* He put his hands on his hips, too, which, if he'd had a pistol tucked in his belt, would have been unmistakable.

"Leason ain't my boy," he said evenly. "And what do you want with Sarah?"

"He works for you, don't he?"

"I pay him, yes."

"What about his mamma? You pay her, too?"

Moody worked hard at keeping his eyes level.

"What's this about, Pickering?"

"I'm just checkin' up on a few things is all. There's been complaints."

"Complaints about what?"

Pudge Pickering turned his head but kept his eyes on Moody, as though trying to figure out how much he could say.

"You know it ain't legal for a white woman and a nigger to . . . to be together," he said.

"How do you mean, 'be together'?"

"You know, to live together, like man and wife."

"Tamsey and I are not living together," he said. "She and her family live up at the cabin, and I stay down here on my boat, when I'm here, which ain't often."

"I ain't talkin' about you, so much. Least not this time. I mean Leason and Sarah."

"Leason and Sarah *are* man and wife."

"They ain't if one of 'em's white."

"What the hell are you talking about?"

"Like I said, there's been reports."

"You said 'complaints.' "

"Same thing. Complaints have been made."

"About what?"

"About them two, Leason and Sarah. Immoral conduct." Pickering grinned. "Fornicatin'."

"Leason and Sarah are married. Just like you and Etta."

"Well, there you go," Pickering said. "Except I ain't black."

"What?"

"And Leason is."

"So what?"

"And Sarah ain't."

"Who says so?"

"She says so. She said so when she applied for that job at Etta's dress shop, wrote it down in plain English, I seen it myself: United States citizen. Etta always asks that. Blacks can't be citizens, so Sarah and Leason can't be man and wife, can they? And if they're living together without being married, then they're breaking the law, and I got to arrest 'em for fornicatin'. So where they at?"

Moody's heart was pounding but he walked calmly to the cabin and reached inside the door for the 12-gauge. There was just birdshot in it, but at close range birdshot could do almost as much damage as buckshot. Pickering's skin was so taut Moody figured it would split if even a pin pricked it. He hadn't felt so strong an urge to do damage to a man since the war in Mexico, not when Millican sold Benah, or even after the encounter with the Judds. He felt virtuous. He raised the shotgun to his hip and aimed it in the general direction of Pickering's massive stomach. Pickering spit his tobacco into the bayou, but otherwise remained where he is.

"You get on your horse and ride on out of here, Pudge," Moody said, "or you're going to find yourself floating down the river after your chaw."

"Threatening an officer of the law," Pickering said cheerfully. "That there's an offense worse 'n fornicatin'. I got half a mind to bring you in, too."

"You only got half a mind at the best of times," Moody said. "If you don't have a warrant you're trespassing, and I can't hardly see you in these shadows. I might think you're a fat thief come to steal Cecil's hog feed for your dinner."

"I'll find 'em," Pickering said, backing off the dock. "Don't you worry about that. We maybe can't keep your coon cargo out of Indiana, but we can damn well keep it out of Spencer."

When Pickering left, Moody hurried to Stokes's cabin and told Stokes about Pickering's visit, and the two of them sat on the porch in a state of suspended animation, waiting for Tamsey and the others to come back from Cecil Fountain's. They told each other that anyone looking at Sarah and seeing a white woman was delusional, but on the other hand, anyone that delusional wasn't going to be easily dissuaded. Etta Pickering knew Sarah wasn't white, Stokes said, so what in tarnation was this all about?

But Moody knew what it was about. He'd known what it was about since the day he let Lucas sell himself. Nothing was forgiven. Some things were forgotten, but damn few, and only for a time. But nothing is ever forgiven.

Where the little river
Meet the great big 'un,
The ole man waits;
Follow the Drinking Gourd.

I.

Leason and Sarah were arrested in Spencer, as they stepped down from the coach that brought them back from Indianapolis. They were taken to the courthouse by Pudge Pickering, with Etta watching from the door of her shop, and placed in separate cells in the courthouse basement. Moody and Tamsey heard about the arrest from Cecil Fountain, and visited the couple the next day, after a long talk with Cliff Parker. They walked up the courthouse steps, entered the lobby through the broad double doors, which now seemed like the heavy gates of a fortress, and down the basement staircase without being challenged. At the bottom, however, a deputy poked through the bag of food Tamsey had brought before letting them in to see the prisoners.

"Guess you didn't find the musket I put in that pork pie," Tamsey said.

"Fifteen minutes," said the deputy.

Leason was clearly frightened. He sat on his cot in the feeble light that seeped through two high, ground-level windows, his arms folded and his head bowed, as though trying to keep himself warm. Moody had seen soldiers sit like that on the eve of a battle they didn't expect to win. Sarah was indignant, no real surprise to Moody, striding back and forth in her cell, impatient for someone to set her world right again. She wanted to know how long they were going to be kept there, "a woman in my condition."

"What the doctor in Indianapolis say, dear?" Tamsey asked soothingly.

"He said I'm fine, a bit high-strung is all. He wanted to let my blood but I told him I was just excited about the baby."

Tamsey told them what each item was as she took it out of the sack. "Catfish from Muddy, potatoes and carrots from Stokes, corn bread and a cooked ham from me." Leason said he couldn't eat, and Sarah said she'd be sick if she even smelled food.

"Lawyer Parker say the bail hearing a week away," Tamsey told them. "Trial in the fall—September, most likely."

"A week!" Sarah cried. "They can't keep us in here for a week! Can they?"

Leason looked at Moody. "What'll happen if they find us guilty?" he asked.

"It's a misdemeanor, according to Parker," Moody said. "A fine, maybe some jail time. But don't worry about that, you won't be found guilty," he added, looking at Sarah. "The thing's absurd."

"But a whole week in here?" said Sarah. "What if something happens to the baby?"

"I'll talk to Sheriff Pickering," Moody said, trying to make talking to Pudge Pickering sound like a reasonable thing to do. He remembered using the same voice to tell Lucas he would talk to Endicot Millican.

"Where'll we get money for bail?" Leason asked.

"We'll get it," Moody said. "I'll put it up and take it out of your hide when you get free."

"If I have any hide left by then."

Moody didn't tell them what Lawyer Parker had actually said, that the penalty would most likely be a thousand dollars each, a year in jail and their marriage annulled. If they didn't pay the fine, Leason could be sold into slavery. Nor did he tell them about an article he'd read in the *Sentinel* that morning, about an Indianapolis couple who were charged with fornication, a white woman and a colored man. A week before the case even went to trial, a mob broke into the couple's house, tarred and feathered the woman and rode her naked down the street on a rail, and ran the man out of town with some of his parts missing. Yesterday a member of the Indiana legislature had stood up in the House and defended the mob: "I say it in all sincerity, without any hard feelings toward niggers, that it would be better to kill them all off at once, if there is no better way to get rid of them." He hadn't told Tamsey about that, either.

All he said now was that he and Tamsey and Parker were doing everything they could. Which was what he'd said to Lucas.

2.

Before Moody went in to see Pudge Pickering, he and Tamsey sat for a moment on a bench under one of the oaks outside the courthouse. People walked past without looking at them, but he could no longer tell Tamsey they weren't seeing her. News of the arrest had spread, and if people weren't looking at them as they passed, it was because they had taken a good look at them from a distance. And seen another white man and a black woman sitting together on a bench. He felt as though they were going into the courthouse to file a complaint. Who would look after Granville and Sabetha when he and Tamsey were in jail, sharing cells with Leason and Sarah?

"I won't be long," he said, standing up. "Will you be all right here? You can always go over to Cliff Parker's office."

"I want to stay close," Tamsey said. She meant close to Leason, he thought, but she might have meant close to him, too.

Pickering was at his desk, scowling at a sheet of paper as though whatever was on it had been written in some indecipherable foreign language he didn't think should exist. He looked up at Moody as if Moody had written it.

"What?" he said.

"Those two kids in the basement," Moody said.

"What about them?"

"A week seems a long time to hold them until you decide to let them out on bail."

"Circuit judge sets bail, not me," Pickering said, "and he don't come through until the third week of the month."

"Couldn't you have waited until then to arrest them?"

"Could have," said Pickering, putting down the paper. "But when a crime's been committed, we tend to want to deal with it right away, not seven days later."

"Hmm. Seems to me that if a crime's been committed," Moody said, "it was committed years ago, when they were married."

"Maybe," he said, "but I only heard about it this week."

"Come on, Melvin. Those are good kids down there. Sarah's in the family way, and Leason works for me and I need him. They ain't going anywhere. How much is bail going to be, anyway?"

"Fifty dollars, most likely," Pickering said. "Each."

Moody took a hundred dollars out of his pocket and planked the amount on the counter. "There," he said. "Let them come home with me now, and I'll personally guarantee they'll be back here for their trial."

"Can't do that."

"Why not?"

The dough around Pickering's eyes rose a little. He stood up and came over to the counter. Moody thought he was coming to take the money, but the sheriff scowled at him.

"Pointing a weapon at an officer of the law, and now attempting to bribe him," he said. "You got any more tricks up your sleeve?"

"Not bribe," Moody said, "pay their bail."

"Their bail ain't set yet. I told you that. And when it is, you don't pay me, you pay the county clerk. This here looks a powerful lot like a bribe."

"How would you know what a bribe looks like?"

"I don't care what kind of amalgamations you got up to down in Texas, Moody, but I'm here to tell you we don't tolerate that kind of thing in Indiana. Whites and blacks together is wrong. That could just as well be you and your lady friend down there with them two fornicators, you know it and I know it, so if I was you I'd shut pan and use this money to hire yourselves a good lawyer, because you're sure as hell going to need one after this."

There wasn't much Moody could do but stare him down like an honest man, which he didn't feel he was, with Tamsey sitting outside waiting for him, so his stare-down faltered a little. He picked up the money and put it back in his pocket, and it did feel like taking back a rejected bribe. Or rescinding a bad bet.

"You're right, Pudge," he said as smoothly as he could manage. "We ain't in Texas. I don't know what you heard about it, but I left the South because I was sick of seeing people punished because they had black skin or didn't believe in the holy institution of slavery. You know what we did to blacks in Texas when they did something we didn't approve of? We put them in jail and left them there as long as we damn well pleased, the longer the better. Now, you tell me how that's so different from what you're doing here."

Pickering looked like he was going to split open and spill grease all over the skillet. "In Texas," he said, "after leaving your blacks in prison until they half rot, you haul 'em outside and lynch 'em. That ain't going to happen here."

"You're sure about that? You read the paper this morning?"

"Not while I'm sheriff, it won't."

"Well, that's a comfort to us all," said Moody. "You faced down a lot of mobs since you became sheriff, have you?"

"They'll get a fair trial."

"How can they get a fair trial if it ain't a fair charge?"

Pickering gave him a look as ferocious as he could make it. It was like being scowled at by a pork pie.

"If you got so much work to do, Moody," he said, going back to his desk, "I suggest you go do it. And let me do mine."

3.

For the next few days, Moody tried to avoid reading newspapers. The news kept him up half the night listening to tree branches scraping on the roof and owls screeching at each other out in the woods. Legislators calling for a higher bond for runaways. Judges sending whole families back to Mississippi. He had a stack of geology books—Buffon, Hutton, Cuvier, Lyell, Dawson—and had recently acquired a set called *American Geology*, by Ebenezer Emmons, the man who named the Adirondack and the Taconic Mountains. He read them into the night, absorbing almost nothing, until Tamsey complained about the lamp keeping her awake. He ended up giving the books to Granville and going back to newspapers. The news exerted a morbid fascination on him. Whenever he thought things were as bad as they could get, the next day they got worse.

For example, the hundred and fifty representatives of the Indiana legislature—including the enlightened gentleman who'd said that killing blacks was the most humane way of handling the state's immigration problem—were going to be meeting in Indianapolis in the fall, around the same time as the trial, to revise the Indiana Constitution. The Whigs wanted public schools, they wanted public officials to be elected and they were calling for a ban on public debt. The Republicans wanted the same things, and accused the Whigs of stealing their ideas. The delegates were supposed to meet in the statehouse, but when it was discovered that the statehouse roof leaked, they debated for three days about whether to repair it in time for the convention or move the meetings next door into the Masonic Temple. When they finally decided to move, they spent another day debating whether the state should incur a public debt by paying the twelve dollars a day the Masons wanted for the use of their building. Moody read these stories aloud to Tamsey, hoping to cheer her up, but they only deepened her despair.

"You telling me," she said, "our lives being determined by people who take three days to decide to move out of the rain?"

"Well," said Moody, "it might not rain, you see."

"It always rain in the fall. They going to hang my baby in the rain."

"No, they're not."

"In Granville's school in New Harmony," she said, "they had a map of the world hanging on the wall at the front of the classroom. Imagine that, a map of the whole world. All the countries different colors, and the oceans blue in between them. Granville show me Africa, and when I saw it I couldn't look at it. You ever see the shape of Africa, Muddy?"

"Yes. I always thought it looked like a side of beef."

"To me it look like a man hanging from a tree. He got a quilt over his head and his elbows tied together behind his back, and his broken neck hanging over to one side. I still can't get that picture out of my head. Africa a hanged man with a sack over his head and a rope tied around his middle."

A week after their arrest, Leason and Sarah were released on bail. Fifty dollars each, which Moody paid to the county clerk. Back in Freedom, the couple retreated to their room in Stokes's cabin and didn't come out for two days, as if they were in hiding. Tamsey said she'd seen the same thing with abused horses. The only thing to do, she said, was to wait it out. Stokes agreed.

"They come out when they hungry," he said, and sure enough, the evening of the second day they emerged as if nothing unusual had happened, saying they were starving, Sarah was going to make pancakes and did anyone else want some? Stokes said he had some maple syrup somewhere.

Moody noted that it was the Fourth of July, which put an edge on their celebrating. There was some strained talk around the table as they ate their pancakes. Tamsey tried to talk Leason and Sarah into letting Moody take them up to Michigan and across to Canada in the *Pelican*. "Everywhere north seem safer than here," she said when there was no response from Leason or Sarah. "They say they's no slavery in Canada, and not no slavery like they have no slavery here, which is just no slavery on paper. Canada the land of milk and honey, if you like your milk frozen and honey you got to cut with a knife. We never should have stopped here."

Leason reached for Sarah's hand as if he'd warned her there would be this talk. "We ain't worried about this thing, Mam," he said. "This just Etta Pickering making sure we don't buy a house next door to hers. When she finds that a house ain't even for sale she'll probably drop the charges."

"It more than that," Tamsey said. "Don't think it ain't."

Moody said they should listen to Tamsey. "We could be in Terre Haute in a week," he said, "and from there we'd take the Wabash up to the new Illinois and Michigan Canal and all the way to Canada."

"How long that take?" asked Tamsey.

"A month, six weeks. We'd there by the end of August," he said. "Your child could be born in Canada."

But Leason said no, not with Sarah in her state. "What if we're caught? What will they do to us? Would Sarah have her child in a prison?"

"You already caught," Tamsey said, "and we know what they want to do to you." Which made Moody wonder if someone had been reading the newspapers to her. "If you don't want to go with Muddy, you can let Quaker Kästchen put you on the Underground Railroad."

Sarah rose from the table and went into their bedroom. Leason looked after her, and then at Moody.

"We ain't going nowhere," he said, "until this baby is born."

Moody had to agree with him. He wished Lucas had said the same thing.

4.

They met with Cliff Parker almost every day, sometimes with Sarah and Leason, sometimes just Tamsey and Moody. He told them that, legally, he couldn't advise the couple to skip bail.

"On the surface of it," he said, "it's such a ridiculous charge that fleeing it would be seen as an admission of guilt."

"There must be something deeper to it," Moody said when Leason and Sarah had left the office, "something we don't understand yet. No one looking at Sarah for two minutes would think she was white."

"She don't think so," said Tamsey.

"And anything that obvious is hard to prove," Parker said.

"What that mean?" asked Tamsey. "You mean you can't prove that tree out there ain't a mule?"

"Exactly," said Parker. "You know it's a tree, I know it's a tree, but what do you do if everyone else suddenly starts calling it a mule?"

"You go to Canada."

"You wouldn't get far," Parker said. Moody remembered saying the same thing to Lucas, and how far did Lucas get?

That night, after he put his book down and before he blew out the candle, he and Tamsey lay awake and talked, keeping their voices low. They knew they were taking a chance by sleeping together, but they couldn't stop themselves. It wasn't only the physical act, it was these late-night talks that he valued. Their days were in such turmoil, and the trial was getting closer. Tamsey told him she felt as though Leason and Sarah had had a terrible accident, like a snake bit them, and told him a snakebite story her Mam had told her from Africa. "Or it like a fire burn their house down," she said, "or Sarah lost her child, and there be no way we could help them." He savored that "we." They were all, even Moody, being swept along by a powerful current and no one knew what was at the end of it. She said she'd spent most of her life fighting upstream, and now she was being told to sit back and let the river carry them along.

"You watch a catfish working upriver against a strong current," she said, "and you see how it use the water, how strong and alive it is in its proper element, and how the fight make it stronger. But anything being carried downstream be tumbled and tossed in the water like a dead thing."

Sarah, who Tamsey had watched grow up, had thrown herself and Leason into this river. Had they been safer in the South? he asked her. No, she said, in the South she'd be cutting Leason down from a tree by now.

"There no sense to what happening," she said. "How can even a lawyer argue what is impossible to reason out?"

"Parker says the only way the State can win this case is to prove that black is white. That's like proving two and two ain't four. It can't be done."

Tamsey said she wished he hadn't said that. "They ain't nothing can't be done," she said.

5.

One afternoon in August, when just Moody and Tamsey had made the trip into Spencer, Parker asked Tamsey about her mother. "Do you remember her at all?"

"She sold when I still a child," Tamsey said, looking at Moody.

"Tell me what you know about her," Parker said.

"Why? This about Sarah?"

"I want to know as much as possible about everyone involved."

"How my mam involved?"

"I don't know. That's why I need you to tell me about her."

"All right," she said.

Moody remembered how reluctant Annie had been to talk about her mam. His own mother had died when he was a child, and he'd thought then that Annie's was the same reverence for a parent she had barely known, a desire to keep an imagined past intact. But with Tamsey it was more than that.

"We was together for a time, in South Carolina. Mam lived in the nigger house and I was brought inside to work in the Big House, I don't know why. Old Massa Lockhart still alive then. He took a shine to me, I guess."

Parker wrote something down. "Do you remember Massa Lockhart's first name?" he asked her.

"Massa Reuben. The old slaves call him that. My mam call him that. I call him Massa Lockhart."

"Where in South Carolina was this?"

"On the Queen Bee plantation," she said. "That all I know of it."

"Please go on."

"I was fetching table linen from the icebox in the cellar when I learned my mam was sold. It was early spring, when the first quail call, but it still cold in the shade, the crocuses all up but not the daffodils. The Queen Bee a big, white house, it seem a mile long to me, with three big chimneys, one at each end and one in the middle where the kitchen was, and fires kept in all three of them. I was humming a tune to myself because there were spiders in the cellar and I always been afraid of spiders. My mam used to tell me stories about Aunt Nancy. One of the laundresses told me to stop sounding so happy, 'cause my mam been sold. I started to cry right away, and ran upstairs and out to the nigger house and my mam not there, and Tilly drag me back up to the Big House and scold me for not getting the linen, and then she set me to cleaning candlesticks, I guess to take my mind off my mam."

"When was this?"

"I don't know. One year pretty much like another back then."

"How old were you?"

"Old enough to know how babies made, too young to have them."

Parker stopped writing. "Thank you," he said. Moody stood up and went to look out the window. "Anything more?"

"My mam come to see me at night sometimes," she said, "after she sold, so I guess she wan't sold far. She sit with me almost till morning, sing to me, show me how to sew, or tell me Aunt Nancy stories until I fell asleep."

"Aunt Nancy?" Lawyer Parker said. "You had an Aunt Nancy?"

"Aunt Nancy the spider in the stories. He make the world and all the people in it."

"I thought God made the world."

"The Lord made Aunt Nancy first. Aunt Nancy like the Lord's overseer, only he on the slaves' side, so maybe he more like a driver."

"Do you remember anything else about your mother?"

"Cliff," Moody said from the window, "why are you so interested in Tamsey's mother? Ain't it Sarah you need to know about?"

"We'll get to her," Parker said. "But I need as full a picture of everyone as I can get. We don't know what the prosecution might bring up."

"What you mean?" Tamsey asked.

"If there's anything to what Sarah says," Parker said carefully, "we need to explore other lines of defense."

Moody returned to his chair. For the first time since the arrest he was beginning to worry that the trial would be more complicated than he thought.

"When I was older," Tamsey said, "I learned she was on the tobacco plantation down the road from the Queen Bee, place called Harrington House. I saw her working in the fields when I went into town with Old Massa Lockhart. She always look up when I passed, like she knew it was me in the wagon. She didn't call or wave, not with Old Massa there, but she watch and watch until we out of sight."

"What color was she?" Lawyer Parker asked.

"Well, I can't rightly say. I can see her standing in the field, shading her eyes, with her hand. She the color of gold-leaf tobacco after it been cured."

"Do you know who your father was?"

"Nobody knows who they father is."

"All the same, do you have any idea?"

"No."

Parker wrote, and she watched the papers pile up on his desk.

"And what about Leason? Who was his father?"

"Like I said."

"Where were you when he was born?"

"I was with Massa Lewis then, in Adair County, Kentucky."

"Lewis. You mean Luce? That's the name on your free papers."

"He a horse trader. He taught us to trust the Lord but to avoid walking behind a horse. He got kicked in the stomach by a horse when he checking its coffin bone, and he died two weeks later. He free Leason and me in his will, so I guess you could say that horse freed us. We got our free papers from Lawyer Temple in Lexington. I walked all the way there with Leason on my back and no free papers."

"All right," Parker said, writing. "Now, what about Sarah? Let's start with her mother."

"Her mother was Sabetha Franklin, wife of Benjamin Franklin. They was friends of ours in Kentucky after we freed. I named my Sabetha for her. They both freeborn blacks. Sarah a freeborn black, too, never mind what she say about being white. The Franklins owned a livery stable and stud farm near Shelbyville, and we worked on the farm for a time. Leason still just a baby when we went there. Sabetha Franklin a small woman, but strong as mule gut and awful kind to us. She took us in off the road after we freed."

"Was she light skinned?"

"Not light like Sarah, but yes."

"Light as you?"

"About."

"Do you know who her parents were?"

"Sabetha Franklin's? She never said."

"Could one of them have been white?"

"One of them could have been purple for all I know."

He wrote that down. "That's good," he said. "We don't have any laws against marrying someone who's purple."

"Look around you, Mr. Parker," she said. "You ever see a fugitive didn't have some white in him? Everybody got some white. Nobody know how much, but how much don't matter."

"It seems to matter to Sarah," Parker said. "Was Sarah already born when you came to Shelbyville?"

"Yes, she the same age as Leason."

"And Benjamin and Sabetha Franklin you say were old?"

"Older than me and James. I don't know how old."

"Does Sarah have any brothers or sisters?"

"Not that I know."

"Could Sabetha and Benjamin have been Sarah's grandparents? Not her parents?"

"It possible," Tamsey said. "But she never said nothing about having another child."

"Leave it with me for now," Parker said. "I'll make some inquiries and let you know what I find."

He passed the pen to Tamsey and asked her to make her mark at the bottom of the last page. She took the pen and made a cross, "like the one the Lord died on," she said, "only falling off to one side, like it might have looked after they took him down." Parker read out what he wrote under it: " 'Thomasina Lewis, her sign.' "

"Are you planning to call Tamsey as a witness at the trial?" Moody asked.

"That's a very complicated question," said Parker. "As you know, blacks can't be witnesses in a trial involving whites. But in this case, it hasn't been established yet that Sarah is white. So I may be able to call Tamsey, if the prosecuting attorney doesn't argue that that would be tantamount to admitting that Sarah is black."

"She is black," said Tamsey.

Parker sighed. "I'll come out to Freedom in a few days," he said.

"What for?"

"I want to see where Leason and Sarah live. And you and Moody."

"Muddy live on his boat," Tamsey said, looking at Moody. "Why you want to see where we live?"

"The prosecution is going to want to see it, so I need to, too. Will it be all right if I come out tomorrow?"

"I guess."

6.

Parker came out in a light gig, like a Virginia dandy. Granville unhitched and dried his horse, a sleek roan Banker that Moody admired when he came onto the porch to greet the lawyer. Tamsey offered him coffee, and Moody took Parker next door to Stokes's cabin while she made it.

The day was warm for September, and Stokes was on his porch, as usual, fanning himself with a newspaper. Leason was down at the *Pelican*, sweeping spilled flour out of the hold, and Sarah was helping him, so the three men had the porch to themselves. Parker took a cursory look inside the cabin, satisfied himself that the couple occupied a single room and a double bed, and came back onto the porch. "I'll go down and look at the boat in a minute," he said, "but I'll wait until Leason and Sarah are finished."

"Always a good idea," said Moody, and Stokes laughed. "Any news of the trial?"

"No date yet," Parker said, "but it looks like late fall. And it's not going to take place in Spencer, as I'd hoped. The attorney general wants it held in Indianapolis."

"Indianapolis? Why there?"

"Politics," Parker said. "Right now, the attorney general is appointed by the governor, but after the Constitutional Convention in October, the feeling is he'll be elected by popular vote, as will the governor, as will the sheriff. Attorney General Fritts wants to be elected, and he expects he'll get more newspaper coverage if the trial takes place in the capital rather than in a little backwater like Spencer."

"He figures it'll be a big trial, then?" Moody asked.

"And he figures he's going to win it handily."

"I thought you said it was just a misdemeanor."

"Well, it's a race issue," Parker said. "These things tend to get blown up."

"Ain't that the truth," Stokes said, waving his newspaper. "Big trials goin' on everywhere. People bein' stole, families flung in jail. I seen it before, never thought to see it up here, though."

"You're referring to the Crenshaw case?" Parker asked.

"That and others."

"John Crenshaw," Parker explained to Moody. "Runs a saltworks up in Gallatin County, Illinois, uses slave labor to work the furnaces. Pretty nasty work."

"I know," Moody said. "I saw saltworks in Virginia."

"Apparently he also breeds slaves on his Hickory Hills estate and sells them down South. A while ago he sold a woman named Maria Adams and her seven children to a slaveholder in Texas, and Maria's husband and her two brothers went after Crenshaw, beat him up pretty good and allegedly burned down the saltworks, which Crenshaw leased from the government. At first there was a lot of public pressure from local whites to have the grand jury indict Crenshaw for slave trading, but after the fire everyone just backed off. Instead, Charles and Nelson, Maria's brothers, were arrested and charged with arson."

"Do I need to ask what happened?"

"Crenshaw got off with a slap on the wrist, and Charles and Nelson went to prison. Maria and her children are still in Texas."

"And the state prosecutor likely the next attorney general of Illinois," said Stokes.

Moody nodded. "Better not tell Tamsey about this," he said, looking at Stokes.

"Why not?" said Stokes. "They need to know what they up against. They's a war on, Virgil. People bein' captured and killed all over the place. Fugitives arming theyselves with hatchets and clubs and pistols, more catchers than trees in the woods. Tamsey and Leason and Sarah need to know that."

"But this trial ain't about catchers or slave breeders," Moody said. "It's about whether Sarah is white or black."

"And you don't think that's about slavery?" Parker said mildly. "What do you think will happen if the jury decides Sarah's black? How long do you think it'll be before catchers show up here in Freedom, probably brought in by Pickering himself? They're taking everyone they can lay hands on. I'm not sure I know what to argue at this trial."

"You going to argue that a tree a mule."

Moody turned and saw Tamsey standing at the end of the porch, silhouetted against the green morning light, holding a coffeepot and a plate of biscuits. He hadn't heard her come up. There was a long silence.

Parker spoke first. "But what if the jury decides to call a tree a tree?"

Tamsey put the tray on the porch floor and went up to where Moody was standing. "Don't you keep nothing from me, Virgil Moody," she said gently. "This my life. Catchers come, they come for me and my children, not for you. I know you want to protect us, and I thankful for that, but you can't protect us all the time. You can't protect us if you not here, or if they twenty of them and one of you."

"Two," said Stokes. "Two of us. And Leason and Granville, that four."

Tamsey smiled. "Lawyer Parker saying the whole state against us. This state, the next state, the state after that. How can you protect us? You remember the Alamo? That us. We the Alamo of Indiana."

"Don't forget me," Parker said. "I'm in this with you, too."

Moody put his hand on Parker's shoulder. "You running for attorney general, Cliff?" he said.

Parker grimaced. "If I win this trial, I'll have to run, all right. I'll have to run for the hills."

7.

The end of September came without a trial date set. On the last day of the month, Cliff Parker once again drove his gig out to Freedom. He tied his horse to the porch rail and came into the cabin in a rush of cold air, trying to appear calm. He sat at the kitchen table, took his hat off and set it on his knee.

"The date's been set," he said to Tamsey. "October 9."

"So soon?" said Moody.

"We ready for it?" Tamsey asked.

"They want it to coincide with the Constitutional Convention, which starts on the seventh. There'll be plenty of reporters in town."

Tamsey shook her head. "Why are lawyers so bad at answering questions? We ready for it?"

"Ready as we'll ever be," said Parker.

"I take that as a no."

8.

The letter came the day before they were set to leave for Indianapolis. Cecil Fountain dropped it off on his way to Vandalia. Moody took it from him and they talked about hog feed for a while, and when Cecil left he opened the envelope. In it were two sheets of paper. The first was from Frederick Heiskell.

"Dear Friend," it began:

I hope this finds you well. The Enclosed came to us by way of the paper, from
your father's Lawyers in Savannah—they discovered your name in our pages
and have asked us to forward the sad news to you on their behalf. Very sorry to
hear of your Loss, and trust that should you again find yourself in or near
Knoxville, that you will come by to see us. Brown and I are, alas, selling the
Register in order to devote our remaining if not actually declining years more
directly to the Great Cause of Emancipation (and me to run for the state legis-
lature), but you will always find a welcome here.

Affectionately Yours, Fred (Heiskell)

He was conscious of Tamsey watching him as he read. "Sad news,"
he told her. "I don't know what it is, though." Although he did.

The second letter, dated a month before, bore the imprint of his
father's law firm in Savannah, Messieurs Harley, Chase and Steele,
informing him of his father's death on the eleventh inst., which
would have been September. Moody tried to think back to that day,
to what he was doing when his father died. Was that the day he and
Leason bought the handkerchiefs for Sarah? Or was it the day Pudge
Pickering came out to Freedom looking for them? The letter went
on to say that, since both his brothers and his mother were also
deceased, the ownership of Plantagenet, the house in Savannah
"and of their goods and chattels," had passed to him.

Chattels. Cattle. He was a slave owner again.

"I'll have to go to Savannah to settle this," he said to Tamsey.

"What about the trial?"

"No, I'll wait until that's over."

"What you do then?"

"Sell the land and free the slaves, I guess."

"Free the slaves," she said, a note of doubt in her voice.

"What do you think?"

"I thinking these days freedom by itself ain't much of a gift.
Leason and Sarah free. You be sending two hundred fugitives up
here where they ain't wanted."

"What would you have me do?"

"Ask them what they want."

"You mean, as I should have done with Annie?"

"Not just Annie," she said.

He wrote to Messieurs Harley, Chase and Steele thanking them for their condolences, although there hadn't been any, saying he would come to Savannah to settle the matter of his father's estate later in the month. Meanwhile, he instructed the lawyers to remove Casgrain as overseer of the plantation, and to assume the running of it themselves until Moody was able to come to Savannah. He sealed the envelope with a grim but satisfied smile, thinking of how this information would be received on Plantagenet. But the thought of Casgrain running the plantation with a free hand was repellent. Even his father had had more humanity in him than that.

9.

Cecil Fountain was to come with them to Indianapolis on the *Pelican*, along with Stokes. He should have arrived the afternoon before their departure, so they could get an early start the next morning. When he hadn't shown up by suppertime, Tamsey urged Moody to go to the farm to see if he was coming.

"I got a bad feeling," she said.

"What do you think has happened?" Moody asked her. She often had bad feelings about things, and she was often right. She still looked for catchers before stepping out of the cabin. Since Zachary Taylor's death in July and Millard Fillmore's assumption of the presidency, things had become even worse for fugitives in the North. Fillmore was pro-slavery and had signed the Compromise bill in September, and even more catchers than usual had flocked into Indiana now that the Fugitive Slave Act had been passed. They walked openly down the streets of Indianapolis and even lounged in

Spencer, and entire troupes of them camped in the woods throughout the state. No one was safe. An entire family, husband, wife and
three children, living near Vandalia, had disappeared only a week
before, and a woman and her child walking home from church, also
near Vandalia, had been saved only when other members of the con-
gregation rode up in a buggy and beat the catchers off. People were
starting to carry guns and avoid traveling alone. Cecil Fountain lived
alone, and his farm was isolated enough.

"Just go," she said. "Look hard."

Moody had been to the farm before, but it always surprised him
to round the bend in the road and come upon cleared land popu-
lated by hundreds of large, white, big-throated birds, some perched
in trees, others settled on fallen logs or walking about like turkeys in
the wire-netted cage Cecil had built at the end of the swamp. The
cage was big enough to house a circus, and the birds flew freely
inside it—otherwise, Cecil had said, they lost their feathers and were
useless to him. Odd, Moody thought, that Cecil made his living
from the very things that would carry his living away from him.
There was a large log barn beside the compound, and Cecil's cabin
set farther into the trees, slightly away from the swamp. Between
the barn and the cabin were two or three smaller outbuildings:
a toolshed, a windowless shack in which he plucked his birds, and
another in which he dried and ground the pelican meat to make
Buzz Crawford's pig feed. Moody checked the barn first. Cecil's
wagon was there, and his two horses, a black and a roan, no hay or
oats in their feed boxes. Moody fed and watered the horses and
opened the door to the corral before walking up to the house.

"Cecil," he called from the porch. "Cecil, it's me, Virgil."

There was a quality to the silence answering his call that told
him the house was empty. He tied his horse to a post, removed the
rifle from its scabbard and approached the cabin slowly. Inside,
there were signs of a struggle, chairs overturned, crockery on the
floor, a water bucket on the counter tipped over and the boards

around the dipper still wet. It was the kind of disorder he and Tamsey had expected to see at New Harmony and not found. Moody had seen it before, in Mexico during the fighting, when whole villages had been emptied for some strategic reason or other. Cecil didn't have much in the way of possessions, but what he did have had been messed with.

Moody went back outside and listened. Pelicans didn't make much noise. This late in the season there were no mosquitoes, although he remembered from previous visits that the swamp was so alive with the insects in the summer that they sometimes killed pelicans, sucked the blood right out of them as they sat on their nests. "Pre-dried 'em for me," Cecil would say. Moody's horse snorted. A crow replied three times, then flew over the clearing, and Moody followed its shadow to one of the sheds. The door was barred from the inside and there were no windows. Someone had taken an ax to the door from the outside, though without success, the bright-yellow splinters in the dark wood almost but not quite deep enough to break through to the bar, as though whoever had yielded the ax had given up just before achieving his goal. The ax was lying in the dirt. Moody picked it up and finished the job.

At first he thought what he was smelling was rotting pelican meat, for this was the shed in which Cecil made his hog feed. But when his eyes became accustomed to the darkness, only slightly lessened by the open door, he saw Cecil lying facedown on the dirt floor, a pistol in his right hand and the right side of his skull rearranged. Three days, he reckoned; it must have happened the night he brought them the letter from the Savannah lawyers. Had the catchers been waiting for him, had he surprised them going through his cabin, drinking his whiskey, taking target practice at his birds?

He remembered a makeshift graveyard in the woods not far from the farm, where a number of men from a road-making crew had died of swamp fever a few years before. He hitched the horses

to Cecil's buckboard, carried Cecil out to it, threw in a shovel from
the toolshed and tied his own horse to the tailgate. Before climbing up to the wagon seat, he went over to the large gate that
formed one side of the pelican compound and opened it. A few
birds waddled speculatively out, then a few more. Soon the whole
flock had seen the open gate and come racing toward it, on the
ground and in the air. Moody watched as dozens and then hundreds of enormous white birds, realizing their freedom, took to
the air, barely missing his head, the thunderous tumult of their
wings filling his ears and their exuberant tempest almost blowing
his hat off. The birds circled above the farm for several minutes,
getting their bearings, then headed south, toward their wintering
grounds in Mexico.

With a sense of grim satisfaction, Moody watched them go,
then returned to the corpse in the wagon.

10.

They tied up in Indianapolis on October 7, two days before the
trial. They managed to secure a room for Leason and Sarah in a
boardinghouse in the negro district. The rest stayed on the *Pelican*.
Stokes would join them before the trial. To offset the gloom of
Cecil's death and their anxiety over the upcoming trial, Moody
wanted to make the next two days as much a holiday as possible, as
though they were spending a pleasant time in the capital before
returning to their normal lives, all six of them, in Freedom.

"You think we staying in Indiana after this?" Tamsey said.

He hadn't thought that far ahead, but yes, that's what he would
have said. Tamsey's question made him realize that he'd been naive.
From the day Leason and Sarah were arrested, though, Tamsey had
known there was no winning this trial. Whatever its outcome, they
could never again feel safe in Indiana.

He took Granville across the common to the Masonic Temple, where the Constitutional Convention was getting under way. "He'll see democracy at work," he said to Tamsey, who replied, "He already seen that." They sat in the visitors' gallery and listened to a discussion about whether the state or the county should be responsible for road maintenance. A few reporters lounged in the gallery, looking bored. One of them jokingly asked Granville what he thought about the debate. Granville told him that whoever built the road should also be responsible for repairs to it, that way the road maker would do a good job in the first place. The reporter said he'd heard more sense from Granville in two minutes than he had from the delegates all day.

"Emmet Burke, the *Sentinel*," he said, holding out his hand.

"Glad to meet you, Mr. Burke," Moody said, shaking it.

"I'm not covering the convention anyway," Burke said. "I'm here to report on the trial that starts in a couple of days, across the street."

"Oh?" said Moody. "What trial is that?"

"You ain't heard?" asked the reporter. "*Indiana v. Lewis and Franklin?* Charge of fornication." He looked at Granville and apparently decided he was old enough to understand the word. "It's going to be a big one. State's attorney arguing the case, and a Supreme Court judge is hearing it."

"Fornication," said Moody. "Ain't that just a misdemeanor?"

"I covered the *Crenshaw* case in Chicago, you heard of that one, I guess. This is going to be bigger than that. It ain't about who's messing with each other, it's about keeping all them goddamn fugitives out of the state so they don't mess with *us*. Begging your pardon, son," he said to Granville.

"What are you going to write about it?" Granville asked.

"Depends how it turns out," the reporter said, and left to rejoin his colleagues.

Granville looked up at Moody. "You still writing to that Kentucky newspaper?" he asked, and Moody nodded. "You going to write about the trial?" Moody nodded again. "Whatever way it turns out?" And again, Moody nodded.

When Tamsey and Sabetha returned to the *Pelican*, Moody took Sabetha to Black's Bookshop and bought her two books, a novel called *Wuthering Heights*, by Ellis Bell, and a book of poems by the Quaker poet he remembered reading at Rachel's, John Greenleaf Whittier. He thought Whittier's antislavery poems would lift everyone's spirits, but they only reminded them of the horrors of slavery, and of the short distance they had traveled from them. " 'Gone, gone—sold and gone,' " Sabetha read aloud. " 'To the rice-swamp dank and lone, / From Virginia's hills and waters; / Woe is me, my stolen daughters.' "

"Least we was wanted in Virginia," Tamsey said.

It seemed there was no escaping the worry. When the children went to bed in the tent Moody had set up on the deck behind the *Pelican*'s cabin, Moody and Tamsey sat on the parlor deck drinking tea. It was a cool night, the stars crisp and sparkling above the quiet city. The captured canal water lapped incessantly against the *Pelican*'s flanks. Tamsey cupped her hands around her teacup for warmth and gazed in the direction of the Masonic Temple, the impermeable roof of which they could just see above the tops of shops and houses. Moody asked her about the boardinghouse she'd found for Leason and Sarah.

"A nice place on Indiana Avenue," she said. "Sarah ain't pleased it in the negro district, but that the only place they could both stay."

"What about Leason's suit?" he said. "Did you get him one at Kästchen's?"

"Black wool," she said. "He look good in it. Like he going to a funeral. Got a silk dress for Sarah."

"Anything for yourself?"

"No, it don't matter how I look."

"You always look good. I don't tell you that often enough, do I?"

"You never told me that at all."

"It's true."

"We old, Muddy," she said. "We too old fools together. That could be us they stringin' up after the trial."

"No one's going to be strung up."

"Or sold."

"Or sold. How was Kästchen?" This was the first time Tamsey had met him.

"Friendly," she said.

"He offer to send you all north?"

"No, none of that."

"See? He knows you ain't runaways, that's why."

"Not tonight we ain't," she said. "Who knows what we all be after the trial."

She squeezed his hand and they went into the cabin. Tamsey slept, but Moody lay awake with a geology book for a while, reading about the steady, relentless reduction of everything to dust.

II.

The next morning, Parker met with Moody, Tamsey, Leason and Sarah in the state legislature building, in a small chamber in the back, down a long, dark corridor lined with photographs of the state's past governors, where the clerks normally took tea but was empty now because everything council related had moved next door to the Masonic Temple, even though it wasn't raining. Parker had lit a coal fire under the kettle, and gave them tea when they got there, and told them the trial was set to start at ten o'clock the next morning, which they already knew. He told Tamsey she and Moody should be there early to get a good seat.

"You're expecting a crowd, then," said Moody, thinking of the reporter he'd spoken to the day before.

"Democracy and justice on trial," he said, "doesn't happen every day."

"I wouldn't say that," said Tamsey. "I would say democracy and justice on trial every day slavery exist. Every time a slave run away and a catcher take him, democracy and justice shrink a little. Least as I understand them words."

Parker gave her a sympathetic look, then told Sarah and Leason to meet him in this chamber a half hour before the others.

"I've talked to Fritts, the state's attorney general," he said. "He's firmly against my calling Tamsey up as a witness. Which means he thinks it will hurt his case. It'll be up to the judge, ultimately. What do you think about it, Tamsey?"

"If it hurt their case," she said, "I'll do it."

"It won't be easy."

"When has it ever been?" She didn't look at Moody when she said it, but he knew that being with him wasn't easy.

They were up the next morning before everyone else, before the sun, which was lingering below the horizon. Tamsey busied herself making food to take for their lunch. He'd bought a chicken and some potatoes at the market on their way back from the meeting with Parker, and she cooked them and made biscuits. When nine o'clock drew near and Leason and Sarah weren't there, she let her mind fly off in a dozen directions at once. "They been caught," she told Moody. "They gone off on Kästchen's Railroad." It was probably only Leason who skedaddled, she said. Sarah wouldn't have gone with him, pregnant as she was, she'd stay in Indianapolis or maybe go to Philadelphia and raise her child white. "I hate thinking that, but the worse the thought, the truer it likely to be." Stokes had told her about the couple who were tarred and feathered and cut up, she said, and she knew there would be some at the trial who'd done the tarring and the feathering and were hoping for another chance to have some fun.

"I don't know what happen if we win, and I don't know what happen if we lose," she said.

"I know," said Moody. "I worry that Parker will do his job and

Sarah and Leason will win this case, but I don't know what winning means. Proving Sarah's black?"

"Like I said," Tamsey said, "whatever happen, we have to leave Indiana."

After retreating to the cabin, Moody laid out the suit of clothes that Henry had procured for him on the *Mary White*. The clothes that had made him look like his father. They weren't as white as they once were, he hadn't worn them since that day, had even forgotten he still had them, but now that he had inherited his father's estate, had literally *become* his father, wearing them seemed appropriate. Maybe it was time to admit to himself what he was. A white man in a world that was increasingly determined by the consequences of slavery. It was time for him to stop acting surprised and indignant whenever anyone suggested to him that the reason he hadn't freed Annie or Lucas was that he had liked it that their relationship was based on ownership, that that was the way he'd been raised, and, hate it though he professed he did, it was the relationship he understood and felt most comfortable with. It had taken Tamsey, whom he in no sense owned, and who made him feel damn uncomfortable all the time, to make him realize that. He could no longer pretend that these plantation-owner's clothes were a disguise; they were his sackcloth and ashes, from his straw hat down to his gray, buttoned spats.

He put them on. Before leaving the cabin, he saw Leason's black hat, the one he'd brought with him from New Harmony. The one Granville told him Lucas had made. He put it on his head. It fit perfectly. Outside, on the parlor deck, Tamsey had the lunch packed in two bailing buckets, Sabetha was clearing the table and Granville was pacing impatiently back and forth along the dock.

"Leason and Sarah here yet?" he asked, just as Leason and Sarah themselves came strolling down the canal path as casually as two aristocrats out for a stroll to look at boats they might buy. Leason looked uncomfortable in his new suit, while Sarah's silk dress made her look like she was going to church. A white church. Moody remembered Parker saying he hoped Sarah wouldn't look too white at the trial, but her dark-blue dress made her skin look whiter than Jersey cream, and under her lace bonnet her hair was piled and pulled to the back of her head in the latest fashion.

"You're wearing my hat," Leason said to Moody.

"Do you mind?"

"Nope. Doesn't go with my new suit."

Walking to the courthouse next to Tamsey, Moody wanted to take her hand, but of course that was impossible. They let Leason and Sarah go on ahead, then hung back behind the rest as though they were going somewhere else and just happened to be on the same path.

12.

By the time they entered the courtroom, it was so full there were no seats near the front. He didn't think Tamsey would like the weight of people's eyes on her anyhow, and she would prefer to sit at the back. He found four seats together, and ushered Granville and Sabetha in first and sat beside Tamsey. Gawkers continued to file in. It was a big room: Indianapolis must have had a lot of Masons, and they all wanted in on this trial. Tamsey asked him quietly if he thought they all had buckets of tar and bags of feathers waiting outside, if maybe they'd acquired a taste for cutting and were looking to do some more of it. He said no, he didn't think so, but there were some hard, clean-shaven faces around them. Etta Pickering was up at the front looking like the judge, jury and avenging angel all in one. But there were some friendly faces, as well. Stokes was there, and Moody nodded to him. Suddenly Tamsey poked him in the ribs and pointed to a tall black man wearing a long coat and a white shirt, a black felt hat resting on his lap. "That Brother Joshua," she said. "What he doing here?"

"Somebody else survived New Harmony," he said, which meant Lucas and Benah might have gotten away, too.

Granville started to get up to go over to him, but Tamsey held his sleeve. "There be time for rejoicing later."

The bailiff came in and said, "All rise," and everyone stood up, and the judge came in through a rear door when they sat down again. His name was Otis Amery. Parker had told them yesterday that he was a good man, honest and smart, which he said was a rare combination. He was a small, round man with a large, nearly bald head and full side-whiskers. He was reasonably assured of being elected to the Supreme Court, Parker had said, and so probably wouldn't see this trial as a publicity stunt. The judge swept into the courtroom almost at a trot and sat down at a table at the front of the room as though waiting for his supper. Leason and Sarah were already sitting at another table, facing the judge, one on each side of Parker. All Moody could see was their backs and Sarah's wavy black hair, Leason's tight curls and Parker's shiny-shouldered black coat. The latter was reading his opening remarks as if he'd never seen them before. The prosecuting attorney, Samuel Fritts, the man with ambitions to be elected state attorney general, sat at another table and gazed over the courtroom like a farmer over his crop. He looked tall even sitting down, and smiled at Judge Amery like they were old friends. He seemed to be saying, *Let's see if we can't get this trial done before lunchtime.*

13.

"Bailiff," said Judge Amery, "will you read out the charge against the defendants?"

"I will, Your Honor. 'The Grand Jurors for the State of Indiana, upon their oath, present that Leason Lewis and Sarah Franklin, on the first day of April eighteen hundred and fifty in Franklin

Township in the County of Owen in the State of Indiana, and from that time to the time of finding this indictment, the said Leason Lewis being then and there a single and unmarried man, and the said Sarah Franklin being then and there a single and unmarried woman, did there and then and during all the time aforesaid unlawfully cohabit in open and notorious fornication, contrary to the form of the Statute in such cases made and provided and against the peace and dignity of the State of Indiana.' "

Amery looked at Parker. "Do the defendants understand the charges against them?" he asked.

"They do, Your Honor."

"How do they plead?"

"Not guilty."

"Both of 'em?"

Parker looked surprised. "How could just one of them be guilty of fornication?" he asked.

Careful, Cliff, thought Moody, as a ripple of laughter circulated in the room.

"Very well," said the judge, "let's get on with it. Mr. Fritts, what is the basis for the charge against the defendants?"

Fritts stood up. He was wearing a hundred-dollar suit with a vest that nicely showed off his gold watch chain, which gleamed as it looped from one side of his abdomen to the other and, unlike Moody's, undoubtedly had a gold watch attached to the end of it. His white shirtfront was starched and his cravat carefully tied, Moody suspected not by him. Did he have a body servant? He looked the kind of man a planter would have over for dinner, whereas Parker looked rumpled and worried, like someone a horse trader might call in to arrange the sale of some yearlings. There was mud on his boots and it looked as though he'd forgotten to shave, and to brush his hair.

"Your Honor," said Fritts, "this may appear, at first glance, to be a simple case of fornication, and little more than a joke to my esteemed colleague, Mr. Parker." He bowed in Parker's direction. "But in fact, Your Honor, Sarah Franklin has been charged with one of the most heinous crimes known to civilized society. I refer, of course, to the crime of having sexual congress with brutes."

There was a murmur in the courtroom—no one seemed to have appreciated the precise nature of the charge as expressed by Fritts. Moody knew that this many people hadn't shown up to witness a simple case of two people living together without being married. They knew that more was going on. Parker was prepared to defend Leason and Sarah against the charge of miscegenation. But what was this about brutes? Moody wanted more than ever to take Tamsey's hand, but refrained.

Fritts turned and raised a restraining hand to his audience.

"Let the ladies in the courtroom stop their ears if they will, and if there be children present let them leave the room. For this courtroom is no place for the faint of heart, nor for those lacking in moral courage. This is not, in the ordinary sense, a crime against the person since, under the law as it now stands, at least one of the defendants is not a person. Nor is it a simple crime against property. Nothing has been stolen, no one has been robbed or murdered. But this woman has most certainly committed an offense against humanity. Do not be misled, Your Honor, by the deceptive neutrality of the terms of the charge, that these two have been unlawfully cohabiting in open and flagrant fornication. That law was never formulated to describe the very contemptible act this woman has willfully committed. How could it have been? How could any decent-minded legislator have anticipated such a circumstance as this? Laws can only be drawn for things we can imagine might happen. If any two white persons, male and female, were discovered in cohabitation without benefit of clergy and outside the bonds of holy matrimony, they would be charged with exactly the same offense, and their sins, though egregious enough, would be answered with a fine and six months' imprisonment, followed by a march to the nearest church. It would occasion a celebration. Law and order would be restored. In similar manner, two negroes living together in such an ungodly and unsanctified manner were so common a thing as to hardly warrant our attention, it would be almost amusing to us, like watching two children playing at house in imitation of their betters, or mongrel dogs coming together in a state of wild and natural innocence. They would be charged, make no mistake, but only to be gently corrected. But a white woman openly consorting with a negro man! No, Your Honor, no church, no law, no society can sanction such an act, for it is by its very nature unnatural, uncivilized, unholy, unthinkable—and unpardonable. And it is the duty of this court to punish what public morality cannot pardon."

Moody looked at Leason, who had turned to Parker. This was worse than anything they had prepared for. Moody was used to seeing slaves being treated like animals, but he'd never before heard them publicly charged with actually *being* animals. Then he remembered how his father referred to his slaves as so many "head," as though they were cattle. Beasts of burden.

"And not only morality, Your Honor," Fritts continued. "Science, too, warns us against the dangers inherent in the mixing of the black and white races. Indeed, most modern scientists agree that when we speak of the black race and the white race, we are in fact speaking about two separate and distinct species of beings, two separate acts of Creation, as different the one from the other as any two species of animals can be, as different, let us say, as is the donkey from the Arabian, or the hyena from the greyhound. Archeology and geology have determined that this separation of the species has persisted since Egyptian times. Negroes and Caucasians could not possibly have descended from the same parents. Negroes, it is now well known, are not descended from Adam and Eve, but are the products of an earlier, and inferior, Creation."

Fritts paused and walked to his table, where he took a drink of water, then picked up a sheet of printed paper and read from it:

"According to Edward Long's *History of Jamaica*, published in 1774, and I quote, 'blacks are lower than the animals; in their natural state, they live in ignorance, idleness and depravity.' He adds that 'there is no other conclusion to be drawn but that the Negro belongs to a different species than our own.'

"A different species, Your Honor. In what ways do they differ from us, apart from the obvious distinction of color, which is as the cockerel differs from the crow? The anthropologist Charles White, in his *Account of the Regular Gradation in Man*, finds, after careful measurement of hundreds of human and humanlike skulls from around the world, that the negro skull has a narrower frontal lobe and is smaller in volume than the skulls of Europeans and even of Indians. Indians, whom we have eradicated from our midst, have bigger brains than negroes. The author also found that whereas whites perspire freely in hot climates, negroes do not. Neither do dogs. Or monkeys. Black women are less troubled by menstruation than are white women, he adds, and again my apologies to the ladies present, and black women give birth without pain, 'like animals,' he writes."

Moody felt Tamsey's shoulder trembling and leaned closer. "Fritts is only doing his lawyerly duty," he whispered to her. "He's just speechifying."

"Is that what you think?" she asked. "That I a kind of animal, that I feel nothing when you touch me? All this time?"

"Don't," he said. "Of course I don't."

"Then what?"

But Fritts had started again, and they turned to face the onslaught head-on.

"No less a personage than the great Swiss scientist Louis Agassiz, one of the foremost authorities in America on the subject of the origins and races of mankind, believes that the black race was created by God separately from the Caucasian race, that it was, as it were, a kind of rehearsal for the real thing. Mr. Agassiz said in a speech delivered just two years ago, in Charleston, Virginia, that, and I quote: 'Viewed zoologically' —that is, Your Honor, viewed from the point of view of the science of—"

"I am familiar with several words of more than one syllable, Mr. Fritts," said Judge Amery dryly, "and 'zoologically' is one of them. *Tendentiousness* is another. Pray get on with it and try to remember that there is no jury present."

"Yes, Your Honor," Fritts said. " 'Viewed zoologically,' writes Mr. Agassiz, 'the several races of man are well marked and distinct,' and he goes on to say that it is wrong to regard Caucasians and negroes as belonging to a single species. He lists more differences between them, psychological as well as physiological, than there can be between members of a single species. He says, for example, that negroes are more submissive, obsequious and imitative by nature, and that it is 'mock philanthropy' to assert that they are equal to whites in any regard whatsoever. 'Imitative by nature,' mark that, Your Honor, as it is germane to my case. His talk was later reprinted in the *Christian Examiner*, Your Honor can read it for himself. In other words, the mixing together of the white and the black races is not only offensive unto heaven, not only destructive of the order of things as ordained by God, but also damaging to the divinely created race of human whites. If we allow a black to breed with a white, you might get a slightly more intelligent black, but you're just as likely to get a defective white."

Moody saw Sarah's hand go involuntarily to her belly.

"No, Your Honor, the crime that this woman has committed must not be taken lightly. She has sinned against God and Creation, a sin no less severe in its potential consequences than that committed by her oldest ancestor, Eve, when she bit into that forbidden apple and had us all cast from the Garden of Eden. A sin against the laws of Moses as well as against the laws of nature, not to mention the laws of Indiana. Will we allow consorting with brutes, and be cast out of Paradise a second time?

"We need not go into the question of whether this couple were joined in lawful matrimony by a recognized minister of the cloth, as I have no doubt my esteemed colleague Mr. Parker intends to do. He'll simply be a-wasting of the court's time, because by the statutes of the state of Indiana no such marriage can lawfully be contracted, and so it don't matter if they were married by the pope himself, the state couldn't recognize it. Shouldn't recognize it. Must not recognize it."

Why wasn't Parker saying anything? Why was he just sitting in his chair like he'd fallen asleep during a preacher's sermon? Moody felt like throwing something at him to wake him up.

"As for the accused man," Fritts continued, nodding at Leason, "I'm tempted, Your Honor, I'm sorely tempted to incline toward leniency. After all, it's probably true that when he first took up with Sarah Franklin, I won't say married her, but when he first took up with her, he believed her to be of the same species as himself. And by the time the truth of the matter became known, there were property issues to consider, and now there is this poor child on the way, and it is entirely understandable that for them the easiest, the least inconvenient, course of action was to take no action at all, as is the usual thing with nigg—that is, with members of the dusky race. So I'm tempted to say, let her feel the full measure of the law for the gravity of the sin she has knowingly committed, but let us show this boy the understanding and forbearance that the apostle Paul showed to the runaway slave Onesimus—you will recall, Your Honor, that after converting Onesimus to Christianity he sent him back to Philemon, his rightful master. We in the state of Indiana are doing the same to thousands of runaway slaves, sending them back to their rightful masters; we have always done our Christian duty toward their kind, and have set an example for others to follow throughout the world. In fact, the very crime for which this boy appears before us today can be seen as the unfortunate consequence of what Mr. Agassiz has identified as the negro's 'imitative nature,' as I mentioned earlier, as well as of our own benevolent attitude toward his species for the past two hundred and some years. For was it not ourselves who taught 'em to form monogamous pair bonds, to cover themselves with decent clothes, to work hard to improve their lot, to want to live in houses and raise children to be better off than themselves?

"That, Your Honor, is my tendency to view the matter. But I am a sentimental man. I am not a judge but an advocate. I fully appreciate that Your Honor may feel duty bound to take both a shorter and a longer view than mine. As my learned colleague here has rightly said, how can only one of them be guilty of the crime of fornication? Your Honor may feel obliged to consider that this man has, knowingly and willingly, as we shall endeavor to prove beyond a shadow of a doubt, broken the laws of this state, nay, of this nation, flouted them openly and publicly, taken our trust and our tolerance and our encouragement and done what with them? Used them to defile our women! Become the viper in the garden, the very personification of the Devil incarnate. Creep like the foul black worm into the pure white flesh of our apple. Your Honor may feel inclined to punish that, and to make of this case an example to the rest of his species already in this state, and especially to those outside of it who may be contemplating coming into it, and there are many thousands of them camped at this very moment at our gates. The court may wish to make it known that in this state we do not take lightly to such abuses of our kindness. Your Honor may feel it necessary to take an even longer view, and consider what Indiana may be like fifty, a hundred, a hundred and fifty years down the line, if every runaway slave and derelict freebooter from Kentucky to South Carolina knew that they could come into this state and flout our laws, make free with our women, impregnate our daughters, sully the purity of the white race, and receive nothing for their hideous actions but a slap on the wrist and an admonition to go and henceforth be good boys, which is what I, a foolish, sentimental old man, would be inclined to recommend. We have an obligation to our future selves. I have no doubt that Mr. Parker, too, will allow his sentimentality to get the better of his rational thinking, and speak to this court about tempering justice with mercy, and leavening the good, honest bread of common sense with the yeast of compassion. Your Honor may feel, and would be right to feel, and will long be remembered for feeling, that yours is the greater responsibility to the future peace and dignity of this state, to the future peace and dignity of this country, to the future peace and dignity of the human race, to take a sterner view of the matter."

Fritts sat down and the room was so silent that Moody thought for a moment the trial was over, that they may as well get up and start putting their lives back together somehow. He heard a few grumbles from the cigar smokers standing behind them, but he didn't look around. Judge Amery cleared his throat and took his pocket watch out of his waistcoat and looked at it.

"Thank you, Mr. Fritts. A fine peroration, and one that has taken us perilously close to the lunch hour. Mr. Parker, if you have no objection, I will declare a recess of one hour."

"No objection, Your Honor."

"Then this court will reconvene at one o'clock."

14.

The last thing they felt like doing was to sit down and eat as if Lawyer Fritts had just told them a story about Brer Rabbit and Tar Baby. Judge Amery hurried out of the courtroom as though he just remembered he'd left his dinner on the stove, but Moody and Tamsey remained in their seats as everyone around them began to talk and file out without looking at them. They sat there alone for a while longer.

"I guess I always knew what white people thought," Tamsey

said. "I just never knew they worked out a good reason for it. They think we have our babies without pain? Didn't my babies come out of me with pain like a bullwhip, all of them? Lashes of pain. And not just where the baby come out, but all over my body. My eyeballs hurt. My back ache. I couldn't use my legs, I near drop Leason when the midwife put him on my chest, I had to hold him with my wrists, couldn't hardly put my breast to his mouth for the pain in my hands. It was sweet pain, dear pain, but it was pain. 'In sorrow thou shalt bring forth children'—does that mean only white women? Does Mr. Fritts think we feel no pain when we are hit with bats, or when we whipped, or shot in places that would not kill us? I have sat with men who been flayed so bad they ribs show through they meat, they groan with pain all night and then go back into the field in the morning so they won't be whipped again."

"Not everyone thinks like that," Moody said.

"Not everyone has to."

"Fritts is a Southerner."

She looked at him. "*You* a Southerner. What do you think?"

"Not that," he said. "I think you're the finest human I ever met."

She sagged a little at that, and almost leaned into him. Then she took a breath. "Get us out of here, Muddy. Get us out of Indiana."

"I will," he said. "Just not yet."

Granville and Sabetha were waiting at the door. Tamsey stood and Moody rose with her. He picked up the lunch pails and took them outside, where he was surprised that the sun was still shining and a light breeze rattled the yellowing leaves on the oaks around the courthouse. The smell of cold vegetation filled his nostrils, but it was a coldness not of death but of preservation. Stokes came over to them, looking like he wanted to say something. Then Cliff Parker, and Brother Joshua with him. Tamsey put her arms around Brother Joshua and began to weep onto his shoulder. He patted her on the back.

"Courage, Sister," he said. "This ain't over."

"Feel like it is," she said. "How can we answer that?" She pushed him gently away and looked up into his eyes. Moody thought he looked like a preacher. Granville shook his hand and Brother Joshua said to him, "Look at you, all growed up. And Sister Sabetha, you still reading everything you get your hands on?"

"This here is Virgil Moody," Tamsey said. "He saved us when we ran from New Harmony. We went back there shortly after the raid, but nobody there. What happen?"

"All the brothers and sisters who weren't took left after the raid," Brother Joshua said. "Twenty-two years, gone like that." He snapped his fingers. "Some took the government ticket to Liberia, some took the Underground Railroad up to Cass County, Michigan, which should be just about as black as Liberia by now, and some gone all the way up into Canada, where slavery been abolished seventeen years and catchers ain't allowed to go, although I hear they do. Not like here, though. I went to Cincinnati with some others, started up a church there, helped a few north. I don't know, time just went by, like it does."

"What happen to James?" Tamsey asked.

"You don't know?"

"Not for sure."

"He killed, Sister Tamsey," Brother Joshua said. "I'm sorry to tell you that, I thought you knew. We found him in the cornfield in the morning."

Tamsey sagged against Moody's arm, and he didn't move. If Brother Joshua saw, he didn't say anything. "He lay in the cornfield all night?"

"Most of us hid in the woods until the catchers left. We buried him in the cemetery along with some mighty good people. Catchers only got about fifty of us."

"Thank you, Brother Joshua."

Moody said, "What about Lucas and Benah? Do you know what happened to them?"

"Lucas and Benah from the North Star?" Brother Joshua shook his head. "Like I said, everybody went off to different places. My guess is, they got away and went to Canada. The fightin' at the Morning Star give 'em time to make the woods."

"Why Canada?"

"That where they were headed when they come to New Harmony, so I figure that where they continue to when they left."

"You don't hear from anyone?"

"I do, from time to time. But I ain't heard from them."

"You have trouble in Cincinnati?" asked Tamsey.

"Trouble everywhere, Sister," he said. "Not like here, though. That convention across the street," he said, looking toward the Masonic Temple, "they makin' every bad thing legal so they can keep doin' it. Ain't that abuse of power?" he asked, looking at Parker.

"Like you say," replied the lawyer, "there's trouble everywhere."

Brother Joshua turned back to Tamsey. "You ain't staying on after this, is you?"

"No, Muddy here taking us to Canada." She looked at him and he nodded.

"Canada the new Promised Land," Brother Joshua said, "they call it the new Canaan because it the land of milk and honey. They got laws there against slavery, that the milk, and none against mixed marriage, that the honey." This time he did look at Moody, and smiled. "Whites and blacks consort freely together," he said, "all according to God's law."

"God's law?" asked Parker.

"Moses married a black woman," Brother Joshua said. "His wife, Zipporah, was Ethiopian, and when Moses's sister, Miriam, spoke against the marriage, God himself come down from heaven in a pillar of smoke and stood in the tabernacle and told Miriam his servant Moses was faithful in all his house, and he would speak to Moses mouth to mouth, not in dark speeches like that Lawyer Fritts, and he ask Miriam was she not afraid to speak against his servant Moses? And the anger of the Lord was kindled against her, and the smoke depart from the tabernacle, and behold Miriam became leprous, turned white as snow. Served her right, too, no offense."

"She turned white?"

"That the leprosy," Brother Joshua said. "You maybe heard of Henry Moss, a slave from Virginia? Happen to him, too."

"What, he got leprosy?"

"Well, no. He just turned white, nobody knows why. He still the same afterward as he was before."

"I might call you as a witness, Brother Joshua," Parker said. "But right now I've got to go look a few things up. See you back in court."

"You do that," Brother Joshua called after him. "We can make this trial a crusade, sweep away these unholy laws that are anathema unto the Lord."

"You'll stay and eat with us, Brother Joshua?" Moody asked, and they sat beneath the skeleton of a bare tree and pretended they were having a Sunday picnic, Tamsey and Brother Joshua, Sabetha and Granville and Stokes. Except it was a Monday and the chicken tasted like dried pelican in their mouths.

15.

When they were back in the courtroom, there was an even greater crush of people than there had been before the break. They saw Solomon Kästchen sitting near the front, beside two women wearing Quaker bonnets. Had he come in case the trial went badly? Ready to send Leason north before the mob got to him? Moody didn't know whether Kästchen's presence was a comfort or a worry to Tamsey. She was inclined to worry.

Parker came in looking like he'd been run over by a post coach. His clothes were rumpled and his hair stuck up at odd angles.

Moody watched him take his place at the table between Leason and Sarah just before the bailiff said, "All rise." He looked like a small-town lawyer who'd found himself caught up in a big-city trial that nothing in his life had prepared him for, and that he could not win. Fritts would bamboozle him. Parker would be a popular man in Indiana if he lost this trial, but he'd be labeled a fool for having taken it on. He'd live out his days in Spencer, probating wills and filing bankruptcies. Moody watched him set a sheaf of papers in front of him that looked as though he'd scribbled them out during the recess. He liked Cliffington Parker, and forgave him already, but he wished he'd stuck it out in law school in New Orleans. He wished he himself could be defending Leason. He corrected himself: Leason and Sarah.

"Mr. Parker," Judge Amery said when he'd settled on the bench. Parker was still shuffling through his papers, looking as though he'd lost the first page. "Mr. Parker," the judge said again.

"Yes, Your Honor?"

"Are you ready to grace us with your opening remarks?"

"I am, Your Honor."

"Excellent. Pray proceed."

More shuffling and Parker put down the papers and stood up. Moody tried to read the expression on Judge Amery's face. It looked interested and disinterested at the same time, like a portrait of a face.

"Your Honor," Parker said, "Mr. Fritts here thinks it's all right to quote to us from scientific books written half a century ago, before we had railroads and telegraph poles, and scientists thought tuberculosis could be cured with tobacco smoke. But I would draw the court's attention to something written a little more recently and perhaps with more relevance. It's an interesting paradox observed by Alexis de Tocqueville some fifteen years ago, in his book *Democracy in America*. 'Race prejudice,' he wrote, 'seems stronger in those states that have abolished slavery than in those where it still exists, and nowhere is it more intolerant than in those where it was never known.'

"Everything Mr. Fritts said earlier is race prejudice, not law," Parker continued, "and certainly not science. He says he's a foolish, sentimental old man, and I am inclined to disagree with him. It's his attitude that is old, not he. And I don't know if he is sentimental, maybe he is, but there is little of sentimentality in his referring to my clients as 'animals.' However, we are not here to explore the depths of Mr. Fritts's heart, we are here to determine to what extent, if any, my clients have broken a law of the state of Indiana—which laws, as we know, are being amended at this moment at the convention taking place across the commons from this courtroom. We can assume, I think, that the stricture against fornication will remain in the new Constitution as it was in the old. So we may proceed. I am not, however, going to have the temerity to instruct Your Honor in your duty or remind Your Honor of what your responsibilities are, as my colleague has spent the morning doing."

"Thank you for that, Mr. Parker," said Judge Amery.

"What I will say, though, is that the entirety of Mr. Fritts's opening remarks were predicated upon one assumption—that one of my clients here is white and the other is black—and it is my duty to point out that we cannot make that assumption. That's why we're here, to find out whether that's the case, and I am not for one minute going to allow Mr. Fritts to proceed as if what we are here to prove has already been proved, to skip over the crime and just get on with the sentencing. To assume such a thing is to make a mockery of the whole judicial system, and I would not presume to insult this court by agreeing to go along with it."

Parker paused and looked at his notes, as though trying to think what to say next.

"Mr. Fritts mentioned compassion, Your Honor. I think that's a fine concept, compassion. For does the Bible not tell us that the Lord is filled with compassion and mercy, long suffering, and very

pitiful, and forgiveth sins, and saveth in times of affliction? I believe
it does. And does it not also say that whosoever hath this world's
goods, and seeth his brother have need, and shutteth up his bowels
of compassion from him, how dwelleth the love of God in him?
Now, I don't suppose Mr. Fritts would have us shut up the bowels
of our compassion from these two people in need, would you,
Mr. Fritts?"

Parker had the room's full attention now. Moody thought he
must have listened to Brother Joshua more carefully than had been
apparent during the break.

"Mr. Fritts also brought in the specter of science, and read to us
some of the *scientific* pronouncements so dear to those Southern
slaveholders in places like Charleston, because they suggest that
chaining up Africans and forcing them to pick our cotton and our
rice and our tobacco for us is no more a crime against humanity
than is the yoking of oxen to the plow or horses to the wagon.
Virginians talk like Frenchmen about freedom and equality because
they have known for centuries that the poor are not going to rise
up in a mob and want some of it for themselves. Mr. Fritts might
be considered a compassionate man in Charleston, but the state of
Indiana rejected slavery in its Constitution of 1816 as an abomina-
ble institution, and most of us who came here from the Southern
states, whites and blacks alike, did so because we were sick of it,
sickened by it. We didn't have a trainload of *scientists* come here
to tell us that it was all right to treat human beings like animals.
We didn't need them in Charleston, either, come to that, because
the people down in Virginia and Georgia and the Carolinas have
been treating human beings like animals for two hundred years
without the blessings of *science* to help them sleep better at night.
I guess they invented bourbon for that.

"But if we ever did bring a scientist to Indiana to advise us on
our proper attitude toward our fellow men, I would rather it not be
a bigot like Louis Agassiz, who made his reputation by studying

fish, as I recall, not human beings. Louis Agassiz, who would not eat food brought to him by a negro servant, or sleep in a bed made up for him by a negro maid, or allow a negro manservant help him on with his coat. I would rather it were someone like Johann Blumenbach, the man who founded the *science* of anthropology to which Mr. Agassiz is but an untrained and opportunistic Johnny-come-lately. Blumenbach was the first scientist to measure human skull sizes and divide all of humanity into the five distinct races we recognize today, based on the size of their heads, the texture of their hair and the color of their skin. The one thing he ever maintained, however, was that the differences he recorded among the various races of man were not differences of quality, nor degree of worth or value, but simple anatomical distinctions. To him, as a scientist, the difference between a black man and a white man is no more significant than the difference between a black horse and a white one. They might look different, but they belong to the same species, and when interbred they produce viable offspring that are also of the same species. I would ask Mr. Fritts, when a white slave breeder sires a child on one of his female slaves, does he believe he has produced a child of a different *species* from his own? Our minds are not equipped to think that he does.

"Blumenbach hated to see his science used by priests, politicians and lawyers to justify slavery. What he said was this, and I'm quoting from memory here so I beg the court's indulgence, he said: 'The assertion is made about the Ethiopians that they come nearer to apes than other men, but if so it is in the same way that the solid-hoofed variety of the domestic sow may be said to come nearer the horse than other sows.' He did not say that one sow was better than another, or that soft-footed sows should enslave solid-hoofed sows, only that the two kinds differed in the structure of their feet.

"Blumenbach also said something else that I find relevant here. He marveled at 'the good disposition of those of our black brethren,' and maintained that in their 'natural tenderness of heart, they can scarcely be considered inferior to any other race of mankind. I say that quite deliberately,' he went on, perhaps anticipating that men like Mr. Fritts here would need convincing, 'their natural tenderness of heart, which has never been benumbed or extirpated on board the transport vessels or on the sugar plantations by the brutality of their white executioners.' Mr. Blumenbach, Your Honor, was a truly compassionate man.

"But, as I said, Your Honor, we do not need to debate the justness or unjustness of slavery. The state of Indiana held that debate in 1816, and is debating it again across the street, and it decided then and will decide again this week that slavery is unjust and inhumane. We are here to decide whether Leason and Sarah have broken the law, and that's where I intend to direct our attention, not to deflect that attention into areas that are inconsequent to it. I intend to prove beyond a shadow of a doubt that they have not broken any law of the state, and I will end my opening statement at this point so as not to take up more of the court's time than necessary."

Parker sat down. There was silence in the courtroom, broken only by the creaking of a chair or the shuffle of shoe leather on the hardwood floor. Judge Amery let the silence hang in the air for a while, then cleared his throat.

"Well," he said, "now that we have heard from the Indianapolis Debating Society, perhaps we can get on with the actual trial. Mr. Fritts, are you ready to call your first witness?"

"I am, Your Honor."

"Good."

"The State calls Isaac Handy as its first witness."

Isaac Handy was a tall, bony man who'd been sitting at the front of the courtroom looking nervous, even from behind. Moody had never seen him before. His ears twitched as he made his way to the chair beside the judge's bench. When he was seated, Fritts asked him to state his name and swear to tell the truth. He cleared his throat twice before finding his voice, and then his Adam's apple

looked like he'd swallowed a bobber and there was a small fish nib-
bling at it. Fritts asked him what his occupation was.

"I'm a farmer."

"And what were you on the nineteenth of April, 1850?"

"Well, I was a farmer and a numerator."

"That would be for the census, then."

"Yes, sir."

"And did you enumerate the township of Owen County in
which the defendants reside?"

"Yes, I did. Them and others."

Lawyer Fritts passed Handy a large book opened to a page close
to the middle, and asked him to "peruse what is inscribed there-
upon." Handy glanced at him. "Read what's written on it."

"Out loud?"

"Yes, if you would be so kind."

"The whole page?"

"Just what you wrote there for the Lewis family, domiciled at
Freedom, if you please, Mr. Handy."

"You mean the one for Virgil Moody?"

"Start with that one, yes."

"Ah, let's see. 'Resident, Virgil Moody, age fifty, boatman.
Thomasina Lewis, forty-seven, housekeeper. Children, Granville,
seventeen, Sabetha, fifteen.' "

Heads turned to take in Moody and Tamsey. Handy had made
it sound as though Granville and Sabetha were Moody's children
with Tamsey. Parker didn't look up from his papers.

"And the next entry?"

"You mean for Randolph Stokes?"

"I do."

"Resident, Randolph Stokes, age seventy, farmer. Leason Lewis,
age thirty, boatman. Sarah Lewis, age twenty-nine, housekeeper."

"Let the court record show that the space for 'Color' after Leason
Lewis's name has an M in it, and that the space after Sarah Lewis's

name has been left blank. What does that *M* signify, Mr. Handy?"

"That's *M* for mulatto."

"And the blank space for Sarah Lewis?"

"Well, it means she's white."

"Blank means white?"

"We're supposed to put a *W* for white," said Handy, "but most everybody in the county's white, so if they's white we just leave it blank. We only fill it in if the person is black or mulatto."

"I see. So, to be clear, the *M* after Leason Lewis's name means he's mulatto."

"That's right."

"And his wife, Sarah, is white."

"That's what it says."

"Thank you, sir. Your witness, Mr. Parker."

Parker stood up and smiled at the witness.

"How did you determine whether to put Sarah down as a blank, Mr. Handy? Did she tell you she was white?"

"No, sir. She weren't at home. There weren't no one home at the Stokes place."

"No one home?"

"Nope. Place was empty as a church on Tuesday."

"So how did you determine what to put in those little boxes?"

"I proceeded to the next closest place down the road and numerated them, and they told me about the Lewises. That's what we was supposed to do."

There was a long pause while Parker allowed that to sink in. "Do you mean to say," he said, "that your assessment of the color of the defendants' skin was based entirely on the say-so of a neighbor?"

"That's what the law says. If a person ain't a-home, I'm to get the information from the next closest neighbor."

"So did you then go back to Virgil Moody's cabin and get the information from Virgil Moody, or from the other members of the Lewis family who were in residence there?"

"No, sir, I did not."

"Why didn't you? The Moody residence is closest to the Lewis residence. You can almost see the Moody cabin from Randolph Stokes's front porch."

"That's right, it's the closest. But the law says I go to the *next* closest, not the *last* closest, and the next closest was the Putnam farm, so that's where I went."

"But the Putnam farm is half a mile from Stokes's cabin."

"'Bout that. I didn't pace it off."

Parker sat down and stared at Handy. Judge Amery appeared to be busy looking out one of the side windows.

"Mr. Handy," Parker said at length. "Do you realize that if you had gone back to the Moody residence, as the law clearly intended you to do, we wouldn't be here in this courtroom today?"

"I done what the law intended," Handy said.

"Your Honor, I move that this case be thrown out on the grounds that the charge against my clients is based solely on hearsay evidence."

"Now, just hold your horses, Mr. Parker, if you please," said Judge Amery. "Like I said, this is a preliminary hearing for a misdemeanor. We got a whole lot of evidence to get through here, and if some of it's hearsay we can throw it out after we hear it."

"But hearsay is inadmissible, Your Honor. Once we hear it—"

"What is inadmissible, Mr. Parker, is that you go on objecting after I've made my ruling."

"Your Honor," said Mr. Fritts, rising from his chair like Satan rising to rescue St. Michael, "I am confident that my learned colleague's reservations will be answered by my next two witnesses. If we may proceed . . ."

"Are you done with this witness, Mr. Parker?"

"I guess so."

"Then let's get on with it. Mr. Fritts, if you please."

"Thank you. The State calls Mrs. Etta Pickering."

Etta Pickering was dressed like a planter's wife, as if she had a garden party to go to after the trial. Despite the fall weather, she was wearing a large, lacy dress and a pink sun hat pinned to her hair, and was carrying a fan. The hat made her appear younger, but she still looked to Moody like a chicken that had just caught sight of a worm.

"Mrs. Pickering," Fritts said when she was in the witness chair and had taken her oath, "you own the dress shop on Main Street, do you not?"

"I do. It's called Mrs. Pickering's Ladies' Finery and Emporium. We sell—"

"Yes, thank you. Did Sarah Lewis enter your shop on July 9 of this year and apply for a job there?"

"She did."

"What did she tell you on that occasion?"

"She told me she was living in Freedom with her husband but they were planning to move into Spencer, Freedom being too much of a constriction for her, she said, whatever that means. She said that when she moved into Spencer she would like to work, and so she was applying for the position of saleslady, as for which I had advertised in the window."

"What did you tell her?"

"I told her she could apply, and that I would let her know when I had made up my mind."

"And did she apply?"

"Indeed she did. She wrote her letter of application right there in the shop. I told her there were certain things I needed to know, such as her age and where she lived. And her nationality."

"And what did she put down?"

"She wrote that she was twenty-two years old, that she lived in Freedom, Indiana, and that she was white."

"But did you ask her to write down her color?"

"No, she wrote 'Nationality: United States.' "

"Not 'white'?"

"It's the same thing. You can't be American if you ain't white."

"Now, Mrs. Pickering, would you be good enough to tell us what happened after this."

"You mean when her husband came in?"

"I mean when Mr. Virgil Moody and Leason Lewis came into your shop."

"They came in to buy some silk handkerchiefs."

"When was this?"

"A week or so later, I don't recall exactly."

"Did they mention Sarah?"

"Yes, they said they were buying the handkerchiefs for Sarah Lewis. I asked Mr. Moody if he was related to Sarah Lewis, and received the shock of my life, the shock of my life, Mr. Fritts, when Mr. Moody's negro servant spoke to me without first having been spoken to, or acknowledged in any manner whatsoever, and contributed the unsought and I must say unwelcome information that the said Sarah Lewis was his wife."

"And do you see said negro servant in this courtroom today, Mrs. Pickering?"

"Of course I do. That's him sitting right there beside Mr. Parker."

"That would be Leason Lewis?"

"That's who he said he was, yes."

"Thank you, Mrs. Pickering. I believe Mr. Parker may have some questions for you."

Parker didn't bother to stand or even look up at the witness stand.

"Mrs. Pickering, if I told you I was an ourang-outang, what would you say?"

"I would say that you were either a madman or a fool."

"Oh? You wouldn't go to your husband and tell him I was an ourang-outang?"

"No, not unless you were married to a white woman."

"You wouldn't believe me?"

"No."

"And yet you believed Sarah when she implied to you that she was a white woman."

"Well, she looks white."

"Thank you. I suppose that to mean I don't look like an ourang-outang. But is it not true that you didn't hire her because you knew that she was a negress, and you only hire whites?"

"No, that isn't why I didn't hire her. I didn't hire her because she was married, and I only hire single ladies."

"Why is that?"

"Because single ladies are more reliable. They don't have husbands and children to look after, they don't come in late and leave early."

"I see. So, after determining that, in your opinion, Sarah Lewis was a white woman, and that her husband was a mulatto, and therefore, in your opinion, she could not legally be married to him, did you then offer her the position?"

Etta Pickering glared at him. "No, Mr. Parker, you may rest assured I did not."

"Why not?"

"Because after determining that she was living in sin with Mr. Lewis, I knew that she was a fornicator."

"Thank you, no further questions."

Mr. Fritts stood and called his next witness. "Mr. Henry Franklin."

Moody did not know who Henry Franklin was, but he felt Tamsey jump when his name was called. "He from a white family in Kentucky," she said to him. "They live near us when we was on the stud farm. I don't know what he doing here. They was a wild and cruel family, and Benjamin Franklin always said it too bad they had the same last name. They bred and sold slaves for profit, just like Massa Luce bred and sold horses."

This reminded Moody of the Judds, and of the poor girl they kept in a cage for breeding purposes, and he wondered if she were now safe. Alabama, Kentucky, it was tempting to think they were well out of them. Tempting, but was it a foolish thought?

Henry Franklin took the witness stand. He was large and uncouth, roughly dressed, unshaven, and his hand, when he set it on the Bible, was thick and calloused.

"Mr. Franklin," Lawyer Fritts began, "you are a farmer in Adair County, Kentucky, is that correct?"

"I am."

"And your farm neighbored onto the stud farm where James and Tamsey Lewis worked, did it not?"

"Still does. My house is about half a mile from where theirs was afore they run off from it."

Moody looked at Tamsey. "We didn't run off it," she said, "we was run off it. Sabetha Franklin died and left the farm to us, but some white lawyers from Shelbyville come out and tell us we can't own property and had to get off it. So we got off it."

"Did you know Sarah Franklin before they ran off?" Fritts asked the witness.

"Yes, I knew Sarah. She used to come over to our house saying as how her born name was Franklin, just like ours, and that she was related to us through my daddy, who used to own her mother."

"What did you take that to mean?"

"Well, what do you think? She was saying my daddy messed with her momma, and he fathered a child by her, and that child was Sarah."

"Did you believe her?"

Franklin shrugged. "Such things happened. Daddy was a hellion, for certain. He used to go all around the county trading horses, and who knows what he got up to? Whenever he saw a child he'd pat it on the head and say, 'You never know but what it might be one of mine.' I used to think he just said it to rile Momma, but I suppose some of it might'a been true. Never seen him do it with a pickninny, though."

"Did Sarah Franklin substantiate or back up her story with any additional information about your father?"

"Yes, she did. She did seem to know a lot about him. She said he used to come visit her momma and bring her things, and she described him pretty good. Said he was a tall man who always wore a white suit and a straw hat, and that was true. Took the laundry woman all day to get that suit white again after he come home from one of his buying trips. Sarah also remembered he wore a diamond ring on his little finger, and he did that. I got it right here," he said, holding up his right hand.

"Your witness, Mr. Parker," Fritts said.

Parker stood up and looked at Sarah as though he couldn't bring himself to look at Henry Franklin.

"Do you recognize Sarah Franklin as your half sister, Mr. Franklin?"

The question seemed to shock Henry Franklin. He looked over at Sarah, who met his gaze and held it.

"No," said Franklin. "I didn't know nothing about her until she come over and started making like she was one of the family."

"So you don't believe her story."

"Oh, I wouldn't say that. I suppose she could be one of Daddy's heifers. But that don't make her one of the family."

"As a matter of fact, Mr. Franklin," said Parker, "it does. What it doesn't do is make her white. No more questions, Your Honor."

Moody began to feel better about Parker. He thought their whole case was based on proving that Sarah was at least mulatto, and Henry Franklin had just confirmed that. Fritts seemed to have come to the opposite conclusion, however, because when Henry Franklin had returned to his seat he stood up and addressed the judge.

"I think we can take it as given that Sarah Lewis née Sarah Franklin is the illegitimate daughter of Sabetha Franklin and Clayborn T. Franklin, Your Honor. If this case goes to trial, I will subpoena documentation from the Franklin household in Kentucky that will attest to the fact that Sarah Franklin's father was a white man. But that only gets us halfway there, because we still have to show that Sabetha Franklin, Sarah's mother, was also at least half white, that is, that she was herself the offspring of one white parent. For in the words of Thomas Jefferson, Your Honor, 'our canon considers two crosses with pure white, and a third with any degree of mixture, however small, as clearing the issue of the negro blood.' In other words, if Sarah Franklin had a white father and a half-white mother, then Sarah Franklin is a white woman. At first I thought this would present certain difficulties, seeing that Sabetha Franklin was born more than seventy years ago, before any records were kept or censuses taken. But diligent inquiry on the part of my office has brought certain factors to light that prove without a shadow of a doubt that Sarah Lewis here, née Sarah Franklin, is the daughter of a white man and a woman who was herself half white."

"Oh, no," Tamsey said under her breath. Moody heard and leaned toward her. "No." She looked up at him, her face wide with anguish. "Sabetha Franklin *was* half white. She used to say her mam belong to a hemp family in Kentucky, but she didn't mean belong the way a slave belong, she meant her mam's family was a family of hemp planters. She say her grandmother the massa's sister who lay with a black man and had Sabetha's mam on the wrong side of the blanket, and they sold her to Benjamin's massa for a hundred dollars just to get rid of her. Sabetha talked about how she and me both gone to horse traders, like a pair of fillies."

Fritts's voice resumed and Tamsey stopped.

"I was eventually put into correspondence," Fritts said, "with a senior member of the Castingay family . . ."

Tamsey stood up suddenly, stepped past Muddy and hurried from the courtroom. Moody followed her. Once outside she let her breath go with a wail that turned heads on Indianapolis Boulevard.

"Castingay," she said to him, "that the name of Sabetha Franklin's family. This ain't going right."

The sun had left this side of the building, and the autumn air was cool in the shadow of the surrounding oaks. Moody took her elbow, chastely, and led her to a bench a short distance from the Masonic Temple.

"If they can make Sarah white," Tamsey said quietly, "what can they not do to Leason? This worse than the lash."

The bench faced across the commons to a corner from which the Anglican church, with its tall, white, cross-tipped spire, guarded the street and the graveyard behind its white picket fence. If they lynched Leason, she said, she wouldn't bury him there.

"Nobody's going to lynch Leason," Moody said.

"There a black church in Vandalia, most of the county negroes go to it. It have its own graveyard, and I might bury him there. It hidden in a tangle of whistle thorn and Virginia creeper, but I know there a road in to it because Cecil told me he drove two small coffins in there after a fire on a sharecropper's farm north of Spencer."

Moody doubted Tamsey would take comfort from a Christian burial. She would not want the kind of comfort that came from words, not after seeing what words could be made to do.

"This come from wanting," she said. "Wanting something tear you open."

"Doesn't it depend on what you want?"

"No. I want you, and that might kill me. Leason want Sarah, that going to finish him. Soon's they find out what you want, they take it away."

"No one's taking me away," he said. And when she turned to him he leaned toward her, pretending to reach for his hat, and kissed her. "And Leason's trial ain't over."

His kiss frightened her so much she drew away as if stung, and looked to see if anyone had been watching. A few white men were gathered on the portico of the Temple, but they were too far away and there was a large, spreading oak between them and their bench. She didn't look at Moody.

"In South Carolina," she said, "if there wan't a good tree handy they truss a man up and lynch him down a well. Tie the rope to the crosstree and drop him down, then watch for the crosstree to bend. They couldn't see him die but they could hear him, choking at the bottom, kicking at the sides, and when the rope stop jerking they call his wife or his mother to crank him up, because cranking nigger work."

"Tamsey," Moody said. "No one's going to lynch Leason."

"I know," she said, looking at him. "They'll take his wife away from him, and his unborn child, and they'll cut him up and put him on the road and make him run until he can't run no more. Like Lucas, Moody, just like Lucas."

"No!" Moody said, too loud. He checked his voice. "Nobody did that to Lucas but me. It was me made Lucas run. It was me killed Annie. I won't let that happen again."

She looked at him with such pity in her eyes it made him sob. "You poor man," she said, touching his cheek. "You can't stop this."

Just then, Stokes appeared at the courthouse door and called to them. "Come in here! They found Sarah white."

Moody and Tamsey sat together for a moment, then Tamsey stood and Moody followed her to the courthouse steps. He was barely able to breathe.

"Lawyer Parker didn't have nothing to say?" she asked Stokes.

"He agree with Fritts. Something's up, I don't know what it is."

"I know what it is," Tamsey said. "Sarah joined up with Lawyer Parker and Lawyer Fritts to rid herself of Leason."

"No, Tamsey," said Moody. "You can't believe that."

"Leason holding her back. Now she with child she wants quit of us. We a shame on her. She want to raise her child white, send him to a white school, get him a white job. You heard what she said."

"She's as frightened as Leason is," Moody said. "I believe she's only now realizing the full import of what she started when she applied for that job."

"She didn't start it."

As they turned to go back inside, one of the men who had gathered on the portico came over to them and removed his hat. Moody recognized him as the reporter who had spoken to Granville the day before, at the Constitutional Convention. Burke, of the *Sentinel*.

"Hello again," said Burke. "An interesting development, don't you think?"

Moody introduced the reporter to Tamsey and explained that she was the mother of one of the defendants, to forestall Burke from saying anything worrying about the trial's outcome. Instead, Burke's interest in Tamsey increased, and he took out his notebook and pencil. Tamsey started toward the courthouse.

"I've just come from the Constitutional Convention across the way," Burke said quickly. "I think you'll find what they're deciding over there has a great deal to do with what is being decided in here."

Tamsey hesitated at the door, and Moody turned to the reporter. "In what way?" he asked.

"They're fixing to do everything in their power to ban negroes from entering the state," Burke said. "Everything in their power. They've raised the bond to a thousand dollars. No exceptions."

"That for fugitives," Tamsey said. "How many times I got to say this? Leason and Sarah ain't fugitives."

"I think the wording's going to be, 'blacks and mulattoes,' Mrs. Lewis. They ain't making fine distinctions anymore. Since President Fillmore signed the Compromise, there's been a general purging of the state. Blacks and mulattoes can't own property. Can't vote. Can't go to public schools. Can't testify in court."

"Catchers still have to bring a person before a magistrate, do they not?" asked Moody. "They have to prove that the person they're trying to kidnap is a runaway slave."

"Yes, they do," agreed the reporter. "And the magistrate has to decide if that person is a runaway or not."

"That's something, is it not?"

"Yes, I suppose it is. But the only evidence'll be the catcher's word. And the magistrate will be paid by the case: he'll get ten dollars for every black or mulatto he sends out of the state, and five dollars for every one he allows to stay in."

"The state has always tolerated illegal kidnapping by catchers," said Moody. "All this means is that kidnapping has been made legal, even profitable. Doesn't seem like much of a compromise, does it?"

As Burke wrote Moody's words in his notebook, Tamsey put her arm through Stokes's and hurried through the entrance into the courthouse.

"You two seemed pretty friendly out there," Burke said to Moody. "What is your relationship with Mrs. Lewis, if I may ask? Just so I get it right."

Moody looked at the portal through which Tamsey had disappeared. He longed to say that he loved her, that she was his wife, that he was going to do everything in his power to keep her safe. But he also knew that not saying that was the best way to keep her safe.

"A friend," he said quietly. "She's a close friend who's going through a difficult time."

16.

Moody took his seat beside Tamsey, this time with Granville and Sabetha on his right, and Stokes and Brother Joshua on Tamsey's left. It was as if they were lining up for a skirmish. There was a restlessness in the room, people checking their timepieces, looking under their chairs for their hats, clearing their throats, as though they considered the trial over but for the sentencing. Fritts made a show of packing up his papers and looking at his watch. Pudge Pickering stood ready to escort the defendants, now the prisoners, out of the courtroom and back to jail. But Parker was on his feet, and Judge Amery was listening to him, and the room hushed again, if a little impatiently, to learn what was coming. If this were to be a tragedy, they were settling in for the final act.

"Now that we have established the racial origin of one of the defendants," Parker was saying, "it remains to do the same for the other, for Leason Lewis."

"Your Honor," Fritts said, standing at his table. "It's as obvious as the nose on Mr. Parker's face what color Leason Lewis is. To belabor the point is a-wastin' of the court's time."

"It may be obvious to you, Mr. Fritts," said Judge Amery, "but the law is blind. Mr. Lewis's race is still to be established. You may proceed, Mr. Parker."

"Thank you, Your Honor. I will remind the court of Mr. Fritts's words, when he quoted the great statesman and slave owner Thomas Jefferson: two white crosses and a third cross with any degree of whiteness, however small, makes a person white. If a person has one white parent, one white grandparent and one half-white or even quarter-white or even one-eighth-white great-grandparent, all on the same side of the family, then, by law, that person is legally white. I intend to prove that that definition pertains to Leason just as much as Mr. Fritts here has shown it pertains to Sarah."

A murmur spread through the courtroom, especially among the reporters, as though a swarm of bees had gotten into the room. Tamsey groaned and shifted uncomfortably in her seat beside Moody.

"You're going to show that Leason Lewis is white?" said Judge Amery.

"I am, Your Honor."

"No," Tamsey said, so low that Moody barely heard. "He can't. Not that, too."

"How do you intend to do that?"

"First of all, I will show the court a document proving that Leason's mother, Thomasina Lewis, was the daughter of a white planter named Reuben Lockhart, and a woman named Betsy, a slave on the Queen Bee plantation, owned by Lockhart, in South Carolina."

"What documents could possibly prove that?" Fritts asked indignantly.

"Reuben Lockhart's diary," said Parker, "which after his death was published and a copy of which I have right here." He held up a slim, leather-bound volume. Moody could see gold leaf on the edges of the pages, and gold lettering on the cover. " 'Memoirs of a Carolina Planter,' " Parker read aloud, " 'by Reuben J. Lockhart.' "

"And Lockhart confesses to fathering children on his female slaves?" asked Judge Amery.

"He rather boasts of it, Your Honor."

"Does he mention the defendant's mother in particular?"

"He does. Shall I read you the relevant passage?"

"You may spare us, Mr. Parker," said Amery. "But hang on to it, in case we go to trial. What other delights have you got for us?"

"As I said, it now remains for us to show that Leason himself is half white."

"And how do you intend to do that?"

"I intend to call Leason's mother, Thomasina Lewis, as a witness."

The murmur in the room, which had begun with the disclosure of the diary, now became a rumbling, as if a storm had come down from the hills, or a posse of catchers were riding hard on a dry road. There was some yelling, some ugliness, among the white spectators. They jumped up and shook their fists at Parker as though they'd been cheated and wanted their money back. A few turned to look at Tamsey, others sat in their seats looking puzzled. Moody knew too much about plantation life to be shocked by Parker's revelations, but these Northerners were catching their first glimpse into the world they would send these fugitives back to, and they were not grateful for it. Tamsey kept her eyes straight ahead, ignoring the crowd. Moody didn't know what to do to help; whatever happened next, whatever she was going to be asked to do, it wasn't going to be good for her. She knew it, and she was preparing herself to do it.

"Do you have a deposition from her, Mr. Parker?" asked the judge.

"A partial one. But I think we need to hear her whole testimony."

"Do you mean, put her on the stand?"

"I do, Your Honor."

Fritts bolted to his feet. "Your Honor," he said, "the law specifically forbids a black or mulatto to testify at the trial of a white person. And we just determined that Sarah Franklin is a white person!"

"The law," replied Parker, "specifically *allows* it. It just hasn't been done in Indiana before."

Judge Amery leaned back in his chair. "He's right, Fritts, the law allows it."

"But there's no precedent," said Fritts.

"Then we'll make one," said Parker.

Judge Amery considered. "This isn't a trial," he said, "it's a hearing. I don't recall any law forbidding black testimony at a hearing. In any case, such a law would forbid black testimony only in a case concerning a white person. Now that we have determined Sarah Franklin is white, the trial no longer concerns her, it concerns Leason Lewis. And we haven't determined yet whether Leason Lewis is white or black, so such a law wouldn't apply in any case. I'm going to allow it. Mr. Parker, you may proceed with your witness."

"Tamsey," said Parker, "will you please step up here to the witness stand?"

Moody squeezed her hand as she stood, as would any good friend, and she began walking toward the front of the suddenly quiet courtroom. By the time she reached the witness stand she was faltering a little. Parker took her arm and helped her into the chair, and when the clerk asked her to place her hand on the Bible and tell the truth she hesitated, but then did. When asked her name, she said Thomasina Lewis clearly, and then Parker began talking as though they were having afternoon tea in his office.

"Now, Tamsey," he said, "you remember we talked about Leason before, didn't we? When you made your statement. But I'm still not clear about a few things. What year was Leason born?"

"I don't know the year," she said.

"There is no record of his birth?"

"No."

"You were a member of the Luce household in Kentucky at the time?"

"Yes."

"How long had you been there?"

"Eight years."

"How long after Leason was born were you freed?"

"Two years."

"That was in 1833?"

"I guess. Yes."

"So you went there in 1823, and Leason was born in 1831. Does that sound about right?"

"About."

"Will you tell us how you came to be in Kentucky?"

"Massa Luce won me."

"How do you mean, he won you?"

"You want the whole story?"

"Please."

"It a long story."

"Make it as long or as short as you like."

Tamsey looked at Parker, then swept the courtroom until her eyes found Moody's. He was careful not to nod. This was her story, and her decision to tell it or not tell it.

"Well," she said, "I already told you my mam was slave to a

horse farmer in South Carolina, name Reuben Lockhart, when I was born. Massa Reuben, we called him, kept me, and when I old enough to work he took me in the Big House, and Mam and me slept in the woodshed behind the kitchen."

"Why was that, do you think?" asked Parker.

"Why was what?"

"Why did Reuben Lockhart keep you and your mother in the Big House?"

"Massa Reuben was fond of my mam, I guess. My mam used to say he fooled her."

"Fooled her? Do you know what she meant by that?"

"He promise to free her. But he never did."

"All right. Please go on."

"When the Lord took Massa Reuben, Young Massa Lockhart, his son, took the plantation and sold my mam to a tobacco farmer nearby, and moved me out to the nigger house until I had my first baby, and after that I was brought back into the Big House and put in the old woodshed again, this time by myself."

"With the baby?"

"No, the baby was sold."

"Again, if I may interrupt, why do you think he brought you inside?"

"I telling this story. Let it come."

"Yes, sorry."

"Young Massa a mean man. He married a pale, red-haired woman from the next county, name of Euphemia Rettis. And Miss Euphemia's brother also a mean man. His name was Hugh Rettis, and he come to live in the Big House with his sister and the young massa."

She stopped and her eyes searched for Moody.

"I was brought inside for him. Nobody said it like that, they said I did for Massa Hugh. But that what I did."

Fritts was on his feet again. "Your Honor," he said, "surely we don't need these lurid details. The ladies, Your Honor, the children."

Moody looked at Granville and Sabetha. "Do you want to wait outside?" he asked them quietly. They both shook their heads.

"Then what happened, Tamsey?" asked Parker.

"When the young missus took over the care of the house, Massa Hugh took what he want and give nothing back for it, did no work, walked in the fields from time to time to see if there was something there he wanted, played cards and drank every night, and there was bad blood between him and the young massa. I was afraid Massa Hugh be sent away and take me with him. My work was in the kitchen and serving at table, and I slept in the woodshed unless Massa Hugh sent for me, which he did most nights. I had another baby that was sold, and that was how things was until the card game."

"What card game was that?" Parker asked when she fell silent.

"I getting to it."

"Would you like some water?"

"No, thank you, I fine."

"The card game?"

"I served at table that night. There were four men, the young massa and Massa Hugh; a neighbor planter named Rufus Pettigrew, who was a widower and often ate with the Lockharts; and another man, Silas Luce, a horse trader from Kentucky who was a friend of the old massa's and still supplied the plantation with most of its horses. They were all drinking and playing *bouillotte*, that a card game, and Massa Hugh drinking more than the others, as usual, and also losing more. At some point Massa Hugh put his cards facedown on the table, set his whiskey glass on top of them and stepped outside, and when he came back he looked at his cards and accused the others of switching his hand. The other men denied any such trick, but Massa Hugh, he was mean enough when he sober, and downright vicious when he had liquor in him, and he insisted, and raised his voice, and refused to sit down. I stayed behind a door, hoping he wouldn't see me. He walked about the room, waving his arms in a fury. I don't think he believed his cards been touched, he just had a poor hand, but once he took a position on a thing he would not back down from it. Young Massa told him sit down and play the hand the Lord give him, and Massa Hugh inflamed to such a height that when his eye fell on me, standing by the door trying to make myself invisible, I knew I was done for. He shout at me, 'You! You saw what happened!'

"I said, 'No, Massa Hugh, I didn't.'

"But he yell at me to get over there. He say I saw them switch his cards! I moved to the center of the room to let him get a better swing at me, as I was taught, and I said, 'I in the room, Massa Hugh, but I didn't see anyone switch any cards. I wasn't paying attention.'

"But Massa Hugh call me a liar, and he hit me hard on the side of the head, but only with his fist, and I thought I might survive this, but then he look about the room, and his eye fell on the laundry paddle lying on the sideboard. I don't know what that laundry paddle was doing there, it belong in the laundry house, but there it was, it maybe Kwaku put it there, but Massa Hugh pick it up and hit me across my back with it. I felt the numbness start at the bottom of my spine, and my legs tingle, and the air leave my lungs. 'I'll put more stripes on you than a *zaybra!*' he said.

"I knew better than to move. I looked to the young massa, but he busy tracing whiskey rings on the table with his finger. It was Massa Luce, the horse trader, who save me.

" 'You ain't a-going to beat her to make her tell a lie, are you, Rettis?' he said.

" 'I'll damn well beat her until my arm gets tired,' said Massa Hugh.

" 'And then what?' said Massa Luce. 'Would you accuse us of cheating on the word of a nigger?'

"Then Massa Hugh stop with the paddle in the air, and lower his arm, swaying slightly on his feet.

" 'Are you, sir,' he said, 'interfering with a man disciplining his own property?'

" 'No,' said Massa Luce. He spoke quietly but there was iron in his voice. 'But I will defend myself from the charge of cheating at cards, no matter who it comes from.'

"My left ear was still ringing from the first blow, but I heard Mr. Pettigrew clear his throat and speak in his high voice: 'Why don't we just shuffle the cards and deal out a fresh hand?'

"Massa Luce gather the cards together and began to shuffle them. Massa Hugh watched him, then set the paddle down on the sideboard and said, 'Good idea,' and he sat down and picked up his glass. He and Mr. Pettigrew and Massa Luce anted, and the young massa deal out a fresh hand, and I thought the worst over. But when I saw how Massa Hugh look at Young Massa, I knew some unpleasantness still on the way, only not what it would be. The young massa had a stack of dixies in front of him and Massa Hugh did not, and when Young Massa look at his three cards and the *retourné* he push the whole pile to the middle of the table.

"From where I standing I could see the young massa had a good hand, three natural jacks. I didn't dare to move around the table to look at the other hands, but I knew they have to be good to beat the young massa's. Mr. Pettigrew look at his cards and shake his head. Massa Luce said he had a pair of Kentucky Thoroughbreds out there worth a good deal more than that, and Young Massa nod.

"When it come Massa Hugh's turn he study his hand so long everyone look at him. He could only win what he put in; if he put in half as much as the others and beat them, he only win half of Young Massa's money and one of Massa Luce's horses. He study his cards again and drank some more whiskey.

"And he said he warrant me worth at least two horses, and Young Massa kept his eyes on his cards and said yes, I was.

" 'What about you?' he said to Massa Luce. 'Will you accept my bet?'

"Massa Luce nod yes, too. My knees trembled so I could barely stand. I knew if Massa Hugh won that hand, he would win a pile of money, two fine horses and me. He would own me outright, and no longer need the goodwill of his sister to keep me. I be his to do with as he please, and I knew too well what please him. For the first time in my life I thought of running away. We taught there nowhere a slave can flee unless it be into the arms of Death, and I learn that lesson here in Indiana, but I was ready that day to take my chances with Death rather than go with Massa Hugh. There was a river run through the farm, and I vowed to myself I would throw myself into it if I could get outside.

"But when Massa Hugh show down his hand, it was weaker than the young massa's: a pair of kings and an ace. Young Massa would show his hand last, but with three jacks, it was better than Massa Hugh's; he would win and my life would go back to what it was before the missus made a present of me to her brother. Young Massa might even put me out with the field workers, to keep me away from Massa Hugh. My heart lift a little. Then Massa Luce showed down his hand, and it was a brelan of tens, which was also better than Massa Hugh's but not as good as Young Massa's natural jacks.

"Massa Hugh knew he lost, but he thought he lost to Massa Luce. He sit back and let out his breath. Massa Luce look at the young massa, waiting for him to show his hand. I felt sorry for Massa Luce, for he was about to lose two fine horses. But instead of laying down his hand, Young Massa look at Massa Hugh and said, 'Sorry, Hugh,' and he fold his cards and threw them facedown on the table.

"Massa Luce was quick. He pull the money toward himself and look up at me and said, 'You got anything to pack you better go get it now. We ain't staying.'

"And that how I come to Kentucky. Massa Luce won me."

There was deep silence in the courtroom. Some of the women were weeping. Most of the men were staring at their feet. Sabetha had buried her face in her hands, and Granville had put his arm around her. How could any of them, Moody wondered, having heard Tamsey's story, not want to rise up as one and condemn the conditions that had made it possible? "A story a story," Tamsey had told him, but this was not a story. "Brer Fox and Brer Rabbit" was a story. This was a tragedy.

"Thank you, Mrs. Lewis," Parker said quietly. He paused, turned toward he table as if to release her, then turned back and addressed her again. "And in Kentucky," he said, "you worked as a house maid, is that correct?"

"I work in the Big House, yes."

"Why was that?"

"What you mean, why?"

"Why didn't Silas Luce put you out to work with the horses?"

"Massa said I wanted inside to look after Missus Luce."

"Mrs. Luce, Silas Luce's wife, Rebecca. She was sick?"

"Yes. She often was."

"What were your duties in the Big House?"

"I was the upstairs maid, chamber maid, kitchen maid for the missus. Cook," she added, looking at Moody. "Anything she want she had me doing."

"What work did that entail?"

"Changing bed linen, dusting and cleaning, emptying the chamber pots, tending to the missus when she in bed."

"They were fairly light duties, then, were they?"

"Compared to what?"

"Well, compared to what your duties would have been out-side."

"I suppose so, at first. Missus thought they was too light, anyway."

"What do you mean by that?"

"She kept finding harder jobs for me to do."

"What kind of jobs?"

"Fetching water. Chopping wood, carrying it up to the upstairs parlor for her fire. Turning the mattresses over. Moving furniture around. Up and down them stairs a hundred times a day. Soon as I come up with a fresh glass of water she send me back downstairs for a slice of toast."

"You were by this time carrying Leason?"

"Yes."

"She must have known how hard these tasks would be on a woman in your condition, mustn't she?"

"She knew."

"She'd been pregnant herself, had she not?"

"The missus never had any children."

"Do you mean that Silas and Rebecca Luce were childless?"

"The missus couldn't have children, that was part of what her sickness was. Every time she tried, she got the sickness and lost the baby."

"That's what happened this time? She was sick and she lost a baby?"

"Yes."

"In other words, Mrs. Luce became pregnant about the same time you did, and you were called into the Big House to look after her. And she subsequently lost her child?"

"Yes."

"Was it before or after she lost her child that she started finding harder work for you to do?"

"Right before, I guess."

"So you were pregnant when she set you these heavy duties?"

"Yes."

"And Mrs. Luce died shortly after this?"

"Yes. I was outside her room when she died, she wouldn't let me come in. The doctor in with her. But we could hear her. She moan like she too weak to cry."

"You say, 'We could hear her.' Who was outside her room with you?"

"Massa Luce. She wouldn't let him near her, neither."

Parker walked over to his table, picked up a piece of paper and brought it to Judge Amery, who pushed his spectacles up onto his forehead and read it.

"More paper, Your Honor," Fritts protested.

"Calvin Luce died in 1835," Parker said, ignoring Fritts, "two and a half years after the death of his wife, which Tamsey has just described, and when Leason was two years old. This is his will, or a copy of it made by Luce's lawyer, Brockton Temple, in Lexington. As you can see, Luce set Thomasina and Leason free upon his death, leaving them his last name and two hundred dollars for their bond. Your Honor will note the wording of the will: 'My wife Rebecca's kitchen slave Tamsey along with the child Lison, her son.' That's what it says here in the copy, that is what Brockton Temple read to Tamsey and Leason when he issued them their free papers." He turned back to Tamsey. "Tamsey, Leason was with you at the time of Calvin Luce's death, is that correct?"

"Yes."

"You'd had six other children before Leason while you were at the Luce plantation, is that right?"

"Hm."

"I'm sorry?"

"Yes."

"What happened to them?"

"They sold when they weaned."

"Why wasn't Leason sold, like the others?"

She sat very still, her hands folded in her lap. She searched the crowd for Moody again. "I don't know," she said. "He was always good with horses."

"At the age of two?" Tamsey said nothing. "Your Honor," Parker said, taking a second paper from his desk and handing it to Judge Amery, "this is the original document, Luce's will, which I have procured from Brockton Temple. Here you will see that the word *her* was written over another word, and the word it is written over was *our*. There has been some attempt to blot it out, but you can see it if you hold the paper so. In other words, Your Honor, the will as originally written by Calvin Luce, the original from which Brockton Temple's scrivener made the copy I read earlier, stipulates: 'My wife Rebecca's kitchen slave Tamsey along with the child Lison, our son ...' "

The courtroom was quiet. Moody searched the walls for a window to see out of, and finding none turned back to Tamsey, not daring to breathe. Tamsey looked down at her hands as though willing them to behave. Then she lifted her head, this time toward Leason, who held her eyes and tried to smile. Moody waited for her gaze to return to him, then he smiled, too.

"Does Brockton Temple have a theory as to who changed the wording of the will?" asked Judge Amery.

"He says it was like this when it came to him, Your Honor."

"Well, obviously it was. I wasn't suggesting Mr. Temple changed it."

Fritts stood up. "Your Honor, this proves nothing."

"I agree with Mr. Fritts," Parker said. "By itself, it doesn't prove anything. Calvin Luce himself might have changed it when he realized he'd made a mistake. But it is strongly suggestive of something, is it not? If Calvin Luce had made a mistake of such magnitude, surely he would have torn up the original document and rewritten it. But he didn't. Maybe he was in a hurry. Maybe he intended to and was disturbed. On the other hand, maybe someone else, perhaps his wife, changed the will without his knowledge, before it came into the hands of Brockton Temple."

"Why wouldn't she simply destroy the will?" asked the judge.

"Because without a will the property would have gone to the Commonwealth of Kentucky. Besides, Brockton Temple had drawn up the will, and so he knew it existed. She might have thought he wouldn't notice such a small alteration, as he did not."

"A lot of maybes," said Judge Amery.

"Yes, Your Honor. But there are likely maybes and unlikely maybes, and all we can do is try to distinguish between them. With your permission, Your Honor?"

"Proceed, Mr. Parker."

"Tamsey, it's really your permission I should be asking for. Will you allow me one more question?"

Tamsey was still looking at Moody. "Yes," she said.

"Was Silas Luce the father of the child you were bearing when you were in the Big House looking after his ailing wife?"

"Yes."

"Silas Luce was Leason's father?"

"Yes."

"Thank you, Tamsey. I have no more questions, Your Honor."

"Well, I certainly have a few, Your Honor," said Fritts, rising to his feet.

Judge Amery glared at Fritts for a second and then turned to Tamsey.

"Mrs. Lewis," he said, "I appreciate how hard this must be for you. Do you want a few minutes to compose yourself? Or we could resume tomorrow?"

"I just as soon get it over," Tamsey said.

"Then get on with it, Mr. Fritts."

"Mrs. Lewis," Fritts began, "you said that before being moved into the Big House to look after Mrs. Luce, you were living in the slave quarters, is that correct?"

"Yes."

"With other slaves?"

"Yes."

"With other *male* slaves?"

Tamsey paused for a fraction of a second. "Yes," she said.

"How many male slaves were there at that time?"

"Not many. It was winter."

"How many, Mrs. Lewis?"

"Maybe five or six, I don't rightly remember."

"Five or six males, living in the same quarters as you before you were moved into the Big House. That's enough, wouldn't you say so?"

"Enough for what?"

"You know what I mean. You testified that before moving into the Big House, you had already had six children, is that correct."

"Yes."

"All of whom were sold."

"Yes. Massa Luce sold horses and slaves in Mississippi."

"And you conceived those babies while living in the slave quarters, I presume."

"Yes."

"Out of wedlock. Without benefit of clergy."

"Is that a question, Mr. Fritts?" the judge interrupted.

"Never mind, Your Honor. Now, Mrs. Lewis, you say you were pregnant again when you moved into the Big House, is that correct?"

"No, I didn't say that."

"I beg your pardon?"

"I said that I was pregnant when I in the Big House. I didn't say I was pregnant before I went in there."

"Well, were you?"

"No."

"You didn't become pregnant when you lived in the slave quarters, as you had six times previously?"

"No."

"How do you know that?"

"Your Honor!" cried Parker. "Not only is that an offensively indelicate question for this witness, it's a damn stupid one."

"Agreed, Mr. Parker," said Judge Amery. "Mr. Fritts, I can see where you're going with this, and I'll remind you again, this isn't a jury trial. The only person you have to impress is me, and I'm not impressed by this line of questioning. Please get to the point, and leave the forensics out of it, if you will."

Tamsey looked steadily at Lawyer Fritts.

"Mrs. Lewis," he said, "is it not possible, in fact likely, that you *became* with child before you were moved into the Big House, by someone living in the slave quarters, and only *discovered* it after you became part of the Luce household?"

"I moved into the Big House in the fall," she said, "when the missus first took sick, and I wan't with child until January. I got my baby just before the missus lost hers. I remember there was snow on the ground, and slaves in the fields breaking hemp in their bare feet. Not snow like you get up here, nothing a person could get lost in, but enough that when you look out an upstairs window wondering what going to happen to you, you see black wagon tracks in the fields, and black slashes in the pastures where the horses kick the snow to get at the grass, and black lines in the laneway made by the horse and buggy when the massa come into the yard for his dinner, and black smoke rising from the chimneys on the slave quarters you wished you'd never left, because you were safe there, and now your whole life changed over again. You think you going along in one direction, you know where you are, where you belong, and then you going in a different direction altogether, and you don't know where that river taking you. Nowhere good, probably. The child will come after the hemp cut and before the tobacco in. My life change when I left South Carolina to come to Kentucky with Massa Luce, and it change again when I came here to Indiana. But there be different kinds of change, there be change that make you stronger and change that rip you apart, and there be change that settle into you and start something growing inside you that you want to keep warm but you wish you never had. That how I know it was January when I found I was heavy with Leason, because there snow on the pastures, and I thought, I be light in September, before the snow start again, and my baby be sold by Christmas."

"Except it wasn't."

"No, not that time."

Fritts remained quiet for a moment. Moody thought he was going to sit down and let Tamsey come back to her seat. But he began again: "So you're saying . . ."

"I never had to do with the men in the quarters," Tamsey said.

"And we're to *believe* that?"

"I took my oath."

"And I, for one, believe it," said Judge Amery.

At that, a second storm broke over their heads. There were shouts of anger and peals of joy, some yelling and stamping, chairs tipped over and feet stamping on the wooden floorboards. The bailiff leaped to his feet—"Order! Order!"—and Judge Amery looked severely at Fritts. Parker was on his feet, calling for dismissal of the charges, and Judge Amery banged his gavel on the table. Everyone was already on their feet when the bailiff called, "All rise," and Judge Amery lit a cigar.

Parker helped Tamsey off the witness stand and she made her way back to Moody. Fritts gathered his papers angrily. Leason and Sarah remained in their chairs, surrounded by the tumult, looking as though they'd just woke up. Then Parker thumped Leason on the back, and Moody took advantage of the confusion to take Tamsey's hand, and she looked at him and shook her head.

When Judge Amery shouted that the defendants were free to go, Leason and Sarah stood up and looked around like children in a forest in which all the trees had suddenly turned to people. They and Parker began to make their way to the back of the courtroom, where Moody and Tamsey were still seated. Fists shook in Leason's face, but other hands patted him on the back. Women clutched at Sarah, their hats dipping like daisies in a high wind. Etta Pickering had vanished. When Leason reached Tamsey, he put his arms around her. "It's all right," he said. "Lawyer Parker says we can go home soon as we get our papers."

"I don't care what they say," she said to Moody, keeping her voice low. "We going to Canada soon as you get back from Georgia."

"Until then," said Moody, "I want you to stay here in Indianapolis with the Kästchens. Stokes, too. I don't want you alone in Freedom while I'm gone."

"And Leason and Sarah?" she asked.

"The whole family," he said. "I'll be back as soon as I can."

PART FIVE

That muddy path to freedom,
Follow the Drinking Gourd.
Pegfoot going to show you the way,
Keep on movin' the Ol' Man say,
Follow the Drinking Gourd.

I.

By 1850, the National Road had been cut, graded and macadamized as far west as Indianapolis. It was passable even when heavy, late-fall rains turned Indiana's other roads into quagmires. Moody remembered the ribbon-cutting ceremony in June, when the governor had made the gathered newspapermen laugh by lauding the new transportation route as a means by which "a white man may now get here from Baltimore almost as fast as a nigger can from Charleston."

October rain was a cold rain, and there was no heat in the stagecoach. He wrapped himself in Robert's broadcloth and thought about buying a proper coat in Baltimore. Tamsey had packed him a bag of chicken sandwiches and cake for the journey, and there were taverns along the way for beer and liquor. They traveled five hours a day. He shared the coach with two commercial travelers and an elderly woman and her niece, who were visiting the woman's son in Baltimore. The son worked for the firm of P. B. Didier and Brother, dealers in agricultural equipment and machinery. The name drew such murmurs of appreciation from the commercial travelers that the woman took from her portmanteau a brochure, sent to her by her son, and read from it aloud: " 'Wheat fans, corn shellers, corncob crushers, straw cutters, hay cutters, fodder cutters, steam reapers of some dozen different patterns, together with minor articles pertaining to the household; viz. churns, sausage cutters and stuffers, butter molds, apple parers, cow milkers, nest eggs, ox yokes, ox bows, ox pins, ox balls' " —here the niece reddened and the woman paused for a moment, then pressed bravely on— " 'traces, tin horns, Damerpatch's Celebrated Yankee Wooden Rake, shovels and spades of all sizes and purposes; in fact, all kinds of garden and fruit tools, wholesale and retail.' "

"Won't be needing ox yokes, bows, pins or the other now that steam's taking over," one of the commercial travelers commented.

"Stagecoaches neither, I guess," said his companion. "I could've taken the train down to Madison and then gone by steamboat up the Ohio to Philadelphia if I wanted, except I ain't got business in Philadelphia."

There was some lively talk about the advantages of steam over horsepower, and of steam power over slave power, in which Moody, embarrassed by his new status as a slave owner, did not join. He felt better since Leason and Sarah had been set free, but not relieved of worry. The North was still full of catchers, legitimized by the Fugitive Slave Act. Kästchen was busier than ever, and Moody felt he and Leason should be on the river, helping. Helping Lucas, who of course was long gone by now.

The coach stopped the first night in Richmond, where he took a room in the tavern that served as the stationhouse, ate a supper of something the tavern keeper called stew, which at least was warm, and then retired to his room to avoid spending any more time with the commercial travelers. At a tiny wooden table set before the dormer window, looking down into the stable yard behind the tavern, he wrote to Heiskell about the trial. He didn't know if Heiskell and Brown were still in the newspaper business, but writing made him feel better. Some. "It is both a victory and a setback for the equality of the races. It means the only way a black man will be accepted is by proving that he is not black." He also wrote of his quandary regarding Plantagenet. If he manumitted his father's slaves, paid their bonds and their passage to Canada and established them in the new Promised Land, it was going to cost money. He needed to sell the plantation and the house in Savannah to raise the capital. But he would not sell the slaves. Would the properties without the slaves sell for enough to pay for their liberty?

As the coach made its way through the cold and the rain, Moody brooded over the trial and its revelations. Tamsey's story continued to haunt him. The thought of her being physically compelled to bear her white owners' children sickened him, and not only because the image that had been pressed into his brain was that of the woman he now loved. It was also because Tamsey's was not an isolated case, and he felt weakened and helpless in the shadow of such enormity, as he had after his dealings with the Judds. Casgrain had perpetrated no less a crime on Annie and others, but Moody hadn't thought it was committed for the purpose of selling their children. Had that been his father's secret money-making scheme all along, to allow Casgrain to "improve his stock" because lighter-skinned children sold for a higher price? And had he, Moody, known it but refused to think about it? Just as he'd refused to consider that Annie had remained with him not because she wanted to, or because she liked him, or even less because she was grateful to him, but because she had had no choice—other than the one she had ultimately taken?

The carriage rattled on, the other passengers fell into a disgruntled silence, and he tried to force himself to think about what he was going to do in Savannah. Without success.

2.

In Wheeling, he spent the evening with Lester Underhill, who was still at the Museum of Natural Curiosities despite his advanced age and diminished health. Moody arranged for the shipment of his and Granville's fossils to the museum, and apologized for not having found a mastodon.

"Pshaw," said Underhill. "Mastodons are a dime a dozen now. Big Bone Lick is a goddamn tourist site; they got booths set up to sell combs and bracelets made from fossil ivory. No, giant reptiles are the new thing, *Iguanodons* and such, at least in England. We have, alas, yet to find any here in America. We seem to have added nothing to the geological record since the formation of the Alleghenies. I wouldn't mind if you found me a fossil reptile before I become one myself."

"Do you still see Tim'n'Tom?" Moody asked.

"He was here not a month ago," said Underhill. "Brought me a wolverine."

"Is a wolverine a natural curiosity?"

"You would think it mightily so if you ever had one attached to your leg."

"A deal of building going on around town," Moody said. He remembered Wheeling as a bustling main street with a metal bridge at the end of it, spanning a channel of the Ohio River over to Zane's Island, but not much else except brag and promise. Now it had hotels and saloons, factories with brick smokestacks, even a train station, although no tracks had yet been laid. Wheeling was still an industrious, if not yet an industrial, town. "Lots of work for fugitives," he said.

"Not as much as you'd think," Underhill replied. "It's all Irish and German labor now, although they work for slave wages, otherwise the owners would bring the blacks back in. There's still lots of fugitives coming through, more than ever, but without work, they don't stay."

"Where do they go?"

Underhill shrugged. "You'd know better than I," he said.

He knew no one in Baltimore, a city of nearly two hundred thousand, counting only the white population. As the train to Washington didn't leave until the next day, he took a room on Booth Street and spent the afternoon walking up and down West Baltimore and Poppleton Streets, peering up at the tall buildings and, out of old habit, at the faces he passed on the sidewalks, thinking of Lucas. He entered a barbershop for a haircut and shave, and scanned the newspapers for coverage of the trial in Indiana without finding a mention of it. Baltimore, he learned from the barber, a man in his sixties with swollen knuckles and skin the color of burnished copper, had become a major stopping place for runaways from the Carolinas and Virginia, so many fugitives flooding the city that the old strictures of slavery had started to burst at their seams. Blacks could live with their own families, own their own houses, run their own businesses, or hire themselves out and work at term slavery, whereby they were owned for a period of time and then freed, "just like it says in the Bible," the barber said. His name was Albert Lacoste, he said, putting his comb in his breast pocket to shake Moody's hand. Moody asked if term slavery wasn't a sign of progress, to which Lacoste replied, "It is—if going back to the way things was two thousand years ago is progress." Fugitives and free blacks still feared catchers, he said, more than ever, and had to be wary of going out alone unless armed. "Look at this here," he said, taking up a pamphlet and reading from it: " 'Vigilance Societies have been organized by antislavery groups to protect fugitives and freed. During the day, black workers toil at the manufactories and the dockyards, with Vigilance Society guards at the entrances, and at night the workers and their families huddle in their neighborhoods, locked in their homes.' "

When he freed his slaves, he wrote to Heiskell that night, would it be into this nightmare?

In the morning, he made his way to the Mount Clare train station and bought a ticket to Washington. It was his first time on a train; he sat in the coach and marveled at the speed at which the built-up countryside flew past his window and disappeared behind him. Huge buildings, their roofs barely glimpsed above tall wooden fences, rows of blank-faced houses, fenced pastures, then more buildings; they all sped by so quickly his neck ached from trying to see them. Surely nothing was meant to move at such velocity. In Washington, walking to settle his stomach after his midday meal, he admired the White House and the Capitol Building, both of which had been built by slaves. The trading of slaves, though not the owning of them, had been abolished in the capital that September, one of the saner provisions of the Compromise, and the vast holding pens on the banks of the Potomac, the former stockyards of Franklin and

Armfield, the biggest slave dealers in the country, were being demolished or converted to cattle pens. The district, surrounded by Virginia and Maryland, both slave states, was like an armed camp under siege. Congress had passed the bill, but even Washington's mayor had opposed it, and slave trading had simply moved out to the nearby town of Alexandria, named after the ancient slave-trading center of Egypt.

On one of his walks he followed the City Canal to the Anacostia River, where, when he reached the Congressional Cemetery, he stopped to watch a group of grave diggers exposing a coffin. Armed guards, army men in red tunics with gleaming brass buttons, stood at attention at the cemetery gates, and he asked one of them, a corporal, who was being exhumed.

"President Taylor," said the corporal.

"Zachary Taylor?" Moody said. Taylor had died in July, apparently of food poisoning. "I served with him in Mexico." God, had it been only three and a half years ago? The Battles of Palo Alto and Resaca de la Palma, smoking corpses, buzzards circling overhead, flags hanging limp from unmanned posts. And then home to Annie and Lucas. Burying Annie. "Why're they digging him up?"

"Moving him to his home in Kentucky. Springfield, they say, but I ain't never heard of it."

"Near Louisburg," said Moody. "Big plantation. Lots of slaves."

"Well, he'll lie more peaceful there, I reckon."

3.

From Washington he traveled south, into the disturbing tranquility of the Virginia countryside. The croplands and plantation houses, slave quarters, quiet, dusty village squares such as he had known in his youth, he now saw with different eyes. He saw fountains and marketplaces where black women purchased food for their white owners, segregated churches and schoolyards in which only white children played. When he stepped down from the stagecoach in Savannah, he felt engulfed by the city's altered sameness. Although the population had doubled to fifteen thousand in the thirty years he'd been away, it still seemed the same size, especially after Baltimore and Washington. The new folk all seemed to have fit into the old houses, the old churches, to lounge in the same taverns and inns along River and Bay Streets. Change came slowly in small places, where townspeople were more inclined to see change as a threat. If slavery were to hold out anywhere, it would be in these small towns and rural areas of America, which was pretty much what the South consisted of. Savannah was encased in the past, he thought as he walked to the offices of Harley, Chase and Steele, located in a dignified set of row houses on Congress Street, and emancipation was the future.

He crossed through Johnson Square, a still oasis in which colored nannies wearing starched muslin dresses pushed white babies in carriages draped in cheesecloth. Autumn was less advanced here than it had been in Indiana. Plum and cherry trees were still in leaf, the magnolias had lost their cups and saucers but stood sedately beside the footpaths, and on the front lawns of the white houses, colored gardeners on their hands and knees troweled weeds from the black earth at the bases of perennial shrubs. God was in his heaven, at least the Southern God was in this meridional heaven. Moody was conscious of his own clothing, which was almost that of a frontiersman; he felt like Natty Bumppo. He didn't know whether to knock on the carved oak door or just walk in. He tried the handle, found it turned, and entered.

He was at the front end of a long hall, with a waiting room on his left and, on his right, a small reception area in which an austere, matronly woman sat at a desk sorting papers. He said his name and that he wanted to see one of the partners about the Moody property. She didn't look up. He took his hat off and watched her for a while, then cleared his throat, realizing too late that in so doing he had identified himself as a Northerner. She would not look up to a Northerner. She pursed her lips and continued sorting, then carried the sorted papers to a filing cabinet and began filing them. Moody retreated to the waiting room and waited. When she had no more papers to file, she turned to him.

"Moody," she said. "That would be Mr. Chase. I'll take you back now."

She led him down the long hall, past an open office in which three visored scriveners labored at high desks, past another open office filled with more filing cabinets, and finally to a closed door with the name Edwidge Chase engraved on it. When Edwidge Chase retired, Moody thought, he would have to take the door with him. She knocked and opened it without waiting for a response, spoke Moody's name and stood aside to let him enter. The man seated behind a polished wooden desk was small, perhaps twenty years Moody's senior, with a full mane of white hair arranged in eccentric swirls on his head. He wore a midnight-blue frock coat over a collarless white shirt, and a gold pince-nez swung from a red ribbon around his neck. Moody recognized him, or rather recognized the red ribbon; before Moody had left home, Lawyer Chase had been to the house many times to consult with Moody's father. Like the city itself, he had grown more corpulent but remained essentially unchanged.

"So," said Chase, folding his hands on the desk, "it has taken a tragedy to bring you back to Savannah. I refer, of course, to the death of your father."

"Hardly a tragedy," said Moody, who thought he could give him tragedies if he wanted them. "He was seventy-eight, and a devil."

Chase frowned. "True. But as I myself am seventy-three, his death puts a theoretical ceiling upon my own expectation. Five years more," he said, looking about the office as though deciding what he would take with him. "I was your father's lawyer for forty years, and it is true he was a devil, but I shall not be yours for nearly so long."

"Just so," said Moody. "As I intend to sell the property, I shan't have need of any lawyer for very long at all."

"What? Sell? Sell Plantagenet?"

"And the town house. All of it."

"But that has been the Moody home for three generations."

"I know, but I am determined to sell."

"And the slaves?"

"Here is what I would have you do," Moody said, taking a chair. "I wish to sell both the plantation and the city property, and to free the slaves."

"Free the—"

"How many are there?"

"Well, barely forty-five at the last census, counting the servants in the city. You would manumit them all?"

"Yes. And more," he said. "I want to take whatever money I realize from the sale of Plantagenet, minus your commission, of course, and divide it among them, perhaps make some provision for those who have been there longest, so that they will not be destitute and forced to flee to places like Baltimore or New York. They can choose what to do with their freedom. Will you do that for me?"

Chase leaned back in his chair and regarded Moody somberly.

"What shall become of them?" he asked. "Have you considered it? As your lawyer, it is my duty to ask you to give that question some thought."

"I have considered it," said Moody. "They shall become free, and they shall have enough money to do as they please."

"Freedom doesn't mean the same thing to them as it does to you and me," Chase said, trying to sound wise but managing only to remind Moody of Lawyer Fritts. "Some of them were born on Plantagenet. They don't know anything else. Sikey was your father's cook before you were born. Would you turn her out with a few dollars in her pocket?"

"If she and the others decide to stay on and work for the new owner, they can do that, we can make it a stipulation of the sale. Since they'll be freed, the owner will have to pay them a wage."

"No one will buy Plantagenet under such conditions," said Chase. "Why would they pay wages to a freedman when they can buy a slave? Unless, of course, they paid him so little he'd be worse off than when he was a slave."

"Nonetheless," said Moody, "I mean to free them. Where's Casgrain?" he asked suddenly. He'd forgotten about the overseer. "I hope you've put him out."

"God beat you to it, I'm afraid," said Chase. "Thomas Casgrain died five years ago. Your father ran the plantation until he became too befuddled in his final weeks."

"No one told me." Moody stood and put his hat on. "Will you draw up the papers?" he asked Chase, who pursed his thin lips and lifted his thin shoulders, as though to say it was Moody's funeral, not his. "Good. I'll send someone over with a list of their names, and come back when the papers are ready to sign."

"It will keep my scribblers busy until week's end."

"If you need me, I'll be at the town house."

"Please relay my sympathies to Sikey."

4.

"Massa Virgil?" Sikey exclaimed, stepping back from the door. "That you? They told us you was coming, but I didn't believe I'd recognize you." She didn't seem to be entirely convinced that it was him. "You don't need to be rapping on your own front door."

"How are you, Sikey?" he said, embracing her in view of anyone looking up from the street. She was smaller than he remembered, but still so big he could barely get his arms around her, and she smelled of a pleasantly familiar blend of bread dough and raw sugar.

"Well as can be, I guess. Been hard times since your daddy passed, but we managing, we managing. Come along inside, it getting chilly in the shade, Lord bless and keep."

She swept him into the house, where his senses were further assailed by reminders of his youth: floor wax, snuffed candles, roast beef, cedar sprigs in the linen closets, an essence of roses that seemed to have lingered in the air since his mother died. The rooms were little changed, some of the furnishings had been replaced, carpets and drapes and a chair or two, but only with newer versions of the old ones. He heard movement upstairs, the maids going about their tasks. His father was two months dead, but the house was obviously being run as smoothly as ever, and Sikey told him it was the same at Plantagenet, "the Gullahs even started planting rice," she said.

"Edwidge Chase thought some of the slaves had run off," he said.

"They come back when your daddy died," she said, and they both laughed.

They were sitting at the big table in the kitchen. Sikey had made tea and placed biscuits on a plate with a pot of Georgia peach preserve beside it. He let her eat two before he took one, and Sikey smiled at that.

"If I didn't believe who you is before now," she said, "you just proved it. You sure ain't your daddy's son."

"Was his death sudden? Was he in a lot of pain?"

"Can't say it was sudden, no. Your daddy in pain all his life, but he wan't your daddy for a long time before he passed, bless and keep. Didn't hardly know where he was half the time."

Moody looked about the kitchen. "So little has changed," he said.

"We been keeping the place going."

"How?"

"Lawyer Chase give us money from time to time."

"I didn't know about Casgrain, either," he said. "You all been looking after Plantagenet, too?"

"We did what we could. But you the young massa now."

"No!" he said, more forcefully than he had intended. He bit into his biscuit. "My plan is to sell this house and Plantagenet, and then go back to Indiana."

Sikey stopped chewing and stared at him. "Indiana?" she said. "Where that?"

"West of here, and north."

"You going to sell this house?"

"I'll free you first," he said. "You and the others. And give you some money."

"Free us?" she said. "We been free since Casgrain died. Not paper free. Is that what you saying, you make us paper free?"

"Edwidge Chase said I'd be doing you a disservice by freeing you. He said that without whites looking after you, you wouldn't know what to do or where to go. What do you say to that?"

She regarded him for another half minute, and then started laughing. She laughed so hard she had to hold on to the table to keep from falling off her chair. Tears rolled down her cheeks, and she wiped them with a corner of her apron.

"White folk looking after us?" she said. "That what they been doing? Looking after us? Oh, Lord! After all our years looking after them?" She was laughing in her anger. "Oh, Massa Virgil," she said, still drying her eyes, "you can free us any time you want."

"Where will you go?" he asked.

"Go?" she said. "Why would I go somewhere?"

"You mean you'd stay here in Georgia?" He experienced a sensation almost of relief that he wouldn't be condemning her to Washington or Baltimore. He wouldn't have to feel guilty about that, too.

"Yes," she said, "I'd stay in Savannah. I'd stay right here in this house, Massa Virgil, right here where I been since I a child, free or not free."

She looked around the kitchen with a proprietary air that seemed to take in all of Savannah, all of Georgia, all of the South.

"Of course, it be better free," she said.

5.

Moody's old room was on the second floor of a wing of the house his father evidently had not ventured into since Moody moved away. It wasn't exactly untouched, it had been dusted and straightened, the curtains drawn and shut regularly, since it overlooked Jefferson Street, but in it were the same spindle bed and dresser, the tall mirror and the spool-legged nightstand he'd had all his young life. There was the mark he'd put in the footboard with his first penknife, and in the wardrobe he found, to his amazement, a shirt, trousers and waistcoat that fit him, and a pair of boots he'd worn when he was eighteen that also fit. No winter coat, and he had forgotten to buy one in Baltimore. The view from the window was the same, too, the trees of course taller, or else different trees, the houses across the street the same but with new occupants, or the descendants of the old occupants. As was he. The dormers in the servants' quarters, high up under the slates, were as blank and dusty as they had been when, as an adolescent, he'd watched them fervently for signs of a woman's shadow against the curtains.

He took the few things he'd brought with him out of his bag, his razor and hairbrush, some clothes that needed laundering, a copy of Hawthorne's *The Scarlet Letter*, which he had read on the stagecoach and would keep for Sabetha. He arranged the toiletries on his washstand, dressed in the clothes that had been in the wardrobe, and left the room to reacquaint himself with the rest of the house. He told himself he was looking for his father's whiskey supply, now his, which had always been kept in a cupboard in the downstairs parlor, along with a decanter and a set of crystal glasses given to his parents at their wedding by his mother's brother, his uncle Patmore. If it was not there he would not ring for a servant, like a master, and would continue to explore the premises. But it was there, the decanter nearly full and an unopened bottle beside it, as though his father had died after laying in provisions for a siege. The glass was as heavy as stone in his hand, the whiskey adding little to its weight.

He took his second drink down to the kitchen, where Sikey was preparing lunch. The smell of rice and beans reminded him of Mexico, *moros y cristianos*, and that made him think of Annie. The six servants seated around the big table were all talking at once, but fell silent and stared down at their plates when he appeared in the doorway. Sikey said she would bring his dinner up to him in the dining room. "Your daddy always took his dinner upstairs." But he said no, he would sit in the kitchen with the others. The servants looked at one another in vexation. He could tell from their silence that Sikey had told them about his plans to free them, and sensed that they would like to talk about it among themselves without him sitting at the table. But he sat anyway.

"In case you have any questions," he said. "Or suggestions."

Sikey introduced them: Bette and Maisie, the upstairs maids; Temperence and Willa, kitchen maids; and Geo and Cane, who worked in the stables behind the house. Geo was old enough to have been there when Moody was, and said he remembered giving the young master his riding lessons. Moody said he remembered that, too, although he did not. Sikey said Geo had worked in the rice fields at Plantagenet until Casgrain died, then had come to the house in Savannah to manage the horses. Cane, his son, was the stableman.

"I'll be wanting to go out to Plantagenet this afternoon," Moody said to Geo. "I can ready my own horse," he said, "but I'd appreciate it if you came with me. Or maybe Cane here. Which of you knows the people at Plantagenet best?"

"I do," said Geo.

"Will you come, then?"

Geo looked at him noncommittally. "You freeing them, too?" he asked.

"Yes."

Geo contemplated this for a moment. "What about the land?" he asked.

For a moment, Moody thought he meant was he freeing the land, too. "My plan," said Moody, "is to sell the land, and this house, and to divide the money among all of you. Maybe give each of you so much for every year you worked for my father. And your free papers, of course."

"So you be selling the land, but not the people on it."

"Yes."

"You ain't going to be living in this house?" asked Geo.

"I hadn't planned on it, no," he said.

"Who be living here, then?"

"Whoever buys it, I guess."

"Where will you live?"

"I've been living in Indiana these past few years," he said. "I've got a family there. I'll be taking them to Canada."

"That little Gullah girl you took from your daddy?" asked Sikey. "I forget her name."

"Annie," said Moody. "No, not her."

There was silence around the table.

After a while, Sikey cleared her throat. "We thank you for our freedom," she said. It sounded like a grace. "We ain't sure about the rest of it. Can we talk about it some more after you see Plantagenet?"

Moody nodded. He felt uneasily that there was something in Geo's question about the land that he had missed. He decided to ask him about it when they were on their way to Plantagenet. He picked up his fork and took a mouthful of beans and rice.

6.

Under the direction of a tall, dignified man the color of a freshly rubbed chestnut, who gave his name as Reverend Ulysses, the slaves had been running Plantagenet for the five years since Thomas Casgrain's death. His father had had less and less to do with the plantation, and when he died in September, Reverend Ulysses and a council of elders had moved into the Big House, where they apportioned work and food as best they could without access to the family's bank accounts and credit. The fall rice had been harvested and sold at market, the canals repaired, the fields replanted, firewood cut and stacked outside the Big House and the slave cabins, and winter clothing distributed. Meals were prepared in the detached kitchen house and served communally at huge harvest tables set up in the barn. Some of the women had established a school in the chapel, where, on Sundays, Reverend Ulysses also preached the Gospel. He showed Moody around, pointing proudly to the results of their work. The house and barns were in good repair, the storage bins rat proofed, the stables clean and well ventilated. Moody was reminded of the North Star and Morning Star communes, and wondered if refugees from New Harmony, Reverend Ulysses himself or perhaps even Lucas and Benah, had made their way to Plantagenet after the raid, instead of going to Canada. His head swam with the irony of it. But the reverend said he had not heard of New Harmony, and knew of no model for what they were doing. They just saw the needs as they arose and found the ways to meet them that worked best.

"How many of you in the Big House?" Moody asked him. They were standing by the stove in the kitchen house, the very room in which Moody had first laid eyes on Annie. *Sumpin' wrong wid y'arm?* The reverend handed him a cup of coffee and they sat at the scarred wooden table on which the jug of cucumber water had sat.

"Six," said the reverend, speaking carefully. "Three men and three women. There was always women in the Big House, as you may recall, but it was generally thought prudent for them to be somewhere else when your daddy come to call."

"My father?" Moody said, divining his meaning. "It wasn't just Casgrain, then?"

"Casgrain," the reverend said bitterly. "No, it was the young men we had to keep from Massa Casgrain."

Moody set his cup down. He remembered the upstairs maids in Savannah who hadn't come down when he'd arrived that morning, who had kept their eyes down at dinner. His father *and* Casgrain. For a terrible second he remembered Silas Judd and the overseer, Sam Lerner, and Judd's semi-insane son J.J., who had come back for the boy Julius but had not taken the girl.

"I am not my father," he said.

"No, we can see that." Could they? Could he? "Geo tells us you plan to sell Plantagenet."

"I intend to free you all," he said. "Would I be doing the right thing?"

"It not too late to seek a better world," Reverend Ulysses said, smiling. "But it don't matter what I think. The council will want to discuss it with you. How long we got?"

"Not long," Moody said. "I have to bring a list of your names to the lawyers in Savannah in the morning."

"Then you be staying the night here?"

"If there's room."

Reverend Ulysses laughed. "We'll find room," he said. "Maybe you can sleep in one of the empty slave cabins."

Moody laughed. He didn't think the reverend was serious.

When they returned to the Big House, the five other council members were sitting around the pedestal table that filled most of the dining room. Moody remembered tense family meals at this same table. Reverend Ulysses and Moody took their seats and the reverend introduced each of them in turn: they were Milo Dingham, Ettamae Cutter, Prissy Porter, Rally Palmas and Jewelle Broadman.

"This here," said the reverend, "is Virgil Moody. Right now, he own this plantation and us, because he inherit us from his daddy."

"Took his time," said one of the women, Moody thought it was Prissy Porter. "His daddy died two months ago."

"Well, he here now," the reverend continued. "What he want to do is free us, sell the plantation, then give us the money from the sale of it, so much to each according to our years of service. He ask me to ask you if we think that a good idea."

There was some chuckling around the table. "He asking the rabbit if it a good idea to shoot the fox and give him the tail," said Milo Dingham.

"And since he ask, I told him it better if he ask us himself. So hear him out. Mr. Virgil Moody, go ahead and ask your question."

Moody looked around the table. Only the women were sitting straight up in their chairs with their hands folded in front of them. The men had pushed their chairs back and crossed their legs, or thrown one arm over the chair back. But they were all waiting to hear what he had to say. He wondered where he would start.

"When I was a young man still living here," he said, "I told my father I would never own slaves, I would never be like him. I didn't know why I hated slavery then, but I did, and I wanted nothing to do with it or this place. I had two older brothers and thought I would never have to test that conviction, because I would never inherit this property. It was easy for me to call myself an abolitionist, because it wouldn't cost me anything. Then my brothers died, and my father died, and now here I am, according to Lawyer Chase and the state of Georgia and apparently the will of God, in whom we trust, the owner of this property and all of you who live and work on it. So what does a good abolitionist do when he finds himself a slave owner? He frees his slaves. And that's what I intend to do."

He looked at the council members in turn.

"I will not own you."

"You could sell us," said Ettamae Cutter, who was sitting directly across from him. "Then you wouldn't own us either."

"I won't sell you," he said, looking straight at her. He took a deep breath, but it didn't help. "I had a wife," he found himself saying. "Her name was Annie, she was a former slave on this plantation. I took her from here thinking I was saving her. We lived together for a long time, first in New Orleans, then in Texas. She had a son, not by me, and I thought I had saved him, too. But I didn't save either of them. I tried to do the right thing by them, but it ended up being the opposite. I didn't free them, and I didn't save them. So I no longer think I know what the right thing is, for anybody. I need you to tell me. I can't go back and undo what I did, but I can try not to do it again. So please, tell me what you want me to do."

"We can't tell you what to do," Reverend Ulysses said quietly.

"Then tell me what you want."

"We can do that. But after that it up to you."

7.

"Please have a seat." Edwidge Chase was wearing a forest-green velvet coat over a pale-yellow chemise and cravat. He smiled at Moody, a cat's smile, not so much an indication of pleasure as a peculiar arrangement of the cheek muscles. The pince-nez swung on its red string, for as Moody entered the office he'd been reading the topmost of a stack of papers on his desk, the first of the free papers his scriveners had completed.

"I can't say this is ill-advised," said Chase, nodding at the papers, "for I myself provided you with good advice not to do it. But here they are."

"I have two more names for you," Moody said.

"Indeed?"

Moody wrote on a sheet of paper and slid the paper to Chase.

" 'Lucas Moody,' " Chase read. "And 'Benah Moody.' "

"I don't know if Benah took Lucas's last name," Moody said. "She probably did."

"This Lucas, he's a relation of yours?"

"I owned his mother."

"I see." Chase frowned, then stood and left the room to take the paper to his scriveners. When he returned, carefully parting his coattails before sitting, Moody leaned back in his chair and folded his hands across his stomach, in not entirely unconscious imitation of the lawyer.

"I have, however, changed my mind about selling Plantagenet," he said.

Chase leaned forward in his chair. "But this is excellent news," he said. "As you know, I think it would be a mistake. You have been out to see the property, I assume?"

"I have. I spent an interesting night there." The slave cabin had whistled and clapped throughout the night like a thing possessed. Moonlight had sifted between the roof slats, and mice had gnawed incessantly at the solid brick foundation behind his head. He had had to get up half a dozen times to put more wood in the stove. Seldom had the crowing of the cocks and the faint gray light of morning seeping through the uncurtained windows been more welcome.

"And you have no doubt seen the shambles to which the place has been reduced since your father's death," said Chase. "It must have been very sad. Your father was a fine man, but he was not a good overseer of slaves. Neither, for that matter, was Casgrain. You would be wise to restore the plantation to its proper condition before putting it on the market. It will fetch a handsomer sum."

"On the contrary," said Moody. "The plantation is in excellent condition. It is being run extremely well and is turning a profit."

"Run by whom?"

"By the people who have been living on it," he said, pointing to the stack of free papers on Chase's desk. He explained about the council of elders. "I intend to give the plantation to them, so they can continue running it."

"Give—?"

"Or sell it to them for a dollar. Whatever makes it legal."

"I don't know that I . . ."

"A freedman can hold property in Georgia, can he not?"

"Well, yes, technically, but . . ."

"This will be a consortium of freedmen," Moody said. "And women. It will be a company, like Pinkerton or the B&O, only instead of producing adulterers and smoke, this one will produce food."

"And the Savannah house? You'll live there without servants?"

"No, I'll still sell that. I've talked to Sikey about it. She and Geo and the others will move out to Plantagenet."

"But where will you live?"

"I'm going back to Indiana," he said. "Town called Freedom, not far from Indianapolis. There's a lawyer in Spencer, Cliff Parker, you can reach me through him. Will you do this, Edwidge?"

Chase looked at him evenly. Perhaps he didn't like the familiar address. But then he smiled his cat's smile and nodded. "I am a lawyer," he said, "you are my client. I am bound to do my best to fulfill your wishes." He removed and polished his pince-nez. "Besides, it isn't often that I get to do something I haven't already done a thousand times." He replaced his pince-nez and looked down at the free papers. "I read the newspapers, too, Mr. Moody, and not all of the books on my shelves are law books. I see the way the world is heading. Emancipation is coming as surely as it came to Britain, although I doubt it will come here as peaceably. The South," he said, looking through his office window onto Johnson Square, "is a leaking ship. *'I sigh for the land of Cypress and Pine, / Where the Jessamine blooms and the gay Woodbine.'* I myself have never kept slaves," he continued, turning from the window, "never mind what my scribblers out there might call themselves from time to time, and like most people I have no particular thoughts about slavery, but I am aware that we are entering a new age, one that favors the North. Machines, manufactories, industry, commerce. Mr. Emerson is right to observe that America is descended from a nation of traders and merchants, that what we do best is to buy cheap and sell dear. How did he put it? 'The English lord is a retired shopkeeper, and we have acquired the vices and virtues that belong to trade. The customer is the immediate jewel of our souls.' Something like that. What he says is no doubt truer of the North than it has been of the South, but it is true down here nonetheless. We certainly bought our slaves cheap, and we will sell them dearly."

"It was also Emerson," noted Moody, "who said that 'If you put a chain around the neck of a slave, the other end fastens around your own.' "

"Your father was much better at selling rice than growing it. He left that to others, and disparaged them for it. But, as you are my client, and therefore," he said, his smile almost detectably increasing in warmth, "the jewel of my soul, I will do what you bid me do."

Moody stood and warmly shook the lawyer's hand, after which Chase pushed the stack of free papers toward him, along with a pen, inkwell and blotter.

"I will correspond with your Mr. Parker," he said as Moody signed the papers. "There will be many more papers to sign and monies to disperse from the sale of the properties. You will let me know your will in these matters, when they arise?"

"I will," said Moody. "And you will let me know how the enterprise at Plantagenet fares?"

"Of course. I myself am very interested in seeing how the new South prospers."

8.

Once again, Moody knocked on the door of the Savannah house, and this time was met by Bette, one of the upstairs maids. She pulled the door open wide and stood behind it, a slight figure in a cotton cleaning frock, her black hair tied back with a white kerchief. When he looked at her she lowered her eyes. Moody told her he had the household's free papers in his satchel, and asked her to tell the others he would like them all to assemble in the parlor.

"Yes, Massa," she said.

"I hope," he said, "that that is the last time you shall call me or any other white man 'massa.' "

She looked at him gravely, gave a small curtsy, and walked back toward the kitchen. He continued into the parlor. While he waited, he let his gaze alight on objects in the room. The clock on the mantelpiece, its face painted with an idyllic Scottish countryside, untouched by the time that revolved constantly over it. The uncomfortable settee on which his mother had crocheted baby caps, which she presented to infants born to her husband's slaves. It was his most constant memory of her. The two pink wing-backed chairs he had not been allowed to sit on as a child, the stolid oak side table bearing two enormous marble vases, always empty of flowers, the glass-fronted gewgaw cabinet that still held, among other things, his father's perpetually unconsulted brass barometer, a sextant, and a conch shell from one of the Sea Islands, Jekyll Island, he thought it was, on which his mother's family had grown indigo before the du Bignon family arrived, introduced slavery and drove the less successful planters, those like his mother's family without slaves, off the island. The old portrait of his mother hung above the fireplace, the original of the miniature he had kept with him since her death. He had held many long, silent conversations with her, and he consulted her now. Did she approve of what he was doing? She gazed upon him fondly, as she always had, and kept her opinions to herself.

One by one, the six members of the Savannah household came into the parlor. He had set their free papers on the oak side table, between the vases, Geo's on top and Sikey's on the bottom. He stood looking through the window onto Jefferson Street, at the large chestnut leaves falling onto the sidewalk, and when everyone was assembled behind him and the rustling had stopped, he turned and began to speak.

9.

He hadn't exactly expected dancing and singing, but still he was surprised by the solemnity with which his father's former servants received their writs of freedom. It had been the same at Plantagenet. They accepted the papers as though they were the payment of a debt so long overdue that the settling of it was more an embarrassment to the debtor than the occasion of joy to the parties to whom the debt was owed. Geo took his free paper with a tear in his eye, but the younger members simply looked at one another and smiled. They had, it was true, enjoyed a measure of freedom since his father's death, and they perhaps saw this settlement more as a confirmation, or completion, of that state than as a new degree of emancipation. They'd all elected to move out to Plantagenet and work with Reverend Ulysses and the council. Sikey said she liked the kitchen house out there, with the apartment above it for herself, and Moody noticed that Geo, though he affected an interest in the brass barometer, could not hold back a small smile when she said it.

When the others left the parlor, Sikey remained behind, and Moody invited her to sit on one of the wing-backed chairs, while he took the other and waited to hear what she wanted to say. She sighed as she settled onto the cushioned seat, put her head back and, holding her free paper in her expansive lap, looked up at his mother's portrait.

"I come in here from time to time," she said, "pretend I'm looking for something or have some chore to do, then just sit here, waiting for the kettle to boil or the bread to rise, and look at her picture. This was her room."

"I don't remember much about her," Moody said. Hers had been an unnerving sense of calm about to be shattered, of peace bitterly gained by sacrifice and surrender. She was, he suddenly realized, the South for which Edwidge Chase had so elegiacally sighed.

"She was kind as the day," said Sikey, "and tough as a turtle's egg. A truly good woman. You was always more like her than like your daddy, which is why your daddy leaned so hard on you. Your mamma spent a lot of time in here, cutting out and sewing for the babies, always had little packages for them when they born, and extra food for they mammas. She tell your daddy, 'Keep them off work for a week, why don't you, let them get they strength back,' and sometimes he did. When she passed he like a hound let loose from his chain. And then his two sons went, too."

"I supposed many of those babies were Casgrain's," Moody said, "but Reverend Ulysses suggested Casgrain's interests lay elsewhere."

Sikey was quiet a moment, looking down at the paper in her lap.

"Thomas Casgrain was no threat to us," she said, "except with the bullwhip. And most often he only use it for show, when your daddy in residence. And mostly on the men."

"Did my father know?"

"About Casgrain? 'Course he did. I think your mamma knew, too. A lot of the boy children was sold young."

Sikey raised her eyes again to his mother's portrait. Moody knew it by heart, each fold of the blue gown, the white lace cap with its trailing ties, the calm gaze that beheld the beholder with confidence and a hint of rebellion. The portrait had been painted in this room, her room, as Sikey said. His oldest brother, William, the one who was killed in New Orleans, was a toddler at her knee solemnly holding a colored ball as if it were the Earth. The conch shell and sextant were behind her on the mantelpiece, the marble vases, like twin urns, on either side of them, and a tea service with its Tudor rose pattern, teapot, pitcher, sugar bowl and a single cup, on an occasional table beside her chair.

"And the girl children?" Moody asked quietly.

"Them a little later," Sikey said.

"Do you remember Annie?" he asked.

"The Gullah girl? I do. You took her to New Orleans. I was glad to see her go."

"Why?"

"She wan't safe here."

"But not because of Casgrain?"

"No." Sikey's fingers were tightly laced above her free paper. She didn't look up at Moody. "But he maybe held her."

"For who?" Moody knew the answer now, but he wanted to hear it. "Not my brother?"

"No," Sikey said. "Massa John had a good wife. She married again and moved to Atlanta. Anyway, Massa John too sick at the end, even before the fever took him. And he wan't mean that way."

"Did you know Annie was with child when she left here?" Moody asked.

"No, I didn't know that," Sikey said, looking at him. "What happened to it?"

"We raised him. Annie and I. He was a fine boy. His name is Lucas."

"He ain't with you now?"

"No."

Sikey was silent. She shook slightly, as though chilled by the way of the world, and glanced at the empty grate.

"Annie never told me who Lucas's father was," Moody said. "I never asked her right out. I raised him like my own. I wanted him to be my own, to be ours. I thought of Annie as my wife, and Lucas as our son. It was easy to do in New Orleans, and easier still in Texas. But it wasn't true. Annie never believed she was my wife, and I never believed she was my slave. She wasn't either."

"No," said Sikey. "She was both."

Moody closed his eyes. He felt the bullet shatter his hip, the bayonet catch on his rib cage. He waited for the pain to subside, but it worsened. The ticking of the Scottish clock was like a thousand muskets being cocked, one after another, aim taken, breath held. His brain darted about in the darkness, touching the conch, the barometer, the sextant, his mother's portrait, the funereal urns, the dark folds in his mother's dress.

Sikey spoke first. "Where Lucas now?"

"In Canada, I hope," Moody said, his eyes still closed against the knowledge of Lucas's paternity. "I sold him, Sikey." He heard Sikey's gasp. He heard Annie stirring in the wing-backed chair, her hand going to her throat, her wild hair, her eyes dull and piercing as ash. Something wrong with his arm. "I thought it was what he wanted," he said, "to be with Benah. But I sold him." He made a gesture with his hand, his palm up, as if to help Annie step out of the river. "And when Benah was sold, too, he ran off after her."

"Ah," Sikey said.

"His mother drowned herself because of it," he said, opening his eyes.

Sikey bent forward and covered her face with her hands. Even his mother looked stricken.

"Who was his father, Sikey?" Moody asked, although by now he knew. "It wasn't Casgrain and it wasn't John. Who was it?"

"It was your daddy, Mr. Virgil," she said, sitting up. "I didn't know she with child by him, but that who it was. That who it always was."

Moody stood and stared unseeingly into the glass cabinet. Sextant, conch, barometer. He thought almost calmly of smashing the glass, grabbing the relics of his mother's ruined island and hurling them out into the street, but he controlled the impulse and sat back down in his chair.

"So Lucas," he said, "Annie's boy—"

"The one you hope is in Canada," said Sikey.

"The one I sold," he said, sparing himself nothing.

"He not your son. He your brother."

IO.

Moody half dozed in the stagecoach, his arms folded across his chest, his hat pulled so low over his eyes he could smell his father's hair oil on the band. It was no longer raining, but the chill had set in and he still had no winter coat. He would get one in Canada. The coach's motion on the macadam rocked him gently against the cushioned side, and each time he felt a slight twinge in his hip, not quite enough to make him shift his position, but enough to bring his father's hated words to mind. Nothing forgiven. He knew now that his father had been right, that forgiveness meant wiping the record clean and that could never happen. After nearly four years his wound was still there, admittedly more like a memory of a wound, bones buried in muscle, but a memory that would never leave him. With his eyes closed, he saw the Mexican boy pressing his back against the tree, his round, dark eyes in the forest's dappled darkness, his hair straight as a waterfall, his skin the color of oiled oak. Tamsey's skin shone in sunlight and glowed in candlelight. The boy was simply raising his right hand in salute to the

Virgin of Guadalupe on his dying day. Moody had made a mistake. An irreversible, unforgivable mistake. He adjusted his position in the coach and saw Lucas sitting across from him at the kitchen table, saying he would be with Benah no matter what, heard himself saying he would not sell him, and then selling him. Everything followed from mistakes, from the fierce desire of one person to be with another. That was love, unspoken, unforgiven. He should have told Lucas he loved him, he should have told Annie, he still hadn't told Tamsey. He felt it, held it so tightly to his chest it was like to burst out of him, and he would never be whole again without her.

When he stepped down from the stagecoach in Indianapolis, Leason was there with the wagon and Moody was glad to see him. He placed a hand on Leason's shoulder and they looked each other in the eye until Leason grinned and looked away.

"Where's your ma?" Moody said.

"Down at the *Pelican*. We got everything ready. Food, ammunition. Kästchen gave us coats and a whole bale of blankets."

"Good. We can hunt and cut firewood along the way. There been any trouble since the trial?"

"Nope."

They climbed up on the wagon and Leason took the reins. "Kästchen says he'll buy the horses and the wagon, we can't just leave them."

"Tell him he can have them, he's earned that and more."

"I been out to Freedom and collected most of our belongings. Stokes coming with us, if we got room."

"We got room."

"How'd it go in Savannah?"

"I'll tell you when we're all together," he said. "But it was good."

II.

Moody watched the shoreline from the *Pelican*'s parlor deck, the spare trees between the water and the low limestone bluffs, the occasional openness of cleared farmland.

"This is slow going after being on a train," he said to Tamsey, who was sitting beside him.

"Slow going after being in jail, too," said Leason, who was at the tiller on the cabin roof. He was able to keep them headed downstream without help from the poles. Granville and Stokes were mainly keeping an eye out for rocks.

Before sailing, they had lifted the stove into the cabin so they would have some heat at night, but the chairs and table were still on the parlor deck, and the thin rug that hid the bloodstain beside the hatch cover. Tamsey was humming a tune almost under her breath as she watched the way the water danced in the low evening light. Moody had come back yesterday with Leason and gone right up to her and put his lips beside her ear.

"Your hair smells good," he'd said. "I love the smell of your hair." And then he said, "I love you." Not loud, not even Leason and Sarah, who were right there, could hear him. It hadn't come easy, he'd had to build up to it on the stagecoach, imagine himself saying it half a dozen ways, but he had said it. She'd looked at him and nodded. "I love you, too," she said, and Leason and Sarah had heard that, and Granville and Sabetha, and maybe even Stokes. And then she'd said, "We better go now."

It was going to be a cold trip, but he expected they'd get to Canada before freeze-up. Brother Joshua had gone on ahead, sent by Solomon Kästchen, and they were to meet up with him at a place called Sandwich. Tamsey admitted to him that going to a place called Sandwich sounded good, even better than a place called Freedom. "You can't eat freedom," she said.

Sarah and Sabetha were in the cabin, Sabetha reading *The Scarlet Letter* and Sarah knitting a blanket for the baby. He'd told them what he'd done in Savannah, and they had agreed that he'd done the right thing. Last night, when they were in bed, Tamsey had said she was glad he had given the land to his father's slaves, but she didn't think that was the end of it. "There one thing I learned from New Harmony, black people only own a thing until some white man want it." He had agreed. He didn't claim to have started any big movement, he said, but he still felt he'd done the right thing.

"You did," she said.

Sailing downstream was easier. It would be harder when they reached the canal and turned north to Terre Haute, and harder still when they got closer to the Great Lakes. But as Tamsey said, "Everything hard," and he'd seen that even after saying it, she'd kept going.

Tamsey was still humming as she watched the land go by, and Moody suddenly thought it sounded familiar.

"What's that?" he asked.

"What what?"

"That song you're humming."

"The Drinking Gourd song?" she said, smiling. "We nearly at the end of it."

It was the song he had heard Annie singing to Lucas. Tull must have been tone deaf. "How does it end?" he asked her.

"*When the little river meet the great big 'un,*" she sang softly, "*follow that muddy path to freedom.* Something like that."

AUTHOR'S NOTE

For the first forty-six years of my life, I thought I was white. Then, at the age of forty-seven, I discovered that I was half African Canadian. My father, who was born to a black family in Windsor, Ontario, in 1925, was light skinned enough to pass for white, which he did. I was raised white. My father never told anyone that he was black— not his wife, my mother, or me, even when I presented him with documentary proof that his family, and therefore he, and therefore I, were black.

In my novel *Emancipation Day*, I presented a main character who was very much like my father: Born into a black family in Windsor, Jack Lewis passed for white when he joined the Canadian Navy in 1943, which at the time did not accept blacks (that policy changed as the war progressed and more cannon fodder was needed). He was posted to Newfoundland, where he met and married a white woman, Vivian Fanshawe, without telling her of his racial background. Like my father, he could have stayed in Newfoundland after the war, living as a white man, but when the war ended, he brought his young bride back to Windsor, where she met his family. Even when she confronted him with what she saw to be the truth, he denied it, telling her that no matter what color his family was, he himself was white.

The tension in the novel (and, according to my mother, in my parents' marriage) began to peak when Vivian became pregnant. She was obviously worried that the baby she was carrying would be black, especially when Jack told her that if it was, he'd know it wasn't his.

Two of the questions explored in the novel are questions I would have asked my father if he'd lived (he died in 1999, my mother three years later), and had he admitted to me that he was

African Canadian: Why did he bring his wife back to Windsor after the war, knowing that she would quickly realize he'd lied to her about his race? And did he himself believe he was white, or did he know he was a black man pretending to be white? They are both profound questions, getting as they do to the psychological heart of passing, but I still don't know the whole answer to either of them. But, as Alice Munro has said, fiction isn't meant to answer questions, only to explore them.

Up from Freedom began to form in my mind when I traced my father's family back to 1835, when Thomasina Grady and her three children arrived in Spencer, a small town in southwestern Indiana close to the White River, which continues east to Indianapolis. There is a small town near Spencer called Freedom. Thomasina and her children were listed as "mulatto" in the 1840 census, and the owners of a small farm not far from the village of Freedom. In the basement of the Spencer courthouse, I found something else: a document from 1850 giving the outcome of a trial involving my great-great-grandparents, Leason and Sarah Grady. They'd been arrested for "fornication," which meant they'd been living together as man and wife without having first been married.

At that time, it was illegal for a black person to marry a white person, and Leason and Sarah were arrested because the State claimed that Sarah was a white woman, and therefore could not legally be married to Leason, a black man. As I read the account of the judgment (there was no transcript of the actual trial), I fully expected to find that the couple had been acquitted when it was proved that Sarah was in fact black. But I was wrong: Leason and Sarah were acquitted because their lawyer proved that Leason was in fact white.

This evidence that my father's family was legally white floored me almost as much as had the original evidence that they were black. Except in this case, I knew it wasn't true: every other document I was able to find subsequent to 1850 still listed the family as either black or mulatto: Leason and Sarah's son, whom they named Andrew Jackson Grady, my great-grandfather, and who arrived in Windsor, Ontario, in time for the 1881 census, is listed as black. As are his children, one of whom was William Henry Grady, my grandfather. In 1920, William Henry married Josephine Rickman, and on their wedding certificate, in the box asking for "Nationality," they were both listed as "Coloured."

When the designations "black" and "white" can be reversed in a court of law, and then reversed again on marriage and death certificates, using those designations as racial signifiers is meaningless. Or rather, they have only the meaning that social custom at the time requires them to have. They are labels of convenience, or inconvenience, depending on whether we want to embrace similarities or dwell on differences.

Whatever the truth of my family's racial heritage, the outcome of the trial was that when the Fugitive Slave Act passed in the United States in the fall of 1850, allowing slave catchers to cross the Ohio River into Indiana to retrieve runaway slaves and drag them back to their Southern masters—and requiring Indiana citizens, sheriffs and judges to help them do so—my family had papers stating that they were white. I have no idea where Thomasina was before arriving in Spencer—there is a record of a Tamsey Grady marrying a man named James in Louisville, Kentucky, in 1829, and Tamsey is a reasonable diminutive of Thomasina—but whether they were free blacks, freed blacks or runaway slaves I don't know. But I do know that they were not white.

In *Up from Freedom*, I have imagined Tamsey's journey from slavery in the South to Freedom, Indiana. I have also imagined Virgil Moody's journey from being a reluctant slave owner in Texas to a willing partner in Tamsey's bid for freedom in the North. As a person who is both black and white, I thought I could explore the tensions and accommodations that inevitably exist between Tamsey and Moody as they learn to live harmoniously together.

I wondered if they were the same tensions and accommodations that existed in my father when he had passed for white. And then I thought that since the United States itself is a confusing blend of black and white, the same tensions and accommodations could be found in that complicated and restless Union. Like my own family, America is more white than black, but since recent surveys have suggested that up to 80 percent of Americans are at least 5 percent black, there are a lot of couples in the United States like Leason and Sarah. White on paper, but something entirely less determinant beneath the skin.

Wayne Grady
Kingston, August 2018

ACKNOWLEDGMENTS

This novel began to form in my mind in 1998, when I traveled to Spencer, Indiana, where my great-grandfather, Andrew Jackson Grady, was born in 1850. In the basement of the Spencer courthouse, I met Roger Peterson, a retired University of Indiana history professor who had devoted his retirement years to sorting out the mountain of town and county records that had accumulated since the early 1800s. Roger had gathered the Grady papers in a file—land purchases, road contracts, marriage licenses, and a brief account of Leason and Sarah Grady's trial for "Fornication," also in 1850. May every family seeker have a Roger Peterson in their life.

Since then I have been aided and encouraged by a great many friends, including Toronto filmmaker Louis Taylor, whose film *Ester, Baby and Me* was an early inspiration; Lawrence Hill, while he was delivering the 2013 Massey Lectures on the subject of *Blood*; the ever-effervescent Derek Burrows, whose documentary film *Before the Trees Was Strange*, about color and family in the Bahamas, helped shape my ideas about racial self-identity; and Sonny Sadinsky, who brought me into the Queen's University law library in Kingston, where I learned that Leason and Sarah's ordeal was far from unique.

The writing was made easier by the generosity of the Canada Council for the Arts, particularly through its sponsorship of the Writer-in-Residence program at Haig-Brown House, in Campbell River, BC. My thanks to Ken Blackburn and Andrew Nikiforuk, who made my stay there a pleasure. And to the largesse of Amazon.ca, whose prize money from the Amazon.ca First Novel Award, given to my previous novel, helped to finance the writing of this one.

I am indebted to my agent, Anne McDermid, who has been patient and enthusiastic throughout this long process. I have received valuable editorial guidance at Doubleday Canada from Nita Pronovost, before she moved to a different publisher, and then from Martha Kanya-Forstner. But it has been my editor, Zoe Maslow, who has most helped me to deepen and expand this novel, and to see things in it I didn't know were there. Thank you, also, to Beverley Sotolov, whose copyediting found a few other things I didn't know were there. And to Brad Martin, Kristin Cochrane, Amy Black, and especially Shona Cook, for their continuing friendship and support.

Louis Taylor once told me, "In the end, all you have to rely on is your family and your community." And so, to my own deepening and expanding family, I extend illimitable gratitude; they are my reason and my inspiration. And of course, as ever, to Merilyn.

UP
FROM
FREEDOM

READING GROUP GUIDE

1. How does your perception of Moody change throughout the book, and why? Do you think he ever becomes aware of his complicity in the cycle of slavery?

2. Moody falls in love with three different women over the course of the novel: Annie, Rachel and Tamsey. What does he learn from each relationship?

3. "It was time for him to stop acting surprised and indignant whenever anyone suggested to him that the reason he hadn't freed Annie or Lucas was that he had liked it that their relationship was based on ownership, that that was the way he'd been raised, and, hate it though he professed he did, it was the relationship he understood and felt comfortable with." What do you, the reader, gain by seeing this family relationship—Moody, Annie and Lucas—from different points of view?

4. In the novel, we see how slavery travels across generations, impacting each one differently over time. How does slavery impact Annie differently than it does Lucas? What about Tamsey and her children? How do you think the history of slavery has impacted the current generation of African-Americans and African-Canadians?

5. Moody notes that black people in the north "are free blacks—a designation that usually signifies a man is free from slavery, but that here has come to mean also a man who works for free. Or for wages so low that he can't afford to do anything about his situation." Do you think Moody's observation has any merit? Is it possible to have the legal rights of a free person, but to still lack freedom?

6. Moody is fascinated by geology—by changes in nature over time, how the natural world is a product of these changes, and how all these changes leave a trace on the Earth. In what ways do memory and human history resemble geology? Is it ever possible to escape our past? How do we reconcile ourselves with our shared history?

7. Parts of *Up From Freedom* are meant to raise ethical and philosophical questions for the reader without necessarily providing answers. What questions did the novel raise for you? Do you think those questions are relevant in the current global climate?

8. Mr. Kastchen tells Moody that many people who oppose slavery—including the Religious Society of Friends—also oppose the Underground Railroad, believing that the most effective way to end slavery is through political channels and legal change. "The Society

believes that helping a few thousand individuals into Canada is nothing compared to freeing four million with the stroke of a pen, but the way I see it, our few thousand will still be alive when the changes come, if it does, whereas if we didn't help them, they almost certainly would not be." When is it better to take legal routes to enact change, and when might it be necessary to take direct action? How does one decide? Where does one draw the line?

9. There are horrific scenes of violence against black people throughout the novel—how did the writing affect you?

10. As you read *Up From Freedom* you meet many characters and then have to say goodbye to them without knowing what their fate will be. What does this sense of unease do to you as you're reading? Why do you think Grady does this?

11. What conclusions about racial divisions based on skin color can be drawn from the trial?

12. At the trial, Tamsey finally gets to tell her story. What effect do you think it has on the outcome of the trial? What effect does her story have on you?

13. Tamsey advises Moody that, rather than simply freeing the slaves on his Georgia plantation, he should ask them what they want. Why do you think she says that? Is it fair to ask the oppressed to come up with their own solutions to the problems of racism? Or is it better to impose the oppressor's concept of freedom on those who seek social change?

14. "Nothing was forgiven. Somethings were forgotten, but damn few, and only for a time. But nothing is ever forgiven." This was Moody's internal struggle throughout the novel. Do you agree with Moody? Why or why not?

15. Who would you recommend *Up From Freedom* to? Why?